THE 2ND
WORLD WAR II

THE 2ND
WORLD WAR II

LAURA DOTHE HELLWIG

TATE PUBLISHING
AND ENTERPRISES, LLC

Published by Tate Publishing & Enterprises, LLC
127 E. Trade Center Terrace | Mustang, Oklahoma 73064 USA
1.888.361.9473 | www.tatepublishing.com

Tate Publishing is committed to excellence in the publishing industry. The company reflects the philosophy established by the founders, based on Psalm 68:11,
"The Lord gave the word and great was the company of those who published it."

Book design copyright © 2014 by Tate Publishing, LLC. All rights reserved.
Cover design by Junriel Boquecosa
Interior design by Mary Jean Archival

Published in the United States of America

ISBN: 978-1-63063-157-4
1. Fiction / General
2. Fiction / Historical
14.03.05

ACKNOWLEDGMENT

A special thanks to my brother, Craig:

For your valuable advice and knowledge and for sharing your love of World War II history.

A loving note to my son, Sven:

For the many hours of research I did online in reference to nuclear energy and weaponry and how to build a bomb and gunpowder and weapons of mass destruction, I am also surprised the FBI didn't come beating down our front door to arrest Mom.

PART 1

THE BEGINNING OF MY LIFE WITH ADOLF HITLER

MEIN JÜNGERER BRUDER, GERHARD

"How could this have happened? Why didn't you do something sooner? Are you telling me you *und* Adolf Hitler had a living *jüngeren Bruder* that no one knew of?"

I lay in the comfort *und* warmth of my *Bett*, with a hunting knife in my boot on the floor next to me, a loaded pistol under the mattress, *und* five *Model 24 Stielhandgranate* stick grenades in my squirrel-skin knapsack under the *Bett*, slowly dying of cancer as my *Mutter* had a lifetime ago. With my beloved Tom, Grace, *und* Louise at my side, I was ready to disclose my story to the world. Those same three questions had been asked by many throughout the years *und* had been deeply haunting me. It had taken a lifetime for me to come to terms *und* feel inner peace within my soul. I was eternally grateful for the love of a good man, whom I credit with helping me overcome an agonizing sense of guilt that I had carried my entire life.

"*Fräulein* Neumann, this interview must be conducted within a timely fashion. Even though Dr. Henry Jackson has informed me I have six to nine months to live, I believe I'll be joining my late husband very shortly. All I ask is that the truth is printed, exactly as I've disclosed. It's extremely important that the world has knowledge of the truth *und* the events which actually unfolded thirty years ago."

"Sure, anything you say. Are are you ready to get started?"

"*Ja*, please make yourself comfortable."

My *Bruder* Gerhard was the seventh *und jüngsten* child of my *Mutter und Vater*. Before Adolf *und* I were born, we had two *Brüder und* one *Schwester*. Sadly, one *Bruder* died in infancy, *und* our other *Bruder und Schwester* died as toddlers of diphtheria. When Gerhard was born on 3 May 1898, he was nine years *jünger* than Adolf *und* two years *jünger* than me. Adolf *und* I were truly blessed with our little *Bruder* who we both adored *und* loved.

From the time Gerhard was born, I played a huge role in his life; in fact, I used to pretend he was my baby. In reality, I was like a

Mutter to him, despite my very *jung* age. Sometimes when the entire *Haus* was perfectly quiet *und* motionless, I would sneak into his room *und* crawl into *Bett* with him to protect him from monsters. You see, those days, my *Mutter* was always tired *und* not feeling well. She usually took small catnaps during the day while my *Vater* was at work, leaving me with the responsibility of Gerhard.

Unfortunately, my *Vater* wasn't much help with any of us. I think *jung* children scared him. *Väter* after-work routine was to stop at the local *Bierhaus* for a *Bier*, come home at 6:00 p.m., *und* sit down with the family for supper. When we were finished eating, my *Mutter* would wash the dishes *und* clean up the *Küche*, while *Vater* retired to the parlor, where he sat in his comfy chair with a cup of *Kaffee und* smoked his pipe. Once he was comfortable, Adolf was instructed to get his homework *und* any *Schule* papers for *Vater* to review. My *Vater* was very strict with Adolf, especially when it came to his schoolwork. The institution that Adolf attended in Fischlam was becoming equally strict with him, due to his developing discipline problems. *Vater* wanted Adolf to do well in *Schule*, to succeed, *und* follow in his footsteps.

Our *Vater* worked in the customs bureau since he was a *jung* man. He became very successful *und* made a good living to support his family. This was his vision for his *Sohn*. For me, however, I always assumed *Väter* prophecy was I would marry *und* my husband would take care of me. Disturbingly, while my *Vater* was alive, we never discussed my future, only Adolf's. While my *Vater* was preoccupied with Adolf *und Mutter* was normally run-down, the care of Gerhard was left up to me. Even at the *jung* age of four, I flourished with the responsibility *und* loved every moment.

"However, *Fräulein* Neumann, our world was about to abruptly change."

"Please continue, you've got my interest."

One cold, early morning in February 1901, Adolf *und* I were suddenly awakened by the sound of my *Mütter* screams. I was so terrified; I flew out of *Bett* with my feet never touching the floor. I immediately knew my *Mütter* screams had something to do with Gerhard. I remember that horrifying vision implanted in my brain that something happened in the middle of the night *und* Gerhard died in his sleep. Adolf *und* I went running into his *Zimmer* only to see both our *Eltern* crying while cuddling *und* holding him.

The next thing I remember, we all jumped into the first *und* only *Automobil* my *Vater* ever owned—the Tatra *Präsident*, which was produced in 1897 *und* was the first motor auto in Central Europe, also one of the first autos in world. That funny-looking motor auto that my *Vater* was so proud of resembled a horse-drawn carriage. It had a bench seat in the front, one at the back, *und* was designed to seat four people. Frantically he drove our family to the nearest hospital in Linz.

It seemed as though we were in the hospital waiting *Zimmer* forever. After hours of torment, the doctor finally came out *und* sat down next to our *Eltern*. I'll never forget the expression on my *Mütter* face while the doctor explained Gerhard's test results. They indicated Gerhard contracted the disease spinal poliomyelitis, better known as polio. He had movement in his arms *und* torso but his legs were severely affected, which was common of this disease. The doctor explained that Gerhard may never walk again. I cried for weeks, probably months. However, very strangely, I don't remember seeing Adolf ever shed a tear. In fact, he didn't appear to have much emotion whatsoever.

Within the next couple of days, per the advice of the doctor, my *Vater* drove Gerhard to another hospital in Switzerland that specialized in spinal poliomyelitis. Polio apparently had been slowly creeping throughout Europe for years, *und* this particular hospital in Zurich was the best. Within a blink of an eye, Gerhard was packed up *und* out of my life. The future for my family was about to be turned upside down *und* inside out.

With everything my family was enduring, needless to say, Adolf began acting very peculiar *und* only added to our troubles. I remember a few comments he made in front of my *Mutter* that reduced her to tears. His harsh comments implied that cripples weren't whole people *und* had no place in society. They had nothing to contribute *und* should be put out of their misery—cripples just took up space *und* were inferior. His comments astonished *und* terrified me. I couldn't understand how his feelings toward Gerhard changed so drastically overnight. From the time my baby *Bruder* was born to the age of three, I witnessed nothing but the adoring love Adolf had for him. I was amazed at the metamorphosis that I saw take place in him without any warning.

As time marched on, Adolf continued to do poorly in *Schule und* constantly spoke of becoming an artist instead of joining the civil service. *Vater und* Adolf, both very stubborn with strong convictions, fought constantly. With the continual turmoil in our *Haus*, one day, out of the clear blue, in 1903, my *Vater*, Alois, suddenly died at age sixty-five.

Two years after *Väter* death, Adolf convinced *Mutter* to allow him to quit *Schule* at the age of sixteen due to his poor grades and without any hope of qualifying for a secondary education. Adolf moved to Vienna with the help of his orphan's benefits *und* some support from my *Mutter*, under the pretense he would study art. My *Mutter und* I both believed Adolf would become a great architect someday, *und* she was content with her decision.

Sadly, my beloved *Mutter*, Klara, died of cancer in 1907, at the age of forty-seven. Adolf *und* I both took her death extremely hard. On her death *Bett*, she revealed that months prior to our *Väter* death, he sent Gerhard to *Amerika* to live with an uncle. Uncle Bruno wasn't a blood relative, just a boyhood friend of *Väter*, who traveled to *Amerika und* became a citizen eight years prior to Gerhard's arrival.

Väter decision to send Gerhard to *Amerika* was in his best interest. In the early 1900s, *Amerika* had become very popular with the care *und* treatment of this crippling disease, because of an overwhelmingly high volume of outbreaks *Amerika* was experiencing. Later the *Amerikaner Präsident* Franklin D. Roosevelt, who also contracted polio in 1921, founded the National Foundation in Infantile Paralysis. *Herr* Roosevelt also founded the Warm Springs Foundation, which he visited often for his personal treatment. The Warm Springs at Pine Mountain State Park was considered state-of-the-art treatment for polio *und* other ailments as well.

Needless to say, I had very bittersweet feelings. On one hand, I was excited that Gerhard was in *Amerika*, receiving the most up to date treatment; however, I also felt very sad at the same time. I was afraid I would never see my baby *Bruder* again. Let's face it: Switzerland is a seven-hour train ride from Leonding, Austria, while *Amerika* is 7,120 kilometers across the North Atlantic *Ozean*.

"I remember as though it was yesterday. I was so young and naive I couldn't comprehend traveling that great of a distance. The entire concept was something out of the land of enchantment."

"I surely can understand how you must have felt. A young girl in the early 1900s who had never been anywhere, you must have felt like Christopher Columbus."

"*Ja, Fräulein*, something like that. But let's continue."

In the beginning, Adolf wrote me several letters about his new life in Vienna *und* portrayed how he was attending the Academy of Fine Arts to study art *und* architecture. He emphasized how excited he was to be planning a career in that field.

During that short period of time, I found myself envying him. For me, there was nothing exciting *und* grand in my life. I was eleven when *Mutter* passed. Per my *Mütter* request, I continued to live in the family *Haus* in Leonding. My *Mütter* dearest friend, *Fräulein* Gabriele, who was a spinster, was asked to move in *und* take care of me. *Fräulein* Gabriele moved out of her apartment in Klagenfurt *und* into my *Vater und Mütter Haus*. The *Haus* was paid off years prior, *und* my orphan's benefits, along with my half of the inheritance, helped *Fräulein* Gabriele raise me until her death in September 1918.

Throughout the years, the only contact Adolf *und* I had was an occasional, unexpected letter he would send, normally with no return address.

"It's funny I was always so excited when he wrote. When a letter came, I flew up the steps to my *Zimmer und* closed the door with such anticipation *und* excitement I could hardly stand it."

"That's a very nice memory of you *und* Adolf," I tenderly smiled at Magdalina with a warmheart.

"*Ja*, for an immature delusional young *Mädchen*."

Needless to say, with every letter, I happily curled up under the covers in my *Bett und* read it over *und* over again. I had a box stored under the *Bett* with every letter in it that Adolf wrote me. At times, when I was feeling lonely or sad, I would grab the box, crawl into *Bett* with the covers pulled up to my chin *und* read through all his letters once again. For some strange reason, this gave me unequivocal peace. Amazingly, to this day, I still have every one of his letters hidden in a secret location.

Unfortunately, I found out, as everyone does, the older you get, the faster time flies by. I hadn't seen Adolf since he moved out of our family home at the age of sixteen, *und* truthfully, I was beginning to forget what he looked like. Our only collaboration was through the mail, *und* every letter I received brought me great joy.

My *Bruder* Gerhard brought me great sorrow. I was obsessed with the thoughts of reuniting. He was so *jung* when *Vater* sent him away I feared he didn't know I existed. However, I blamed Bruno; he had our address *und* knew that Gerhard had an older *Bruder und Schwester*. I always assumed Gerhard wasn't aware that he had family living in Europe. If he knew of us, he surely would try to get in touch.

The next couple of letters Adolf mailed were filled with all his accomplishments *und* how well he was doing at the Academy of Fine Arts in Vienna. He bragged about himself so much it became virtually impossible to believe everything he wrote. Even though I knew he embellished things, I still was very proud. I wanted to believe that my *Väter* dream of his success would happen *und* Adolf would do it his way.

"Sadly, the gullible young woman I was found out a few years later that he wasn't accepted into the academy *und* never studied architecture or art."

Then shortly after the Great War broke out on 28 July 1914, I received another letter from Adolf. He informed me he had moved to Munich the year prior with the money he received from the final part of *Väter* estate. Proudly, he enlisted in the Sixteenth Bavarian Infantry Regiment as an Austrian citizen. My first reaction to this news was of extreme fear for his safety *und* well-being, although deep down inside, I was extremely proud. Adolf was my only blood relative in Europe, *und* with my growing fears of Adolf fighting in the war *und* possibly dying on the battlefield, I began pulling double duty. In order to survive with half my wits, mentally I had to shut down *und* realize I may never see Adolf again, *und* unfortunately, I was giving up all hope on Gerhard as well. For all I knew he could have died in *Amerika* from his polio illness. Then on top of those negative feelings, Adolf never tried to get in touch with me the entire time he was in the infantry, making it impossible to stay positive. During those years, I prayed every night to *Gott* to keep Adolf safe *und* out of harm's way.

Unforeseeably, four years after Adolf enlisted, I received another letter from him. I remember before I could open the envelope, I broke down weeping in a typical female hysteria. Receiving that letter after so long restored every ounce of my being. The letter started off with my *Bruder* so humbly proud of the three metals awarded to him—the Iron Cross Second Class that he received in 1914, the Iron Cross First Class, *und* the Black Wound Badge, both of which he received in 1918. Once again, I was overwhelmed with pride. I remember feeling like a little kid at Christmas, the anticipation of seeing Adolf in full uniform with his metals pinned to his jacket was mind boggling.

"Magdalina, I can't begin to imagine how you felt. You literally prepared for the worst, *und* the unexpected actually occurred."

"*Ja* however, that was the good news. The bad news, Adolf was in a Red Cross hospital located in the town of Pasewalk in Mecklenburg-Vorpommern, *Deutschland*. He was hospitalized because he was temporarily blinded with mustard gas. After speaking with *Fräulein* Gabriele, we both made the decision to take the train to Pasewalk *und* surprise him with a visit."

Fräulein Gabriele *und* I rode our bicycles into town *und* purchased two train tickets. After a very scenic eight-hour train ride through *Deutschland* to Pasewalk, *Fräulein* Gabriele *und* I anxiously waited for Adolf to join us in the waiting *Zimmer* of the hospital. Five minutes later, a nurse brought him to us in a wheelchair. Horridly, the expression on his face wasn't what I expected. He looked at me exacerbated *und* in shock at the same time. His expression of belligerent anger over the fact we came so far only to see him in his present state reduced me to tears. I would assume when he saw my stupid feminine emotions in full swing, he finally calmed down *und* became a human once again. After all that drama was finally behind us, we then engaged with pleasant conversation for about hour, *und* then Adolf proudly showed off his metals.

However, surprisingly within a split second, once again Adolf became embittered when I mentioned my sadness over *Deutschland* defeat. He boisterously explained to us his profound belief in the *Dolchstosslegende* (the "stab in the back" legend), which meant the *Deutsch Armee* that he was inconceivably convinced to be undefeatable had been stabbed in the back by civilian leaders *und* Marxists wanting social change. Adolf seemed to be so passionate with his views it was dreadful. After a two-hour bittersweet reunion, as I fought back the tears, we hugged *und* gave each other a big kiss on the cheek while saying our farewells. He tenderly assured me he would be leaving the hospital soon *und* would visit me at our home in Austria.

Sadly, as I thought back to my hospital visit with Adolf, it was abundantly clear that his mood swings had become much worse through the years *und* were beginning to frighten me. The boy I knew when we were very *jung* was smart *und* kind; in fact, he was considering the possibly of becoming a priest when he got older.

"It's strange, I didn't realize it until that moment. The turnabout in Adolf's personality actually began when our *Bruder* Edmund died of measles at the age of six," tears filled my eyes as I looked at *Fräulein* Neumann and noticed her eyes filling as well.

"*Oh mein Gott*, another sibling died? How many *Kinder* did your *Eltern* have?"

"A total of seven—Gustav was born 10 May 1885 to 8 December 1887, Ida 23 September 1886 to 2 January 1888, Otto 1887 to 1887, then of course, Adolf was born 20 April 1889, Edmund on 24 March 1894 to 28 February 1900, then me *und* Gerhard. Unfortunately, out of seven *Kinder* my *Mutter* gave birth to, there are only three of us who survived."

Adolf was very close with Edmund, even though there was five years' difference between the two of them. Strangely, when Edmund died, Adolf began to get closer to Gerhard, who was only two at that time. I believe in my heart, Adolf somehow felt that Gerhard could take the place of Edmund, but sadly, he never got over Edmund's death. That was predominately around the time the family began to

THE 2ND WORLD WAR II

notice a big change in him, in his schooling, and in his attitude *und* discipline problems. He seemed to have lost interest in everything, except art.

I held onto the hope *und* love in my heart that Adolf at the age of twenty-nine would become a great man someday, just as *Vater* had dreamed. Unfortunately, as fate would have it, there would only be two more correspondences from Adolf *und* I wouldn't see him again for another twelve years.

BRIGHT RED FLAGS

"Looking back now, this is around the time I should have realized something was brewing."

With hearing the scuttle buff in town, people were concerned of the recent changes that were taking place in *Deutschland*. Our main concern was the uprising of a powerful political party, the *Deutsch* National Socialist Workers Party quickly sweeping throughout *Deutschland*, along with Adolf's recent interest *und* his newly gained political power.

The next letter I received from Adolf explained that shortly after he left the Red Cross hospital, he moved back to Munich. This confused me; he had given me the impression he was doing well with his studies of architecture before he enlisted. Therefore, I presumed once the war was over, he would finish his education *und* obtain a degree.

"Obviously, that was nothing but an illusionary dream on my end."

Adolf stated in his letter he left the academy *und* abandoned a promising career in architecture to go into politics *und* live in poverty. Needless to say, my bubble had burst. As immature *und* naive that I was, I had unrealistically envisioned him returning to our Leonding, Austria, *Haus und* working as an aspiring architect. Once Adolf was settled into a new way of life, the two of us would work together gathering information concerning Gerhard *und* bring him home to Austria. The three of us would live happily ever after as a family.

"Yeah right. Who in their right mind could ever image in their wildest dreams the future unfolding as it did," Ella looked at me and laughed."

Adolf's letter was different than his prior correspondence. It wasn't his normal lengthy letter bragging about himself *und* embellishing the truth. Actually, it was fairly short. Not only was it very disturbing to hear how he gave up his studies, but due to his recent political interests, he adamantly urged that I forfeit my surname of *Hitler*.

I was told to assume my childhood nickname of *Wolff*. This was a name I acquired as a child, *und* for whatever reason, it seemed to have stuck. Everyone knew me as Magdelina Wolff; other than family *und* teachers. I'm not sure if anyone knew my birth name. Adolf loved me *und* was a good man he wouldn't ask this unusual request unless it was important.

Amazingly, a few years later, a letter postmarked from Philadelphia, United States of America, addressed to *Herr* Alois Hitler, was mailed to my *Haus*. I very calmly tore open the envelope, pulled out the letter, *und* as I began to read it, my eyes filled with tears. I quickly realized that Bruno had written this correspondence. Obviously, he was unaware my *Vater* died twenty-nine years ago. I *dankte* the Lord with all my heart for that letter—it was the answer to my prayers, *und* I was gleaming with joy from head to toe. Finally, after a lifetime, I had an address, along with some optimism. I could write Bruno on Gerhard's behalf. My childhood dreams were about to become a reality. However, as the saying goes, "Be careful what you wish for."

"Magdalina, would you like to take a short break?"

"*Nein*, I'm fine. I do, however, want to read this letter to you all."

2 April 1932

Herr Alois Hitler
Michaelsbergstrasse 16
Leonding, Austria

Dear Alois,

I know we agreed that there would be no correspondence between the two of us for the well-being of Gerhard; however, I feel obligated to share some recently obtained information. I'm haunted with this knowledge *und* feel it's extremely important to bring it to your attention. First, let me inform you of your *Söhne* health *und* accomplishments. Gerhard has come a long way working extremely hard *und* has made a milestone of progress. However, he still needs the aid of crutches *und* braces to walk. Nevertheless, the most important thing is, he is mobile. He has grown into a handsome, kind *jung* man. He's healthy; *und* just recently married a good woman of Italian decedent. Gerhard has a job in a military factory not too far from home. Proudly, he became an *Amerikaner* citizen when he was twelve *und* is fluent in *Englisch* as well as *Deutsch*. I wanted to teach him *Deutsch*, in case he ever decided to return home to Austria.

Apparently, Adolf has tracked Gerhard down *und* knows the address of the apartment that he shares with his wife, Christine, in Philadelphia. He has confidentially been corresponding with Gerhard for a year, *und* needless to say, I'm very concerned. Gerhard has been acting strangely this past year. I cannot quite put my finger on it, but he hasn't been himself for some time.

Every Sunday since the two of them have been married, I join them for supper at their apartment. Two weeks ago, after supper, we all retired to the parlor. I was sitting on the sofa having *Kuchen und Kaffee*, talking with Christine, when my hand innocently ran across an envelope stuffed between the sofa cushions. When Christine *und* Gerhard left me alone to go into the *Küche* for more *Kaffee*, I tucked the envelope in my trousers' pocket. I then excused myself to use the *Badezimmer*.

The letter was written in *Deutsch und* was in some sort of shorthand or code. From what I could decipher, I believe Adolf is sending Gerhard a sizable amount of *Deutsch Reichsmark* that he apparently is smuggling out of country. It seems as though Adolf has requested Gerhard to buy a large piece of property somewhere in a remote area in Philadelphia. There was more written; unfortunately; I couldn't make sense out of it in the short time I was in the *Badezimmer*. After the salutation of his letter, Adolf stated that there will be future correspondence with further detailed instructions *und* under no circumstances can anyone have knowledge of these letters. He also reminded Gerhard the importance of keeping secret his newly acquired relationship with Adolf.

My dear *Freund* Alois, you have to speak with Adolf. I know he's a grown man; however I'm seriously concerned. We're hearing stories in *Amerika* of his politics in Berlin *und* how he's shaking things up in the *Vaterland*. Gerhard is a good, law-abiding *jung* man with a bright future ahead of him. I don't want to see Adolf influence Gerhard with becoming involved in something corrupt. I maybe an old man overreacting; this may end up as an innocent mistake. However, I cannot shake this eerie feeling I'm getting in the pit of my stomach.

Enclosed is my address. Gerhard *und* I no longer share an apartment since his marriage to Christine; however, I live in the same building downstairs. Please keep this between you *und* me. I wouldn't want Gerhard to have knowledge of this sneaky thing I have just done. I'm a very old man *und* don't have much time left. Gerhard is proudly the only family I have. I regard him as my blood. His well-being *und* safety is all I'm concerned with.

Please get back to me as soon as possible. I hope all is well with you, Klara, *und* Magdalina. I want to reassure you, Gerhard had no knowledge of his family in Europe before Adolf got in touch with him. I did as you requested *und* raised him as my own *Sohn*. I have given him a good life, *und* with the *Schilling* you so kindly sent me, along with a good job I've held for years, he has had every advantage a boy growing up in *Amerika* could dream of.

Enclosed is a copy of my most recent photograph of Gerhard. I took this at city hall in Philadelphia right after he *und* Christine wed.

Dein Freund,
Bruno Dietrich
1602 Lombard Street
Apartment A-3
Philadelphia, Pennsylvania
United States of America

I read my *Väter* letter several times to try *und* grasp the information. I remember my brain feeling like mush between my emotions of fear, joy, confusion, *und* sadness; I didn't know what to do next. With Adolf telling me to change my name, along with the contents of that letter, I was feeling like a top secret spy. For whatever reason, I felt an alarming urgency to dig a hole in the backyard *und* bury the box that was stored under my *Bett* for years, containing every letter Adolf wrote. Without giving it much thought, I decided to include my *Väter* letter from Bruno to the safety of the letterbox as well. I immediately walked down the cellar steps *und* grabbed my *Väter* garden shovel *und* strolled out the back cellar door to the corner of the yard alongside the blackberry bush *und* dug a large deep hole to lodge my letterbox. Immediately, I filled the hole in *und* walked back to the creek located at the rear of the property. After locating the largest boulder in the creek that I was able to carry, I placed it directly on top of the hole to mark the area. While trying to catch my breath, I sat on the ground next to the rock *und* meditated for hours.

"Amazingly after all these years, *und* here on my death *Bett*, I can still smell that beautiful warm spring afternoon air, *und* hear the sound of the birds singing in the trees barely camouflaging the sound of the creeks flowing stream."

What a perfect day that was; however, I found myself carefully contemplating thoughts of possibly hiding other items of sentimental value in the very near future. I couldn't shake that uncanny feeling of urgency to get prepared for something significant. After returning the shovel to its rightful place in the cellar, I went upstairs, made my supper, *und* sat in the parlor, eating with a fire radiating in the stone fireplace, recapping on the day's events.

"I wish I would have been smart enough to have listened to my inner voice that day."

I remember questioning my sanity several times in the preceding months. I now realize I was acting out of sheer anxiety of the unknown. Things were changing in *Deutschland* drastically, *und* I dreaded the thought this change would find its way into Austria. For the first time in my life, I was living alone with no one to speak rationally with. The situation may have played out differently if I didn't allow my girlish imagination to dictate all the time.

"My denial sense in those days was so powerful; I actually was very talented with this emotion. Although the haunting reality is there really wasn't anything different I could have done to make the events turn out differently. We all tried *und* did the best we could with what we had to work with. I will go to my Maker with that sense of peace, as I believe the others all have done as well."

VALUABLE TIME PASSES TOO QUICKLY

Unfortunately, it took me a few months to sort through my emotions *und* get my head wrapped round all that drama. In the wake of my recent acquired knowledge, even more valuable time had passed. Furthermore, due to my financial circumstances, I had very little free time. Since my inheritance was depleted, I had to take on more work as a domestic. At the time of *Fräulein* Gabriele's death, I just celebrated my twenty-second birthday *und* was in need of more work to support my household. I very gratefully took over the families *Fräulein* Gabriele worked for. I was working six days a week *und* very long hours. For the first time, my beautiful blond-*und*-white cat Brigitte *und* I were living off my income only. Needless to say, I learned very quickly how to be frugal with my *Geld*.

I knew I had to do something in reference to Bruno's letter. However, even though I was young *und* immature, somewhere along the line, I learned to take time *und* don't act out of urgency when important decisions have to be made. With the evidence I buried in the backyard *und* my knowledge of Adolf *und* Gerhard's alleged secret business, I finally came to the realization that I must come out of hiding *und* take the bull by the horns. I was between a rock *und* a hard place. Do I get in touch with Bruno, or do I go directly to *Deutschland und* talk with Adolf? If Adolf *und* Gerhard were truly involved with something of a corrupt nature, I would do whatever I could to prevent my two *Brüder* from engaging in any wrong doing.

Nonetheless, once again, more time passed with nights spent tossing *und* turning in *Bett*. After pondering between the two ideas for a few more weeks, finally, I smartened up with a more sensible objective. I would take the easy *und* more practical road *und* simply respond to Bruno's letter as he had asked my *Vater* to do in confidence.

After my normal Sunday trip into Linz for groceries, my inner turmoil battle got worse. Thanks to the townsfolk, I had just become a little more educated on the seriousness of my *Brüder* involvement in *Deutsch* politics. Strangely, he apparently renounced his Austrian citizenship *und* became a *Deutsch* citizen in February 1932. From the early 1920s, *Deutschland* had already been experiencing a tidal wave of different politics, the Socialist, Bolsheviks, *und* Marxism. Much to my surprise, around the year 1921, my *Bruder* became heavily involved with the Socialist Party, which later he changed to the National Socialist *Deutsch* Workers Party, *und* one of the main topics was the Jews. With all the different political parties *und* the Jewish situation that was escalating, the country was in complete upheaval during those years.

It seemed as though I wasn't the only one confused in my own little corner of the world. While walking through town *und* listening closely to people's conversations, it was abundantly clear; concerns were focused on the *Deutsch* chaos. Those days were hard; I remember keeping to myself as much as I could. I gladly dropped my *Väter* surname; in fact, I ended up hiding my birth certificate in my treasure box as well. I remember having extreme feelings of fear for Adolf's well-being, which haunted me every day. All I wanted to do was hide my head in the sand *und* forget whatever activities both my *Brüder* were engaged in. After all, they were both grown men *und* sure has heck didn't need me metaling in their lives. A few days later, I received what was to be my last correspondence from Adolf.

"*Fräulein* Neumann, would you like me to read this letter as well?"

"*Ja*, your letters will help me understand the entire story."

"Great, I'll do one better. Once this interview is finished, you can have the box of letters. I have them in chronological order."

25 June 1932

Fräulein Magdalina Wolff
Michaelsbergstrasse 16
Leonding, Austria

Dear Mags,

I hope this letter finds you in good spirits, healthy, *und* safe. I have to stress this topic once again. It is imperative you stay in Austria *und* under no circumstances are you to get involved with any problems of the *Vaterland.* I want you to promise to stay away from the radio, the news, *und* the opinions of others in reference to *Deutschland* politics. Stay put in Leonding—I promise you will be safe there. Try to stay away from town as much as possible. The people will be forming opinions of me, which I don't want you to hear; it may influence you negatively. I wish I could tell you more, but it's better to keep things as they are.

I have a great dream of the reunification of the *Vaterland und* Austria. *Deutschland* will become the greatest most powerful country in Europe, as *Amerika* is in the West. *Deutschland und Amerika* will be the two dominating countries of the world, while the other nations will continue to be inferior.

Once my business is completed in *Deutschland,* I'll come back to Leonding *und* visit for a while. Maybe the two of us can go on *Urlaub* together for a week or two, someplace nice.

I *liebe* you,
Adolf

I decided it was time to write Bruno, *und* in doing so, I would kill two birds with one stone—discuss how he would like me to handle the situation with Adolf *und* obtain information on Gerhard. Since I wasn't smart enough to jot down Bruno's address before burying my treasure box, I decided to wait until it got dark *und* dig it up. My *Haus* was fairly secluded; however, it did sit close to the road. My road was off one of the main roads leading into town. It was a one-lane dirt road *und* is normally only traveled by the locals on bicycles. However,

I wanted to be smart *und* not take any unnecessary chances of anyone seeing me.

While I sat on a lawn chair out back, drinking a cup of tea on that beautiful sunny day, I was desperately trying to compose a letter to Bruno. As normal, I started to daydream just like I always did as a child. In my mind, I had created a rather pleasant adventure.

Gerhard *und* his wife would travel to Europe *und* live in Austria. My *Väter Haus* is a modest size; however, the property it sits on is two acres. We could add onto the main *Haus* or build a second *Haus* outback so they could have privacy. *Gott* willing, they would have *Kinder und* I would be blessed with niece's *und* nephews. The *Kinder* would all have their own *Schlafzimmer, und* we would have a tire swing hanging from the old walnut tree out back. They would swim *und* fish in the creek down the slope of the backyard in the summer, *und* my nephews would learn to hunt in the woods across the creek. Adolf would move in as well *und* design Gerhard's new *Haus*. Adolf could have our *Eltern* old *Schlafzimmer* upstairs, since that *Zimmer* is the largest. My *Schlafzimmer*, which is next to theirs is the second largest, *und Fräulein* Gabriele's old *Zimmer* would continue to be a guest *Zimmer*. The small *Schlafzimmer* downstairs would be used as Adolf's office, where he could sit at his drawing desk *und* design new buildings. We would make the office very professional looking for his clients who needed work done. Adolf would be transformed into a successful man, *und* we would all be together.

"Isn't it amazing how talented I am with daydreaming. I can really tell some whoppers sometimes."

"*Nein*, I don't think there's anything wrong with wanting to keep your family together."

"It's funny. I was so naive *und* childish. I also daydreamed about Adolf *und* I traveling to *Amerika und* playing out the same scenario in the New World. I firmly believed that the possibilities were endless in *Amerika*. Many of us haphazardly were under the illusion that the streets were paved with gold. *Fräulein* Neumann, I can assure you they are not."

Sadly, it was my life's ambition that we would all be together someday. After *Fräulein* Gabriele's death, I was so lonely out here in the sticks by myself. An hour bicycling trip into Linz once a week for groceries didn't give me an opportunity to make many *Freunde*. I made a cold, hard decision that day; I lived like a hermit long enough. I ended up inviting Esther Rosenburg to supper that following Sunday, *und* graciously she accepted. After all, she was my best *Freund* since grammar *Schule*. We lost touch sometime after we graduated high *Schule*, *und* she moved into town away from this desolate area.

After spending hours on that lawn chair, daydreaming *und* rationalizing my life, I realized the sun had begun to set *und* darkness would soon follow. Since I virtually got nothing accomplished, once the treasure box was dug up, I would then put all concentrated efforts into composing my letter, *und* stop the nonsense, which consumed the entire day. Time was running out that evening. I needed to go to *Bett* early because the next day was an early morning at *Frau* Koch's *Haus*—it was the dreaded laundry day.

17 August 1932

Herr Bruno Dietrich
1602 Lombard Street
Apartment A-3
Philadelphia, Pennsylvania
United States of America

Dear *Herr* Dietrich,

I want to apologize for not writing sooner. Also I have some bad news; my *Vater und Mutter* have been dead for many years.

Since my *Vater* is dead, I felt it was proper that I would write you. I have not mentioned your letter to anyone; in fact I have it hidden. My *Bruder* Adolf *und* I haven't seen one another since he was in a Red Cross hospital with injuries inflicted from the Great War. He writes me from time to time; however, as time passes by ever so quickly, the letters are fewer. I have to say the last few letters he sent me were alarming. I'm beginning to feel the same fear as you concerning Adolf's involvement in

Deutschland. I want to assure you I followed your instructions *und* Adolf has no knowledge of this.

Danke for getting in touch—my prayers have been answered. I'm hoping you'll send me Gerhard's address so I can rekindle a relationship with my baby *Bruder.* If that's not possible, could you please give him my address *und* tell him I *liebe und* miss him. Please ask him to get in touch with me.

In your letter, you stated to my *Vater* your concerns with the relationship between Gerhard *und* Adolf. I wasn't aware Adolf had been in touch with him. I'm amazed that I had no clue the two of them have been corresponding with one another *und* left me out. I'm very angry with Adolf over this; he's well aware how I've yearned for my *jüngeren Bruder.* I have waited twenty-two years. Does Gerhard even know I exist?

Please let me know what you would like me to do. I have no one else to speak with about these matters, *und* I'm frightened. Adolf has got me so paranoid I don't trust anyone, *und* I'm not sure if I trust him anymore.

Sincerely,
Magdalina Wolff
Michaelsbergstrasse 16
Leonding, Austria

Surprisingly, four weeks later, I came home from a very hard day at work, *und* there was a letter from the United States of America lying on the floor from the mail slot in my front door. My heart sank immediately, *und* I was sickened. Stamped very large across the address read, Return to Sender–Deceased. Although I really didn't know Bruno that well, I was too *jung* when he left Austria to go to the New World, I still felt anxious *und* very sad with the news of his death. Later that evening, with uncontrollable tears running down my cheeks for someone I really didn't know that well, I dug up the treasure box from the backyard *und* dropped my returned letter into it to accompany the others.

"I remember like it was yesterday. It's amazing how my gut talks to me sometimes," and as I look up at Ella, I suddenly got that eerie feeling in the bit of my stomach once again.

Without giving it any thought, I immediately ran upstairs to my *Schlafzimmer und* gathered up the few pieces of jewelry that my *Mutter* left me *und* a small amount of *Schilling* I had saved. Those items also made a home in my treasure box. The ground was replaced, *und* the large rock was once again placed over top of the area.

Once again, I tossed *und* turned all night with Brigitte cuddled up next to me, deep in thoughts of Gerhard. The wind had been literally taken out of my sails. Now with Bruno dead, there was only one person who knew of Gerhard's whereabouts in *Amerika*.

"Although, I had Bruno's address, *und* I knew he lived in the same *Komplex* as my *Bruder*, there was one huge problem, I didn't speak or understand *Englisch* those days."

My heart was so heavy; it was inconceivable I got that far after a lifetime, only to have my dreams come to an abrupt halt. All I wanted was to get some backbone *und* take the train into *Deutschland*, hunt down Adolf, *und* insist he help me reach out to Gerhard.

The following morning, I left for work earlier than usual. I had a very long day scheduled at *Frau* Koch's *Haus*. It was Wednesday, which was the loathsome laundry day, once again. I literally spend all day washing *und* ironing. I was so exhausted—she must have been saving her laundry up for weeks. After my supper, I changed into my night clothes, made a cup of *Kaffee, und* turned the radio on. I snuggled into my *Väter* comfy chair, as he did every evening when he was alive. It was amazing—at that point, it dawned on me I hadn't listened to the radio in months. Adolf had me so neurotic. I just wanted to listen to some music; my record collection wasn't the best *und* my record player was in desperate need of a new needle.

I felt so guilty turning that stupid radio on. Adolf was hundreds of kilometers away in Berlin *und* would never know I was listening to music. Within seconds of turning it on, much to my amazement, I heard Adolf's voice bellowing from the box, like he was sitting in my parlor. I knew he was very involved in politics, *und* of course, I have heard the controversy from the people in town; however, I was still shocked to hear my big *Brüder* voice broadcasted to the world. I remember feeling so intimated with his loud, stern voice bearing so much anger *und* passion at the same time; it was mind boggling.

Unfortunately, by the time I turned the radio on, I had come into the end of his speech, so nothing he said had any relevance at that point. I decided right then *und* there, I would no longer allow myself to be ignorant *und* the only person who had no idea of the current events, despite what Adolf wanted me to do.

Timing was perfect, my *Freund* Esther was coming for Sunday supper. That was a great opportunity to ask her to travel to Brandenburg, *Deutschland*, on 27 July 1932 with me. Adolf was scheduled to give another speech in person, *und* I wanted to be there to witness this event. I had a few weeks to save the train fare *und* the cost of a nice supper in Brandenburg. Esther *und* I would make a day of it. After all, the last time I went anywhere other than work *und* into town for groceries was the train ride into *Deutschland* with *Fräulein* Gabriele to visit Adolf in the hospital.

"I felt as though I should have been called Monk Magdalina, instead of Magdalina Wolff."

Two days later, I was standing in front of the ironing board in *Frau* Volkmer's kitchen when I overheard *Herr* Volkmer *und* his *Bruder* Richard engrossed in a very serious conversation in the next *Zimmer*. They were expressing their concerns over the possibility of Adolf Hitler becoming chancellor of *Deutschland*. Their conversation was so intense, *und* I, of course, found myself straining to hear what they were saying. The Volkmer *Brüder* agreed—if Adolf was appointed the next chancellor, *Deutschland* could suffer greatly. With his involvement in the National Socialist *Deutsch* Workers' Party *und* their dreadful anti-Semitic ideas, that could be a recipe for difficult times ahead. They were convinced evil was lurking in the air *und* would drift into Austria. The two *Brüder* immediately left the *Haus und* spun off in Richard's auto to speak with the people in town.

Frantically, I finished the ironing as quickly as I could. My hands were shaking vigorously *und* my eyes were filling up with tears. I had to get home before I completely broke down. I was so afraid that *Frau* Volkmer would see right through me *und* figure out my true identity. For the first time in my life I was concerned for my wellbeing. I was soon tormented by thoughts of my *Vater*. If he was still alive I doubt any of this would be happening. My *Vater* would never allow anyone to tarnish the Hitler name, considering it took most of his life to legitimately acquire that name.

Three weeks later it was time for Esther *und* I to board the train in Linz *und* travel to Brandenburg *Deutschland*. Esther graciously suggested I take the window seat since I had been living a rather secluded *und* sheltered lifestyle. The scenery was breathtaking. *Deutschland* had the most beautiful countryside in the world. I was so excited to leave my little domain, *und* the thought of actually traveling with a *Freund* to a new place was beyond belief. I felt like a little *Mädchen* left loose in a candy shop.

After Adolf's speech on that warm, perfect July afternoon, in the beautiful courtyard in Brandenburg, Esther *und* I looked at one another with horror in our faces. There was no doubt my *Bruder* was born to be a speaker. His monotone *und* gestures, just his enthusiasm alone, made him so powerful. I couldn't believe how the crowd was so mesmerized by him. However, as Esther *und* I walked around observing the people, it was abundantly clear not everyone agreed with him. I desperately fought off any urges to run up to him *und* give him a big hug *und* kiss. As much as I loved my *Bruder*, he obviously had changed drastically *und* began to scare me. I kept it on the back burner whether or not to see him afterwards *und* speak with him about Gerhard. Adolf was obviously too far gone in his convictions, but if there was a remote possibility I could save Gerhard, I was *Hölle* bent on doing so.

However, after Adolf's speech, he was quickly whisked away. Any thoughts I had of confronting him quickly dissipated. Esther *und* I sat under a golden weeping willow tree in the beautiful *Blume* gardens alongside the courtyard *und* talked for hours. Therapeutically, we shared the same thoughts; something bad is going to happen, we could feel it deep in our bones. We were concerned, Esther was half Jewish. Her *Mutter* was an Austrian Catholic, *und* her *Vater* was an Austrian Jew. From what we heard in Adolf's speech *und* the rumors circulating, Esther *und* I were seriously considering leaving Austria, just as my next-door neighbor, the Rubins, had two weeks prior. We spoke about booking passage to *Amerika* like Bruno did years ago.

Gratefully we had a slight advantage, Esther knew someone who spoke some *Englisch*; Gretel Hubert who was an old *Freund* of her late *Mütter*. All Esther knew of Gretel was that she lived in Munich *und* we could ride the train from Linz to the Austria-*Deusch* border *und* straight into Munich. We didn't know if this *Frau* was still alive; however, it was the only plan we could think of at the time. Neither Esther nor I knew anyone else who spoke the *Englisch* language. Esther promised she would go through her *Mütter* belongs *und* try to find an address or a telephone number for Gretel. The more we spoke of it, the more appealing *und* exciting this plan was sounding.

I remember feeling that bittersweet feeling once again. I was sad with the possibility of leaving my home but extremely relieved with the thought of no longer looking over my shoulder *und* having to control my tongue *und* emotions at all times. To be constantly on guard every day, all day long was a very difficult *und* exhausting challenge. The burden I carried of someone discovering my true identity was becoming overwhelming. However, once we were in *Amerika*, I would be free of those worries.

For this extravaganza, I would have to retrieve my birth certificate from the treasure box *und* forge the name Magdalina Wolff. To make the deal even sweeter, between Esther *und* I, we had enough *Schilling* to at least get to *Amerika*. Once there, Esther *und* I would both get jobs, a small apartment somewhere *und* share all expenses. After we were settled, I then would concentrate on locating Gerhard *und* conduct my business at hand.

"I've got to tell you, the mere thought of that adventure for two *junge Frauen* in those turbulent days was enough to scare anyone to death. Although as strange as this is going to sound, the thought of that adventure scares me more now as an old lady, *und* obviously I know how it all played out."

We were leaving our home *und* family, our jobs *und* our native language, only to willfully walk into uncharted waters. Although, the original plan was temporary as Esther *und* I spoke fondly of returning someday to Austria once the dust settled in *Deutschland*. However, in all practicality, there is no returning to an old way of life. As time marches on, life of course is constantly changing *und* moving forward with or without us willfully participating, however not always for the best.

THE MAKING
OF A DEVIL IN DISGUISE

 After Adolf's fancy speech in Brandenburg, *und* that lovely day I spent with Esther with all the plans *und* dreams we discussed, I decided to make some major changes in my life. I would no longer allow Adolf to dictate or intimidate me. I chose to continue to use the name of Wolff because of the affairs in Europe as they were, *und* the feathers he was ruffling among some of the Austrian people, I knew that was for the best. However, Adolf's other requests, I chose to ignore. I was a grown woman *und* was going to live my life as I saw fit.

"I hate to say this *Fräulein* Neumann, but Tommy *und* Grace will get a little chuckle at my expense on this one. Somehow, I courageously gained some chutzpah *und* enforced a bold new routine."

After supper every evening, I listened to the radio for music *und* also the news. I traveled into town more often than before at least three to four times a week. I began buying a newspaper every time I was in town *und* purposely focused into what people were saying. Thankfully, I was not that shy little *Mädchen* any longer *und* afraid of engaging in conversation with others. I had become more knowledgeable *und* felt comfortable speaking with people in reference to current events. I was actually beginning to make some *Freunde*. Bottom line was we were all concerned the troubles of *Deutschland* would invade Austria *und* affect us all. It seemed as though, every week our little circle of concerned citizens became larger.

I even went one step further; I invited Esther to live with me. Fortunately, the lease on her apartment was due to run out at the end of the month. We utilized the weekend to move her belongings into my *Haus* with the help of *Herr* Rosenburg. Her *Vater* drove into town with his farm truck *und* helped us load it to the brim with her belongings. After two trips the apartment was completely empty. We then made space for her belongings among my things in the *Haus*. Once Esther was no longer paying rent each month *und* the two of us began sharing expenses, we were able to start saving *Geld* for our adventure. That ridiculous, childish illusion of my two *Brüder* moving back home *und* all the daydreaming I was engaged in was obviously all in vain and a big waste of time. It was long overdue that I grow up *und* join the rest of the world. I firmly believed straightforward that *Gott* had another path for me to walk.

After Esther *und* I were both comfortable with our new living arrangement, we contacted Gretel in Munich. We knew time was running out, the leaves finished falling from the trees *und* the nights were growing longer. It was late November, *und* winter was inevitably just around the corner. If we didn't meet with her before Christmas, we probably would have to put the meeting off until early spring. If you don't drive, the winter season can be brutal with just a bicycle for transportation. The only traveling I normally did in the winter months was to *und* from work each day *und* what was absolutely necessary. In order to visit with Gretel, we had to ride our bicycles into town *und* take the train to Salzburgerland. Gretel's *Sohn*, Frank, would then drive over the *Deutsch*-Austrian border *und* pick us up at the train station. We then had to drive back over the border *und* an hour to Frank *und* Gretel's apartment in Munich.

As luck would have it, we were able to coordinate one of the last Saturdays before Christmas. Gretel *und* Frank graciously welcomed us into their very spacious three *Schlafzimmer* apartment. Amazingly, I could tell at first sight the Hubert's came from *Geld*; just the furnishings alone were incredible. We didn't know anything about these people; only that Esther's *Mutter* was very close *Freunde* with Gretel, *und* they went out of their way to make two strangers feel incredibly welcome.

We made ourselves comfortable in the parlor, enjoying *Kaffee und Kuchen*. Their parlor was lovely; there was a variety of house plants along each side of a large picture window, with a bird cage housing a yellow parakeet nestled within the plants, *und* family photographs all over. The warmth in the *Haus* allowed us to feel as though we knew the family forever.

After conversing for a few hours, we finally got down to business. The logical approach was for Gretel to call the United States *und* ask the operator for the telephone number *und* or address for Gerhard Hitler. I remember Gretel expressing her concerns; she was scared that she didn't know enough *Englisch* to converse with an *Amerikaner* telephone operator *und* was very intimidating to her.

Esther *und* I found out later in the evening that Frank also knew some *Englisch*. His *Mutter* taught him as a *Kinder* what little she knew. She was always pushing him to study the language *und* learn more; however, as a teenager he didn't have the time or ambition to continue on. Frank never understood why it was important to her. At the time, he had absolutely no interest in learning a foreign language *und* his unprecedented view was that *Englisch* had no place in his future, so why bother.

"I must say, that narrow-minded philosophy came back and bit him in the *Arsch* later. I got such enjoyment out of teasing him about this," and as I began to laugh, *Fräulein* Neumann joined in.

After a couple attempts, Gretel was able to get in contact with a very nice *Amerikaner* telephone operator *und* asked for the number of Gerhard Hitler. Minutes later, the operator got back on the line *und* informed Gretel there was no listing for a Hitler in Philadelphia. The operator even went so far as to look in other areas of Pennsylvania since the name wasn't common. Gretel thanked the operator *und* hung up. My heart dropped to my feet as we sat in the parlor looking at one another like we all had two heads or something, not knowing what the next step should be.

Suddenly out of nowhere, a thought popped into my brain. When I was very *jung*, I was captivated with the stories of my *Väter* childhood. He was considered illegitimate, *und* at birth, his *Mutter* gave *Vater* her surname of *Schicklgruber*. Years later, his *Mutter* married Johann Georg Hiedler, who became his *Stiefvater*. However, my *Vater* was never adopted *und* still used the name Schicklgruber. After his *Eltern* died, my *Vater* went to live with Johann Nepomuk Hiedler, who was the *Bruder* of his *Stiefvater*. Johann Nepomuk made sure my *Vater* became legitimated in front of three witnesses. My *Vater* had a legal baptismal register made up with his name Alois Hiedler. However, throughout the years, there was confusion on the spelling of *Väter* name, *und* somehow, Hiedler became Hitler.

Since we had no luck with Hitler, I assumed Gerhard was using the surname of Hiedler. Gretel so graciously placed another call to the operator, *und* within minutes, we had Gerhard's address. Unfortunately, he didn't have a telephone, but most important is we had the address.

"I still remember feeling so surreal at that point. It seemed as though I prayed for that moment my entire life. Strangely that very second, I developed butterflies in my stomach. I was scared to death."

I was very apprehensive; all the planning Esther *und* I had been engaged in for five months was becoming a reality. My comfort zone was certainly being challenged.

Gretel made sure we parted with a scrumptious sauerbraten-*und*-potato supper before Frank drove us back to the train station. Gretel was a wonderful *Frau und* a perfect hostess to two people who started out as complete strangers, *und* six hours later, I felt as though we were close *Freunde*. Esther *und* I *dankte* her for a lovely supper *und* the tremendous amount of help she gave us. As we hugged *und* said our farewells, I felt a warm feeling inside for the Hubert family.

Once the three of us arrived at the station, Frank sat with us as we waited for the train in the cold night air. In the short time we sat on that uncomfortable bench under the lantern in the freezing night air, Frank *und* I talked nonstop. It was as though there was no one else in the world, just the two of us. Unfortunately, the train arrived at the station on time *und* our conversation came to an end. Esther *und* I boarded the train *und* watched Frank as he stood there until the train pulled out of the station.

With the long train ride home, I enjoyed spending quiet time, reminiscing back to that moment over *und* over again in my brain. Unfortunately, the moment was quickly spoiled when I realized hours later that Frank *und* I monopolized the conversation *und* were very rude to Esther. Even though she never said a word on the contrary, I felt compelled to make it up to her at some point; she was too good of a *Freund, und* I sincerely didn't want to hurt anyone's feelings on my behalf, especially Esther.

With the way the day unfolded, *und* the joy I was feeling knowing I had an address, I decided to confide in Esther my secret treasure box buried out back. We immediately removed the rock *und*, with much difficulty, dug an area next to my treasure box in the brisk night air by what little light the oil lantern was illuminating. This task was difficult; the ground was beginning to freeze. Esther gathered her valuables *und* any *Schilling* she could spare *und* placed her valuables in a box my *Vater* had in the cellar, filled with assorted old nails *und* screws. We placed her treasure box next to mine, irretrievable for the winter months, then covered the hole *und* replaced the rock on top. Esther *und* I then walked down to the creek *und* carried up a few more rocks *und* strategically placed them alongside the bush.

Our hiding place looked more authentic than it ever did. I proudly couldn't image anyone examining the backyard *und* determine that there was something buried—not even my *Bruder* Adolf, in all practicality, if he was ever to return home. I'm sure he would remember that ugly overgrown blackberry bush; however, the landscaping alongside of it would never raise any flags.

"Grace *und* Louise, I want to remind you both while I'm thinking of it. My treasure box is still buried there. Inside the box are a few pieces of antique jewelry that was my *Mütter*. When you're ready, dig it up. I want you both to have her jewelry. Someday, you can pass it to your daughters as well."

"Of course, *Mutti*, we'll take care of that immediately."

"*Danke*, my beautiful *Liebchen*."

Esther and I decided to purposely put off writing Gerhard until after Christmas. After all, it was our first Christmas together, *und* I wanted that year to be special. Esther grew up with Christmas *und* Hanukah. Her *Eltern* practiced both religions, so a *Tannenbaum* wasn't out of the ordinary. Esther *und* I crossed the creek in my backyard *und* walked into the woods with my *Väter* axe *und* cut down the perfect tree. After we struggled to get the tree into the *Haus und* set up, I dragged up the old decorations from the cellar. On the stove in the *Küche*, we popped corn kernels *und* sat in the parlor in front of the fire with a bowl of popcorn, eating some *und* stringing the rest to make garland for our *Tannenbaum*. After working all day on our tree, it was finally finished *und* was so beautiful.

I hadn't seen a tree in my parlor since *Fräulein* Gabriele died. It was tradition. Every year, she *und* I would cross the creek *und* cut down a tree, just as my *Mutter und Vater* had done for many years. Christmas was always so magnificent in my *Haus*, *und* how I missed the smell of the pine, just the whole atmosphere of the holiday. Happily, *Herr* Rosenburg, Esther, *und* I celebrated an old-fashioned Christmas with a big supper *und* all the trimmings to boot. That year was so special for me.

"Oddly, to this day, despite everything that happened, I have always cherished Christmas of 1932."

Unfortunately, all that joy was short lived. Just as most Austrians feared, Adolf Hitler was appointed the new chancellor of *Deutschland* on 30 January 1933 by *Präsident* Paul von Hindenburg. On that gloomy, cold, *und* snowy evening, Esther *und* I were trying to relax in the parlor while we listened to the news program on the radio. With the announcement of my *Brüder* newly acquired fame *und* glory, my heart sank down to my feet *und* Esther began to cry. The fear of the unknown overwhelmed the two of us tremendously. Austria was considered a federal state of *Deutschland und* was united with the *Vaterland* until the allies split us after the Great War. With the fire blazing in the fireplace, me in my *Väter* comfy chair *und* Esther on the coach, we decided to stop drinking the tea she just made *und* have some schnapps instead. The two of us ended up talking *und* drinking until the wee hours of the *Morgen*.

Once the holidays were completely behind us, inevitably, it was time to sit down *und* compose a heartfelt letter to Gerhard. Fortunately, for the first time in my life, I actually consciously choose my words very carefully. I had great concerns with not knowing if he would inform Adolf of my letter. Obviously, I didn't know him; we were complete strangers to one another. Once again, my inner voice was telling me to play it safe.

"As my *Kinder* know all too well, my favorite expression is, "Assume the worst *und* hope for the best." This next letter that I'm about to read to you all is actually a carbon copy of the original I sent to Gerhard.

With age, it's quite smudged. However, once I start reading it, the words should come back to me as though it were yesterday. I'm old with cancer, but my brain and memory is sharp as a tack."

6 February 1933

Herr Gerhard Hiedler
1602 Lombard Street
Apartment B-4
Philadelphia, Pennsylvania
United States of America

Dear Gerhard,

Gott sei dank, I was finally able to track you down. I have so lovingly thought of you through the years. I'm your *ältere Schwester* who lives in Austria, where you were born. I'm sure you don't remember me; however, I have very fond memories of you. *Vater* took you away from us when you were only three years old to receive the best medical care for polio. There hasn't been a single day in my life that I haven't thought of you.

I saved some *Geld.* A *Freund und* I are planning to book passage on the steamship *Rotterdam.* We have to take the train from Linz, then board a second train that will take us to Rotterdam in the Netherlands. A steam tug will pick us up *und* transport us to the NASM Hotel situated on the opposite side of the wharf. Then we will board the steamship in four to five days. It'll take six weeks to cross the North Atlantic *Ozean und* sail into the port of Ellis Island in New York. I need to know if Esther *und* I are welcome so we can plan our trip to *Amerika.* As you can imagine, there is much preparation we have to do in order to make this trip successful. Please get back to me as soon as possible.

Liebe,
Magdalina Wolff
Michaelsbergstrasse 16
Leonding, Austria

Very enthusiastically *und* with butterflies in my stomach, I mailed my letter to Gerhard. At that point, Esther *und* I jumped the gun somewhat we immediately started planning the trip in further detail. We arranged a ride with Esther's *Vater* to the train station, *und* he graciously offered to watch over my *Haus und* take care of Brigitte while we were in *Amerika*. I gave him a key to the front door but decided to take Brigitte to Gretel *und* Frank's apartment. Gretel loved cats, *und* at that particular time, she was mourning the death of Mocha, her male orange-*und*-white tabby who unfortunately only lived for six years. I knew my Brigitte would give Gretel much pleasure *und* would be well taken care of in their home. The Huberts were very good people; Gretel was also kind enough to lend me her *Deutsch–Englisch* Dictionary to help us with *Englisch* once we arrived in *Amerika*. Furthermore, by taking Brigitte to Gretel's, it gave me an excuse to see Frank once again. I had feelings that I never felt before *und* didn't understand.

"I'm almost embarrassed to admit this, but at that age, I honestly never had an encounter with a boy before or a date. I was what you call a late bloomer. From my shortcomings, Esther got great pleasure from teasing me. Like she would know any different. Well, at least that's what I thought during those days. *Oh mein Gott*, did I say that?"

"*Mutti*, that was quite a sly little dig."

"*Ja*, Gracie, my mouth sometimes blurts out stuff before my brain catches up. Anyway, let me go on with the story while I'm still feeling well."

Esther used to tell me all the time, when we got back from *Amerika*, she was moving in with her *Vater und* we would go into business together. After all, when we were *jung*, we saw each other just about every day after *Schule*. I loved going to her *Haus*. Her *Väter* farm looked somewhat different those days than it does now. The original barn out back was torn down about fifteen years ago, *und* we built that huge thing in its place. Although the small slaughter *Haus* off to the left *und* the smoke *Haus* off to the right side were still original.

The Rosenburg's always had many different animals when we were growing up. *Herr* Rosenburg's pride *und* joy was his two Black Forest horses *und* a Rhinelander. Every morning before *Schule*, I helped Esther feed the pigs *und* chickens. Faithfully, every Saturday, we cleaned the stables so we could spend the rest of the weekend riding. After her *Mutter* died, her *Vater* sold all the animals *und*, unfortunately, allowed the place to deteriorate.

Our business plan was to plant corn in the fields *und* buy more animals. We would slaughter the chickens *und* pigs *und* sell the meat *und* produce to the market in town. We would fix up the old barn *und* board horses *und* give riding lessons. The entire time I knew Esther, I never realized she was a dreamer as well. The two of us becoming farmers seemed more practical than any of my farfetched dreams *und* was much more appealing than spending the rest of my life doing domestic work. Our business venture was something I was looking forward to, at least until the great transformation took place. Her vision defiantly sparked my interest, *und* to this day, I'm beholden to her for planting that seed in me.

"*Ja*, but, *Mutti*, credit needs to go to you *und* the others. Not to her."

"Louise, you're right, but I want *Fräulein* Neumann to know where the idea originated from."

It was mid-autumn of 1933 *und* very sadly I still hadn't heard back from Gerhard. After all the work Esther *und* I put into planning our trip to *Amerika*, I had gotten very discouraged *und* literally began to give up. I hadn't heard anything from Adolf, either, which, under the circumstances, was for the best. I gravely feared how he would react if he knew I contacted Gerhard *und* was planning something of this magnitude behind his back. However, on the flipside, apparently, Gerhard hadn't informed Adolf of my plans. There was no doubt in my mind if he had, I would have had a visit from a very angry, distraught, *und* out of control man. Esther *und* I, of course, were becoming very antsy; we had been planning our trip for a year *und* were ready to go.

I started to become extremely concerned; traveling in Europe was becoming more difficult as each day passed. Both Esther *und* I were feeling an overwhelming sense of urgency to act quickly before it was no longer possible to leave Europe. Then on top of all of that, *Herr* Rosenburg was extremely upset with Esther *und* I when we informed him that we had crossed the Austrian border into Munich to see Frank *und* Gretel a few times. Strangely, the presence of military officers had become astounding within the three visits we made to their apartment.

Very noticeably the *Sturmabteilung* (SA) stormtroopers, also known as the brown shirts, were walking around the train stations *und* the streets in the towns of *Deutschland*, acting like big shots. They were nothing but big bullies. I hated how they spoke down to people *und* tried to intimate them. Several times, we witnessed the Brown Shirts beating people with their night sticks in broad daylight, in front of witnesses in the streets. *Gott* forbid you would try to help someone—they would only turn around *und* start beating on you. We also witnessed innocent people arrested for no apparent reason. According to Frank, the Brown Shirts had been around for a long time; however, they were never that noticeable or violent.

Esther was beginning to feel very apprehensive with the thought of visiting Frank *und* Gretel in *Deutschland*. Upon our last visit, Gretel informed us the Brown Shirts stopped by their apartment *Komplex*, harassing everyone. She was terrified with the possibility that Frank would not hold his tongue *und* give them a reason to arrest him. Apparently, it didn't take much to anger these guys, *und* they appeared to have free rein to do as they pleased. *Gott sei dank*, after about an hour, they left the *Komplex* without incident. Gretel was very intimidated *und* was petrified the Brown Shirts would return. I immediately offered Frank *und* Gretel my *Haus*; they could stay with us, *und* once Esther *und* I booked passage to the New World, they would have the entire *Haus* to themselves. They decided to take me up on my generous offer; however, Frank *und* Gretel needed a couple of weeks to pack the basics, their family heirlooms *und* some other valuables. Everything else would stay behind in their apartment until such a day they would return to *Deutschland*, when better days were upon us all.

"Unfortunately however, as you are about to find out *Fräulein* Neumann, things didn't quite play out that way."

PART 2

OUR EXPERIENCE WITH THE SECOND WORLD WAR II

REALITY VS. DENIAL

 In what seemed to be a frantic state of mind, very nervously, *Herr* Rosenburg invited Esther *und* I for Sunday supper at the farm.

"Esther, do think your *Vater* is all right?"

"Sure, why do you ask? I know he's acting somewhat strange, but I'm sure everything's fine. He's probably just a little anxious over all this nonsense in Europe these days."

"*Ja*, I hope your right."

Very pleasantly, Esther and I enjoyed a scrumptious *schnitzel-und-*boiled-potato supper with white asparagus, just as Esther's *Mutter* used to make when she was alive. I was pleasantly surprised that Esther's *Vater* is such a tremendous cook. It's as though this meal was going to be the last supper. While Esther *und* I washed *und* dried the dishes *und* cleaned up the *Küche*, *Herr* Rosenburg sat at the *Küche* table, drinking his *Kaffee und* nervously smoking one *Zigarette* after another.

"I want you *Mädchen* to get out of Austria. I fear *Deutschland* may end up going to war once again. Please don't hesitate. Go to the *Amerika*, just like you both have been planning for the past year."

"*Herr* Rosenburg, my *Bruder* hasn't responded to my letter, *und* without Gerhard, this trip is impossible. The only way Esther *und* I can enter into the country is to have an *Amerikaner* citizen sponsor us. With Bruno dead, there's no one, *und* after all the time that's passed, I sincerely doubt Gerhard has any intentions of getting in touch with me."

With all that said, *Herr* Rosenburg is not letting me off the hook quite that easily. He will not allow me to make up any excuses; Esther *und* I have no choice—we are traveling to *Amerika* whether we like it or not.

"Magdalina, I understand that you haven't heard back from your *Bruder und* that's the reason nothing has progressed. However, snap out of it, *Schatz*. Write your sister-in-law. Maybe she can help. I'm very serious, *Mädchen*. I want you both on that steamship when it's scheduled to leave port again in two months. Esther, you need to start wearing your *Mütter* crucifix, *und* don't ever take it off from around your neck. I also want you to change your name. Start using your middle name Ingrid, *und* drop the burg in your surname. You are now Ingrid Rose with no middle name.

"Papa, what are you saying, I don't understand. Why are you acting so strangely tonight?"

Esther sat down next to her *Vater*, as I cautiously looked into *Herr* Rosenburg's blue eyes and suddenly felt the blood from my face leave, making me very lightheaded. I prayed he wouldn't remember my surname *und* that *Deutschland's* new chancellor, Adolf Hitler, was my *Bruder*. I had never heard Esther's *Vater* speak with such a stern, serious voice, *und* that look on his face was indescribable. I could tell he meant business *und* we had no choice in this matter. Unfortunately, I had a feeling there was going to be many more tossing *und* turning, sleepless nights curled up to Brigitte ahead of me.

Esther *und* I left *Herr* Rosenburg's farm *und* bicycled back to my *Haus*. It had become quite chilly after sunset, and I decided to ignite a small fire in the parlor fireplace. Surprisingly, Esther *und* I haven't spoken a single word the entire way home. I walked into the *Küche*, pulled out a bottle of schnapps from the cupboard, *und* poured two night caps. The two of us sat in the parlor in front of the fireplace, sipping our drink *und* staring into space in complete silence. Any discussion about our evening with *Herr* Rosenburg clearly isn't happening tonight.

"Esther, maybe we should call it a night. Let's get a good night's sleep, we can discuss this tomorrow morning."

"I agree. In the morning, things may be clearer."

"*Gute Nacht*, Esther. Don't let the bed bugs bite."

I picked up Brigitte from the rug in front of the fire, closed the fireplace screen, walked upstairs, *und* went to *Bett*. As suspected, I tossed *und* turned all night long, with the vision of *Herr* Rosenburg's eyes planted in my brain.

Even though I got very little sleep last night, morning came quickly. Esther decided to take the next day off from work, *und* as it turned out, I lost my Monday work a week ago. The Schmidt family, with whom I was employed with for the past three years, out of the clear blue, packed their family up *und* moved to Switzerland. Regrettably, with losing my Monday work, this will seriously affect my finances. People are scared right now, *und* no one will hire a domestic with the fear of another war lurking in the mist.

Esther *und* I were both exhausted; neither one of us got much sleep. After everything her *Vater* expressed to us last evening, we need some time to sort through *und* digest it all.

"Esther, do you think we should go back to your *Väter* later today *und* talk some more?"

"*Nein*, I have never seen papa act like that before. There's nothing more to talk about, *Schatz*."

"Okay."

When the logical thing would have been to sleep last night, I spent the evening not only tossing *und* turning, but thoroughly thinking through our conversation with *Herr* Rosenburg.

"Esther—I mean, Ingrid, I believe your *Vater* is very rational *und* wise, *und* we both need to respect his wishes. Late last night, I decided to take your *Väter* advice *und* try again. This time, however, I'll write my sister-in-law, Christine. Although, I'll need your help. We can use the dictionary that Gretel lent us to translate *Deutsch* into *Englisch* the best we can. Once we have completed this task and Frank *und* Gretel still haven't moved in, I think we have to go to their apartment one last time *und* have Gretel correct it."

Still in our nightclothes, we lounged around in the parlor, ate breakfast *und* drank *Kaffee*, *und* talked until early noon. We decided to dig up the two treasure boxes one more time to retrieve the crucifix *und* anything else we may need for our long journey to *Amerika*.

Thankfully, it was a beautiful sunny day *und* the ground wasn't frozen. Ingrid and I decided to retrieve some of the *Schilling* we have been saving. I did another walk through the *Haus*, gathering the antique jewelry my *Mutter* left me, *und* placed them in my treasure box as well. Ingrid placed some old family photographs in her box *und* her *Mütter* wedding ring. We covered the ground over the area once again, replaced the rocks, *und* walked back into the *Haus*. After lighting a fire in the parlor fireplace, Ingrid *und* I sat on the floor in front of the glowing warmth. We pulled the pillows off the sofa *und* placed them surrounding us. The atmosphere was so surreal, warm, *und* cozy, as we attempted to tackle this next letter.

10 November 1933

Frau Christine Hiedler
1602 Lombard Street
Apartment B-4
Philadelphia, Pennsylvania
United States of America

Deer Christine,

I Gerhard's older Magdalina. I from Austria. I know not English. My friend Ingrid Rose *und* I want to come. I rite Gerhard long time ago I no hear back. We will come by ship in 2 month. Please let me no if we are welcome. I have no telephone, can you please to wright me.

Thank,
Magdalina Wolff
Michaelsbergstrasse 16
Leonding, Austria

"Ingrid, *Dank* for your help. My letter is short and sweet, but to the point."

"*Ja*, I agree. That was hard enough just those few words."

"I know what you mean. I hope Gretel doesn't have to spend too much time correcting it."

Christmas came *und* went once again. Frank *und* Gretel still haven't physically moved in; however, most of Gretel's family heirlooms *und* valuables have been moved into my *Haus und* are scattered throughout. This year, Ingrid *und* I didn't bother with a *Tannenbaum* or decorating; neither one of us felt like going through the trouble.

Everyone walked around town going about their business in a somber state. Distraughtly, the SA are in Austria as well, everywhere you look. There's also been violence in our streets. No one talks to anyone; you don't know who to trust anymore. Everyone walks around with their heads hung low, minding their own business. I haven't seen anyone look me in the eye for some time now.

To make things worse, the families I did work for no longer need me, most of them have left the country. The Volkmer family gave up on their quest. They packed up everything they could, sold the rest, *und* left for Switzerland. Ingrid *und* I decided to sell most of our belongings as well, which made more room for Gretel's things. At the present, Ingrid *und* I were down to the bare essentials. She was still working as a secretary in town, *und* thankfully, I managed to pick up another family who has the means to pay me for my services. At the present, Ingrid *und* I were just getting by.

Time was passing very quickly; I still hadn't received a response from my sister-in-law. Regrettably, once again, I found myself giving up hope. I was beginning to come to the realization that bad times might haunt us in Austria *und* we needed to get prepared.

Amazingly, the second I no longer allowed myself the pleasure of denial *und* accepted the reality that Ingrid *und* I were stuck in Austria, I came home to a letter lying on the floor by the front-door mail slot. The return address was United States of America. I leaped for joy. I picked up the letter *und* sat down on the hallway steps, staring at it as though the letter was going to magically pop out of the envelope *und* read itself to me. Ironically, at the same time, Esther walked in the front door *und* looked at me like I had just grown two heads.

"What's wrong, Mags?"

"I don't know, I'm frightened, this just came today," Esther smiled and gave me a cute little wink.

"Well what are you waiting for, open it, *Liebchen?*"

April 13, 1934

Fräulein Magdalina Wolff
Michaelsbergstrasse 16
Leonding, Austria

Dear Magdalina,

Danke for writing. I apologize for taking so long to respond. After receiving your letter, I immediately sat down *und* composed a response. Unfortunately, I don't know *Deutsch*. I composed a letter in *Englisch* then took it to a friend who owns a print shop located two blocks from where I live. He's a very kind *älter* gentleman who immigrated from *Deutschland* years ago *und* is fluent in the language. He then translated my *Englisch* version into *Deutsch*.

It was so delightful to hear from you. I didn't realize Gerhard had a *Schwester*. I only know of an *älteren Bruder* who got in touch with Gerhard a couple of years ago. I don't even know his name. Gerhard's guardian, Bruno Dietrich, never mentioned anything about Gerhard's family in Austria.

We would *liebe* to have you *und* your friend visit. Please come to *Amerika und* stay as long as you like. You will need an *Amerikaner* sponsor in order to enter the country, which I will be more than happy to accommodate. I have already applied *und* received the paperwork for this procedure. I'll fill it out *und* send it back once I know the actual departure date. The day you're scheduled to arrive in New York at Ellis Island, I will be there to pick you up. Once you book your trip, please get back to me with the number that is assigned to your passage. This way I can keep track of the exact day *und* approximate time you'll be arriving in port. Please don't worry about the transportation part, I'll handle that. You just get to *Amerika und* I'll take care of the rest.

I'm so excited to finally be meeting family of Gerhard's.

Fondly,
Christine L. Hiedler
1602 Lombard Street
Apartment B-4
Philadelphia, Pennsylvania
United States of America

As excited as I was to receive Christine's letter, unfortunately, tragedy unfolded in *Deutschland*. *Präsident* Paul von Hindenberg died 2 August 1934, *und* Adolf Hitler became *Führer* and *Reichskanzler* of *Deutschland*. Another group of men, this time dressed in grey uniforms, wearing red armbands on their left arms with the swastika displayed have been present in many of our towns in Austria. It appears as though the SA stormtroopers in the brown uniforms have disappeared *und* have been replaced with the *Schutzstaffel* (SS), who are more visible *und* violent. With these thugs walking our streets, Ingrid *und* I realize precious time is running out. Once this turmoil turned into the recipe for war, traveling across the *Ozean* would become impossible.

After breakfast the next morning, Ingrid *und* I rode our bicycles into town to use the pay telephone that sat in front of the barber shop. I called Gretel to let her know our plans were becoming a reality *und* that Ingrid *und* I would be leaving in two weeks. I invited the Hubert's to Sunday supper to discuss a few last minute details, also to light a fire under Gretel's butt, in hope that she'd also see the situation for what it is *und* move quickly. Due to the fact that Frank owned and drove an auto should make their trip a little easier; they only have to deal with the border crossings. It seemed as though overnight, the train stations had become swamped with SS presence, making it very uncomfortable for people to travel these days.

Ingrid *und* I tried to make the Hubert's feel as welcome as they had us so many times prior. After supper, we retired to the parlor where we ate *Pflaumenkuchen und* drank *Kaffee*. Unfortunately, with much dismay, Gretel was still dragging her feet somewhat *und* wasn't quite ready to physically move in. Despairingly, I gathered up Brigitte's belongings *und* her cat food for Gretel to take back to her *Haus* in *Deutschland*.

"Gretel, I was hoping you would be ready this time. I know you see what's going on. I feel you're literally running out of time. If anything really bad happens in *Deutschland*, I believe you'll be safer here. Please just leave your stuff. When times are better, you can go back for it. It's just stuff. Gretel I'm sorry to say, but you're in denial."

"Mags, I agree with you whole heartedly. My *Mutti* is a very stubborn *Frau*. I promise in two weeks we will move in here, if I have to drag *Mutti* kicking and screaming."

"*Vielen dank*. At least now I'll have one less thing to worry about as we're sailing kilometers across the North Atlantic *Ozean*."

The four of us sat in the warmth of a blazing fire in the parlor *und* were engaged in pleasant conversation. To give us peace of mind, Frank graciously offered to drive into Austria once a week to check up on *Herr* Rosenburg *und* my *Haus* until the time they're officially moved in. Frank promised Ingrid, once he's living in my *Haus*, he'd visit her *Vater* a couple times a week *und* help him with whatever is needed. I knew Ingrid worried; *Herr* Rosenburg was an old man who lived alone, *und* with the current events that were happening in Europe those days, Frank's offer gave her tranquility.

Remorsefully, I handed Brigitte over to Gretel as my eyes filled up with *Wasser*. I tried desperately to hold back my emotions; however, I burst into tears. That cat had been with me for nine years. We said our good-byes, hugged, *und* promised that we'll see one another again in better times. I watched Frank help his *Mutter* into the auto *und* laid Brigitte on her lap. Strangely, I found myself wishing Ingrid *und* I didn't have to leave. I really liked Frank. He started to walk around to the driver's side when I noticed he stopped, looked at me deep in my eyes, *und* started walking back toward the front door where I was standing. Shivers went down my spine. He put his arms around me *und* hugged me tight. I stood there mesmerized as I returned the hug.

"Can I kiss you good-bye?"

As I heard those beautiful words, I felt the blood go to my head *und* my legs felt like Jell-O. I've never in my entire life felt anything like that before. Although I was petrified, I wanted to kiss him. I was ashamed to even think about it, but I'd never kissed a man before *und* didn't know what to do.

"*Ja*, Frank, that would be lovely."

We kissed for want pleasantly seemed forever. I didn't want this precious moment in my life to ever end.

"Magdalina, can I have the address of your sister-in-law in *Amerika*? If it's all right with you, I would like very much to write you *und* stay in touch."

"Sure, give me a moment. I'll go in *und* write it down."

With my hands nervously shaking uncontrollably, I walked back outside, grinning from ear to ear. My face must had illuminated all the different shades of red. I very tenderly handed Frank the address.

"I'm going to write you—you better write me back."

"Of course, I will. *Danke*."

We passionately kissed one more time; I felt this incredible sensation running through my entire body. Frank pulled away *und* looked deep into my eyes.

"*Auf Wiedersehen*, until we meet again."

"*Auf Wiedersehen*, Frank."

Sadly, I watched this glorious man walk away from me, jump into his auto, *und* drive out of my life. Needless to say, I once again tossed *und* turned all night long; however, this time, with such empathetic feelings, I actually didn't want to sleep. I just kept replaying the scenario over *und* over in my head. Unfortunately, my companion Brigitte isn't snuggled up next to me this time. This is going to be quite an adjustment on my end.

The following afternoon, Ingrid *und* I bicycled over to her *Väter Haus*. *Herr* Rosenburg was sitting on his front porch like he knew we were coming *und* is waiting for us. Ingrid *und* I walked into the *Haus und* went into the *Küche* to put the tea kettle on. Once the *Wasser* boiled, we made some tea *und* brought three cups back outside *und* joined *Herr* Roseburg.

What a glorious September afternoon! The sun's rays radiated incredible warmth with a faint sweet breeze. The three of us sat on the porch drinking our tea *und* talking for hours. *Herr* Rosenburg nervously smoked what seemed to be a full pack of *Zigaretten* in the short time we were visiting.

"Papa, I want you to come with us to the New World."

"*Nein*, I cannot, *Liebchen*. I have to stay here with the farm. She'll be yours someday soon. I'm going to fix things up around here for that glorious day you return. I *liebe* your dream of returning to Austria *und* the two of you becoming farmers. Work the land—the soil is rich *und* the possibilities are endless. This is my legacy to you."

"Papa, I don't care about all that."

"Esther, of course, you do. When the time is right, fulfill your dreams *und* live a happy, prosperous life. I know you'll make something great out of this old place. That will give me the strength to continue on."

"Papa, please."

"*Nein*, I'm an old man, my place is here."

He got up, took Ingrid by the hand, *und* the two of them walked back into the *Haus*. A few minutes later, they joined me back outside on the porch. Ingrid showed me a photograph of her *Mutter und Vater* on their wedding day.

"Magdalina, I also have something for you. My wife's broach that you *und* Ingrid so adored as *Kinder*. I want you to have it. Please always remember us."

"*Oh mein Gott*, I can't."

"*Ja*, you can."

My eyes filled up with tears as I hugged him with a long, powerful embrace. It was everything I could do not to break down in a silly *Mädchen* hysteria.

"*Vielen dank, Herr* Rosenburg."

"You're welcome. Now, *Mädchen*, I want you both to go home before it gets dark. We'll reunite once again when things are better in the near future. I *liebe* you both, *Auf Wiedersehen*."

Ingrid cried the entire bicycle ride back to the *Haus*, *und* I was speechless. Never would I, in a million years, ever expect this to be so difficult. We're only going to *Amerika* for a long visit. We'll travel back to Austria in a year or so when Europe's troubles were far behind *und* Ingrid Rose could safely become Esther Ingrid Rosenburg once again. The future was grand; we just had to get through a couple of rough patches.

CALM WINDS *UND* FOLLOWING SEAS

 The next *Morgen*, I woke to the sound of birds singing happily *und* the whisper of a clean, sweet breeze blowing through my *Schlafzimmer* windows. I wanted to lay in *Bett* all *Morgen und* drink this in; however inviting me downstairs was a wonderful aroma enticing me to the *Küche*. Ingrid made *Kaffee*, scrambled eggs, bacon, *und* toast. I was famished *und* was not shy to inhale my food.

"This is wonderful Ingrid. Why didn't you wake me? I would have helped with this incredible farewell breakfast."

"Don't worry about it, Mags. I had trouble sleeping last night, so I decided to get up early. I cleaned a little *und* already took my bath. Please, let's eat before it gets cold."

"Sure, everything looks great. *Danke.*"

"Mags, after we're finished breakfast, I'll do the dishes. Take a bath, *und* get yourself pulled together. We have much to do this morning—this is our big debut."

"Sure, no problem."

After two helpings of eggs, about one-half pound of bacon, *und* two pieces of toast, I was finally full *und* busting at the seams. I walked back upstairs *und* drew a warm bath. As I sat in the tub in deep thought, staring into space, I began to show signs of a shriveled prune. I dried off *und* walked back into my *Schlafzimmer*, finished packing my bags, *und* made my *Bett*. As I sat at my vanity, putting my face on *und* fixing my hair, my mood became gloomy *und* my eyes began to fill. I immediately got up and walked over to my *Bett*, sat down, pulled my stockings up, *und* fastened them to the garters. I slipped into my favorite white silk petticoat *und* put on my pink suit. Immediately, I walked over to the dresser *und* took out a second pair of white gloves *und* placed them in my pocketbook *und* pinned *Frau* Rosenburg's broach to the lapel of my jacket.

I took one last look around my *Raum und* found myself instinctively tidying up somewhat. Once I realized I was acting neurotic, I closed *und* locked the windows *und* pulled the curtains open. I walked down the hall to *Fräulein* Gabriele's old *Zimmer* to make sure the window was locked and the curtain was drawn as well. Without giving it much thought, I checked Ingrid's *Zimmer*; however, not surprisingly she's already taken care of everything. I gathered my things, walked my bags down the stairs, *und* placed them next to Ingrid's by the front door.

Ingrid *und* I walked around the *Haus*, checking every nook *und* cranny, making sure the place was secure *und* we didn't forget anything. I walked out to the backyard *und* looked around as well. The *Haus* was perfect, both inside *und* out. I decided to walk across the street to the cemetery *und* visit my *Eltern*. With the fear that this could be the last time I'd able to visit their graves for an indefinite amount of time, I stood fighting back the tears.

"*Mutti, Vater*, I'm sorry I have to leave for a while. I'm going to *Amerika* to see Gerhard *und* his wife, Christine. I pray I'm able to bring Gerhard home someday, so he too can visit you *und* I can show him where he was born. My decision to leave for *Amerika* is for the best. I *liebe* you *und* miss you both."

As I bent down to remove the old, dried-up flowers I placed on their graves last week, I notice *Herr* Rosenburg's truck parked in front of the *Haus*. Ingrid *und* her *Vater* were loading our suitcases into the truck *Bett*. I quickly walked back to my *Haus* with butterflies in my stomach. We'd been planning this moment for so long, *und* now it was really happening. I have to say, I was scared to death. This was such a large leap into the unknown.

I locked the front door, picked up my pocketbook, *und* walked down the stone walkway towards *Herr* Rosenburg's truck. I stopped for a moment, turned around *und* took one last mental picture of the scenery. For a quick moment I had to remind myself that this is for the best. I know in my heart Ingrid *und* I are doing the right thing, furthermore her *Vater* will never allow us to back out now.

Herr Rosenburg helped Ingrid *und* I into his truck *und* took off down the dirt road heading into Linz. We had thirty minutes before the train was scheduled to pull into the station. *Herr* Rosenburg retrieved our suitcases from the truck *und* placed them on the ground next to the bench. He then sat down between us in silence, as we patiently waited for the train to arrive.

"Huh, five minutes late. Not so bad. You *Mädchen* make me a promise."

"Sure, Papa, anything."

"Don't return until you know things are better in *Deutschland*."

"Okay, no problem."

"*Nein*, I mean it—no matter what happens; you have to promise to respect my wishes."

"I promise, Papa, anything you say."

With all that said and done, the train pulled into the station *und* the passengers got off. Ingrid *und* I jumped up from the bench *und* grabbed our suitcases *und* pocketbooks. *Herr* Rosenburg helped us carry our suitcases over to the tracks to board the train. The mood is so surreal. This truly was one of the hardest things I've ever done.

"Esther, I *liebe* you."

"I *liebe* you too, Papa."

"Esther, you are *mein kleines Mädchen und* always will be. Mags, please take care of my baby."

"Of course."

"Papa, I'll write you once we get to Ellis Island."

"That would be great. I look forward to hearing from you. Don't forget everything I've told."

"We won't, Papa. I promise."

With tears running down all three of our faces, totally ruining the makeup which took me twenty minutes to apply, Ingrid *und* I took turns embracing *Herr* Rosenburg with long hugs. I have to keep reminding myself that this is a temporary situation, we'll come back someday *und* life will go back to normal. Although, I really wish Ingrid *und* I could have convinced *Herr* Rosenburg to join us in our adventure. Although Frank has promised to check in on him periodically, I'm also worried. My *Vater* has been dead for many years, deep down inside I may be looking at Esther's *Vater* as a substitute.

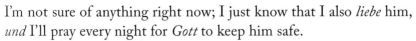

I'm not sure of anything right now; I just know that I also *liebe* him, *und* I'll pray every night for *Gott* to keep him safe.

"*Auf Wiedersehen Mädchen.*"

"*Auf Wiedersehen, Papa.*"

"*Auf Wiedersehen, Herr* Rosenburg."

We picked up our suitcases *und* quickly boarded the train. Delightfully, the *Waggon* is fairly empty so we sat towards the back. The conductor helped Ingrid and I place our suitcases on the rack above the seats *und* we got settled in for a long ride. Ingrid graciously offered me the window seat, *und* I happily preoccupied myself with the beautiful scenery of the countryside. I cannot imagine *Amerika* having this kind of plentiful beauty. From what I've heard *Amerika* is a huge country of flat *und* dessert type dry lands, with dust *und* tumbleweeds everywhere. The streets maybe paved in gold, however *Amerika* will never come close to the natural beauty of Austria and *Deutschland*.

Ingrid *und* I sat for hours with nothing to say to one another as the train stopped at every scheduled location for passengers to depart *und* the new to board. The entire time we spent on the train, I could faintly hear Ingrid sobbing, indiscreetly. After a few hours, the train conductor politely walked up to where we're seated *und* informed us the next stop was where we need to get off. Once we got off this train, we had to walk to another platform that was located on the other side of the station. We're to purchase our tickets to the Netherlands *und* wait thirty minutes for the international train to Rotterdam.

Forty minutes later, we boarded the second train. Unfortunately, this train was very crowded. The entire time I was sitting there with nothing to do, my imagination once again kicked into high gear *und* was out of control.

"Ingrid, do you think all these people have the same plan as we do? Maybe they're all leaving for *Amerika* as well, *und* there won't be enough room for us."

This scenario seemed very strange, even for my daydreaming expertise. There were at least fifteen *Waggons* filled with people.

"Don't be silly. Things aren't that bad. It's not a life or death situation to flee to *Amerika*. These people are going to other destinations for entirely different reasons."

"*Ja*, of course, you're right. You know me when I get started," I turned away *und* chuckled to myself.

Ingrid fell asleep, *und* I ended up in a conversation with a very nice *ältere Frau* sitting next to me across the aisle. *Frau* Krause was alone *und* probably relished the idea of having someone to talk to as much as I do. It's a far better way of passing the time versus silly, girlish daydreaming. She also purchased a ticket to *Amerika* on the steamship *Rotterdam*; however, her ticket was stamped first class. She lived in *Deutschland und* had family who lived in *Amerika*. After much persuading, she finally decided to leave *Deutschland* to live with her *Sohn und* his wife in the New World. This was actually her second trip in five years; the first time she went was for a three-month visit when her *Sohn* was getting married.

Frau Krause informed me that there would be anywhere from two hundred to three hundred emigrants who will board the steamship from *Deutschland*, Austria, Switzerland *und* Italy. Typically, emigrants purchase tickets for the steerage section, which is the lowest deck of the ship. Of course, first *und* second classes have the top sections *und* all the privileges to boot. She never asked me what ticket I purchased. I had to assume she was perfectly aware that it was steerage *und* was trying to be polite. Although, I would have never considered myself an emigrant; I was just a passenger. *Frau* Krause assured me that once we arrive at the hotel, we'd be provided with more information. After talking for an hour, I ended up falling asleep as well.

Suddenly, Ingrid *und* I were woken to the sound of the train whistle. *Frau* Krause very kindly informed us that this was our stop. As we said a heartfelt good-bye to one another, I gave her a quick hug *und dankte* her for the pleasant conversation. Ingrid *und* I gathered our baggage *und* pocketbooks *und* exited the train. Another very pleasant train conductor with the Holland America Line was outside, shuffling us like cattle toward a steam tugboat tied up at the dock in the wharf.

Apparently, there were several *Waggons* that were only assigned to the people who were taking this trip. The rest of the train carried other passengers with different destinations, which explains why the *Waggon* we were riding in was so crowded.

Ingrid *und* I started to get very excited. You could see the NASM Hotel across the wharf *und* a riverboat with more people entering. I overheard two gentlemen conversing about the local train *und* riverboat that would be bringing more people the next couple of days before our departure. At this point, Ingrid *und* I were feeling nothing but excitement *und* pure bliss.

"See, Ingrid, everything is working out beautifully. This is the best decision we could have possibly made."

Once we crossed the wharf, we were shuffled off the tugboat *und* escorted to the hotel where we're assigned dormitories. Families are together while single men have the back *und* single women are assigned the front area. *Gott sei dank*, Ingrid *und* I have two other women bunking with us, who were our age and seemed very nice. This was a blessing, considering we'll be spending five to six days in these dormitories before we sail. Each dormitory had four to six iron berths *und* were separated by partitions that were open on the top. On the opposite side of the *Zimmer* was the same setup. In the center between the two partitions was a wide open space with tables *und* chairs. There were windows *und* ventilators on every side. The *Badezimmer und* washrooms were located off the vestibules close to each dormitory.

"Ingrid, this is one of the strangest hotels I've ever seen."

"Yah, Mags, just exactly how many hotels have you stayed at?"

"Very funny. Point well made," Ingrid *und* I immediately began laughing until our sides hurt.

Once we received our assigned *Zimmer*, we were then shuffled to a large auditorium for a presentation. During this hour's presentation, it was explained that the hotel was designed *und* built for the sole purpose of exporting emigrants across the North Atlantic *Ozean*. The hotel was part of the Holland America Line. This entire trip was a carefully designed package, which included the train to the wharf, the steam tugboat that took us to the hotel, the accommodations, *und* the steamship sailing to *Amerika*. The hotel was a holding place for emigrants before we can board the ship *und* sail out of port.

Every steerage passenger will be seen by a physician who'd be coming around daily, inspecting us on cleanliness, bathing, disinfecting, *und* any other sanitary issues before we could become a prospective citizen of the United States. The dormitories will also be inspected. Anyone not passing an inspection will be held at the hotel in quarantine *und* later sent back to their point of origin. The day prior to boarding, an inspection will be done at the hotel of the steerage passenger's baggage. All *Federbetten und* pillows will undergo vigorous steam disinfections.

The last medical inspection will be conducted by the ships surgeon, an *Amerikaner* physician. Once we pass through his inspection, we will have our inspection cards stamped with a rubber seal of approval. At that point, we will finally be approved to board the ship with our baggage in one hand *und* our inspection cards in the other. As we enter the steerage section, our inspection cards will be checked one more time. We then will be vaccinated by the ship's surgeon *und* will be ready for the long journey across the North Atlantic *Ozean*.

"I must say, Ingrid, a funny *und* happy thought just popped into my brain. Years ago, I read one of *Fräulein* Gabriele's books about Western cowboy's *und* the *Amerikaner* frontier. I now know how those poor cows must have felt as they were being shuffled to the slaughter."

"Very funny, but I don't see any humor in any of this."

"Ingrid, I promise you everything will be all right."

Once my brain thoroughly processed the hotel's presentation, I began to understand why they put us through this torture. Ingrid, on the other hand, was having difficulties coming to terms with this procedure. In fact, after the presentation, as we were escorted to our assigned *Zimmer*, she complained the entire time.

"Mags, I'm returning home tomorrow. I'm so upset with this whole thing. I don't understand—I'm clean. I bath everyday, just like they do. How dare they assume that we're dirty *und* are diseased? Why, just because we're from Europe? I'm so humiliated."

"Ingrid, you're taking this information out of content. They're just taking precautionary measures. They want to be sure someone isn't infected with something *und* unknowingly brings it into the country where it can spread *und* infect *Amerikaner*."

"Yah, I guess you're right. I'm acting *kindisch* once again. See, that's why I need you. You have to keep me grounded."

"No, not *kindisch*, Ingrid, just a little over sensitive, *und* you're understandably scared. I'm scared as well, but how wonderful the country of *Amerika* must be. They take all these precautions to protect their citizens *und* are also protecting *und* welcoming foreigners. Ingrid, I think you *und* I are really going to be happy in *Amerika*. Please don't go home. We got this far. Once all these procedures in the hotel are behind us *und* we're actually on the ship, everything will be so much better."

Five days later, Ingrid *und* I boarded the steamship *und* were getting settled into our berths in steerage. Once we were settled in, we proceeded to walk up on deck to witness the ship pulling away from the wharf *und* out into the North Atlantic *Ozean*.

"Ingrid, I'm so excited I could scream," I said, as the smile on my face is from one ear to the other.

"*Ja*, me too."

"This is the most incredible adventure of my life. I just wish your *Vater* could have been here to see this."

The cool salty *Ozean* air smells so delicious, *und* the sound of the seagulls with the breathtaking beauty of the sun beginning to set was overwhelming. We walked around, proudly drinking in all the sights *und* sounds. The ship was so clean *und* immense. There were so many passengers it might take an hour to walk from bow to stern to experience this picturesque sight. I thought I could literally live on deck until we pull into Ellis Island; however, it's the end of September *und* the nights in the middle of the *Ozean* were going to be extremely cold. Furthermore, I was a steerage passenger *und* we were only permitted limited, scheduled times on the ship's upper deck.

As quick as that, my bubble burst. Needless to say, our first night aboard ship was extremely interesting. It was almost impossible to sleep; we were packed in like cattle, *und* with all the different sounds, smells, *und* people snoring, it was devastating. Sleeping on deck, freezing my *arsch* off, was looking more appealing with every passing moment. I could tell Ingrid was having problems sleeping *und* was upset. For the first time in my life, I was actually afraid to say anything to her; I lay on my *Federbett* on eggshells, pretending I was asleep. We had to fixate in our brains that this was a temporary situation; we had to go with the flow *und* get accustomed to our new living arrangements. This wasn't the end of the world. Once we were in *Amerika*, life would be grand.

Unfortunately the next day, we found out rather quickly the ship's deck was primarily reserved for first-*und* second-class passengers only. Life aboard ship for steerage was completely different. We were scheduled deck privileges for a short time, normally when first *und* second class were in the dining area. Our quarters below were cramped *und* dirty. There was a severe lack of sanitation *und* facilities *und* no washing or bathing areas. With each passing day, the stench was getting worse. People were getting seasick, *und* the smell was impossible. Much to my dismay, I even witnessed rats running about. As cold as the nights have been getting, the days cooped up down below with all these people was uncomfortably hot. I was beginning to fear the tangibility that Ingrid *und* I weren't used to this type of atmosphere *und* might not survive this torture.

With everything we were presently dealing with *und* the conditions of steerage, disgruntledly, Ingrid had become very standoffish in the past couple of days. Ever since we boarded ship *und* sailed into the *Ozean*, she had become very distant. Most evenings, I could hear her weeping when she thought I was asleep. Alarmingly, I was now second-doubting myself *und* becoming extremely discouraged *und* frightened with negative thoughts of this trip. Maybe we made a mistake leaving Austria.

I could not imagine how bad things could really get in *Deutschland*; however, I was sure the changes my *Bruder* was trying to make would end up for the best. My *Bruder* Adolf was a good man, with a good heart *und* a good head on his shoulders.

As quickly as that daydream went through my brain, I came back to reality. Since Adolf became chancellor a year ago, *Deutschland* had been sliding downhill. Two months ago, when he became the *Führer-Reichskanzler*, the country's problems were getting worse.

Bottom line was, my *Bruder* was a dictator with bad men working with him. People were scared; *Deutsch*-born citizens were leaving their homeland, especially the Jewish population. According to the recent newspapers, Austria had taken in an overwhelmingly amount of *Deutsch* Jews into the country.

I could not allow myself to be that naive *und* believe there was nothing wrong. There were too many good *Deutsch* people who were brainwashed into thinking the new *Führer* was the answer to *Deutschland* problems. I believe these people would end up suffering for their stupidity. Furthermore, I didn't understand how Adolf, an Austrian-born citizen, could denounce his citizenship *und* become a *Deutsch* citizen *und*, that quickly, the *Führer* of *Deutschland*. I would imagine that *Gott* specifically didn't intend women to have a head for men's politics.

Shake this off. We're doing the right thing, I thought. Ingrid *und* I would go on deck tomorrow, sit down, *und* rationalize the pros *und* cons of our decision to leave Austria. I'd make her understand our situation was temporary. Hopefully, the weather would continue to be nice *und* we would arrive in Ellis Island, New York, within a week. Once we get to *Amerika*, the possibilities would be endless. One day, years from now, Ingrid *und* I would reminisce about our travels to *Amerika und* remember this small amount of inconvenience *und* suffering we were experiencing right now. I was sure once this was behind us, we'd feel nothing but shame due to the fact that we were so selfish not to see the bigger picture *und* be grateful. I had to put all my concentrated efforts into snapping her out of this deep depression she was currently in.

The next afternoon, when the ship's steward came down below to invite the dungeon people on deck, Ingrid *und* I walked up together. Thank *Gott*, once again it turned out to be a beautiful sunshiny day with a perfect sea breeze. It was a little chilly for early October; however, I would assume that's to be expected in the middle of the *Ozean*. I put my winter sweater on *und* enjoyed the limited time granted to us on this spectacular day. We only had an hour of scheduled deck time, *und* I planned on making the most of it.

In a split second, I happened to look over the port side of the ship, *und* out of the corner of my eye, I noticed a school of dauphines leaping in the *Ozean*. I was so excited that without a thought, I screamed for Esther.

"*Oh mein Gott*, I cannot believe I just said that. Ingrid, I'm sorry, it just slipped out of my big mouth. I pray no one heard."

"Mags, relax. Who cares who heard what?"

"Ingrid, you have to come see this."

Ingrid ran over to where I was standing, *und* the two of us stood there captivated, watching these incredible creatures leaping in *und* out of the *Ozean* with such grace. It's as though they were racing against the ship *und* having so much fun keeping up. Unfortunately, our dolphin experience only lasted a few minutes; they must have gotten bored *und* went someplace else. However, Ingrid *und* I continued to watch the sea directly overboard. Happily, within minutes, our pleasure was restored with the sight of a large school of stingrays also swimming in unison with the ship. Ingrid *und* I stood there looking overboard the entire time we were privileged with this valuable deck time.

This isn't how I planned the day. I wanted to sit on the deck chairs in the warmth of the sun *und* talk some sense into her. After our precious allotted time was up, the dungeon people were quickly gathered *und* instructed to walk back down to the black hole *und* get settled in for the rest of the day. For the first time in a week, I could actually see a smile on Ingrid's face. While both of us had been lifted beyond words with the simplicity of the sea's treasures, I was now convinced I'd keep my big mouth shut for the time being. Maybe those dolphins *und* the beautiful stingrays were a gift from *Gott*, something we both needed to lift our spirits once again.

Gratefully, *Gott* has been watching over the dungeon people; the weather continued to stay nice with calm winds and following seas, allowing the steamship an early arrival. The ship steward walked down into the black hole *und* informed us that the next morning, the *Rotterdam* would be sailing into Ellis Island. We all jumped for joy. In the ten days that we'd been at sea, this was the first time I'd seen the dungeon people happy. A few gentlemen pulled out their violins from their suitcases *und* began playing old Italian folk songs. People sang all night long, keeping our spirits flying ever so high.

Just as promised, the next morning, we entered the harbor at Ellis Island. The ship's captain came over the radio *und* informed us that the passengers of first *und* second classes would depart first. The stewards would then come down into the black hole *und* organize the dungeon people. We'd then divide into sections *und* lineup. Each section would form a single line, *und* a steward would lead us up on deck. Once we passed through Ellis Island *und* were processed, our new lives in *Amerika* would begin.

Two hours later, Ingrid *und* I were starring at the Statue of Liberty in total amazement, standing on the shores of Manhattan. We heard so much about her; however, I could never imagine being a part of this extraordinary sight. Obviously, I was terribly wrong in thinking that *Amerika* was flat *und* dirty. With this view as the first impression *Amerika* had shown us, I was anxious to see every inch of this incredible country. This beauty had given me an uncanny feeling of peace *und* tranquility, which I haven't felt in a while.

REALITY HITS ME UPSIDE THE FACE

 As Ingrid *und* I were preoccupied looking around, with our bags on the ground next to us, captivated by the hustle *und* bustle of Manhattan, our pocketbooks clinched to our sides, it suddenly dawned on me Gerhard's wife was nowhere in sight.

"Ingrid, we may have a little problem here. Christine is supposed to meet us at the *Hafen* in Manhattan. We have no idea what she looks like, *und* stupid me, I neglected to ask in my letters."

"Don't worry. What are you always telling me? This too shall work out."

"*Ja*, you're right," I said half heartedly, with the feeling I could slap myself upside the face for being so stupid.

With all the emigrants standing around, talking *und* looking for their contact people, *und* hundreds more being transported to shore, I could not imagine how Christine would ever locate us. Ingrid *und* I might end up standing here all day. Unfortunately, this was the only detail of the entire trip I didn't think of. My last correspondence with Christine stated the steamship *Rotterdam* was scheduled to arrive in the New York *Harbor* on 30 September 1934. I also gave her the number assigned to this particular trip, per her request. Yesterday, there should have been an itinerary for that number broadcasted on the radio of the actual date *und* time the *Rotterdam* was expected to sail into the *Hafen* at Ellis Island.

"What a fool I am. This detail should have been a no brainer."

"Magdalina, please stop. Don't ruin this moment."

"*Ja*, of course, Ingrid. I apologize."

Minutes later, Ingrid *und* I noticed a large cardboard sign held over the heads of the crowd, reading "Magdalina Wolff *und* Ingrid Rose." This must be our sign from *Gott*. We quickly picked up our suitcases *und* desperately scrambled through the crowd over to the large sign. A tall, thin beautiful woman, with flowing long dark hair *und* a slight olive complexion, was standing with her arms reaching to the sun, holding the handmade sign. We immediately dropped our suitcases *und* embraced Christine. Next to her is an *älteren* gentleman whom Christine brought along as our translator. Richard Bergmann was a *Freund* who was born in *Deutschland und* had lived in *Amerika* for the past ten years. He owned a print shop two blocks down the street from where Gerhard *und* Christine live.

"Hi, I'm Magdalina, but everyone calls me Mags."

"Welcome Mags, I'm Christine. I apologize for arriving late. Last evening, conformation was broadcasted on the radio, informing us that the ship would be arriving into the harbor sometime today. We were instructed to call the Ellis Island office for an arrival time this morning. I walked down to Richard's print shop to borrow his telephone and was told that the ship had just sailed into the harbor. Richard and I immediately flagged down a taxi and were taken to the train station in Philadelphia. Unfortunately, we had to wait an hour for the next train that was scheduled to arrive in Manhattan. I hope you and Ingrid haven't been waiting too long."

"*Nein*, of course, not. It took hours to check in *und* pass through customs *und* get a ferry to Manhattan. Ingrid *und* I have been pleasantly occupied with the sights of the Manhattan coastline."

"Great, let's get out of here and go home. I took a couple days off from work to help you and Ingrid get settled in. Richard and I would like to take you sightseeing sometime tomorrow. Richard has also taken a few days off from work. He has graciously volunteered to be our tour guide and token translator. Gerhard will not be home until 6:00 p.m. However, once he arrives, we have a surprise for you both."

"*Danken*, Christine, for everything. I cannot wait to see my *Bruder*," I said in a nervous, crackling voice as I stumbled over my words.

Two hours, later we departed the train at the Philadelphia train station *und* caught the first available taxicab. The driver stopped in front of a four-story apartment building in the city, nestled among other various-size dwellings. Christine paid the taxi driver; he opened the trunk of the auto *und* walked our suitcases up the cement path leading to the steps *und* placed them all together. Christine *dankte* the gentleman as he sped off for his next fare. Richard immediately picked up the two suitcases, *und* we grabbed the others *und* followed Christine. We walked up the front steps, entered the building, *und* were led halfway down the hallway.

"Magdalina, please put your suitcases down in front of this door and follow me."

"Of course, Christine, *kein* problem."

As Richard also placed the two suitcases on the floor alongside the others, Ingrid *und* I looked at each other, slightly confused. We proceeded to walk up one flight of stairs *und* down the hall. Christine took a key out of her pocketbook *und* opened the apartment door. She graciously invited us into her home. Christine humbly showed us around her small immaculate one-*Schlafzimmer* apartment, trying to make us feel welcome with every step. It's amazing to see the difference between their tiny apartment *und* Frank *und* Gretel's extremely large three-*Schlafzimmer* apartment in *Deutschland*. I'd always lived in a single *Haus*, so the concept of apartment living was new to me. Gerhard's home was barely large enough for two people. In retrospect to the accommodations we recently experienced on the steamship, needless to say I was extremely concerned.

The four of us happily sat in the parlor *und* drank *Kaffee und* ate French mini pastries that Christine purchased from the baker down the street earlier this *Morgen*. We talked *und* got acquainted for hours with the help of our translator, Richard. Gratefully, Ingrid *und* I experienced such a lovely day with Christine *und* Richard; they both went out of their way to make us feel welcome.

"Everyone, please make yourselves comfortable at the table. It's 6:45 p.m. Gerhard is forty-five minutes late, and I don't want supper to dry out."

"*Vielen dank*, Christine. Everything looks and smells perfect."

Christine was an impeccable hostess. The table was perfectly set with fresh yellow mums *und* baby's breath in a crystal vase placed in the center. The food smelled delicious, *und* I was famished. Ingrid *und* I hadn't had a decent meal since Gretel *und* Frank were at my *Haus* to say our farewells. We quickly picked up the cloth napkins neatly folded at the place setting in front of us *und* placed them on our laps.

Christine's supper menu consists of an *Amerikaner* beef pot roast in a rich dark gravy with carrots *und* new potatoes, buttered baby peas, *und* warm buttermilk biscuits. Ingrid *und* I were so famished we scarfed our meal down like we hadn't eaten in weeks. When no one was looking, I think I probably licked my plate clean. What a wonderful supper.

I couldn't help but think how rude of Gerhard not to show up for this delicious meal on my first day in *Amerika*. Christine obviously went through a lot of trouble preparing it. When everyone was finished, Ingrid *und* I immediately jumped up from the table *und* helped Christine clear the dishes while Richard sat in the parlor smoking a *Zigarette*. Christine washed *und* I dried. Ingrid kept clearing the table, bringing dirty dishes into us. It almost seemed as though those dishes were multiplying.

For the first time today, I was beginning to feel a little eccentric. I was not sure what to do once the dishes *und* the *Küche* were finished. However, Christine always seemed to be one step ahead. She asked us to retire to the parlor as she brought out freshly brewed *Kaffee und* a pack of *Zigaretten*.

"I'm sorry I didn't make dessert. Is that all right?"

"*Oh mein Gott*, of course! We're stuffed to the gills. What a great supper. You cannot begin to imagine what they were feeding us on that steamship. I felt like a farm animal."

"Good, please join me for a cigarette."

"*Danke*, but I don't smoke. Neither does Ingrid."

"That's fine. Do you mind if I have one?"

"*Nein*, of course, not."

"Oh dear, look at the time. You girls must be exhausted. Forget the cigarette. I have something I want to show you."

"*Danke*," I looked at Christine with admiration.

The four of us got up, walked out the door *und* down the flight of steps. We walked back down the hallway to where our suitcases were still sitting in front the apartment door. We were so engrossed in conversation and good food I completely forgot about them.

Christine took another key out of her skirt pocket *und* opened the apartment door, graciously invited us in, *und* turned on the light.

"Gerhard and I were planning to surprise you. I was hoping he and I could do this together. However, you girls need to get settled in and go to bed. Tomorrow is another day."

Christine seemed very excited to show us around. The apartment was a very spacious, well-kept two-*Schlafzimmer*, double the size of Gerhard's *und* completely furnished.

"Magdalina, this apartment and the furnishings once belonged to Bruno. This is where your baby brother grew up."

"*Oh mein Gott*, this is wonderful. I feel as though I have a small piece of my *Bruder*."

After Bruno's death, his estate went to my *Bruder*. Gerhard was able to purchase the entire apartment *Komplex und* reserved this particular apartment. Originally, he intended to move in right away; however Gerhard had been so busy with his other business venture they just haven't had the opportunity to pack *und* move. Later, when Christine received my letter, they agreed that this apartment would be perfect for Ingrid *und* me. I was surprised Christine *und* Gerhard didn't switch apartments before we arrived. This one was so much nicer. However, I was not looking a gift horse in the mouth; this was a wonderful surprise, *und* more important, Ingrid had smile on her face. After that great supper *und* this wonderful apartment located in this beautiful country, I was sure I'm going to toss *und* turn tonight. Just as I'd been saying all along, things were going to get better now that we were in *Amerika*.

"You girls get some sleep. Richard and I are going to leave now. I'll come by sometime later tomorrow morning, and we'll go from there."

"*Danke*, Christine *und* Richard. *Gute Nacht*."

Ingrid *und* I stood in the parlor in an incoherent state of mind, looking at one another not knowing where to start, *und* too exhausted if we did. We decided to go directly to *Bett*, when we get up tomorrow *Morgen* we'll deal with a new day. We left our suitcases in the parlor, *und* each of us chose a *Schlafzimmer*. Remarkably, considering the days events, I had no problem falling asleep; I think I was asleep before my head actually hit the pillow.

Much to my surprise, I woke exceptionally early *und* very excited with my first full day in *Amerika*. After making my *Bett*, I closed Ingrid's door so she could sleep longer *und* went into the *Küche* to look for some *Kaffee* or tea in one of the cupboards. The *Küche* was quite lovely *und* very modern. The cupboards were white metal, the counters emerald green, *und* a cream linoleum floor with specks of deep orange and emerald green. There was an electric percolator on the counter alongside the white icebox *und* a tin container filled with *Kaffee*. I made a full pot of *Kaffee und* began snooping around. Apparently, Christine recently purchased some groceries for us. There were a few items in the icebox—a wax carton of milk, eggs, orange juice, a couple bottles of Coca Cola, butter *und* some cheese. One of the cupboards was filled with a variety of canned goods. Another smaller cupboard had a ridiculous amount of spices stored in it. We have a box of Cheerios *und* a loaf of bread in another cupboard. The cupboard under the sink housed the dish detergent *und* cleaning supplies. The only item in the freezer was two ice-cube trays. Obviously, Ingrid *und* I would have to go to the market sometime today *und* stock up.

I poured a cup of *Kaffee und* walked into the parlor *und* looked around. The parlor was a large *Zimmer* with beautiful hardwood shinny floors and a large green area rug. A dark gold sofa sat under a large window draped with blue, green, *und* gold floral ruffled curtains, swagged and tied back at each side, with white ruffle shears underneath. Two high-back chairs matching the floral curtains sit in front of the sofa with a cherry *Kaffee* table between the sofa *und* chairs. Two matching cherry end tables sat next to each end of the sofa, with tall brass candlestick lamps *und* matching ash trays. There's a beautiful mahogany antique mirror hanging on the wall on the right with a matching high vanity table directly under it, *und* a set of three mahogany bookcases on the opposite wall.

I walked over to the bookcase *und* I'm pleasantly surprised with the amount of books written in *Deutsch*. I found one book titled *Deutsch auf Englisch*, pulled it out, *und* placed it on the *Kaffee* table. This book, along with Gretel's *Deutsch*-English dictionary, would be a great learning tool. I was beginning to feel much anxiety realizing that Ingrid *und* I would have to learn *Englisch* promptly. I sat on the sofa sipping my *Kaffee*, reviewing the book *und* trying desperately to pronounce *und* memorize these *Englisch* words. I thought, *This is probably going to be more difficult than I could ever imagine.*

An hour later, Ingrid woke up *und* joined me in the parlor. I immediately jumped up *und* walked into the *Küche und* poured her a cup of *Kaffee*. When I came back into the parlor, I noticed she too was looking over the same book. We decided when we see Richard later today for our sightseeing tour we'd speak to him concerning the best way of learning the *Englisch* language. Perhaps he might be interested in tutoring us. Ingrid *und* I finished our *Kaffee*, took turns taking our baths, *und* proceeded to get ready for our first bona fide day in *Amerika*.

I just finished making myself beautiful, *und* as great timing would have it, there's a knock at the door. Anxiously, I leaped for the door with much anticipation. Surprisingly, there was a handsome tall young man standing in the hallway. Bewildered, I stared at him for a moment, having no idea who he was; however, as my eyes glanced down his body, I noticed the metal crutches he's leaning on. Of course, at this point, I realize there was a strong possibility that my baby *Bruder* was standing in front me, like a dream come true.

"Are you Magdalina?"

"*Ja.*"

"*Hallo*, I'm Gerhard."

"*Oh mein Gott.*"

I threw my arms around him with such force I almost knocked him off his feet. Seconds later I began to hysterically cry. I got myself so crazed I began feeling somewhat lightheaded. I walked over to the sofa *und* sat down to regain my equilibrium. Gerhard immediately called for Christine, who was standing down the hallway out of view. They both walked into the parlor, holding hands with huge grins on their faces, *und* sat down next to me. Gerhard so tenderly wrapped his arm around me as the two of us sat there babbling on *und* on. Before I knew it, Gerhard *und* I had totally monopolized the conversation.

"Magdalina, since you and Gerhard are engrossed in conversation, I'll take Ingrid down the street to Richard's. We'll pick him up, and the three of us will walk to the market and purchase food for your kitchen."

Once Gerhard translated what Christine said, I gave her a huge hug *und* a *Küss* on the cheek, with appreciation for her uncanny prudence of the situation.

"*Danke*. If you don't mind, that would be great. I can't get enough of Gerhard's wonderful childhood stories."

Joyfully, Gerhard *und* I sat in the comfort of my new parlor, conversing to one another *und* catching up from a lifetime. We spent the entire day speaking in *Deutsch*, telling each other about our lives. I was delighted he was so diverse with the language *und* remarkably had the Austrian-*Deutsch* dialect down almost perfect. Bruno did a great job; Gerhard was also fluent in *Englisch* with a faint accent.

"Magdalina, I also took a few days off from work. I own the apartment *Komplex*. Therefore, I'm the landlord, *und* with such, there are a few perks. Unless there's a problem in the building, we can spend some uninterrupted quality time together."

"That's wonderful. I have so patiently waited for this day. Now that it's here I feel as though I'm dreaming. Is this reality, or am I going to wake shortly from a very pleasant dream?"

"Mags, I can guarantee you're not dreaming. I suggest we all wake up bright *und* early tomorrow morning. Richard, Christine, *und* I are going to show you *und* Ingrid around town. Since the day has already gotten away from us, we'll postpone our little sightseeing adventure until tomorrow. Also, Christine's taking you to the factory where she works as a sewing machine operator at 12:30 p.m. Somehow, she was able to convince her boss to give you both jobs, even though you don't speak *Englisch*."

"Wow, Gerhard, I'm really excited and scared in the same breath. I can't imagine how Ingrid *und* I can work with others if we can't speak *Englisch*."

As Gerhard explained, there were other immigrants who work there as well, predominately *Deutsch*, Italian, Irish, *und* three Polish *Frauen*. Christine assured us that there are two, very kind *älteren Deutsch Frauen*, who currently spoke limited *Englisch und* were learning the language as well. They could actually be a tremendous help with the language barrier. I had to learn quickly; I was actually looking forward to the day I can converse with Christine without the help of Richard or Gerhard.

It didn't take long for Ingrid *und* I to get settled into our new home, in our new country, *und* into a whole new way of life. Living in the city was very convenient; everything was within walking distance, not like my *Haus* in Austria, where there was an hour's bicycle ride into town for supplies *und* human interaction. The market was one block down the street. Richard's printing business was two blocks in the opposite direction, *und* the factory where the three of us worked was located around the corner.

Our jobs were going relatively well for the most part. Almost all the *Frauen* who worked at the factory were nice, very understanding, *und* patient with the language barrier, with the exception of a few older Irish *Frauen*. They didn't seem to like us *und* refused to display any kind of friendship. Christine was constantly reminding us not to take it personally; this was just the way they are. These *Frauen* treat every new arrival the same way. They apparently were prejudice against the *Deutsch und* Italians who work in the factory. Once I could speak *Englisch* better, I planned to look for another job. However, I was very grateful for this job; obviously, you do what you have to do.

"Christine, I can never *danke* you for the tremendous help you've been. You're like our guardian angel. However, Gerhard on the other hand, has completely disappointed me."

"I know, Magdalina. I wish there was something I could do to knock some sense into him."

"*Nein*, you've done enough, I just have to except things for what they are."

Sadly, as I looked back and remember the first three days Gerhard *und* I spent together, it was a dream come true. We spent every waking hour together getting to know one another. Those precious three days would be imbedded deep in my soul for the rest of my life. However, reality hit me upside my face all too quickly. After the three days, everything changed drastically, like night *und* day. Any interest Gerhard may have had in materializing a relationship with me seemed to abruptly come to a halt. My *Bruder* would literally come *und* go all hours of the day *und Nacht*.

Christine revealed that Gerhard had purchased many acres of ground in a very remote rural area *und* had a gigantic warehouse built on it two hours away, somewhere in the farmlands of Pennsylvania. Gerhard took Christine there once when the warehouse was first built. In fact, he learned to drive *und* purchased an auto shortly after the warehouse was constructed due to the great distance. Unfortunately, Christine had no knowledge of the purpose this warehouse served *und* what type of business Gerhard was involved with. She was extremely concerned of where the *Geld* came from to make such a large purchase between the land, the building, *und* the auto. Bruno only left Gerhard enough *Geld*, which bestowed him the means of purchasing the apartment *Komplex*. She was also very concerned of the amount of time he was away allegedly at this secret business venture.

Our first year in America flew by, and fortunately, Ingrid and I, with the help of Richard, were learning English quickly. However, during the short time Ingrid and I had been living downstairs from Gerhard, I had noticed him hanging around some pretty shady-looking fellows; that was when he was actually home. Their demeanor almost reminded me of the brown shirts, without the uniforms, of course. Needless to say, I was very concerned; I prayed he was not involved with something illegal.

I did often wonder if Adolf had been in touch with Gerhard and had been aware that I'd been living in America in the same building as our baby brother. Christine had informed me on several occasions there'd been no letters sent to her address, postmarked "Berlin, Germany," ever since Gerhard purchased the acreage for the warehouse. Even if Adolf was aware I was living here, what difference would it make? He must be too busy running a country to be keeping tabs on me, especially with the news we'd been hearing from Germany these days.

Richard had a younger brother who still lived in Berlin. Han's wrote Richard every couple of months, keeping him abreast of the current events. From what we've heard, the events unfolding in

Germany were disgraceful. Nazis were everywhere and had been taking over the country. Jews, and anyone deemed undesirable, were being deported to any country that would accept them. Austria's chancellor, Kurt von Schuschnigg, agreed to accept fifteen thousand Jewish refugees, which proudly made my old home the nation that accepted the most amount of people. Word is, America hadn't taken anyone. This really confused me, considering America had been accepting immigrants from Europe well before World War I and was proudly doing so today.

Han's also informed us that Adolf pushed through the unification of Austria and Germany. Much to my amazement, Austria held voting polls and an astronomical amount of the people voted to unite. I thought this to be very strange; I was always under the impression the Austrian people where happy after the allies of World War I separated us. I was beginning to understand why Mr. Rosenburg was so adamant that Ingrid and I come to America and why Esther had to change her Jewish name. However, I didn't understand why she had to continue with the façade—Ingrid Rose, a good Catholic German immigrant—now that we're settled in America. I was terrified for the people of Europe. The latest rumors circulating were giving us the impression that another war was inevitably going to happen. Considering Germany hadn't financially recovered from the Great War and lost so much, the thought of more conflict was crazy. I could not believe my brother was that stupid to start another war. I prayed these rumors were just that and there was no possible truth to any of them.

To make things worse, Ingrid hadn't heard from her father in almost a year. Her numerous attempts to contact him had been in vein. Her letters had gone unanswered, and every time she would borrow the telephone in Richard's print shop, the calls would never go through. I had to constantly remind her that we both promised him no matter what would happen in Europe, we'd stay put in America. Once we knew things were better, we then could return back home. I prayed every night for the safety of Mr. Rosenburg, Gretel, and Frank. I had never spoken a word to Ingrid, but because they were Jewish, I was very concerned for their well-being.

Strangely, Frank and Gretel had never written us, either. Although, Frank seemed so excited when I gave him Christine's address on that romantic last evening we shared, the night before Ingrid and I left for the Netherlands. I didn't understand, and unfortunately, I was irresponsible, having neglected to get their address in Germany. I just assumed they would take me up on my offer and move into my house. The letter I wrote Frank and sent to my address a little over a year ago also went unanswered. None of this made any sense, unless Austria, for some odd reason, had lost its mail service.

Then to top it all off, the few times Gerhard had actually been around in the last couple of years, I had always tried to speak with him concerning these matters. He was adamant not discuss any European politics with me. In the same breath, every time Richard would receive a new letter from Hans, the three of us would walk down to Richard and his wife Jutta's apartment for supper and the reading of his latest letter from Berlin. Richard was a good man and wanted us to stay informed with the current events in Europe, especially since we still had family and friends who lived there. Richard had no idea that Gerhard and I were the brother and sister to Adolf Hitler. He knew Gerhard to be Gerhard Hiedler and me as Magdalina Wolff. Fortunately, since I had been living in America, I no longer had to worry about someone discovering my true identity. After all, the only people who had knowledge were Gerhard, Ingrid, and me.

To the best of my knowledge, even Christine, wasn't aware of our blood ties to Adolf. If she indeed knew, she never spoke of it. Christine had given me the impression that she was the type of person that could be beaten to an inch of her life and would still go to her grave with a secret. Although I had only known her for a few years, I could very comfortably say that I trusted her beyond a shadow of a doubt. I knew Ingrid would never reveal the truth, either; my insurance policy was that she also had a secret identity. I had known Ingrid my entire life, and she was my best friend. I trusted her as I know she trusted me.

Gerhard, on the other hand, I was conscience-stricken to say I didn't trust him. Although in all practicality, Gerhard could not implicate me without implicating himself. Unfortunately, there were many skeletons in the closet that needed to stay behind a closed, locked door. I had one brother who was a bloodcurdling dictator on the verge of destroying Germany and another brother who had a talent for the illusion of being sweet and nice in a diabolical way. When all was said and done, even though the Hitler brothers had been a devastating disappointment, I could not help but feel unconditional love for them both.

CONFLICT, AGGRESSION, AND BLOODSHED—A PERFECT RECIPE

 September 1, 1939, "Germany Invades Poland from the North, South, and Western Sides of the Country," was the headline in the daily *Philadelphia Inquirer*. Ingrid and I sat in the parlor both feeling melancholy and total disbelief. Adolf's invasion of Poland would certainly trigger another war in Europe.

"Ingrid, inevitably, at some point, America will begin food and gas rationing as Britain smartly did during World War I. Because I'm so peculiarly anal, I think we should start buying larger quantities of canned goods and nonperishables each week. If food rationing begins, we'll be well ahead of the ballgame."

"Alright, where will we store extras?"

"Every apartment has an enclosed storage area down in the cellar. We can buy a padlock for the door and literally begin stock piling food, batteries, and any items we can think of in case of an emergency. I would rather be ridiculously paranoid than underprepared."

Ever since this headline appeared in the *Philadelphia Inquirer*, Ingrid was adamant to return home. However, fortunately for her well-being, this would be practically impossible. Steamships that had been transporting people to and from Europe for over a hundred years had pretty much come to a halt. Sixteen days after Germany invaded Poland, Russia also invaded Poland from the eastern side. As the *Philadelphia Inquirer* had stated, all European nations, including America, were on alert and acting vigilantly.

"Ingrid, don't you think it's strange that Gerhard hasn't returned home, especially with the news of Poland? If for anything, just to comfort us, especially Christine, under the circumstances."

"Yah, but obviously he doesn't care. His poor wife has been living alone for the past eight months. What's up with that?"

"I don't know. He drove off one morning to work at the warehouse, and unfortunately, that was the last time any of us saw him. At least he's decent enough to send Christine a sizable amount of money each month for expenses. I can't imagine what she would do without it, considering the apartments are always in need of repair."

As good fortune would have it, Richard and Jutta recently gave up their apartment four blocks away and moved into one of the vacancies on the first floor. Richard retired and sold his printing company; however, he now had assumed the superintendent's job of the complex. We all pulled together and pitched in to help Christine with the daily operations of the complex. Amazingly, I actually considered Christine family more than my own brother. Gerhard was blood, which—I had disturbingly realized—sometimes meant absolutely nothing. Blood was irrelevant in some families. It seemed both Gerhard and Adolf were so wrapped up in their own world and apparently share the same family values—they simply don't care about anyone but themselves.

Uneventful weeks quickly passed with little word about Europe. Life in the city of Philadelphia was marching on as usual. Ingrid and I woke to a beautiful sunny brisket Saturday morning and decided to utilize this wonderful November day. We bundled up and walked down to the park to watch the children play while waiting for the market to open. After purchasing our weekly groceries plus the extra for hording, we proceeded to struggle carrying the bags of groceries down the street without having an accident. Just in the nick of time, a strange but familiar voice yelled out our names from across the street. We stopped dead in our tracks and watched a very handsome tall man with dark hair walking towards us.

"You girls look like you need some help."

"Oh my god! Frank Hubert—is that really you?" I immediately placed my bags on the sidewalk and threw my arms around him.

He returned a tight embrace and literally lifted me off my feet. "Magdalina I have been looking for you for months."

"Frank, what are you doing here? Forget that. Why are you in America?"

"I'll explain everything once I help the two of you get your groceries home, over a cup of hot coffee."

"That would be lovely," I looked at Frank with excitement from head to toe.

"Wow, are you girls feeding an army or something?"

Without giving it another thought, Ingrid and I invited Frank for Sunday supper. As the three of us walked down the sidewalk carrying the bags of groceries, I felt as though I just swallowed a fistful of butterflies. I opened the front door; Frank walked into the parlor and stood there looking around for a couple of seconds and then walked into the kitchen to help us put the groceries away. I pulled three Coca Colas from the icebox and started brewing a pot of coffee and joined Frank and Ingrid in the parlor. After I quickly gulped down the Coca Cola, and with Ingrid and Frank engrossed in small talk, I anxiously excused myself. I ran out the front door and up the steps to Christine's apartment.

I was so excited; I felt like a little kid in a candy store. I nervously knocked on her door, and happily, Christine agreed to join us for Sunday supper at 5:00 p.m. I then ran back down the flight of stairs and down the hall to Richard and Jutta's. I knocked on their door and invited them as well. This was going to be the greatest supper ever. Later, I would send Frank and Richard up to Christine's to borrow her folding card table and two folding chairs and set them up in my parlor since our dinette set could only seat four.

"Frank, can you escort me to the Italian butcher five blocks north? I want to make something special for our reunion supper."

"Sure, let's go now," as I looked at Magdalina, it suddenly dawned on me, this woman is even more beautiful than I remember.

"Ingrid, hold that thought. We'll be right back."

I asked Mr. DeLuca to slice sirloin paper thin in three-by-six-inch strips. I also bought a pound of bacon. When Frank and I got back to my apartment, Ingrid and I went to work preparing a traditional German beef roulade and spaetzle with a brown onion gravy and fresh peas. Frank sat on the stool next to the kitchen counter as Ingrid and I worked on supper. The three of us were pleasantly engaged in conversation; however, after an hour of chitchat, I brazenly blurted out the question that had been tormenting my brain since I first saw Frank.

"Frank, why haven't you written me? You gave me the impression you were anxious to stay in touch. I gave up on you."

"Please accept my apologies for not writing. There's actually a very good explanation and my mysterious presence in America as well.

"Days after you and Ingrid left Europe in 1934, I was at a friend's house, having a couple of beers and in the interim, the Gestapo showed up at my mother's apartment complex. The entire building was raided and ransacked one floor at a time. They literally tore the place apart. People's valuables were stolen and loaded onto two big trucks that sat in front of the complex heavily guarded. Thank God, most of my mother's family heirlooms were already at your house prior to this invasion. However, unfortunately, we didn't work quickly enough. She had two fur coats and a large jewelry box filled with valuables from her mother and grandmother confiscated."

"Oh my god, your mother must have been devastated," I looked at Frank with much sadness in my heart.

"During the time the Gestapo ransacked the complex, my mother was visiting a sick friend down the street and witnessed the commotion. People informed me she ran home and was arrested on the spot, along with other neighbors. They were loaded onto the trucks and driven to the train station, where a freight train transported them to a concentration camp called Dachau. My resources informed me that this particular camp was constructed for political prisoners, which Heinrich Himmler, one of the Gestapo's big shots, is responsible for and has full command.

"I haven't seen my mother since that terrible day. Rumor was circulating that she was arrested because she's Jewish. My mother's maiden name is Bloomberg. My late father was a German Protestant, and my mother is a German Jew. However, my parents brought me up as a Christian. I know very little Judaism. I remember my grandparents on my mother's side visiting us on Jewish holidays every year. I was very young and didn't remember much of those days. My grandmother and grandfather died when I was nine, and after that, my mother and father didn't bother with Jewish traditions. I'm sorry my mother and I never conveyed this to you, but things were getting weird around that time, and we decided to keep it under our hats."

"Don't be silly, I would have done the same thing," I quickly turned away from Frank and wiped away the tears in my eyes. "I'm sorry, please go on."

"German friends of our family warned me to flee the country while I still could. With Hitler and the Nazis expressing hatred and negativity towards the Jews, it was inevitable hard times were surely coming.

"When I finally wised up and swallowed my pride, I contacted a friend who was the leader and founder of an underground organization. He, along with many other good German Samaritans, formed an underground and was dedicated to smuggling Jews and anyone of need out of the country to safe havens. At that point, Germany stopped the deportation of citizens due to the fact no other countries would accept them. They then arrested and transported anyone they pleased to the newly constructed concentration camps."

"Oh my god, how in the world can people get arrested for no reason," Ingrid and I looked at one another horrified. "I'll stop interrupting, please finish."

"The underground forged a new set of papers and gave me a uniform, allowing me to masquerade as part of the ship's crew. If the ship was stopped and searched, I would blend in with the others. This disguise also allowed me illegal entry into America. With the help of an anonymous inside-crew member, four of us were smuggled aboard ship, which was exporting goods to America. Thankfully, we were able to take this voyage undetected by burying ourselves in the hay that was nestled around each crate to protect them from moving.

"Once I arrived in America, I rode the train to Philadelphia in search of you and Ingrid. Unfortunately, the address you had given me was irretrievable once the Gestapo ransacked my mother's apartment. This is why I wasn't able to write.

"I'm presently renting a room at the Young Men's Christian Association in Philadelphia. They're very understanding and patient with me, considering my English is limited. I plan to become an American citizen as soon as possible. Fortunately, I befriended a man who also lives at the YMCA and is teaching me to speak, read, and write the language."

"Ingrid, can I tell Frank who you really are?"

"Sure, Mags. Knock your socks off."

"Believe it or not, Ingrid is half-Jewish as well. Her father, unforeseeably, was adamant that we leave Europe. We believe somehow Mr. Rosenburg had insight to what was going to happen in the future. Ingrid's real name is Esther Ingrid Rosenburg. Her father is a German Jew, and her mother was a German Catholic. Very strangely, a few months before we made the trip to America, Mr. Rosenburg made her promise to wear her mother's crucifix and change her name. For five years, Esther has been known as Ingrid Rose. No one has knowledge of this except me and now you. Mr. Rosenburg had fraudulent identification papers made for Ingrid so she could continue this facade after we relocated in America."

"Don't worry, ladies. Your secrets safe with me. Now that you've brought up Ingrid's father, there's something I need to share. A week after my mother was arrested and sent to Dachau, I became friends with Mr. Rosenburg the first time I drove to Leonding to check on Magdalina's house. He actually greeted me with a shotgun. Fortunately, I was quick on my toes and convinced him I wasn't a burglar, obviously because I had a key. Mr. Rosenburg graciously decided not to fill my butt with buckshot that day, and the two of us ended spending a pleasant afternoon sitting on his front porch drinking a few beers and shooting the bull.

"Caught completely off guard, upon my trip back to Germany that evening, the Salzburgerland Border Police detained me for a period of time, interrogating me. After an extremely traumatizing experience and realizing my fears of a possible arrest at the border was warranted, I decided it was time to take up permanent resistance in Leonding, Austria."

"On the drive back to Austria, I was very fortunate. I had no problems at the German and Salzburgerland borders. After I got back to your house and unloaded my bags into your parlor, I went directly to bed. When I woke the next morning, I decided to pay Mr. Rosenburg another visit and share with him my experience at the border. I patiently knocked on his front door. However, there was no answer. I scurried around to the back of the house and noticed his truck was still parked outside the barn. Anxiously, I walked back to the front and opened the door. It wasn't locked, which struck me as very peculiar. I let myself in and cautiously walked around.

"Quite noticeably, the kitchen seemed to be the primary spot of a crime scene. Broken dishes lay on the floor, the table and chairs were knocked over, and the water from the faucet in the sink was still running. Every day that I stayed at your house, I drove to Mr. Rosenburg's praying that this would be the day. I would drive up, and he would be sitting on the front porch smoking a cigarette and drinking a beer. Unfortunately, that day never materialized."

While Frank barely got those words out, Ingrid immediately stopped what she was doing and ran into the parlor in tears. "Are you alright," as I looked at my best friend, I could feel her sadness as well.

"Yes, I know my father will be just fine. Frank what happened next?"

"I had only been living in your house less than two weeks when I woke one morning very early and happened to look out the bedroom window. Strangely, I noticed a truck parked further down the road. There were five Nazis walking around the property. As panic stricken as I was, and realizing I probably wouldn't see my mother again for a very long time, I decided if I was able to avoid arrest, I would contact my friend with the underground and leave Europe for good. Thankfully, fifteen minutes later, the Nazis drove off. I immediately ran upstairs and threw my things into two duffle bags and frantically drove myself to the train station in Linz. Without any further thought, I parked my car in the parking lot, locked it, and sadly deserted it. I immediately purchased a one-way train ticket to Brandenburg, Germany, where my friend has a small apartment and the underground has an undisclosed location.

"Thanks to the underground, five days later, I was a stowaway on that cargo ship heading for the America. Nine weeks later, the gentleman whom I befriended from the YMCA informed me that Hitler had just invaded Poland. I cannot begin to explain the gratitude and relief I felt at that exact moment that I was settled in America. I would assume after the invasion of Poland, traveling overseas became a thing of the past, even the illegal kind."

"That's an incredible story, Frank. Thank God for your friend and the underground. Did your friend leave as well?"

"No, Mags, unfortunately, he stubbornly insisted on staying behind. He and his group are determined to continue their work and help as many people as they can."

"God bless him. Let's hope he's safe and someday you'll go back to Brandenburg and visit him."

Unfortunately, as time marched on, Frank and I didn't see each other again after that wonderful reunion. Neither one of us had a telephone, and in addition, the YMCA was forty-five minutes from my apartment. To make the situation more difficult, I ended up starting a new job at the military firearms and weaponry factory in Kensington, Philadelphia. I was hired due to their increasing need of labor because of America's part in the war effort for Europe by supplying Britain with arms and munitions for the war.

As time flew by ever so quickly, and the war in Europe was in full swing, we still hadn't had any word from Gerhard. My brother Adolf was on the front page of every newspaper in America constantly. Unfortunately, Richard's letters from Hans abruptly stopped, and our pipeline of news from Berlin sadly came to a halt. We now had to rely solely on American journalists reporting the news, which we discovered early on was not always thorough and correct.

—⟨⟨⟨ ⟩⟩⟩—

Once again, Ingrid and I woke to horrifying headlines in the *Philadelphia Inquirer*. On December 7, 1941, the headline read, "Japanese Attack Pearl Harbor." The following morning, December 8, 1941, the *Inquirer* read, "President Roosevelt Declares War on Japan." Ingrid and I, as probably every American, nervously listened to the news on the radio for days, basically never turning it off. Four days later, December 12, 1941, the front-page headline in the Inquire read, "Hitler Declares War on the United States of America."

Within that very second, I could feel deep down in my bones Ingrid was beginning to look at me differently and was becoming very standoffish. I immediately excused myself and went for a very long walk through the park alone. Even though the morning was extremely bitter cold, and I was freezing to death, the coldness in my apartment was probably much worse. I ended up spending the entire day away from home. I had to reassure myself I did nothing wrong and I could not help the fact that I was born into the Hitler family. I was terribly ashamed of my two brothers; all I want to do was crawl into a hole and die. Although no one had knowledge of my true identity other than Gerhard and Ingrid, I was beginning to feel extremely paranoid. My god, I left Europe and endured much sacrifice to travel to America with nothing but good intentions; now I felt as though I need to runaway someplace else and hide my head in the sand.

Within a short time, life in America was beginning to get very difficult. Anyone of Japanese descent, even if they were born in America, were gathered up and transported to camps that were built outside the city in the farmlands of Pennsylvania. Disturbingly, rumors had been circulating that the police had started taking groups of Germans away to these camps as well. I didn't understand how Japanese Americans and German Americans are being stereotyped and hated by the American people so drastically. American boys and men of all nationalities, including Japanese and German, were lining up enlisting in the military. Thousands were being deployed to Europe, and very disturbingly, thousands will lose their lives and return in body bags.

Once again, I woke to another headline in the morning *Philadelphia Inquirer*:

> D-Day, the Invasion of Normandy, at 6:30 a.m. on Tuesday, June 6, 1944

It seemed as though overnight, the men who worked in the factory had all magically disappeared. They were either in boot camp or deployed somewhere overseas. The factory had nothing but women workers, young and old, who were producing larger quantities than ever before of army equipment, tanks, weapons, and ammunition daily. There were no men left in America these days, only young boys and old men. The country continued to move forward and thrive due to the female population.

Thoughts of Frank were raddling rampantly through my brain. I wonder daily where he was and what he was doing. At our last reunion, he spoke of becoming an American citizen. My curiosity was overwhelming me as to whether or not he had also enlisted and was possibly deployed somewhere in Europe, killing Germans. Horridly, I could not begin to imagine how this mentally worked. If I was in the army, I could kill a German Nazi or anyone of that mentality level, no matter what nationality he was, without giving it a second thought. However, how do you kill German military servicemen who were fellow countrymen who had enlisted with pride in the German armed forces for a career in defending the beloved fatherland? These men weren't Nazis and didn't start Adolf's war and didn't agree with it; nonethelesss, they were stuck dying for it.

I willfully became an American citizen; however, I was born and raised in Austria, which technically was a part of Germany. I feel confused and ashamed that I didn't honestly know where my loyalties deep in my heart, beyond a shadow of doubt, are. They were divided, maybe not equally; however, bottom line was, they were divided. Thank God, women were on the home front, keeping things going, and not in Europe on the frontlines.

—◦◦◦◦◦—

After months of voluntarily working fourteen hours a day, six days a week, needless to say, I was feeling very proud to be an American citizen contributing positively to the war effort in my own small way. However, as I left work on this very cold late January evening, after a very long fourteen-hour workday, and proceeded to walk down the steps to catch the underground train, I was suddenly startled. Two gentlemen in double-breasted gray-and-blue suits walked up to me, standing directly in my path.

"Excuse me, miss, is your name Magdalina Hitler?"

I froze dead in my tracks. I took a deep breath and paused for a moment to gather my thoughts as I desperately tried not to show any emotion on my face.

"No, sir, my name is Wolff."

I felt the blood run from my head. I must have turned as white as a ghost; the two gentlemen immediately took me by my arms and very kindly escorted me to a nearby bench on the underground train platform. After the blood flow in my head returned and I had a second to recollect my thoughts, I looked at the younger gentleman in the blue suit with tears in my eyes.

"Yes, my name is Magdalina Hitler. I apologize. I haven't heard that name in a very long time. I've always been known as Magdalina Wolff. What can I do for you this evening?"

"Miss, I'm sorry we have to bring you into the police station for questioning. It shouldn't take too long."

"Why? What did I do wrong?"

"We don't know. We're just following orders."

The two officers escorted me to their police car and drove off as I sat in the backseat, doors locked and a cage between the front and back. I had never been so petrified and humiliated in my entire life; I thought, instead of going to the police station, they would have to drive me to the nearest hospital for a heart attack. Once we arrived at the police station, I was escorted by the same two gentlemen to a private interviewing room. They asked me to have a seat and offered me a cup of coffee. The man in the blue suit walked out of the room to get the coffee, and three other gentlemen walked in and sat down in front of me.

"Is your birth name *Magdalina Hitler*?"

"Yes, just as I explained to those two gentlemen."

"Don't get cocky with me, lady. Just answer my questions. Why do you go by the name of Magdalina Wolff?"

"It's just a nickname given to me when I was a child."

They began asking me all kinds of strange questions pertaining to my last name and whether I had any loyalties to America. As a few pain stacking hours passed by ever so slowly, and the feeling of extreme exhaustion came over me like a ton of bricks, the questioning began to get more intense and frightening.

"Are you from Germany?"

"No, I was born and raised in Austria and had been an American citizen for the past six years."

"Are you a spy?"

"No! Of course, not. I'm nothing, just a plain ordinary American citizen working in a factory that produces military weapons and arms for the war effort."

"Are you related to Adolf Hitler?"

"Yes, he's my older brother."

"Older, how many brothers do you have?"

"One other—Gerhard is my younger brother. He is also an American citizen. He has lived in America his entire life and has been a citizen since he was a child. What's going on here? Why do you ask me the same questions over and over again? Can I please go home? I have work early in the morning and have to get some sleep."

"No, miss, I'm sorry to say you're under arrest for suspicion of espionage. When we locate your brother, he'll be arrested also—you can bet your last bottom dollar on that."

"Es...pio...nage? I can't even pronounce the word. I have no clue what it means."

"Nice try, lady. Stop acting like Snow White. We know your kind."

"My kind—what does that mean? I don't have a kind. I haven't done anything wrong."

"Eddy, stop with the insulting, intimidating remarks. I apologize, Ms. Hitler, for Eddy's insensitive and mean demeanor. He can't help it. He was born that way. His mother probably dropped him on his head. *Espionage* is another word for 'spy.'"

"Spy, I'm not trying to sound stupid or anything, but I'm not sure if I know what a spy is."

As I sat there dazed and confused, one of the officers who originally picked me up, handcuffed me, while the three men who interrogated me for the past four hours left the room. The two men from the train station sat with me as I cried hysterically and kept whimpering on and on.

"I did nothing wrong. I wouldn't know the first thing about being a spy. Why is this happening to me? I did nothing wrong."

I cannot begin to fandom how I could get arrested just because my brother was Adolf Hitler, whom I hadn't seen in ten years and lived 1,126 kilometers across the North Atlantic Ocean. I didn't understand what that had to do with me. I was a hardworking, tax-paying American citizen.

"Sir, may I ask you a question," I looked at him with tears in my eyes, as I readjusted the handcuffs that were digging into my wrists.

"Miss Magdalina, of course, you can."

"How in the world did you ever find me and suspect my surname is *Hitler*?"

"I'm not sure, miss. We have agents all over questioning anyone of Japanese or German decent. All I know, someone who apparently knows you well was questioned early this morning at the factory where she works. She has given you up and a woman named Christine Hiedler as well."

"Christine, where is she now?"

"She has also been arrested. She confessed that she's your younger brother's wife."

"Confessed…confessed to what? The only thing in life she ever did wrong was marry my brother."

"I don't know, miss. All I know is that many good immigrants who were patriotic enough to become American citizens and learn the English language are being persecuted and put into camps. I'm sure once the war in Europe comes to an end, things will go back to the way they were. I personally believe President Roosevelt is scared and doesn't know what else to do with you people. Please don't worry. I hear they treat everyone in the camps with respect and are very good to them."

"Thank you, sir."

After hours sitting in that dungy, smoked-filled room, the two officers who picked me up at the underground station escorted me back into their police car. They drove me to my apartment, where I was escorted by an officer and allowed ten minutes to pack some clothes and personal affects. As I walked into the apartment, I noticed Ingrid's bedroom door was shut. This was strange; she had never closed her door. Although, I would assume she must had come down with a very bad and fatal case of the dreaded guilt disease for her ungodly betrayal to her two close friends.

I quickly gathered my belongings and climbed back into the police car with my handsome escort. I tried desperately to stay awake; I had to see where they're taking me. However, no such luck; my eyelids would not cooperate. I awoke two hours later to a picture-perfect view. Beautiful tall mountains were in the background and nothing but rolling hills and open fields. There was a creek with fresh springwater flowing off to the right, and on the left was a long dirt road leading up to the camps. As I was suddenly mesmerized with this incredible scenery, I noticed two very large camps, one for the Japanese and one for the Germans. Once the car stopped, I was quickly escorted by one of the camp guards to a large building with a sign hanging in the front of the gates: German Women Only.

After I was taken to a small office and processed, the guard walked me to my living area. It had a neatly made bunk, with a wool blanket and one pillow. There was a partition on the left side with a couple of shelves for my clothing and personal effects.

"Hi, my name is Mary Sabatino. Please don't be scared. Everything will be all right."

"Thank you. My name is Magdalina Wolff," I said in a terrified, crackling voice.

Miss Mary was a beautiful tall woman, who looked my age and seemed very nice. She allowed me the time I needed to put my things away. Although, only having ten minutes to pack, needless to say, I didn't have much to put away. Miss Mary and I then walked back outside past another building as she showed me where the water-closet building was located. There were twenty large standup showers with shower curtains for privacy. On the opposite wall were toilets with flimsy curtains in front of them, and the back wall was what resembled a long horse trough with many water faucets coming out of the wall. The washroom was surprisingly very clean, considering how many women apparently used it.

Miss Mary then escorted me to the mess hall, which was located past two other housing buildings. The mess hall was another very large building, with a kitchen in the back and long tables arranged in rows in the eating area.

"Ms. Wolff, camp rules are everyone signs up for daily work duties. Your choices are breakfast, lunch, and dinner cook or bakery duty, daily dining cleanup, or housekeeping for the mess hall and washroom."

"Miss Mary, can I please sign up as a cook?"

"Of course."

We were also required to keep our beds made daily, wash linens once a week, and keep our clothes clean and our living quarters spotless. The guards routinely came around every morning at 6:00 a.m. sharp to check everyone's living space while we were in the mess hall for breakfast. We were to shower every other day, at which time, we have to wash our hair.

As strange as these regimented rules seem at the present, I was happy the camp had strict rules. Enforced cleanliness would prevent disease when there's a large amount of people all living together in small quarters. With everything I'd just been introduced to, it didn't seem as though it would be that awful here.

I literally had to take the attitude—if I could survive that long, tedious trip across the North Atlantic Ocean on a steamship to America, in all practicality, this should be a cakewalk. However, I would still be praying for a quick end to the war. I could not wait for the day, life would be restored to some kind of normalcy and I would have the opportunity of confronting a backstabbing, betraying, no good so-called best friend.

WAR RELOCATION INTERNMENT CAMPS

 Miss Mary kindly informed me that the mess hall would be closing in a half hour. The cooks had to clean up the dining area and start preparing for lunch. She encouraged me to immediately walk over to the food line and get something to eat while the food was still out. This was a wonderful idea, considering the last time I ate was lunch at work yesterday. I brown-bagged a peanut butter and jelly sandwich with an apple and purchased a Coca Cola from the vending machine. Needless to say, I was famished. I picked up a tray and rapidly went through the food line, feeling as though I hadn't eaten in weeks.

Sadly, my eyes were telling my brain the portions were too small, while my stomach was telling me this meal won't even put a dent into my hunger. I sat down at an empty table and started to inhale my food. I ate so fast I had no idea if the food was appetizing. Suddenly, out of the corner of my eye, lo and behold, I saw Christine walking towards me. I immediately jumped up and ran over to her. We threw our arms around each other and wept simultaneously.

"My god, Christine, what's going on? I can almost understand why I'm here, but you?"

"Apparently, someone has been speaking with the American intelligence officers, who have been snooping around the apartment complex all week. They're collecting information on everyone. Someone apparently told them I'm married to Gerhard Hiedler, and after questioning me for hours, they arrested me and brought me here. I've been here for two days. I wanted to warn you and Ingrid but had no time. After I was arrested the police drove me home, I had ten minutes to pack. A couple hours later, I was incarcerated in this war relocation internment camp for German women. Jokes on them, however—I'm not German. I'm of Italian descent and first generation in America."

"I know, dear. They did the same thing to me."

"Mags, what do you think Gerhard's up to? The only reason I was arrested is because I'm married to him."

"I don't know what in God's name he has done, or is presently up to, but I have much to explain. I was arrested because my biological name is Magdalina Hitler, not Wolff. My older brother is Adolf Hitler, the *Führer* of Germany, and my younger brother's true name is Gerhard Hitler, not Hiedler. We all bear the shame of my poor father's name. No one would have discovered my ugly secret if it wasn't for Ingrid.

"She maliciously betrayed us both. Noticeably, she began acting strange when Europe went to war. Then on that glorious day we ran into Frank, she seemed a little distant. Frank believes her father was arrested because he's Jewish. I expressed to Ingrid that I thought Adolf was leaving Austria alone since it's his birthplace, even though he reunited the two countries. I believe deep down inside, she blames me for her father's disappearance."

"That's ridiculous, you love that man just as much as her."

"On top of all that, after the incident occurred at Pearl Harbor, Ingrid's attitude seemed to have gotten much worse, and was becoming noticeably more distant from me. We barely spoke to one another and I didn't see much of her. She started coming home late after I was already in bed, and left for work before I woke in the morning. Ironically, she wasn't home on the weekends either; I have no idea what she was up too or where she was staying. I was beginning to think maybe she had a boyfriend and was staying with him. However, that didn't make sense. Neither one of us were raised that way. Her father would have killed her. Christine, just between the two of us, my best friend Ingrid has a little secret of her own."

"Do tell, Magdalina."

"No problem, it'll be my pleasure to expose that backstabbing, betraying sack of horse manure.

"When Ingrid and I were still living in Austria, before we came to America, Ingrid's father insisted she wear her mother's crucifix and change her name from Esther Ingrid Rosenburg to Ingrid Rose. Her father sensed something was brewing with the Jews in Europe and must have feared for the Jewish population in America. I personally haven't witnessed that kind of prejudice with Jewish people in America. However, I've witnessed extreme prejudice and segregation between the Negroes and the whites. I've sadly heard of segregation in the military as well. I wonder when white men and Negro men are fighting side by side and dying on the battlefields, does the army segregate them as they literally fall in action and courageously die for the same country? Or is there one battlefield for Negroes and one for whites?"

"I have no idea."

"I know, Christine, I'm sorry. Here I stand on my soapbox, so self-righteous. However, in retrospect to the serious troubles in Europe, which is affecting the entire world, how can America stereotype ethnic groups of people for prejudices in Europe that the war is centered around? I'm bewildered. This country has serious issues that hurt so many people, and now extreme hatred is growing among the Americans toward Japanese Americans and German Americans. How can the people in this country justify this behavior? Aren't they contradicting themselves?"

"Mags, I suppose that's for another day."

"Of course, you're right. Although, please promise you'll keep this information to yourself. As much as I'm devastated with Ingrid's betrayal, and hatred runs deep through my bones, I'll not lower myself to her lack of morals. Truth be told, I really don't want to see any harm come to her, just a little revenge."

"My lips are sealed."

Once I was finished eating, Christine walked me around camp, introducing me to a few women she'd become friendly with in the short time she'd been here. She kindly asked the older woman next to my cubicle if she would change places with her so we would stay together. Fortunately, the woman was very nice and accommodated our wishes immediately.

—◁▥ᒡᒧ▥▷—

From what I've noticed, the camp seemed to be pragmatic, and in all practicality, neither Christine nor I should die from this experience. Miss Mary, who was our favorite guard, worked Monday through Friday, 6:00 a.m. to 5:30 p.m., and seemed to be the kindest and most compassionate guard employed here. The other guards weren't very nice; they had no respect for us and didn't seem to care about anything except collecting their paychecks at the end of the week.

Miss Mary's family originated from Italy. Her grandparents were Italian immigrants, who became American citizens and learned to speak, read, and write English fluently. They settled in and raised a family in East Stroudsburg, Pennsylvania. Because of Mary's family she could relate and feel compassion for the wrong that had been done to us.

However, time was flying by so quickly. As organized as this war relocation internment camp was, there was never enough food. Christine and I were losing too much weight and were beginning to look unhealthy. In the time that I'd been locked up in this camp, I found myself always hungry. I went to bed hungry and woke up hungry each and every day. Sometimes at night, the growling in my stomach was embarrassingly loud, and I had fears of keeping everyone awake.

However, spring finally sprung, and life in the camp was not the same. Per Miss Mary's suggestion, Christine and I dug up and cultivated a large patch of ground outback of our building. We planted a vegetable garden, with seeds that Miss Mary smuggled in for us. Our beautiful garden consisted of rows of tomatoes, corn, lettuce, carrots, and fall butternut squash. I also collected some old sprouted potatoes from the mess hall that were uneatable and placed them in rows, three inches into the ground, to produce hearty plants for an abundant amount of potatoes. On a daily basis, I also collect coffee grounds, eggshells, onion skins, and various pieces of garbage for composting.

Quite remarkably, since none of us knew anything about farming, and I never considered myself to have a green thumb, throughout the summer and into the early autumn months, we were picking delicious homegrown vegetables, which we humbly shared with the other women. When the guards weren't looking, we also tossed some of our crops over the fence into the Japanese women's internment camp.

Now that the harvest was finished and the winter months were upon us once again, Miss Mary also sneaked us in food from home whenever she was able. She knew as well there wasn't enough food for everyone and, therefore, desperately tried to do whatever she could to help us. Warmheartedly, Christine and I had befriended a wonderful woman.

At a blink of an eye, our second spring approached. Christine and I were organizing every woman who was physically able to dig, turnover, and cultivate their own patches of ground outback of their barracks. Happily, as I glance over to the Japanese women's camp, the women there were doing the same. We all saved the seeds from the vegetables we grew the previous year and dried them out. I prayed the men's camps had also been fortunate enough to have the same opportunity. Their camps were further away, and unfortunately, we couldn't see what was going on there.

"Have you heard the latest rumor circulating around camp?"

"No, Christine, what's going on now?"

"Supposedly, the guards will be releasing the German prisoners soon."

"Really, wouldn't that be a blessing? Although, I'm not sure if I could survive in the outside world again," I silently shudder at the thought.

Despite the happiness Christine and I were feeling with the news of this latest rumor, very distraughtly, none of us had any idea what was going on in the outside world and the progression with the war. Miss Mary had tried to communicate current events with us as much as possible, but guards weren't permitted to interact with the inmates and she had dangerously stuck her neck out very far on many occasions.

Five days later, out of the clear blue, minutes before sunrise, we're woken to the warden's voice over the loud speaker. We had thirty minutes to pack our belongings and line up in the courtyard located by the front gates. While standing outside in military formation, freezing our buns off, very noticeably there were trucks filled to the brim with Negroes. The voice over the loud speaker instructed us to form a line in twos. We'll then be escorted outside the camp. Once outside, we were to sit down in a large group in the cleared portion of the field opposite side of the trucks. Once the trucks were completely empty and the Negro people were inside the camp's barrier, we'd then be told when to board the trucks.

"Look at those guards and how they're dressed" I whispered.

"They're scary looking. I don't want to go with them." Christine gripped my arm.

"I know. I don't, either."

Remarkably, it seemed as though history was repeating itself. The outside guards were wearing very handsome gray-tailored uniforms, with a red band around their left arms displaying the swastika as clear as the nose on my face. I found myself literally doing a double take and questioning what my eyes had just viewed.

"Christine, I don't understand this. These uniforms the guards are wearing are extremely similar to the SS I remember seeing in Austria and Germany before Ingrid and I left. What in God's name is going on here?"

As instructed, Christine and I sat on the cold ground in a fearful, confused state. Although the morning temperature was in the low thirties, we both seemed to be sweating bullets as we tightly held one another's hand. The entire four years she and I had been living together in this internment camp, either one of us had ever muttered a word about Adolf, Gerhard, Ingrid, or our actual identities. My brain was telling me this sight had something to do with my brothers. A very terrifying uneasy feeling came over me as I tried to imagine what we could possibly be in store for next.

"No matter what happens we need to stick together," I kissed Christine on the cheek as I tenderally took hand.

"I agree, I'm scared to death."

"Me too, but I'm not going to let you out of my sight. Keep holding my hand."

As hundreds of us sat on the field terrified and freezing, waiting for the Negroes to get off the trucks and march into our camp, I strangely felt a faint tug on my shoulder. I turned around sharply, and much to my surprise, Miss Mary was sitting behind me. I barely recognize her; she was dressed in street clothes and looked much different out of the guard's uniform. Her beautiful long jet-black hair was flowing at her shoulders.

"Girls, please be extremely quiet, grab your bags very quickly, and indiscreetly follow me."

"All right, Miss Mary."

"Now that we're on the outside, please stop calling me Miss Mary. Mary is good enough."

"Thank you."

Mary, Christine, and I literally crawled through the dense, dead wheat field without speaking one word or making a sound. Once we could no longer see the big trucks or the people sitting in the clearing of the fields, the three of us stood up and began running. At this point it began to flurry, and as we continued to run for what seemed to be for dear life, the flurries turned into wet snowflakes.

The three of us ran for a couple of miles until we came to another clearing. As I stood in the clearing trying to catch my breath, I noticed a beautiful red Plymouth parked on the side of the road. Mary took out a key from her pocket, opened the doors, and we all climbed in. She shifted the car out of park and began to speed off down the road. The three of us, huffing and puffing to catch our breath, with our hearts racing a mile a minute, sat in complete silence for what seemed to be a thirty-minute drive.

Mary pulled up to a beautiful very large farm and drove her car around back and parked it alongside the barn. We immediately jumped out of the vehicle and followed her around front to the main house. She unlocked the front door and invited us into a very spacious parlor with beautiful shiny wood floors and antique furnishings. Christine and I made ourselves comfortable on the sofa in front of the huge stone fireplace roaring with a warm blaze. Mary left us for a few moments and walked into the kitchen to make a pot of freshly brewed coffee.

"Oh my god, do you hear that? It sounds like there are other people in the kitchen."

For a split second, my stomach dropped to my feet as I became lightheaded and got very nervous. My hands began to sweat and shake uncontrollably. I wanted to literally slap myself for being so gun-shy and foolishly feeling mistrust and suspicion of a good woman.

"Magdalina, relax. We can trust Mary. Just because Ingrid betrayed us doesn't mean Mary will."

"You're right. We've known her for four years, and she's been very good to us."

Mary came out of the kitchen with the coffee and three other people, who immediately sat down and joined us in front of the fire.

"Girls, I want to introduce you to my parents, Alfonso and Carlita Rizzo, and this handsome gentleman is my husband, Antonio Sabatino."

"Oh my god, Mary! You could knock me over with a feather. I can't believe you're married. Christine and I never suspected. I know that sounds really stupid, but you don't wear a wedding ring, and you don't look like your married. Although, I don't know what a person looks like when they are. Anyway, congratulations all the same."

"Thank you, Magdalina. But all joking aside, there's a lot I need to explain to you both. I couldn't in good conscience allow you girls to get on that truck. One day last week, after work, five men dressed in gray uniforms with red bands around their left arms were waiting for a group of us to leave work. I overheard these men talking to a few guards who were interested in becoming part their organization. Apparently, there's a new plan taking effect in the immediate area. The uniformed men have been rounding up Negroes in our neighboring towns outside the city. From what it sounded like, they're transporting Negro men to the German internment camps to undergo military training.

"We also heard all Negro women, children, and elderly are transferred to North Carolina to holding camps, where large barges will be used to deport them back to Africa at a later date. All Japanese who are presently in the Japanese internment camps are also being deported back to Japan for a peace treaty. The German men, women, and children who got on those trucks this morning are, as we speak, being transported to a nearby military installation located somewhere in a remote area outside the mountains. The men will be trained for military, while the women and children work in the factories."

"Why in God's name...what's going on here...those poor families," Christine compassionately put her arm around me in solace.

"No one knows what exactly is going on. There has been nothing printed in the newspapers. We haven't seen anything broadcasted on the television nor heard any news on the radio. It seems as though this is taking place confidentially, and only a few camp guards have actual knowledge of the situation.

"My family and I spoke a few days ago, and we all agreed it was time to get you girls out of there and bring you home with me. Fortunately, the camp supervisors haven't maintained good records of the men, women, and children who were brought into the internment camps. Last Thursday, I snuck into the administrative office while the supervisors were at lunch. Fortunately, I had enough time to go through the file cabinet and pulled your records and stuffed them into the waistband of my skirt. That evening after work, I brought the files home, and we burned them in the fireplace. You should be safe here. I don't believe anyone will miss you."

"Gee, thanks, Mary, for the encouragement."

"Oh my goodness, Magdalina, don't be silly. You know what I mean. My family encourages the two of you to stay with us on the farm, at least through the winter months. Hopefully, by then, World War II will come to an end, and we can all get back to normal. You should be safe here. As you can see, we're very secluded out here. We own seventy-five acres of farmland, and our nearest neighbors to the southwest are four other farms with the same acreage. Heading toward the northeast, strangely, there's a very large building that resembles a warehouse, which was built about ten years ago. This building is located right outside the mountain range, about a half-an-hour drive from our farm."

"Oh my god!" What do you mean a 'warehouse'?" I looked at Christine with the same expression that was written all over her face.

"We don't know what exactly this building is. It's just the way we describe it."

"Mary, please go on."

"We have driven out there several times and tried to observe what's going on. The location is very strange for what appears to be a warehouse. It's completely surrounded by an eight foot wire fence with barbed wire on the top. There are guards who patrol the perimeter with guns, dressed in what seems to be the same gray uniforms and red armbands as the guards we saw early this morning. The building is nestled within the woods, with the mountains in the background, and isn't easily visible to the naked eye.

"In the past couple of years we'd driven out there, we'd always park our car in a well-camouflaged area near the building. We'd then unnoticeably sneak through the woods with binoculars, conducting a surveillance of the property, as my father keeps a log with dates and times of the activities. Strangely, we had witnessed many guards dressed in full uniform, and an abundant amount of workers seemed to be employed there as well. Apparently, these guards and workers must have been living on the premises. The closest town is an hour away, with no reported strangers living among the townsfolk. However, once a month, the same three gentlemen have been observed driving a very large truck into town for food and supplies. They spend an abundant amount of money, so everyone looks a blind eye. Although this has been the topic of conversation for years and everyone is curious, but no one takes the bull by the horns."

"Oh my god, this story is unbelievable! Christine and I are forever in your debt. I don't know how we could ever thank you and your family for the generosity that you all are showing us."

With everything Mary had informed us of in reference to this building, its location, and the uniformed guards, I suddenly developed a nauseous feeling in the pit of my stomach. As I gingerly look over at Christine, I could tell she was feeling as squeamish as I.

"Have you personally seen these men who drive into town once a month," as the words rolled off my lips, Christine grabbed my trembling hand.

"Yes, we make periodic monthly trips into town ourselves, especially at harvesting time. From what I've personally observed, for years, it has always been the same three gentlemen. However, about six months ago, I noticed that the younger blond-haired man had been replaced with a dark-haired man about fifteen years older. They keep to themselves and don't normally speak to anyone. They come and go and mind their own business."

"Christine, I don't know about you, but I have a bizarre feeling."

"This is scary, I think I maybe reading your mind."

"I don't know about that, but I think we need to pull one skeleton out of our closet and share it with the Rizzo's and Sabatino's. Christine's husband, who is my younger brother, bought property near the mountains ten years ago and had a very large warehouse built for an unknown business venture. Once the warehouse was completed, Gerhard drove Christine to the site one time to show it off. I remember her explaining the long drive from their apartment located in the city to the warehouse location directly outside the mountains. Christine, do you remember this conversation you and I had shortly after I arrived in America? You also felt it was a strange location for a business, and we were both very concerned."

"Yes, of course, I do, Mags. I remember that long drive, having no clue where I was half the time. I also remember what the place looked like. However, at that time, there wasn't an eight-foot fence with barbed wire. The building was hidden with trees and forest surrounding it. Before we left, Gerhard took me inside for a tour. It was just a huge empty space with four walls. Obviously, it wasn't much of a tour.

"I remember asking him why he had the building constructed and what his intentions were. Horridly, I'll never forget his response. It actually gave me a very uneasy feeling inside and goose bumps. He just flat out told me it was none of my business and I'll know soon enough. It has always haunted me why would he take me there to show off his new investment if he had no intentions of explaining the building's purpose. Mags, I get it. I think I know where you're going with this."

"I'm sure you do, we seem to be on the same wavelength. Four days after I arrived in America as an immigrant from Austria, my brother drove off in his car one morning and didn't come back until three weeks later. Within my first year in America, Gerhard was coming and going constantly and staying away from home longer periods of time.

"Ironically, the one time I actually had the chutzpah to question him, he bellowed that he was starting a business and when it got off the ground, we'll all know then. He pacified me by telling me he didn't want to jinx his plans by speaking about it too soon. Then when the two of us got arrested and detained in that internment camp, Christine and I agreed we wouldn't think about any of this hogwash any longer and wouldn't speak of him for the duration we were incarcerated. Mary, may I ask a favor?"

"Of course, what's up?"

"The next time you go into town, can Christine and I go with you? I need to see these three gentlemen for myself."

"Sure, Mags, not a problem. However, I would prefer you both stay in the car and out of sight. We cannot afford to have anyone in town noticing two strangers, in case the authorities may have noticed you're missing and are looking for you. When I return to work Monday morning, I'll try to snoop around and get some more information. Although, I would assume most of the guards who are still working at the camp probably won't have anything to do with me at this point. The guards who have been recruited seem to stick together, whispering among themselves in secrecy."

"Thank you, Mary. You're a dear friend. Christine and I both love you."

"You're quite welcome. Bring your bags, ladies. Let's go upstairs. I want to show you to your room. You'll have to share it, but it's a nice-size bedroom with two comfortable single beds. Not like those bunks in camp you are both used to sleeping on. We need to get the fireplace going in your room immediately. It gets extremely cold upstairs in the evening if you don't keep the fire constantly lit. This house was built in the 1800s, so there's no heating furnace. We heat the entire house with the fireplaces that, thankfully, are in each room. The water closet is also upstairs. Get cleaned up. My mother and I will start supper. We eat supper in the winter months around 6:30 p.m., which is the time I get home from work every day. In the spring, summer, and fall months, we normally don't eat until dusk, when my father and Antonio come in from the fields. Please take your time. I'll be downstairs in kitchen."

Christine and I washed up and changed into clean outfits. We quickly walked back downstairs to help Mary and Mrs. Rizzo prepare supper. Antonio was preoccupied with starting a fire in the large brick floor-to-ceiling fireplace in the kitchen, while the fire in the parlor was still blazing pretty much heating the entire first floor. After inhaling a delicious supper of fried chicken, mashed potatoes, and gravy, and once the dishes were washed and put away, Christine and I turned in early, remarkably, for the first time in four years, without the sounds of growling and grumbling in our stomachs keeping us awake.

What an extraordinary day. So much had happened, and there had been too much information to process. My head was spinning out of control.

"Christine, are you still awake?"

"Yes, as tired as I am, I don't think my brain is going to let me sleep tonight."

"I know what you mean. As nice as these people are, we can't stay here. We have no money, and because we're fugitives, we can't get a job in town. We have to go back to our apartments in the city. Maybe we can get our old jobs back. Can I stay with you temporarily until I'm working and able to afford a small apartment on my own?"

"Yes, of course. Stay as long as you like. I doubt Gerhard will be coming home anytime all too soon. And if he does, so what? For all I care, he can pound sand."

"Thank you. Obviously, I can't go back to my apartment. I'm afraid if I see Ingrid again, I'll tear her ugly face off and throw it in the gutter."

The next morning we woke to three feet of snow. Christine stayed inside, helping Mrs. Rizzo, while I put my heavy coat on and walked outside to look around. It was like a scene from one of Norman Rockwell's paintings; it was incredibly peaceful and beautiful here. I sincerely prayed that before I die, I could have the opportunity to travel and see the sights of this enormous, beautiful country. I was still amazed I was that naive and ridiculous to believe America was flat, brown, and dirty, with tumble weeds blowing in the wind. I had no idea where that vision ever originated from. That stupid vision was embarrassing. I thought I'd show good sense and keep that thought to myself and never own up to it.

While Christine helped Mrs. Rizzo in the kitchen, Mary and I walked into the barn to feed the horses. They had twelve horses and twenty stalls. Mary explained that this was horse country. Her father buys and sells horses along with planting and harvesting corn. That's how they make their living. As quickly as that, a light bulb went off in my brain. I decided to offer my services. I could clean the stalls and take care of the horses daily. I was good with horses and knew what I was doing, thanks to all the years I spent after school helping Ingrid. This idea allowed me the luxury to feel so much better. I could actually earn my keep and be useful until the appropriate time Christine and I venture back home.

Meanwhile, I knew in my heart staying here temporarily was for the best. Reality dictates we'd already been arrested once and don't need to go through that again. Furthermore, I really wanted to see those three men drive into town. I had an eerie feeling and had to see firsthand.

THE GREAT ESCAPE

 The six of us were comfortably sitting in the parlor after supper, drinking our coffee and listening to the radio, unwinding from a very long and strenuous day. While Mary was at work, Christine and I helped Mr. Rizzo and Antonio plow the fields for the May 15 planting. Christine and I were sitting next to each other on the sofa, exhausted and struggling to keep our eyes open long enough to listen to the evening news before retiring for the evening.

Thank you for tuning into our radio program, *You Can't Do Business with Hitler*, with John Flynn and Virginia Moore.

Today, May 8, 1945, will go down in history as V-E Day, Victory in Europe Day. I'm pleased to announce on May 2, 1945, Col. Gen. Alfred Jodl of the German Army signed an unconditional surrender for Germany. We also have news that the German leader, Adolf Hitler, was pronounced dead by a self-inflicted gunshot wound through his mouth on April 30, 1945. With the surrender of Germany, the war will be coming to an end.

Pres. Harry S. Truman is demanding an unconditional surrender of Japan. Japanese citizens would rather commit suicide as opposed to being taken prisoner or bearing the humiliation of a surrender. The people have been promised by their emperor that any civilian who dies for Japan has an equal spiritual status in the afterlife along with Japanese soldiers who have perished in combat. Emperor Hirohito publicly states, "Their intent is to fight on to the bitter end and to the last man."

Please tune in next Sunday at 7:00 p.m. for our regular program, *You Can't Do Business with Hitler*. This is John Flynn and Virginia Moore signing off. Thank you and God bless America.

"Praise the Lord! This calls for a celebration! Carlita, go into the kitchen and grab a bottle of wine and some glasses. Antonio, please change the radio station to music. I feel like dancing."

"Right away, Alfonso."

"Magdalina, come dance with me, instead of sitting there like a party pooper."

"No, thank you, Mr. Rizzo. I'm exhausted. Please don't mind me. Go on celebrating."

Mr. & Mrs. Rizzo were smiling from ear to ear, with a gleam in their eyes as they start dancing towards the front door. Mary and Antonio began dancing as well; they opened the door, and the two couples danced their way through the doorway into the moonlit, warm night air. Christine and I exhaustedly looked at one another, sipping our wine in silence.

Suddenly I felt the urge to excuse myself, as the tears in my eyes began to flow uncontrollably. I ran upstairs to my bedroom, closed the door, and lay on the bed, crying into my pillow for the loss my brother. Thankfully, Christine didn't follow me; she was complaisant and allowed me sometime to grieve alone.

Adolf would forever be known as an evil madman; however, he was still my brother and I loved him. I put the pillow over my face to muffle the sound as I cried myself to sleep that evening. I had to be very careful not slip and say anything or show any kind of emotion in front of the Rizzo's and the Sabatino's. Mary and her family were wonderful, kind people. I never wanted them to know who I am. I'd go to my grave with the humiliation and guilt of the love I had for my brother.

I wish it was possible to travel back to Germany to find Adolf's body and have him buried in the cemetery next to our parents in Leonding. However, I know this was unrealistic; the newspapers had informed us that Berlin was completely demolished and there were dead lying in the streets everywhere. The Soviets were presently taking over the city. I prayed they didn't decimate my brother's body, like what the Italians did to Benito Mussolini. The Italian people were so disgusted they lynched Mussolini and his girlfriend in Milan. They then hung the two of them upside down and left their bodies on display for the public to view. I got to let this go; there was nothing that could be done. I wished I knew where Gerhard was. I needed to speak with him—Adolf was his brother as well.

Sadly, forty-five days passed by with no positive news of Japan's surrender. With Adolf's death and Germany's surrender, World War II still cannot come to an official end. Unfortunately, America and the Allies were still fighting the Japanese. However, with the months flying by so quickly, at least I had had time to process my brother's death and come to terms with it. I no longer feared my emotions or facial expressions would give my skeleton in the closet away.

"Mary, can you and the girls drive into town and purchase the household biweekly groceries and supplies?" Mary's mother asked.

"Sure, Mamma. It'll do the three of us good to get out for a while. Magdalina, is that all right with you guys?"

"Of course."

On that very hot, sunny Saturday in July, Christine and I climbed into Mary's red Plymouth to drive into town for a few hours. Mary's mother decided not to go with us this time; she was making a strawberry cake with the tons of strawberries Christine and I picked earlier this morning from the patch they had outside their kitchen backdoor.

Since I was consumed with the obsession of personally witnessing those three gentlemen in the big truck, we always accompanied Mary and Mrs. Rizzo into town. Christine and I were no longer in fear of being noticed. Now that Germany had surrendered and the war was winding down, we felt comfortable walking the streets and into stores in full view. When asked, however, Mary would lie and explain that we were her cousins from Ohio, staying with her family for a while.

The three of us strolled out of Sam's Market, each carrying three grocery bags, and proceeded to walk across the street to where the car was parked. As we started to load the groceries into the trunk, much to my surprise, as I turned and glanced up, noticeably, there was a large truck driving into town.

"Oh my god, Mary—is that the infamous truck?"

"Yes, it is. We've just hit payday."

Christine, Mary, and I quickly finished loading the groceries and locked the car. Immediately, we proceed to walk down the sidewalk following the truck, trying to look as inconspicuous as possible, blending in with the rest of the town's people.

The vehicle parked outside of Herman's Hardware Store. Two gentlemen got out and walked into the store, while one man stayed seated in the truck, and the fourth stood outside leaning up against the side of it, smoking a cigarette. We swiftly crossed the street and walked over to the hardware store.

Mary and Christine made themselves comfortable on the bench that was located directly in front of the store, as I advanced very cautiously, slithering into the store, following the two gentlemen. I purposely kept my sunglasses on and walked over to the aisle where locks and keys were displayed. In a panic, I picked up a box with a lockset for a front door and started to read the instructions on the back, while keeping a close eye on the two gentlemen.

One of the men was up front paying for batteries, while the other was walking towards the counter with electrical wires and fuses. I took one good look at this man and tore my sunglasses off my face in such a fury I almost took an eye out. I could not believe what my eyes were seeing.

"Oh my god, it's Gerhard!"

With shaky hands, I immediately returned the box to the lock display and ran out of the store in a frenzy. Panic-stricken, I grabbed Christine and Mary to get out of view as quickly as our feet would take us. While briskly walking past the truck, I happened to look in and saw a very familiar face sitting there, staring into space. I immediately started running like an unnerved whirlwind. I ran down the street about a block when I suddenly began to feel lightheaded; my knees buckled, and my world went black. A man walking by caught me right before I hit the cement. He picked me up and carried me to the bench in front of the men's apparel store. Christine and Mary, frightened out of their wits, sat down beside me and held my hand.

Fortunately, I regained consciousness immediately and thanked the gentleman who saved my face from becoming a part of the sidewalk. I literally sat there for a few minutes in total shock, trying desperately to wrap my head around what my eyes had witnessed. Once I felt the blood flow through my body normally again, I took Christine aside and explained that I had just witnessed Gerhard at the counter in the hardware store and I believed Adolf was sitting in the truck. Mary was sitting next to me with a perplexed, confused look on her face completely in the dark.

"Mary, I promise Christine and I will explain everything to you and your family after supper. You all deserve to know the truth."

I watched the truck with baited breath pull out of its parking spot and proceed to drive slowly down Main Street. This time, the truck parked in front of Sam's Market. Three of the gentlemen got out and walked into the store. I didn't notice the fourth; I assumed he was still sitting inside the truck. Christine and I were frantically trying to figure out what to do next, realizing we don't have much time to come up with a solution. If we didn't act now, we might never get this opportunity again. I know for a fact the one gentleman was Gerhard, but the man in truck would haunt me terribly. I had to confront him and find out if he was indeed my dead brother.

"Mary, will you please walk back to your car and wait for us there? Christine and I have to handle this alone."

The two of us walked over to Sam's Market. Christine sat on the bench in front of the store, and I walked over to the truck. The windows were down, and the man was sitting in the passenger front seat, reading something. I decided to speak to him in German.

"*Entschuldigen Sie*, sir, may I *sprechen* to you for a moment?"

Startled *und* taken by complete surprise, he immediately dropped what he was reading *und* glanced over at me, seemingly recognizing my voice. I looked him square in the eye *und* stuttered in disbelief. He immediately opened the truck door *und* jumped out. We threw our arms around each other *und* embraced in a huge hug, *und* I, of course, started to ball my eyes out.

"*Oh mein Gott*, Adolf, what are you doing here? I thought you were dead. We heard on the radio…it was on the television…it was printed in every newspaper. I don't understand," at that very moment I got lightheaded and leaned up against the truck and took a deep breath.

"Mags, slow down for a second. I never thought I would see you again. Gerhard informed me you've been living in *Amerika und* in his apartment *Komplex* in the city. However, under the circumstances, we both thought it was wise to have no contact. Gerhard *und* I have a *Hölle* of a lot of explaining to do. Right now, he's in the market with two other men, purchasing food for our compound. Wait until he returns. The three of us will go someplace safe to talk."

"*Gut*, what do you want me to do right now?"

"Get into the truck with me *und* lie low."

"All right, I just have to talk to that woman sitting over there. I'll be right back."

Adolf climbed back into the truck *und* closed the door as I walked over to the bench where Christine was patiently waiting for me.

"Christine, please go back home with Mary. I'm going with Adolf and Gerhard to a private location for a meeting. I'll ask Gerhard to drive me home later after we're through. This is mind-boggling. I have to get to the bottom of this, or I will have no peace."

Christine gave me a hug *und* a kiss on the cheek *und* very reluctantly walked down the street to where the auto was parked.

I immediately scurried back to the truck; my *Bruder* opened the door, *und* I climbed in next to him. A few minutes later Gerhard *und* the other two gentlemen walked out of Sam's Market with boxes of groceries. Gerhard opened the backdoor *und* the three of them loaded the boxes into the truck. They then walked back into the store *und* made a second trip. Once the groceries were loaded, Gerhard jumped into the driver's seat *und* looked over at me, white as a ghost. He immediately instructed the other two gentlemen to crawl into the back of the truck. The three of us decided to hold off any conversation until we would arrive at our destiny *und* could sit in privacy.

Thirty minutes later, we turned off the road *und* onto a grass-lined driveway running into a forest of trees. About 4.83 kilometers down the driveway, I noticed the outline of a very large building. We stopped in front of two huge security gates as Gerhard pulled out papers from his pocket *und* handed them to the guard. I noticed the guards were all wearing gray uniforms with red armbands around their left arms. Displayed on the armband is a black swastika. The first time I noticed the swastika armbands, the SA brownshirts in Europe were wearing them. The SA became disempowered after my *Bruder* ordered the Röhm-Putsch in 1934 *und* were replaced with the SS Nazis wearing gray uniforms with the armbands. I certainly didn't understand why these uniforms with a swastika were in *Amerika*. I assumed I would find out very shortly.

After the guard inspected Gerhard's papers, they immediately opened the two front gates *und* allowed us entry. Gerhard pulled around back *und* parked the truck into a large garage at the back of the warehouse on the left side. The three of us jumped out of the truck's cab *und* walked two kilometers to a side door leading into the warehouse. As I walked through the door *und* quickly browsed around, I immediately stopped cold dead in my tracks in complete amazement. There were twenty-five men who looked like scientists in white lab coats diligently testing something. There was a small pond of water *und* blackboards hanging on the walls, with math equations written in chalk. The entire time we were there, no one seemed to look up or cared that we were there.

As I followed my *Brüder* up a large open steel staircase, I noticed on the right side a very large *Zimmer* with several assembly lines. I could not quite make out what the assembly lines were producing; there were too many workers blocking my view. At the end of each assembly line was a worker packing large wooden crates with the items coming off the line. I also noticed the workers are speaking *Deutsch*. Very peculiarly, since I first climbed into the truck with Adolf, I hadn't heard a word of *Englisch* spoken.

At the top of the steps was a small conference *Zimmer*. Gerhard instructed me to have a seat at the beautiful large mahogany table, waxed to a high gloss finish, with twelve large cushioned armed chairs on wheels sitting around it. A very large red flag with a white circle in the center displaying a black swastika hung from the ceiling against the wall in front of the *Zimmer*.

As I waited patiently for my *Brüder* to return, the door opened *und* a woman in a gray uniform jacket with the red armband *und* a matching skirt wheeled in a cart. She carefully placed a pitcher of iced water on top of a metal tray that sat at the center of the table with three glasses around it. She then reached for a hot plate *und* placed it on the table with a coffee urn, three cups, teaspoons, along with cream *und* sugar. She immediately wheeled the cart back out the door without saying a word.

As Gerhard *und* Adolf walk back into the *Zimmer*, they were also wearing the same uniforms with red bands. Adolf's uniform was proudly displaying the Iron Cross and the Wound Badge from the Great War and the gold Nazi Party pin that he wore on a daily basis in *Deutschland*. As they sat down next to me, they took off their hats *und* placed them on the table in front of them.

"Okay, Mags, where do you want us to begin?"

"With you, Adolf. You're dead—I cried for you forever," my hands began to tremble.

"All right, just sit tight *und* listen. This is going to get a little complicated. However, before I get started explaining things, I need you to sign this affidavit swearing you to secrecy of what is mentioned in this *Zimmer*."

"You're kidding, right?"

"No, Magdalina, I'm dead serious. I staged my own death to get out of Europe. When I ordered the attack on Poland, I did so for the sole purpose of taking back some of the land that was stolen from *Deutschland und* given to the Pols after the Great War. The *Deutsch* government was forced to give away 13 percent of its territory, which meant 6 million *Deutsch* people were living in the newly acquired Polish territories. Also as a result, *Deutschland* lost approximately 65 percent of its iron ore, 45 percent of its coal, 72 percent of the zinc, *und* 10 percent of *Deutsch* factories. In addition, Poland was mistreating the *Deutsch* people who lived in these territories. I desperately tried to negotiate this peacefully *und* was only asking for the portions of the *Deutsch* territory back. However, Poland refused to negotiate, which didn't leave me much choice.

"After the invasion of Poland, Britain *und* France declared war on *Deutschland* but, surprisingly, didn't care that the Soviet Union had also invaded Poland on 17 September 1939. My main intentions were the reversal of the Treaty of Versailles with no bloodshed. You have to understand, at that particular time, *Deutschland* had to except responsibility for starting World War I *und*, as a result, was forced to sign that ridiculous treaty."

"I agree. Under the circumstances, that was a good decision," Adolf looked at me with a surprised expression on his face, as I sat there like I knew what I was talking about.

"The treaty was unfair, *und Deutschland* was forced to repay reparations at a total of $6,600 million. The treaty also put a strict blockade on the *Vaterland* which eliminated all imports. The *Deutsch* people were literally starving to death as a result of this blockade. There were also unreasonable military restrictions put into effect, which meant the *Vaterland* would be left defenseless. I violated this treaty, the embargo was lifted, *und* the military became abundant *und* strong. The unemployment percentage was lowered, *und* some of *Deutschland* wealth was restored along with portions of the stolen land. My intentions were for the welfare of the *Deutsch* people.

"After our victory in Poland, SS officers rounded up thousands of young, strong men *und* were taken to Berlin. I used the Pols as laborers to add a second level to the underground *Reich* Chancellery Air-Raid Shelter. Originally, this shelter had one level. The *Vorbunker*, which was built in 1936 for my guards, servants, *und* myself, is located beneath the large reception hall behind the old *Reich* Chancellery building. This portion is connected to the new *Reich* Chancellery building. It was later used as a bomb shelter for my upper senior, support, medical *und* administration staff. The lower level was designed as the *Führerbunker* for privacy *und* was built in 1943. That particular section is 2.5 kilometers below the first level *und* is located beneath the gardens of the old *Reich* Chancellery building, about 120 meters north of the new *Reich* building, at a total of 8.5 meters underground.

"The two sections are connected by a staircase *und* closed off by a large bulkhead steel door. The emergency exit is located in the gardens of the *Reich* Chancellery building. I had *Deutschland* best architects *und* engineers design *und* build it. The *Führerbunker* was designed as a safe place for me, *und* anyone I choose, to live in for an indefinite amount of time. Between the upper *und* lower levels, the bunker houses thirty *Zimmer*, which are *Schlafzimmer*, conference *Zimmer*, *Badezimmer und Küchen* with full pantries. In order to get into the *Führerbunker*, you needed a special identity card. Three of *Deutschland* top scientist's *und* six physicists where given cards, along with my senior SS officers.

"Later, I had an emergency tunnel constructed. The entrance is behind a hidden locked door in my study in the *Führerbunker*. The tunnel leads into Leonding, Austria. I had a *Holzbrenner* (wood-burning) Volkswagen placed near the entrance of the tunnel in Berlin. Proudly, this auto is another one of *Deutschland* greatest inventions. What little fuel *Deutschland* had went primarily to aviation *und* military tanks. Due to the gas shortage, the *VW KdF-Wagen und Armee Kuebelwagen* were also converted."

"That's interesting, Adolf. How in the world can an auto run on burning wood?" I turned my head and snickered to myself.

"Wood logs are heated to a temperature hot enough to decompose it. Once gas is produced, it is stored in a chamber *und* injected into the cylinders of a regular internal combustion engine. Amazingly, these autos actually run for a long time problem free. The trip in the tunnel by auto is 523.6 kilometers, about an eight-hour drive. I had the exit from the tunnel built in the cellar of our *Eltern Haus*. The plan was stupendous. I assumed you still lived there, *und* once the workers broke through the stone wall of the cellar, my men could come *und* go without your knowledge. I remember how you hated those steep steps *und* that dingy, musky smelling cellar as a *Kinder*. Once construction was completed the architects, engineers, *und* workmen were all executed. It was crucial that the *Führerbunker und* tunnel remained top secret. I couldn't take any chances. There's a much larger plan at stake."

"What do you mean a much larger plan?" I immediately took a deep breath and kept my composure to give the illusion, that none of this is fazing me.

"On 16 January 1945, I came to the realization that *Deutschland* was losing the war. Physicists who had the proper identity cards consisted of Dr. Erich Schumann, Walter Trinks, Kurt Diebner, Abraham Esau, Walther Gerlah, *und* Walther Bothe. Chemists were Klaus Clusius, Otto Hahn, *und* Paul Harteck. They were all admitted into the *Führerbunker*. My longtime girlfriend, Eva Braun, *und* our

German shepherd, Blondi, also joined me. A week later, I gave the order for the scientists, physicists, *und* my personal physician to be transported through the tunnel into Austria. Once they entered the cellar, they closed off the entrance with *Väter* old tool cabinet *und* exited through the back cellar door. They were then instructed to walk 3.22 kilometers northeast to an abandoned farm. The old man who lived there was taken to a concentration camp years prior. We used the farm to grow corn, which was part of the façade.

"These men would stay at the farm for a couple of week's *und* were given new identity papers. They then changed their appearances *und* dressed in farmer's attire. Three weeks later, they used the old man's truck, which was earlier converted to wood burning, loaded with bushels of corn, *und* drove into Slovenia under the pretense of selling corn to a distributor in Ljubiljana. Once in Ljubiljana, the truck was driven to the coast where an *unterseeboot*, the XXI *elektroboot*, was waiting. The captain then submerged into the Adriatic Sea *und* traveled into the Ionian Sea around Palermo into the Mediterranean *und* then into the North Atlantic *Ozean* to *Amerika*.

"In the middle of the night, the *unterseeboot* emerged where a dingy was waiting, *und* my men were rowed to the shores of Wilmington, North Carolina. Gerard picked them up in the truck *und* transported them to this location. This plan of evacuating everyone was carried out over a three month interval. Heinrich Himmler, Hermann Goring, Joseph Goebbels, Reinhard Heydrich, Klaus Barbie, Adolf Eichmann, Theodor Eicke, *und* I were the last to leave. We carefully planned *und* staged our deaths. The people of *Deutschland und* the enemy had to believe we were dead. We used many doubles *und* left them where they would be seen by the public. Some were left hanging or blown up by grenades, but the majority of the doubles were staged with the allusion of suicide. Time was of the essence, the Soviets were very close to taking over Berlin. Because we were considered the most valuable, the enemy would have gone to great lengths to capture, torture, *und* mutilate us. I also felt it was imperative that the *Deutsch* people *und* what was left of my military believe that I was dead as well. I was terrified that the *Deutsch* people would do to me what the Italians did to Mussolini."

"I've got to tell you, not only was I distraught by your so-called death, but that same thought entered my head and tormented me."

"Well, in all honesty, my fellow countrymen ended up having pure hatred for me. Through the years, I had been informed in many reports of a prayer *und* a very popular saying among the *Deutsch* people: "Dear Lord *Gott*, keep me quiet so that I don't end up in Dachau." There were many unsuccessful assassination attempts on my life, dating back to before my seizure of power in 1930. The last was Operation Valkyrie, with Colonel Claus von Stauffenberg, a *Deutsch Armee* officer and Catholic aristocrat who was one of the leading members. I must say that last attempt by von Stauffenberg pierced through my heart. He was a highly decorated colonel *und* a casualty of war whom I respected *und* admired."

"*Oh mein Gott*, Adolf, I can't believe you cheated death that many times *und* escaped Europe unharmed."

"*Schwester*, my death was easy. I married Eva on 30 April 1945. The next day, Eva *und* I sat next to each other in the parlor of the *Führerbunker*. As a test, I first gave our German shepherd, Blondi, a cyanide capsule, *und* she died immediately. I then gave Eva a capsule, which had the same effect. Once Eva was dead, one of my officers brought in a peasant from the streets of Berlin. He sat next to Eva, not realizing she was dead *und* was ordered by gunpoint to drink a cup of tea tainted with a cyanide capsule. Once he was dead, I opened his mouth *und* shot him. For authenticity purposes, I placed my favorite pinky ring on his right hand *und* a picture of *Mutter* in his jacket pocket.

"As preplanned, the two *Deutsch* officers who were standing outside the *Zimmer*, waiting, were ordered to take both bodies outside the emergency door of the bunker. The two bodies were then placed lying together in the gardens of the old *Reich* Chancellery building, doused with petrol *und* then burned. The man's body was burned beyond recognition. However, Eva had to stay somewhat recognizable. The two officers who carried out my orders, I later shot *und* killed. No one could know the truth. The first rumor was I died in battle fighting the Soviets, defending Berlin. Later, the bodies would be discovered *und* the world would believe that Eva *und* I committed suicide.

"I changed my identity, wore a pair of eye glasses, *und* shaved my moustache. I dressed in farmer's work clothes, as did all my senior Gestapo officers. I too made the long trip across the North Atlantic *Ozean* with my senior officers in the XXI *Elektroboot.*"

"Adolf, that is the most unbelievable story I've ever heard. This is going to take some time for me to digest all this information. What does the swastika on the flag mean?"

"The red represents the social ideas of the Nazi movement, the white disc represents the national idea, *und* the black swastika represents the mission of the struggle for the victory of the Aryan man. In 1935, I replaced the black-red-*und*-gold flag with our Nazi flag. This beautiful flag is the national flag of *Deutschland*. I think I've explained everything. It's now your turn, Gerhard."

"Are you all right, Mags? Do you need a break?"

"*Nein*, please tell me your story," not like I'm terrified enough at this point, lets bring on more, my brain was telling me.

"As you are well aware, Bruno Dietrich was my guardian. I grew up in the apartment that you *und* Ingrid share *und* was raised as Gerhard Hiedler. I knew nothing of my biological family in Austria. Bruno raised me as his own. I had a wonderful childhood, *und* I loved him dearly. I was thirty-three, was engaged to Christine, *und* had just signed a lease for the one-*Zimmer* apartment upstairs for Christine *und* me. Ironically, as I was packing my belongings into boxes on day, I innocently came across papers hidden between the books in the parlor bookcase. One was my original birth certificate, along with a fictitious one *Vater* made up so I could enter into *Amerika*. The name on the original certificate reads Gerhard Hitler, *und* my origin of birth is Leonding, Austria. As you can image, I was extremely confused.

"Once Bruno arrived home from work that evening, I confronted him with the paperwork. Our *Vater* sent me to *Amerika* for an advanced, state-of-the-art treatment for polio *und* lovingly arranged for me to live with Bruno. *Vater* wanted me to become an *Amerikaner* citizen *und* live a happy life in the New World *und* have no knowledge of my family in Austria.

"Remarkably, one month later, I heard a speech that Adolf gave on 25 February 1932, after he was appointed administrator for the state's delegation to the *Reichsrat* in Berlin. For some unforeseen reason, I actually paid attention that time, as opposed to other speeches he made in the previous years. Bruno always tuned into the *Deutsch* station on the radio every Sunday after supper. Poignantly, it hit me like a ton of bricks, after hearing Adolf's speech, that possibly we were related. I immediately wrote him *und* mailed the letter to Berlin without Bruno's knowledge. Adolf wrote me back, which started a long-distance business relationship between the two of us. Although I'm an *Amerikaner* citizen, I still share Adolf's views for the *Vaterland*."

"Gerhard, would you please pass the *Wasser* pitcher." I gulped down a glass of *Wasser* relieving the dessert feeling in my mouth.

"Six months later, I began receiving *Reichsmark* from *Deutschland und* was asked to purchase fifty acres of ground in a very remote, inconspicuous area somewhere in Pennsylvania. I was then instructed to have a large building constructed according to the blueprints which were sent to me. Once that project was completed, I was to travel to New York City; Washington, DC; Annapolis, Maryland; Charlotte, North Carolina; Los Angeles, California; *und* Augusta, Maine, *und* follow the same instructions.

"In 1934, when Adolf became *Führer und Reichskanzler*, I began receiving more *Reichsmark*, with more complicated instructions. Around 1940, I began receiving packages with gold, silver, platinum, precious stones, *und* furs apparently confiscated from the Jews who were taken to the concentration camps from *Deutsch*-occupied countries in Europe.

"I was so overwhelmed I had to move out of my apartment in the city. Trust me, I didn't want to leave Christine alone, but knew I couldn't bring her here. Christine would never understand or accept the master plan, *und* I feared she would hate me for it. Christine is better off without me in her life for the time being. Someday, in the near future, when the master plan is in full swing, I'll come back for her. Come to think of it Mags, what are you doing here, so far from home?"

"I was supposed to visit a sick *Freund* for the day. I took a bus to Mount Davis, Somerset County, with the last stop in the town of Elk Lick. Once I got off the bus, I was to call my *Freund und* her *Mutter* was to pick me up. She lives somewhere in Elk Lick. Innocently, I was walking down the sidewalk looking for a telephone when I recognized a ghost sitting in the truck. As you can imagine, I felt as though my eyes were playing tricks on me."

"It's getting late. You're better off sleeping here tonight. Tomorrow after breakfast, Adolf *und* I will take you back into town. Meanwhile, *Fräulein* Scholz will escort you to an empty *Schlafzimmer* upstairs *und* get you settled in for the evening."

"*Gute Nacht*, Mags."

"*Gute Nacht*."

Adolf *und* Gerhard walked out of the conference *Zimmer, und* minutes later, Gerhard strolled back in with an *älteren* woman. Her overall appearance *und* demeanor was stern *und* stiff like a military general. She was dressed in a gray uniform jacket with a matching skirt *und* red armband as well. Her face looked as though she hadn't smiled in years,—very serious, like a bulldog. Gerhard introduced us *und* assured me that she'd take good care of me. I followed *Fräulein* Scholz down the hall to a door. She pulled a key from her skirt pocket, unlocked the door, *und* escorted me into my *Schlafzimmer. Fräulein* Scholz then quickly left the *Zimmer und* came back minutes later with night cloths for me to change into.

I was so exhausted; this had been too much information for my brain to grasp. In fact, my brain was fried. I know one thing: as exhausted as I was, I'd probably have problems sleeping tonight, with all this hogwash dancing around in my head *und* my adrenalin at an all-time high. I predicted a very groggy start the next morning.

WATCH WHAT YOU WISH FOR

 I woke the next *Morgen* extremely early. As suspected, I got very little sleep; I tossed *und* turned all *Nacht* with all this information running rampantly through my head. I cannot begin to imagine what my two *Brüder* are up too. I laid in *Bett* wide awake in a dumbfounded state of mind for a long time, trying desperately to digest everything. I knew one thing—I had to get out of here. This place, along with these people *und* my two *Brüder*, was beginning to give me the heebie-jeebies.

I was saddened over the thought. I promised Christine yesterday I would inform her *und* Mary's family of any knowledge I would acquire. However, things were different now. I was truly frightened, not on account of signing that stupid affidavit, but because this was a nightmare. I had no clue how to put into words my recently acquired knowledge. As I lay in *Bett*, draining my brain, my stomach began to talk to me. I was starving. We were so absorbed in conversation we never had the opportunity to eat supper last *Nacht*. There was no clock in the *Zimmer*, *und* unfortunately, I neglected to put my watch on yesterday before we left the *Haus*.

"No problem, I'll walk down the hall to the *Badezimmer und* start snooping around. Maybe I can to get a cup of *Kaffee* as well."

I leaped out of *Bett und* put my dress, stockings, *und* shoes back on. I quickly shuffled over to the door, *und* much to my amazement, I was not able to open it.

"*Oh mein Gott*, the door is locked! I can't believe they locked me in this *Zimmer*."

Now I was truly petrified. They had locked me in *und* had me sign a confidentiality affidavit; I felt as though I was part of something top secret *und* highly classified. Panic-stricken, I stood at the door, yelling for my *Bruder*. Seconds later, I heard a key in the lock *und Fräulein* Scholz was standing outside the door with an agitated look upon her face. She angrily escorted me to the *Badezimmer und* then walked further down the hall to the dining area. Much to my surprise, sitting at a large table in a private dining area was Gerhard *und* Adolf, in full uniform, sipping their *Kaffee*. As I sat down next them, *Fräulein* Scholz brought a cup of *Kaffee und* placed it in front me. I was so enraged *und* humiliated with the thought of being locked in a *Zimmer* all *Nacht* like a prisoner I could not see straight. I literally wanted to tear both their heads off.

"Why the *Hölle*, was I locked in last *Nacht?*"

"Magdalina, it was for your own protection."

"Adolf, what does that mean, 'for my own protection'?"

"We never had the opportunity to show you around. Gerhard *und* I were afraid if you woke early or in the middle of the *Nacht und* left your *Zimmer*, you could easily get lost or hurt. Don't be angry. Breakfast will be served at 0500. It's a beautiful *Morgen*. Pick up your *Kaffee*, and let's go out back to the balcony *und* have our breakfast. When you're finished breakfast, *Fräulein* Scholz will escort you back to your *Zimmer*. She laid out a new outfit for you to put on."

"All right, but please remember you *und* Gerhard have to take me back to town this *Morgen*."

The three of us walked out to the balcony *und* sat at a glass umbrella table. Adolf was right—what a glorious day! As I sat there glancing around, the view of the mountains was breathtaking. Minutes later, we're served a traditional *Deutsch* breakfast of *Brötchen* with jam, soft boiled eggs, and ham *und Deutsch* sausage. After I finished, as instructed, I followed *Fräulein* Scholz back to my *Zimmer* to get changed. As I walked through the doorway, I noticed a gray uniform jacket *und* matching skirt neatly pressed lying on the *Bett*. Next to the jacket was the same red armband everyone is wearing. I took off my dress *und* hung it up in the small closed on the right *und* put the suit on. Without a doubt, the suit was beautiful, well tailored, *und* formfitting. The armband, however, I left on the *Bett* —I refused to put that on. I knew enough that the Nazis are evil, *und* now that I had a better understanding of what the swastika means, I wanted absolutely nothing to do with it or their silly flags. Next to the closet was a small sink with a cup holding a tube of toothpaste *und* a new toothbrush. I brushed my teeth *und* rejoined Adolf *und* Gerhard back on the balcony.

As the three of us sat in front of a beautiful mountain view, enjoying a second cup of *Kaffee*, pleasantly content with listening to the sound of the bird's joyfully singing *und* a slight warm breeze of clean fresh air moving ever so tenderly across my skin, I was mesmerized with this perfect *Morgen* tuning everything else out.

"Magdalina, please finish your *Kaffee*. There's something I want to show you."

"Sure, can you *und* Adolf give me a few minutes?"

The three of us walked down the steps of the balcony *und* toward a jeep parked alongside a storage shed directly underneath the steps against the back wall of the warehouse. Adolf climbed into the front passenger side, *und* I climbed into the back. We drove toward the mountain on a very rigid dirt trail. Fifteen minutes later, Gerhard stopped, *und* the three of us piled out of the jeep. We walked in the direction of another very large building nestled within the trees directly in front of the mountain. In front of this building was what seemed to be a designated area for military training that went on for miles. There were twenty-five uniformed instructors *und* hundreds of men split up into *Gruppen* on different areas of the field. I could not help but think how organized *und* professional this all seemed.

"Gerhard, job well done! You've certainly exceeded my expectations."

"*Danke*, that really means a lot to me."

"Adolf, Gerhard, what's going on here?"

I was speechless by this sight *und* the enthusiasm Adolf had expressed. Since neither one of my *Brüder* answered my question, my thoughts *und* fears of what they might be doing here was overwhelming. I tried desperately to keep my emotions from showing on my face. Adolf *und* I followed Gerhard into the building. This building was nothing but a long *und* narrow barracks with hundreds of cots lining the walls on each side. At the foot of the cots were small storage chests.

"Gerhard, how is the training field *und* barracks working out? Is there enough room in here for the amount of men we presently have?"

"*Ja*, with room to spare."

"Wonderful."

"What do you think, Magdalina?"

"How should I know? I have no idea what's going on."

Adolf *und* Gerhard walked around the perimeter of the training field, watching and commenting on the different groups of trainees, while I stood alongside the barracks, wondering what to do next. My feet were telling me to run like *Hölle*, while my head was telling me to stay put and don't move a muscle. After about thirty minutes, my *Brüder* came back for me, *und* the three of us jumped into the jeep *und* headed back to the warehouse.

We walked in the side door and into the science lab. Again, no one looked twice at us. Adolf *und* Gerhard then escorted me to the other side of the building where the factory was set up. Impressively there were six long assembly lines, with ten women workers per line. Apprehensively, I walked up closer to get a better view, *und* I was shocked at what my brain was telling my eyes. Semiautomatic rifles (Volksstrum-Gewehr VG 1-5), automatic rifles (Sturmgewehr StG 44), rocket launcher (Panzerfaust), MG 42 machine guns, 88 mm Flak guns, *und* submachine guns (MP 38 and MP 40) were coming off the assembly lines *und* packed into large wooden crates. These crates were then loaded onto dollies *und* taken to a ramp leading down below the building. I knew these weapons; they were some of *Deutschland* best. When I worked in the military factory in Philadelphia, we learned about them. *Amerikaner* engineers were trying to duplicate these weapons, *und* then their goal was to produce a better product.

I abruptly excused myself to use the *Damentoilette und* splash my face with some cold *Wasser*. I desperately needed a couple of minutes to regroup; I felt my breakfast beginning to dance around in my stomach and talk to me. As I walked out of the *Damentoilette*, my mouth dropped down to my feet—I could not believe my eyes. There in plain view was Frank Hubert, with a group of men walking down the hallway in single file *und* in perfect formation toward the factory. He immediately saw me as well, *und* the two of us embraced in a huge hug.

"Frank, what are you doing here?" I said with such excitement.

"We don't have much time to talk. A couple of months ago, a group of soldiers came into the city in the middle of a pitch-black *Nacht und* raided the YMCA where I've been staying. These soldiers were rounding up all the *Deutsch* men *und* women in the city one building at a time. Somehow, they knew in advance where we all lived. This all went down so quickly, *und* the raid was well organized. Amazingly, it didn't arouse suspicion from any outsiders. At gunpoint, we were recruited to join their organization *und* were loaded into trucks *und* brought here. The men are undergoing extensive military training while the women work on the assembly lines fifteen hours a day. No one knows what's going on. However, we all have our own theories, but needless to say, none of them are good. Magdalina, are you a prisoner also? The last time I saw you was four years ago. I went by your apartment several times, but no one was ever home."

"Frank, I can't explain. It'll take too long. Where are they keeping you?"

"There's a military barracks a couple of miles away at the foot of the mountain range. If you walk straight across the training fields, you'll see the barracks. Although, I have to warn you, every inch of this place is heavily guarded."

"Okay, I'll figure out something. *Auf Wiedersehen.*"

Frank ran off to catch up to the rest of the men as I inconspicuously walk back to where I left my *Brüder* standing by the assembly lines examining the product. I don't believe they could have seen me engaged in conversation with Frank. The *Damentoilette* was located clear across the building *und* down a narrow hallway. Immediately, I disguised any enthusiasm I maybe showing on my face for bumping into Frank. *Gott sei dank,* no one can see my heart doing back flips.

Once I rejoined my *Brüder*, the three of us walked up the iron staircase to the second level *und* into the *Esszimmer*. Adolf then lead Gerhard *und* me through his private *Esszimmer und* back outside on the balcony, where the three of us sat at one of the glass umbrella tables once again. We placed our lunch order *und* sat in the warmth of the sunlight *und* quietly ate. The scenery was so tranquil; it was unimaginable that all this abnormality was taking place within all this beauty.

THE 2ND WORLD WAR II

"Gerhard, please take me back to town after lunch. I need to catch the next bus to Philadelphia."

"Mags, I'm sorry that's not going to be possible."

"What do you mean 'not going to be possible'? You told me last *Nacht* you would drive me back after breakfast. *Und* it's well after breakfast," my heart dropped to my feet.

"I know. I apologize for deceiving you."

"Gerhard, I need to go home."

My heart pounded in such a way I thought it might literally leap out of me chest. As my eyes filled up with tears, I turned away for a minute to regain control *und* not let my *Brüder* see fear in my eyes or tears that were now slowly running down my face.

"You know, Gerhard, in complete honesty, I'm really not surprised with this at all."

My head and heart were once again in a battle. I didn't know exactly what's going on here, but I was smart enough to realize one thing—my current knowledge was too great. At that very second, a dismal feeling flowed through my body with thoughts of my *Brüder* executing me due to this knowledge.

"Everyone, leave. I need some privacy with my family."

"Sure thing, *mein Führer*."

The three officers who were also on the balcony, eating lunch, quickly picked up their plates *und* walked back inside to leave Adolf, Gerhard, *und* me alone on the balcony.

"Magdalina, we want you to know this was never the plan."

"Okay, Gerhard, what exactly is the plan?"

"Adolf *und* I never had any intentions of bringing you into this. You have a nice apartment, a good job, *und* a great relationship with Christine. I know you will both take care of one another if the time ever warrants. This is another reason I had to leave. I wanted to protect you *Mädchen*. I had to get as far away from you *und* my wife as possible.

"Unfortunately, now things are different. Adolf *und* I were up all *Nacht* discussing this matter. We both feel that we have no other choice. We're going to draft you into the master plan. However, until you prove trustworthy, you'll only be granted limited knowledge *und* clearance. You'll live here temporarily. I'll have *Fräulein* Scholz bring you some personal items *und* put them in your *Zimmer*. Make out a list of things you need, *und* she'll pick them up for you immediately. If everything goes according to plan, you'll be able to return home in a year.

"Tomorrow *Morgen* at 0500 sharp, you'll eat breakfast in the mess hall with the others, *und* at 0600 you're to report to *Herr* Sven Hirsch. He'll train you to work *und* oversee the assembly lines in the factory. Later, when you've proven yourself, we'll upgrade your security clearance to something more challenging. Temporarily, you have a security clearance 1, which is the lowest. You're only permitted upstairs in your *Zimmer*, the *Badezimmer*, mess hall, *und* downstairs in the factory part of the building only. Security clearance 1 allows one supervised break outside, but within the perimeters of the building. *Herr* Hirsch will show you around *und* get you acquainted with everyone. When you're finished with *Herr* Hirsch, see *Fräulein* Scholz to get your *Zimmer* in order. Adolf *und* I will meet you back here on the balcony for supper promptly at 1800. Mags, don't look so scared. Trust me, everything will be fine."

"If you say so, Gerhard. It doesn't look like I have a choice in the matter," yeah right, over my deadbody, I mumbled under my breath."

As instructed, I followed *Herr* Hirsch around the factory as he introduced me to the other workers *und* showed me the ropes for the next two hours. He was a very kind, helpful, and attractive man, nothing like the other people here, especially *Fräulein* Scholz. She had as much personality as a dead fish. I'd never seen that woman crack a smile or have any kind of an expression on her face other than always looking angry.

Once we were through for the day, I went up to my *Zimmer und* lay down on the *Bett* before supper. I had a pounding headache all day, probably due to brain overdrive. I don't think I slept that *Nacht* for any more than an hour. Within seconds, I ended up falling asleep *und* didn't wake until the next *Morgen* when I heard my door unlock *und Fräulein* Scholz came into my *Zimmer* at 0500. I arose immediately, *und* once again I was escorted down the hall to the *Badezimmer*. I bathed quickly *und* put another perfectly ironed *und* starched gray uniform on which *Fräulein* Scholz had laid out on my *Bett* once again. *Fräulein* Scholz escorted me down to the mess hall, where I joined my *Brüder* for breakfast.

Directly after we were finished, *Herr* Hirsch walked into Adolf's private dining area *und* escorted me down the steps to the assembly lines. All the women workers were dressed in workmen's uniforms; *Herr* Hirsch *und* I, along with two other guards, seemed to be the only people dressed in military uniforms. I once again purposely didn't put the red armband on; it sat on my *Bett* exactly where it sat yesterday. Later that day, *Herr* Hirsch asked me to go up to my *Zimmer und* put the armband on. He convinced me that this was in my best interest.

"Magdalina, please listen closely. These people who have authority around here can be very persuasive. Don't step on anyone's toes—do as you are told, *und* don't ask any questions. Most importantly, don't trust anyone, especially Olga Scholz. She's a spy *und* reports directly to the Hitler *Brüder*, along with a few of the other guards. I'll point them out to you later. If someone is defiant or tries to escape, they're taken outback *und* immediately hung. The poor slob is left hanging there for a week for us all to view. Trust me, this is serious. These people aren't messing around."

"*Danke, Herr* Hirsch, for that important information."

"Magdalina, please call me Sven. *Herr* Hirsch is my *Vater*."

"No problem, Sven. *Danke* all the same."

With all the confusion I was presently feeling *und* everything that was happening around me, I was very concerned of what Christine *und* Mary were thinking about my absence. I was sure they're worried by now; I had been missing for two weeks.

There has got to be some way out of here. I have to escape *und* warn the authorities of the potential dangers unfolding. However, if I'm able to pull off a successful escape, who the *Hölle* can I speak to? No one is going to listen to an Austrian immigrant woman with such an unbelievable, horrendous story.

As the weeks quickly passed, Sven *und* I were becoming close *Freunde*. I could see Frank from a distance every day, promptly at the same time; however, we hadn't had an opportunity to speak again. Like clockwork, supper was promptly at 1800, *und* at 1900, I was locked in my *Zimmer* for the remainder of the evening. At 0500, Olga would come in *und* lay out a fresh uniform on my *Bett*. It seemed as though her only purpose in life was to take care of me, but I knew better—she was indiscreetly watching *und* spying on me.

I haven't spoken with Adolf *und* Gerhard since we had lunch together my second day here. Recently, anytime I'd see Adolf, he seemed to always be in the company of *Herr* Himmler *und* some of the other big-shot Gestapo officers. I constantly saw Gerhard *und* those other two men coming *und* going with the trucks. They were always loading *und* unloading the trucks with large wooden crates. Gerhard *und* his partners would be gone for days *und* weeks at a time. Last night, after Olga so promptly locked me in my *Zimmer*, I stood glancing out my tiny window, which faced the left backside of the compound, *und* saw Gerhard *und* his accomplices drive the trucks around back to the garage area. He immediately jumped in the back of the truck *und* drove out a large army tank with the swastika displayed on the front. The other two gentlemen did the same. Once the tanks were out of the trucks, the three of them returned the trucks to the garage *und* locked it. Surprisingly, the three tanks sat there in plain view overnight.

I woke fifteen minutes before Olga was due. I jumped out of *Bett und* looked out the window. The three army tanks were no longer sitting there. I could not help but feel the seriousness of this situation. I wondered if I could trust Sven. I didn't care if I was an Austrian immigrant—I had to escape *und* warn someone, maybe those two detectives who arrested me. They seemed very nice *und* understanding; I felt they might have had some empathy for me *und* the situation.

My brain was in battle; part of me wanted to take a chance *und* speak to Sven, although if he turned me in, my neck would be the next one on display. With that thought, the sound of Olga's key was in my door once again.

After thinking about this all day, I decided to take Sven's advice *und* trust no one, not even him. Tomorrow, I thought, when I get my scheduled break outside, I'll indiscreetly walk around *und* study the grounds. Frank *und* I have to come up with an escape plan. I cannot continue to stay here in this compound *und* live with this nightmare any longer.

Once my door was locked at 1900 for the evening, I sat down on the *Bett und* proceeded to write Frank a note with the pad of paper I stole from the assembly line earlier today. I'd pass the note to him tomorrow when the men come in from the training fields for supper. This was the only time they were permitted in this building. At 1700, like clockwork, the men were escorted down the long hallway *und* up the iron steps to the mess hall. I'd leave the assembly line at 1700 as well *und* walk to the *Damentoilette*.

In my note, I'd explain that every Monday *und* Thursday, I'd leave the factory floor *und* walk to the *Damentoilette* exactly at 1700. This way, we could secretly correspond with one another. Olga was never around for that hour; she ate supper with the other security clearance 3 supervisors in the executive dining area between 1700 *und* 1800. She then would escort me at 1800 to the security clearance 1 dining area *und* walk me back to my *Schlafzimmer* promptly at 1900. With having one hour free of Olga every day, this plan could actually work.

Thursday, at 1700, I walked back to the *Damentoilette* as stated in my note to Frank. While I walk down the long hallway, I passed Frank. We didn't acknowledge one another, *und* without a single word, he passed me a note. I quickly walked into the *Damentoilette und* stuffed the note into my bra. At 1900, when Olga locked my door for the evening, I sat on the *Bett und* pulled out the note.

> Magdalina, I'm so happy you got in touch with me. You must have read my mind. I too have been surveying the grounds *und* the situation. Our barracks are on the outer backside of the training fields at the foot of the mountains. There is an eight-foot fence that encloses the barracks, *und* another eight-foot barbed wire fence that runs the perimeter of the entire compound. It seems the only way out will be to tunnel under both fences *und* fill the dirt back in, leaving no evidence behind. This will buy us sometime the next *Morgen* before we're missed. Right now, I'm trying to find an area in the barrack's fence that has limited visibility. Once we're on the other side of the compound fence, there's nothing but dense forest leading up

the mountain. I don't believe this compound goes any further than the barracks. The mountains appear to have a very rugged terrain. So our attire will be of the utmost importance.

There are four guard towers, two in the front *und* two in the back, located in all four corners of the perimeter. The one in the back, on the left side, is directly located approximately two miles from the backside of that humongous garage where they keep the three trucks. The light on that tower faces *und* lights up the back, looking onto the training fields *und* the barracks *und* about a mile beyond the foot of the mountain. The other tower located on the right, in the back corner directly outside the barracks, lights up the entire back area all the way up to the warehouse.

Out front, when we first arrived right before sunrise, I studied the area *und* noticed there's one guard posted at the double gates. There's a tower located in the front left corner, *und* that light shines more left to front. That's where there's a slight blind spot. The garage is tall, *und* there's a discrepancy; it limits the light from the back right light, *und* the front left isn't quit angled correctly. As a result, it bypasses the corner *und* the back of the garage. I can get out by tunneling under the first fence; I just have to figure out the best location for that. Once I'm on the other side, I believe I can make it to the back of the garage without anyone noticing. We need to synchronize a time *und* meet behind the garage. Once we're in that location, we'll then tunnel under the perimeter fence *und* run like *Hölle.*

However, getting you out of that locked *Schlafzimmer* is going to prove more challenging. You'll have to find a way to get out the door. Beware you cannot walk down those stairs. I've heard it's extremely guarded because that area is visible from the steps *und* is the science lab. There are shifts of scientist's *und* guards working around the clock seven days a week.

Keep studying the area. Between the two of us; we'll come up with a plan to get you out. I'll see you next Monday. Please take care of yourself *und* be safe.

Liebe,
Frank

After reading Frank's note twice, I sat on my *Bett* trying to think of a plan. As Frank stated, my door was locked. I had tried to pry it open *und* pick the lock but had been unsuccessful, so far. The window was so tiny. I might be able to jimmy out, although once I was on the outside, I was not sure what to do. I would have to confiscate a long heavy rope *und* shimmy down to the bottom. Alarmingly, this level was probably forty feet from the ground. If I'd fall, I surely won't have to worry about that noose—I'd be part of the landscape. The only thing that made sense was the balcony where I had eaten a few times with my *Brüder*.

Tomorrow, weather permitting, during my afternoon scheduled outside break, I'd inspect the back of the building in more detail. Just for the heck of it, I'd study the distance from my window to the ground, then the ground to the back of the garage. Although, shimming down a rope wasn't my first choice of escape; I had never been good with athletic things. Since my first choice was the balcony located on the right side of the building, I'd put more effort into that.

I lay all *Nacht* wide awake, staring at the door with strange thoughts running rapidly through my brain. Just as I began to fall asleep, out of the clear blue, remarkably, an idea hit me like a ton of bricks. I jumped out of *Bett und* walked over to the door. The bolt from the lock going into the door jamb on the right side was impossible; however, the hinges of the door were screwed into the doorframe from the inside. I wonder if I could pry that bolt out of the hinges. Unfortunately, with much effort, I could not feasibly budge it with my fingers. After drastically glancing around the *Zimmer* for something that's thin enough to wedge between the bolt head *und* the hinge, I came up empty. I decided I'd look around tomorrow in the mess hall *und* the factory *und* see if I could find something.

I was bursting with energy *und* excitement for the first time in months; I actually felt a sense of hope. With excitement flowing through my body, I literally forced myself to lie back down in *Bett und* desperately tried to fall asleep. For the time being, I had to put this on hold; Olga's 0500 face would be gracing me with her presence in no time flat.

At 0530, as I finished my breakfast *und* began to get up from the table, a light bulb suddenly went off in my brain. Nervously, I looked around the dining area for anyone watching me *und* slowly slid my hand from my place setting to the edge of the table *und* shoved the butter knife into the sleeve of my jacket. Feeling guilty as sin *und* scared to death, I continued sitting there, trying desperately to look normal as I waited for *Fräulein* Scholz to retrieve me at 0600. Once again, my prompt *und* predictable fearless leader approached the table *und* escorted me to the stairs. While walking down the steps, following Olga closely, I slid the knife from my sleeve back into my hand *und* placed it in my bra without her noticing.

The clock seemed to stand still; work went on forever. Finally, with much anticipation, it was time to go outside for my afternoon break. Amazingly, the second I walked outside, the drizzle changed to rain, with sporadic sounds of thunder hovering overhead; although, I didn't care—I was on a mission. As I walked around to the back from the side door, noticeably there were six uniformed men outback as well. However, I was sure they were too busy checking the contents of the wooden crates that were about to be loaded onto the trucks to pay me any mind.

As I strolled around trying to look inconspicuous, I noticed a small rock on the ground. I bent down to pick it up *und* very quickly *und* cautiously turned *und* placed the rock in my bra, between my two breasts. I then stood there for a few seconds *und* stared at the back of the building. Quite noticeably, my *Schlafzimmer* window, along with a row of eight other *Schlafzimmer* windows, was housed in the flat stucco back wall of the building, forty feet from the ground. Realizing an escape out my window wasn't practical, I then glanced over at the balcony on the right side *und* recalled when I ate lunch with my *Brüder*.

The Hitler *Brüder* had a private *Zimmer* off the right side of the mess hall dining area. The entire dining area was broken off into three sections. The largest section was on the left side *und* wrapped around in an L shape for the security clearance 1 workers *und* the trainees. There was a smaller long *und* narrow *Zimmer* in the center towards the back behind the L shape part. This *Zimmer* was reserved for security clearance 2 *und* 3 supervisors. Then the third was the large private dining area for Adolf, Gerhard, *und* the other senior Gestapo officers, who all have the highest security clearances, which are 4 *und* 5.

On the back wall of this private *Zimmer* were large glass windows *und* a glass door leading out to the balcony. I remember this *Zimmer*; Adolf, Gerhard, *und* I sat at one of the tables *und* had *Kaffee*, and then we moved outside onto the balcony for breakfast. That was my first day here. Also, what came to mind, while we were seated inside, I recall looking around *und* drinking it all in. The *Zimmer* was so beautiful *und* tastefully decorated, *und* most importantly, I never saw the presence of any security guards being posted or entering the *Zimmer*; it gave me the illusion of complete privacy.

Once again at 1900, Olga locked me in my *Schlafzimmer*. I immediately undressed *und* changed into my *Nacht* clothes *und* unpacked my overstuffed bra.

"I have a rock *und* a butter knife, small boobs once again *und* a wild idea."

I waited an hour after the prison warden locked me in. I have to be extremely careful; I believe Olga's *Schlafzimmer* may be located next to mine. I took the butter knife *und* tried to insert it between the bolt head *und* the hinge of the door. I then took the rock *und* hammered it once, making a very uncomfortable loud bang. I immediately walked over to the *Bett und* took the summer blanket off *und* covered the metal hinge with it. Very apprehensively, I hammered it once again, this time successfully muffling the sound. I hit it again a few more times.

"*Oh mein Gott*, what a great idea! This is really working."

I took out the top *und* bottom pins *und* shimmed the middle pin halfway. I could not believe my eyes—this could actually work. I'd literally take the door off the hinges while it was locked *und* escape through the left side. Once I was out in the hallway, I would lean the door back into its hinges. I could not, of course, replace the pins; however, if Olga should walk out into the hallway in the middle of the *Nacht*, she won't suspect anything was wrong until the next *Morgen* at 0500. She'd put her key into the lock, *und* the door would literally fall into my *Schlafzimmer*. At that point in time, Frank *und* I would have to be as far up that mountain as humanly possible. Once my *Brüder* had knowledge that I had escaped, I'd then be dog meat.

With trembling hands, I replaced the pins back into the hinges. I opened the window *und* hide the rock *und* the butter knife on the window ledge outside. I felt like a little kid at Christmas; I was so excited I could hardly stand it. I immediately sat down on my *Bett und* wrote Frank a note to slip to him at 1700 on Monday.

> Frank, good news. I was able to take the pins out of the hinges of my door, which means I can get out of my *Zimmer*. Once outside I'll walk down the hallway to the mess hall *und* into Adolf's personal *Esszimmer*. The *Zimmer* has no locked inner door allowing me access. There are large windows on the back outer wall *und* a glass door leading outside to the balcony. If the windows open I'll try to shimmy out one of them, however if I cannot, maybe I can take the glass door off its hinges as well. Or another option, I can break the glass *und* run down the balcony steps *und* meet you behind the garage. Please take a look at the balcony location *und* tell me what your thoughts are. I'll try to sneak into Adolf's *Esszimmer* sometime this week *und* examine the windows *und* door up close. Please write back.
>
> *Liebe,*
> Magdalina

Monday, at 1700, I walked to the *Damentoilette* unnoticed as usual. As Frank *und* I passed one another with no eye contact, I slipped him the note. The next *Morgen*, I anxiously ate my breakfast quickly. As I sat at the table, with my heart pounding in my chest so hard, I feared everyone could hear it *und* read right through me. Nervously, I looked around *und* didn't see anyone of any significance. Normally, I had freedom from Olga this time every day for ten minutes. Quickly *und* cautiously, I strolled over to Adolf's private *Zimmer*. Thankfully, no one was in there; in fact, I hadn't seen either one of my *Brüder* for a few weeks. I immediately walked over to the wall *und* carefully studied the windows. They were sliding windows with locks inside. Perfect, I was small enough to fit through one of them. I quickly turned around *und* vigorously started walking out of the *Zimmer* when suddenly I noticed the grisly silhouette of Olga watching me. My heart dropped cold dead to the floor.

"What in *Gottes* name are you doing in here, Magdalina?"

"I'm looking for my *Brüder*. I was hoping they were on the balcony eating breakfast. I need to speak with them about something important."

"They're not in the building, *und* you're well aware this *Zimmer* is off limits to you."

"I know, Olga, but like I said, I thought my *Brüder* might be out there. I have personally been out on the balcony with them before," at this point I'm now petrified.

"I don't care about any of that. Leave now, or I will force you to leave, *und* you can bet your last bottom dollar, I'm reporting this incident. Guaranteed, there'll be repercussions, *mein Liebe*."

"I didn't do anything wrong, *Fräulein* Scholz."

Within split seconds, I saw her put her right hand at her waist *und* grab the handle of her pistol. I walked out of the *Zimmer* quickly, as she closely followed behind. I was completely intimidated *und* terrified; I was really in deep trouble now. No doubt, she surely would tell Adolf when he'd return. They were so strict with these crazy security clearances I wondered if you could get hung for something this trivial. I've got to get in touch with Frank; we needed to take action immediately. However, if my fate was hanging on the gallows, I would rather die trying to escape, as opposed to walking into a *Zimmer* that was deemed off limits. I'd write Frank another note this evening *und* pass it to him tomorrow, one day early. He won't be expecting me, but Olga had given me no choice. I felt incredible anxiety, knowing that we were up against the clock this close.

> Frank, I'm sorry but we have to do this tonight. Olga caught me in Adolf's private *Esszimmer* yesterday *Morgen*. She's already threatened to turn me in. Although my story sounded very innocent, they'll probably execute me. I'm terrified; if you're not able to escape this evening, I'm sorry to say, I'll be leaving without you. I'll meet you in back of the garage tonight as the

LAURA DOTHE HELLWIG ◀

guard change takes place at 2130 promptly. I sincerely hope to see you than.

Liebe,
Magdalina

For the last time, I was locked in my *Zimmer* at 1900. *Gott sei Dank*, neither one of my *Brüder* showed up today. I prayed Frank was able to meet me; I didn't relish the thought of escaping alone. I might have to, however, accept the fact that I was going to die no matter what I do, but with *Gott* as my witness, I did not intend going down without a fight.

As that thought came and went through my brain, another thought entered. Antonio *und* Mary owned a small hunting *und* fishing cabin somewhere in this immediate area further up the mountain.

"I wish I would've been more attentive when they told Christine *und* I where it's located."

What a shame we never got the opportunity to indulge in that long weekend fishing trip we were planning. That would have been too perfect.

"First things first, get this stupid door off its hinges *und* get as far away from this this fiasco as possible."

I took the canvas bag out of my jacket that I swiped from the assembly line earlier this *Morgen*. I packed everything that would fit, keeping in mind there was only one more month of summer left *und* winter would be here shortly. I put on a pair of trousers *und* laced up the heavy workman's boots that Olga just picked up for me last week. At least she was good for something.

As it had for my two practice runs, the door came off with ease. I slid out with my bag *und* leaned the door against the hinges. Surprisingly, it seemed to be fairly sturdy; I assumed it shouldn't fall until Olga would try to open it at 0500.

"What a priceless picture! What I wouldn't do to see that *dumme Kühe* face."

With that vision implanted in the back of my brain and a small smile on my face, I quietly ran toward the mess hall. Behold, there was not a soul in sight; however, the sounds of the people downstairs

142 ◀

und the assembly lines running was predominate. I very cautiously walked back to the outer wall of Adolf's private *Esszimmer und* opened the window next to the door. Fortunately, there seemed to be no one walking around outside, *und* directly under the balcony was a locked storage shed, so no one can feasibly be standing there out of sight. I threw my bag onto the deck *und* slipped out the window. I quietly closed the window behind me *und* lay flat on the deck for a few seconds, looking out into the yard with my heart palpitating, sweating bullets on this extremely cool evening.

I now understand what Frank was referring to. The light bypassed the back of the garage, *und* therefore, the woods along that area should be a safe exit. I glanced at my watch *und* noticed my timing was perfect. However, now came the hard part; I had to get across the yard to the garage without being seen by the guards in the watchtowers. The balcony steps shouldn't be a problem; the light from the watchtower just barely missed them. Once I was down the steps, I would have to tightly snug the back of the building *und* wait until exactly 2130 for the guard change in all four towers. As the guard change took place, I would then have to run like holly *Hölle* to the back of the garage.

As I proceeded to come off the last step, crawling on my hands *und* knees, heading to the back wall of the building, faintly in the pitch darkness of the night, I noticed a silhouette. I immediately stood up *und* began creeping down the back wall, snugged in as tightly as possible. Dreadfully, as I crept closer, I noticed the silhouette was actually a man leaning up against the wall, also out of view of the lights, smoking a *Zigarette*. My heart totally stopped. I was busted, *und* I gave up. He dropped the *Zigarette* to the ground *und* smashed it out with his boot. Within seconds, my eyes focused enough to see that the man smoking was Sven Hirsch.

"What are you doing here, Magdalina?"

"I'm escaping, so go ahead *und* turn me in. I accept my fate. I'll be hanging here tomorrow *Morgen* with that other poor fellow. At this point, death has got to be better."

"Don't be ridiculous. I'm not going to turn you in. I happen to have very strong feelings for you, lady."

"*Danke*, but what are you doing out here?"

"I have a security clearance 3, which allows me outside smoking privileges beyond my two scheduled breaks. In fact, that's the only reason I took up this filthy habit—to get out of that horrible building as often as I can. Are you escaping by yourself?"

"*Nein*, I have a *Freund* who is to meet me behind the garage at 2130."

"Mags, how did you get out on the balcony?"

"The window next to the door opens. It's the only one that does. Fortunately, I was able to squeeze through it."

"Listen up, I have an idea. If you want me to keep my big mouth shut, then I'm escaping with you."

"Okay, what's the plan, Sven?"

"I've been a prisoner at this compound for five years. I was part of the first group from town that was hired to work the assembly lines. We were given free housing on the premises during the week, *und* on the weekends, the trucks would take us back to our apartments in town. We made good *Geld*, *und* everyone was treated well. However, that only lasted for a year. Things slowly started to change for the worst, but we kept working because there were no other jobs in Somerset at the time. A year ago, right before Adolf Hitler joined his *Bruder*, everything changed drastically. Uniformed guards appeared, security got real tight, work hours were increased, *und* those ridiculous Nazi *Deutsch* flags that hang all over appeared overnight.

"Barbed wire fences went up, *und* the guard towers were constructed. People were being hung *und* executed for no viable reason. I planned to escape a few times. However, it seemed as though something would happen to prevent it. After you arrived *und* we started to become *Freunde*, you prevented my escape. I felt as though I had to stay to protect you *und* keep you safe. These people are monsters. I believe they're planning to attack *Amerika*. If we can get out of here alive, there may be a chance we can still get to the authorities *und* warn them before something drastic happens."

"Sven, that's exactly what I've been planning the entire time I've been here."

"Great, we're on the same page. Now let's high tail it out of here. Unfortunately, I will never fit through that window. But give me a couple of minutes. I have an idea. I'll pack a few things *und* throw it out window onto the balcony. Meanwhile, go back up with your bag, lay down flat, *und* wait for me to return back outside as a precaution, just in case one of the other supervisors comes out for a smoke. When I come back down from my *Zimmer*, I'll bum a *Zigarette* from the other supervisor. I'll tell him I dropped my *Zigarette und* couldn't find it in the dark, went up to my *Zimmer* for another pack, *und* didn't have any left. I'll then walk back outside under the pretense I'm going to smoke. If it's still safe, I'll signal you to come back down with my bag as well.

"Promptly at 2130, we'll leave together *und* run to the back of the garage. If your *Freund* isn't there at that time, we'll have to leave without him. I grew up here. My *Eltern* emigrated from *Deutschland* when they were *jung*. My *Vater* bought a small horse farm, which is a two day walk from here. I know a great place to hide out for a while until the heat is off. It's a cave that is located behind a waterfall. When I was a *jung* child through my later teenage years, my *Vater und* I would camp at this cave *und* spend a couple of days hunting *und* fishing. In fact, this is the perfect location. We still have supplies stored up there, *und* it's far up the mountain in a very remote area. It'll take us all *Nacht* to get there on foot. However, once we're at the cave, we'll be safe *und* no one should be able to find us. When spring arrives *und* we're no longer top priority, we'll venture back down, retrieve my *Vater*, *und* travel southwest into Garrett County, Maryland, *und* get some help."

"*Danke*, I'm grateful you're joining us."

At exactly 2130, the first shift of guards started climbing down the tower latters. As they stepped onto the ground *und* the two front guards were halfway back to the barracks while the second shift were inching their way up, it was now time to flee. Sven grabbed my hand, *und* the two of us ran like a bat out of *Hölle*, trying to reach the back of the garage in those few precious minutes that was downtime. Remarkably, we made it behind the garage just as the guards got settled into their crow's nest.

As Sven *und* I walked around the left corner of the garage, we immediately were startled by the contour of a man standing a few yards down at the other end. Sven instantly dropped his duffel bag to the ground *und* very calmly pulled out a pistol from the holster he had buckled around his waist *und* pointed it at Frank.

"*Gott sei Dank!* I was so afraid you wouldn't be able to make it in time."

"Magdalina, is this the *Freund* you were telling me about?"

"*Ja*, please put that pistol away. Frank, this is Sven Hirsch. He's a *Freund*. He'll be traveling with us as well. Sven, this is Frank Hubert."

Sven immediately pushed the safety on the pistol *und* returned it to his holster. As the two men shook hands *und* greeted one another, the three of us were suddenly spooked by the sound of footsteps in the dry leaves. My heart sunk down to my feet, as my eyes were flabbergasted at the sight of Olga, standing there, grinning at us as though she just hit payday. Out of sheer instinct, Sven lunged for her *und* simultaneously grabbed her gun with one hand *und* put his other hand over her mouth as she tried to pull her pistol out from its holster. Sven then broke her neck *und* killed her instantaneously. Her lifeless body dropped to the ground without hesitation. Sven immediately unbuckled the holster from her waist, returned the pistol to the holster, *und* handed it to Frank.

"Magdalina, Frank, I'm sorry you saw that, but I had no choice. This woman is pure evil. She would have gone to great lengths to make sure that the three of us were hanging over there next to George first thing in *Morgen*. Let's get on our way. We have a lot of ground to cover this evening, *und* with limited moonlight, this will slow us down."

Frank immediately started to dig under the eight-foot wire fence with a metal window bar he was able to jimmy loose from his barracks.

"Frank, hold up for a second."

"Sure, Sven, what's up?"

"I may have a better idea to get us out of here quicker. The first time I was planning my escape, I took a lot time to study the fence. I propose we climb over. Frank, do me a favor *und* help me take Olga's jacket off."

Very confidently, Sven climbed the fence to the top *und* placed Olga's wool jacket over the barbed wire, along with the wool blanket he took off his *Bett und* was wearing like a scarf. He stayed at the top *und* waited for me to reach him. Once I was at the top, he shoved me over the barbed wire that was somewhat protected with Olga's jacket *und* the blanket. I then quickly climbed back down the other side. Once Frank was over the barbed wire, Sven too hoisted himself over. When Frank *und* Sven reached the ground, noticeably, Sven had many cuts on his body from the barbed wire, which had started to penetrate through Olga's jacket *und* the blanket with the weight of the third person. The cut on his leg was fairly deep *und* was bleeding considerably through his torn trousers. I immediately took out my winter scarf from my duffel bag *und* wrapped it tightly around his leg. The three of us then proceeded to walk quickly through the woods, following Sven *und* the flashlight he stole from one of the security clearance 4 guards the first time he attempted to escape.

THINGS AREN'T ALWAYS AS THEY SEEM

Sven, Frank, *und* I exhaustedly walked all *Nacht* long, almost in pitch dark. The only light illuminating seemed to becoming from the stars that were guiding us. Thankfully, it was an incredibly beautiful evening; the sky was clear *und* loaded with stars. However, for late in August, the night air was becoming extremely cool in the mountains, *und* obviously, the further we hiked up, the colder it became.

"Magdalina, you're freezing. Your milky white skin is turning a shade of blue right before my eyes." Sven compassionately looked at Frank, and said, it's time to stop for a couple of minutes *und* take a short break."

"*Danke*, Sven."

"Hey, guys, we're no longer in the compound. Let's speak English now—that's if we still know how."

"That's a great idea, considering it took me so long to learn what little I know."

"Well, Frank, whose fault is that? Your mother was always on your case about it," at that second, I completely lost control and began to laugh.

"Ha, ha. You girls always stick together."

Utilizing the precious few minutes we have, I took out my heavy winter sweater from my makeshift duffel bag and put it on, along with my winter hat. Gratefully, between the sweater and the hat, I was ready to push on and keep up with the boys. We continued to traipse through the heavy blanket of forest brush for another two hours. Suddenly we came to an abrupt stop in a small clearing and sat down on the cold ground to take a break. Thank God, my feet were killing me. I unlaced my boots and slid them off to expose my feet to the cold brisk night air. I was silently grateful for this break, as I'm sure Frank was as well. Sven seemed to have the stamina of a bull.

"Frank, Magdalina, take a ten-minute break and rest. I know I've pushed you hard. However, please understand once the Nazis realize we escaped and killed their kingpin, stool pigeon Olga, they may not rest until they have our hides. One thing I've witnessed in the five years I've been imprisoned is that the Nazis don't take too kindly to anyone trying to escape. Let's continue on, guys. We should reach the waterfall by the break of dawn."

Thank God, Sven was right. I don't think I could have gone on much further. We reached the waterfall just as the sun began to rise, which gave us welcomed light and a little warmth. Frank and I sat on the ground, resting our feet for an hour, hypnotized and fully absorbed in this phenomenal view. As the three of us sat so peacefully in the small clearing of the forest and observed the waterfall, all I could see was the magnificent water falling from the rocks twenty feet above. The water literally fell directly in front, concealing anything located behind the falls. Every detail of this location was exactly as Sven described.

After a long rest and our fill of ice-cold fresh water, Frank and I followed Sven and gingerly climbed the rock staircase to the middle of the waterfall. Sven graciously and proudly escorted us to the inside, behind where the water was cascading. We walked down a long, wide rock ledge that led to the cave's entrance. As we entered the cave, I was totally dumfounded and speechless. This cave resembled a cozy, warm, and very spacious hunting cabin. There were two double cots set up on the far back wall.

Sven pulled out two sealed large wooden storage containers from underneath both cots. Each container was holding a rolled-up sleeping bag, pillows, wool blankets, towels, and a spare single cot folded and stored inside. There was also a sleeping bag rolled up tightly lying on top of each cot. Between the cots was a padlocked large wooden chest, with an oil lamp sitting on top. Sven pulled up the black bearskin rug lying on the rock floor in front of the fire pit and grabbed a key. He opened the large chest and showed us its contents. There was a full arsenal stored inside this chest, consisting of two rifles, two shotguns, and about a dozen boxes of ammunition. Also stored in the chest were four hunting knives, two axes, some heavy extra-strength ropes, two bows with a large supply of arrows, and two sets of binoculars.

"Holy cow, Sven! Are you guys expecting the world to come to an end or something?"

"No, of course, not, Frank. We just used to come up here a lot. Are you all right, Magdalina?"

"Yes, I'm fine. Thank you. Just a little tired."

The wall on the right side of the cave had a folding card table with four folding chairs. Next to the table was a large mahogany shelf; on the top shelf were two full bottles of vodka and one half bottle of whiskey, a can of coffee and four glasses. On the second shelf lays a large dishpan, containing a bottle of dish detergent, two tubes of toothpaste, three rolls of toilet paper, a bottle of shampoo, and three bars of bathing soap. There were also six bars of laundry soap. On the next shelf, neatly stacked were dishes, coffee cups, glasses, and some silverware in a brown paper bag. There were also two pots and a large cast-iron frying pan, a tea kettle, and three empty water jugs.

The bottom shelf had an old wooden produce crate filled with flashlights, batteries, seven boxes of stick matches, different-size sewing needles, and several spools of nylon thread. Also stored on the shelf is a first aid kit, a tackle box, two large bottles of lamp oil and a metal bucket. Leaning next to the shelves were three fishing rods, two pairs of skis, and snowshoes. On the left hand side of the cave was a large metal trash can with a lid that Sven and his father used for fresh drinking water. Alongside that was a funny-looking homemade large wooden rack. Next to the rack on the floor lay another wooden produce crate strangely filled with boxes of salt.

"Wow, Sven, I must say this place is an escapee's paradise? Everything but the kitchen sink. Or is the sink someplace else?"

"Very funny, Frank, you're quite the comedian."

"All kidding aside, what's up with this place?"

"My father and I, and a boyhood friend and his father used to camp up here every year in the autumn, early winter, spring, and some summer months. We used this place for hunting and fishing. Our preferred hunt was always deer and black-bear. However, when my mother was alive, my father also used the cave as a getaway from her for a couple of days, sometimes weeks.

"This location is a seven-hour walk up the mountain from my father's farm. Because of the distance, we always stayed for a few of days. In fact, about twenty years ago in late September, we were snowed in for almost a week. My father and I learned the hard way what is needed for survival in the wilderness. After that experience, we literally made it a priority to make sure the cave is always well stocked for any emergency. It's easier to keep everything stored here and just schlepp food and clothing as needed.

"Speaking of food, Magdalina, why don't you lie down and get some rest, while Frank and I gather firewood and try our luck at fishing. I don't know about you two, but I'm famished, and unfortunately, as you can see, there's nothing to eat."

"All right, I'll take a short catnap. Later, I'll get up, clean the place, set up the third cot, and make three beds."

"Thanks, Mags. Frank, we better shake a leg and not waste another minute of daylight. The Nazi soldiers are probably just realizing we've successfully escaped. This mountain is huge and can take a patrol three to four weeks before they may even come close to approaching the vicinity of our location. To get here, we traveled southwest. However, logic dictates the Nazis will head straight up the mountain and toward the north because of the location of Olga's body. They'll then notice the blind spot behind the garage. That is one of the reasons I left her there for them to find. The terrain is easier on the northeast side. It makes perfect sense to assume we would head in that direction, especially since we're traveling with a woman."

"Excuse, me!" I looked at Sven with a sly little grin.

"Sorry Mags, no pun intented. I'm calculating we have one week that we can safely hunt with the rifles and shotguns. The sound doesn't travel far, but I don't want to take any unnecessary chances. After a week has passed, all hunting will be done with bows and arrows. The good news is, however, I happen to be an excellent archer, and we have a very good supply of arrows. With that said, within the next two weeks, I'll train you both on archery and how to make arrows to keep our supply plentiful for the winter.

"We'll save the ammunition for any intruders, both animal and human, and use it only as needed. Believe me, I've seen many black-bear and coyotes hanging out around here. Especially bears, this is a prime location for fish. The Casselman River flows northward from Grantsville, Maryland, into Somerset County, Pennsylvania, and falls twenty feet into a deep hole in front of the waterfall and continues on its way to the Youghiogheny River. Realistically we'll need to kill at least three black-bears before the winter months fall upon us. Their hides make excellent winter coats, and the meat we can freeze in the meat cooler stored outside on the caves ledge by the entrance.

"Unfortunately, the one thing my dad and I don't have stored up here is winter clothing. However, we have three months before hibernation. Typically, there'll be black-bears congregating to this area. Instinctively, they engorge themselves as much as they can before hibernation. Another optimistic fact is we have the winter months on our side. We're high up, and it will snow unseasonably early for this time of year. This is to our benefit. We can keep the meat frozen and, with any luck, keep undesirable Nazis down the mountain."

"Sven, I have to ask this question, just for kicks and giggles. I have friends who own a small cabin up here somewhere. Do you think we should try to find it since we're going to be here all winter?"

"No, hun, I'm sure you're referring to Antonio Sabatino's place. His cabin sits four miles up the mountain and ten miles southwest past the compound. If the soldiers can withstand the mountain terrain and the bad weather, which will be upon us shortly, they'll surely run across his cabin. When we were kids and went on our hunting exhibitions, Antonio and his father always joined us at the cave. The cave is more secluded and spacious and is a better location for fishing and hunting. The location of Antonio's cabin is good for a weekend getaway, but not from hiding from the bad guys. My goal is to get as prepared as possible and hunker down here.

"Meanwhile, Frank and I need to winter-proof the cave better. First thing on the agenda is to replace this old, rotted door. It was originally put up as a temporary fix during that long week my father and I were snowed in. We can make a new door, stronger and more weatherproof. Frank and I will cut down some trees first thing tomorrow morning and get started with the construction. The new door will be designed to enclose the entrance. However, we'll leave a small opening in the upper right-hand corner, close to the fire pit. This opening will allow the smoke and toxic fumes from the fire to escape for ventilation. With the amount of energy the falling water creates, the smoke will dissipate and won't be visible from the other side.

"However, with this opening on the door, it will also allow the cold air to enter. We'll have to make sure the fire is burning constantly. Believe me, when that fire is out even for a short time, it would become unbearably cold in here in the middle of the winter and we could literally freeze to death. Our two top priorities are building up a decent food supply and reconstructing the door. However, for the time being, let's just catch supper for tonight and get some shuteye. I feel like I'm going to fall over soon."

"You got it, boss. I'm so hungry I could eat a bear."

"Frank, I'm assigning you the job of the century—our daily comedian."

"What do you think, Mags?"

"I agree with Frank. Now get the heck out of here. I have stuff to do."

While the boys were out fishing, I ended up falling asleep on one of the double cots. I so eagerly wanted to keep up with them and prove myself as worthy; however, once they left me alone, I just literally passed out. When I woke a few hours later, they still hadn't returned. To make myself useful, I cleaned up the place and took out the extra cot from the storage container and set it up next the other two. I brought out the pillows and the heavy wool blankets and made the three beds for our first evening in the wilderness. I wish I could take the pillows and blankets outside to air them out in the sun, but unfortunately, I didn't know how to get out of here alive.

About an hour later, Frank and Sven walked back into the cave with stacks of firewood in their arms. After neatly stacking the firewood against the wall next to the fire pit, Sven showed me how to safely exit the cave. Although the rock ledge behind the waterfall was very wide, it was smart to snug close to the cave's wall, away from the falling water. The further in from the waterfall, the dryer the ledge, and the possibility of slipping and falling over the edge into the falling water and down into the deep hole in the river was less.

Frank and Sven escorted me back outside to six rather large fish lying on the enormous tree stump down below, alongside the waterfall, which resembled a table and was smartly used as such. They caught two bass, a trout, and three pike with Sven's old fishing lures. Sven handed me a knife and showed me how to clean the fish. After we were finished, he stressed the importance of thoroughly rinsing down the tree stump with a bucket of water and always throwing all the fish heads and debris back into the river.

"There are many wild and dangerous animals living in these woods, especially bears and coyotes. They have a keen sense and smell for any fish oils that are left on the wood stump, and they'll most definitely pay us a visit. Also, if the Nazi soldiers are lucky enough to get this close, we certainly don't want to leave any trace of human inhabitance," Sven explained. This was one of Sven's golden rules for survival.

The three of us thoroughly cleaned everything up and walked back into the cave with the catch of the day for our first supper. Frank started a fire in the pit as I roasted off the fish in the cast-iron frying pan that looked like it had been here since the cavemen and dinosaurs. Incredibly, much to my surprise, fresh fish and cold springwater was a very tasty first night's supper. The only thing that could have made this meal complete was if we had some potatoes. After we had finished eating and I had washed the dishes and put them away, Frank pulled out a small batteryless radio from inside his jacket's pocket."

"Where did you get that?"

"I feel horrible about this, but I stole it from my friend Elmer, one of the other trainees in the barracks. There's a loose floorboard by the front entrance where he hides it between the floor joists. To listen to it, Elmer had to put it on the windowsill and point the large wire antenna outside. This little radio has been a godsend for us all. We listened to music sometimes, but for the most part, we had it tuned into a news program. The entire time I was a prisoner, we were always deeply saddened that nothing was ever reported in reference to the activities of the compound or the Nazis."

Before turning in for the evening, Frank, Sven, and I decided to venture back outside with the radio to see if we could get reception up here. Frank set up the radio on the tree stump and successfully found a news program that didn't have static. Remarkably, this was the only station we're able to receive. Although the news has already begun, we were at least in time for the tail end of a speech President Truman was making.

> ...Feel confident that World War II will shortly be coming to an end.
>
> The first bombing took place on August 6, 1945. A uranium bomb known as the Little Boy was dropped on Hiroshima. The second was on August 9. A plutonium bomb known as Fat Man was dropped on Nagasaki. These two major Japanese cities have been destroyed.
>
> With the success of the Manhattan Project, I see no reason why Emperor Hirohito will not surrender.
>
> Thank you, and God bless America.

Frank, Sven, and I sat in complete silence looking at one another, traumatized in total disbelief. Although we didn't hear the entire speech, we didn't know what to make of this.

"Oh my god, all those poor innocent Japanese people! I don't understand why Japan didn't surrender after Germany. This horrific atrocity could have been avoided."

"Mags, please don't get upset. I'm sure President Truman felt this was the only way of assuring a surrender and world peace. These bombs probably did nothing but scare the emperor into submission."

"Frank, do you really believe that? I personally think the president could have done something different without having so much bloodshed on his hands. But then again, maybe this is why women aren't in politics. As I find myself saying this a lot these days, I guess you men know what's best."

For the next couple of days we had the radio on nonstop. Frank and Sven built the new door with the radio on the entire time; we even fished with the news. Finally, a week later, we heard a broadcast announcing that Japan has surrendered and a cease-fire was declared on August 15, 1945. The three of us jumped for joy and were embarrassed in a huge group big bear hug.

"I'm so excited! Maybe this nightmare we've been living in will finally come to an end. Maybe the three of us should walk down the mountain into Maryland and into civilization before the winter weather strikes? If we're in Maryland, we're far enough from the Nazis. They won't find us. It would be nice not to spend the winter roughing it in the wilderness."

"Magdalina, I'm sorry, but that's not a good idea. We'll stay put and ride out the winter right where we are. The surrender of Japan has absolutely nothing to do with the current events that have been unfolding in Somerset County."

"Yah, Mags, I happen to agree with Sven."

"Okay, the boys have the majority," I said half-hearted, knowing darn right well their both right.

Weeks later, the news program announced that the war had officially ended on September 2, 1945. Needless to say, I was beginning to feel some hope. Especially with the war over and the United States military returning home shortly, maybe now Adolf and his Nazi friends would be rounded up and deported out of America.

The next morning, winter arrived two months early. Without warning, we woke to a heavy snowfall, with blistery winds and freezing temperatures.

"Look, boys, today is officially our first snowfall, September 5, 1945. How beautiful, I'm going to document this date in my journal."

"Mags, I didn't realize you're keeping a journal."

"Yes, I actually just started. I permanently borrowed one of Olga's notebooks and decided to document our adventures. If for anything, we'll have stories to tell our children someday."

"Are you trying to tell us something?"

"Ha ha, Frank, very funny."

The snow continued falling heavily throughout the rest of the day, but thankfully it was a dry snow and shouldn't accumulate. However, our first snowfall was a rude awakening that we're beginning to run out of time. Mother Nature and her fully fury was lurking around the corner.

The next day, after our first snow came to an abrupt end, and as the afternoon sun peeked through the clouds, the boys decided to teach me how to fish with lures. I have very fond memories of fishing with Adolf in the creek behind our house with nightcrawlers we dug up in our backyard when we were very young. Unfortunately, that was the extent of my fishing career. I must say, however, this way of fishing was very interesting. The technique was difficult to learn at first, but the reward was gratifying. In a few short hours, we caught one bass and three northern pike.

Remarkably, we were so engrossed in the solace of our day together we barely noticed when the solace suddenly came to a halt. A huge black-bear innocently came strolling out of the forest to pay us a visit. He must have smelled our catch and was interested in eating an early supper. Sven instinctively and immediately, without hesitation, picked up his rifle, which was lying on the ground next to him, and shot the bear dead with one bullet. I must say I haven't been that terrified of dying since I came down those balcony stairs, crawling on my hands and knees and scooting down the back warehouse wall, only to be greeted by Sven and his cigarette.

I immediately ran over to Sven and threw my arms around him and gave him a huge huge bear hug. Frank stood there motionless; I could tell he's embarrassed. He must feel like a fish out of water up here. He grew up in the city; he couldn't begin to compete with the likes of Sven. That poor enormous bear just wanted to join us for supper, and now we're so excited to have fresh meat tonight. Thankfully, the nights had been getting cold enough to keep the meat preserved. Frank and I were now going to get our first lesson in skinning an animal and tanning the hide. Thank God, when I was a child, I used to sneak into the slaughter house and watched Mr. Rosenburg. Hopefully, I could maintain my dignity and composure and not come apart at the seams with the first sight of blood and guts.

Sven had been an incredibly patient instructor in teaching us everything he knows about survival in the wilderness. I had no idea what Frank and I would have done without him. We probably would be hanging from the gallows next to George. We had been up here for eighteen days, and in this short time, Sven had shot two large black-bears and one buck. Thankfully, we had enough meat for a couple of months. I spent every day sewing our black bearskin winter coats. The deer skin was too small for a coat; however, I intended on making a pair of men's hunting trousers from it. We only need one more bear for the third coat; however, Frank and Sven have decided it was time to cease firing the weapons; they were now only going to hunt with bows.

With much anxiety, the boys had been spending their days fishing in the river before it freezes, stockpiling as much fish as possible. The fish and meat were stored in the large meat cooler which sits on the ledge outside the cave. The nights had been getting so cold that the meat was freezing and, thankfully, was staying frozen throughout the day. The ledge where the cooler sat was predominately safe from bears. Even if they could smell it, there was no way they'd be able to maneuver themselves through the long passage behind the falling water. Bears are quite instinctively cautious of their surrounding and their size. Coyotes and bobcats, on the other hand, could probably get back here, but Sven assured us that all the years he and his father had stayed in the cave, they had never seen an animal come back. If a coyote or bobcat was to venture back, there was no possible way for them to get into the cave and make supper out of us.

Sven and Frank finished the new wooden door, and the entire cave was now completely closed off. We had a stockpile of firewood next to the pit from top to bottom and also on the opposite wall, next to the funny-looking rack that Sven used for tanning hides.

"Magdalina and Frank, I want to tell you how proud and grateful I am. We're right on schedule. It's late September, and within a few weeks, the ground will be covered with snow and the surface water on the deep part of the river will freeze and possibly the waterfall as well. It's hard to believe, but I remember a few times it got so cold up here that the falling water also froze. When it gets that cold, we'll be cave bound, except for walking out to the ledge and retrieving fresh water from the waterfall daily.

"Frank, I think we should take the next couple of weeks and do more hunting with the bows. My goal is to bring back at least five months' worth of meat. This way, if we're to get snowed in for any length of time or if the enemy is in the area, we'll be prepared and won't have to set foot outside the cave."

"Sure, Sven. Whatever you want, I'm you're amigo."

"Thanks, buddy. I just want to reassure you both that once spring arrives, we'll walk down the mountain into Maryland and into civilization. We'll inform the authorities about the compound and what's been going on. God willing, the Hitler brothers will be arrested and deported back to Europe, and we have an early spring."

"That sounds wonderful, Sven. I can't wait until spring. From the time I was a little girl, I always hated winter. Winter's in Austria get pretty bad also."

I prayed Sven was right, and just spilling our guts to the authorities would correct this unbelievable situation. All I wanted was to go back to Mary's farm and pick up Christine. Then the two of us would travel back to our apartments in Philadelphia and live in peace; a little comfort wouldn't hurt, either.

A BIZARRE BUT WELCOMED REUNION

 "Sven, you sure were right. It's getting cold up here and fast. For some crazy reason, I thought you were exaggerating. When I lived in Philadelphia, it didn't get cold until December or January, and even then, it wasn't this cold."

"Stick with me, kid. I'll steer you in the right direction."

After spending two weeks doing nothing but hunting, Frank and Sven managed to bring back another black-bear and more meat than the three of us could eat. Frank actually hunted and killed a deer and several cottontail rabbits with his bow and gave Sven much needed help taking down the oversized man-eating black-bear.

"Frank, I'm amazed how quickly you've mastered archery skills. Thanks for your help with the bear. He was definitely giving me a run for my money."

"Oh…my…God, Sven, you're so welcome."

At that point, I looked at both men with all the testosterone in the air, and very pleasantly laughed to myself in silence. Frank's on cloud nine; I would assume he's had more fun in the past sixty-five days than he probably had in his entire life. Frank explained that his father died before he was a teenager, leaving his mother to raise him on her own. His family were city people; even when his father was alive, he wore a suit and tie to work every day. Neither his mother nor father was the type to get their hands dirty. The only fishing and hunting for food they ever did was at their local butcher.

The morning started out cloudy and brisk, with a predominate smell of rain in the air. I had just finished skinning the deer, while Sven and Frank were still working on the bear, when we were suddenly terror-stricken with the sound of footsteps rustling in the dry leaves nearby. Without delay, the three us threw down our hunting knives and picked up our rifles. We ran for cover in the dense part of the woods alongside the clearing, aimed our weapons, slid back the bolts, and chambered our bullets. As we lay in the forest debris, with our rifles aimed towards the sound, I was suddenly blown away by the sight of Antonio and Christine boldly parading out of the woods. We all immediately disengaged our rifles as Sven ran up to his best friend and embraced him in a huge manly bear hug, while I through my arms around Christine.

"What are you doing here, Antonio?"

"Sven, this is a very long story over a bottle of bourbon." Antonio quickly pulled out a bottle from the large sack he was carrying and held it up in the air, enticing us, like hanging a bone over some dogs.

"Sounds good. Who's that?"

"This is Christine Hiedler. She is a friend of Magdalina and Mary."

"Pleased to meet you, Christine."

"Antonio, take the girls inside. Frank and I will clean this mess up and meet you in the cave shortly. Please do me a favor. Rekindle the fire in the pit. It should only take a couple of minutes to warm the cave back up. We have enough firewood in there for a month of Sundays."

"Sure, boss, no problem."

Frank and Sven finished taking the meat off the bear carcass and cleaned the entire area spotless; the only thing left was to tan the hide. Surprisingly, they decided to leave the tanning for tomorrow morning. The bear hide would take hours to prepare for the rack and the drying-out stage; therefore they dug a large hole and buried the hide for safekeeping overnight. The plan was to get up early and finish the process first thing in the morning. After they were finished, they picked up the deer hide and brought it back with them to the cave to prepare it for the rack.

"Antonio, can you salt down the deer hide, while Frank and I put everything away. I'm very anxious to hear your story. Although, I must say, I'm feeling very concerned in the same breath. Surprisingly, I have just broken my cardinal rule of mountain survival: never leave anything for the animals or evidence of human habitat behind. Although in good conscience, the bear hide should be undetectable by both animal and human because of the current weather conditions."

After Frank and Sven finished putting everything away, they sat down on the black bearskin rug in front of the fire and warmed their bodies. Meanwhile, Christine and I continued working on supper, as Antonio poured a glass of bourbon for us all, and diluted it with a little water.

"Okay, Antonio, what's going on? You've got me on pins and needles. But more important, did anyone follow you?"

"Sven, you know me better than that. Of course, not."

"Great. Where's your wife?"

"This is an unbelievable story, so hunker down, everyone. Here it goes. As you're aware, my wife is employed as a guard at one of the internment camps that President Roosevelt authorized for the Japanese after Pearl Harbor. Originally, these camps were designed for the Japanese. However German Americans were also gathered up and taken to these camps. After four years, the refugees of both camps were let go. The Germans and Japanese were then replaced with Negroes from Elk Lick and our neighboring townships in Somerset County. Apparently, convoys of military men worked their way south, one township at a time, while heading into the city of Philadelphia.

"These convoys rounded up and transported Negroes in the middle of the night into the two camps for holding. They built training areas with barracks outback of each camp. Young Negro men are going through extensive basic training to get prepared for military battle. The women, children, and older Negroes are taken to Wilmington, North Carolina, where several barges are waiting to deport them back to Africa. All this is done in the middle of the night successfully undetected."

"Yah but, how in the world did they know where the Negroes were?"

"Just hold your pants on, Sven. I'll get to that."

"Once the Negro men are thoroughly trained, they're then transported to camps located in other states, also for holding. As the camps became empty and all the Negroes from Philadelphia to Somerset County were rounded up, trained, and shipped out, the army convoys began rounding up the Jews. The same sequence applied. They invade Elk Lick first, next our neighboring townships, and move south, raiding all the townships between here and Philadelphia. These military convoys are very organized. I assume due to the US Census Bureau that started in 1940, they have knowledge of where people live, which allows the Nazis to come in, collect everyone, and leave without arousing suspicion. To date, there are two different groups of people, the Negroes and Jews, consisting of thousands who are extracted from their homes right under our noises. No one seems to know what's going on. Nothing's been printed in the newspapers or broadcasted on the radio or television in reference to this bizarre activity.

"My wife, sadly, has stuck her neck out way too far on the chopping block, despite my constant forewarning. She has taken too many chances sneaking around, gathering information. Three days ago, she went to work and never returned. Mary's parents and I drove to the camp that evening, looking for her, and of course, no one knew anything and barely gave us the time of day. The next morning, I was out in the fields, harvesting corn all day. Sadly, as I came off the fields at the end of the day and walked into the backyard, as plain as the nose on my face, I saw my in-laws hanging from the old elm tree. I have to assume, if I hadn't been that deep in those fields, my scrawny carcass would be hanging next to them as well. I immediately ran into the house, gathered up all the guns and ammunition from the locked cabinet in our cellar, grabbed some supplies and my winter apparel, and proceeded to run out the backdoor."

"Wow buddy, I'm sorry to here about Mr. and Mrs. Rizzo. Let's just pray Mary's safe," Sven looked at Antonio deeply saddened.

"Thankfully, Christine had just been dropped off by her friend when I noticed her walking toward the backyard to take the laundry off the clothesline. Christine and her friend spent the entire day in town searching for any news of Mary and Magdalina. At that point, Magdalina had been missing for two months prior to my wife not returning home from work. I desperately tried to stop Christine from walking any further and witnessing that horrendous sight. Unfortunately, it was impossible. Within seconds she immediately broke down in hysteria and began screaming. I grabbed her, pulled her to the ground, and put my hand over her mouth. I was feeling much anxiety, not knowing if the guilty people were still around. After Christine calmed down, I instructed her to go into the house and quickly pack winter clothes and any supplies she may need, although only as much as she could carry.

"When Christine wasn't in view, I pulled out my hunting knife from my boot and cut my in-laws down from the tree. I quickly grabbed the shovel from the barn and buried them next to their beloved strawberry patch.

"Christine and I fled the farm quickly and began hiking to my cabin thirteen miles southwest. My thoughts were focused on the Nazis from the camps, who may have the blood of Mary's parents on their hands. They knew we stopped by the camp the night before looking for her and asking a lot of questions. They probably came by the house sometime the next morning after I was already out in the fields, with the intention of executing the three of us. Since they're probably looking for me, I thought my cabin would be safe. It's nestled within the woods in plain view. That is, if you know where to look. Mount Davis-Negro Mountain is large. The likeliness of someone stumbling onto my cabin is implausible."

"I don't know, buddy, maybe they found it through the US Census Bureau as well." I said to Antonio in an upbeat, cocky type of way.

"Anyway…my haphazard plan was for Christine to stay in our room and I would get some shuteye on the sofa. First thing in the morning, I would very cautiously walk back to Meyersdale and search for Mary. With the possibility I could actually find her, presuming it was safe, the two of us would go back into the house for Mary's belongings and at the same time I would grab as much food as possible. Unfortunately, things didn't work out quite the way I planned. Once Christine and I arrived at the cabin, it was obvious that someone committed arson. There was nothing left worth salvaging. The place was ransacked and then set ablaze. This apparently took place a couple of hours prior to our arrival. The wood was still warm and smoking.

"I must say, Sven, the walk to the cave this time seemed much longer and strenuous than I remember as a teenager. However, I'm pleasantly surprised Christine was able to keep up without too much trouble. I promised her once spring rolled around, we'll walk down to your father's farm and borrow his truck to search for Mary and Magdalina. I cannot begin to image how anyone could have located my cabin and torched it at least an hour before the two of us arrived. It doesn't make sense. How did anyone know I owned a hunting cabin and were able to find it that quickly? This is the part of the puzzle that has me baffled and concerned."

"I think I can explain what happened".

"All right, Sven, what's the scoop?"

"Presumably, your cabin was torched because of Magdalina, Frank, and me. There are Nazi patrols presently looking for us. The three of us escaped two months ago from a military compound located twenty miles northeast from the foot of the mountain. I'm assuming they have patrols searching the north and eastern areas of the mountain, with patrols in our neighboring towns as well. These three areas are the most practical locations for someone traveling with a woman this time of year. There's no doubt they're looking for you as well. However, Frank, Magdalina, and I must have a very hefty price tag on our heads. Between the three of us, we have too much knowledge of this Nazi organization and what they're potentially up to. Magdalina, do you mind if I tell Antonio and Christine your story?"

"No, Sven. Christine already knows, and Antonio's your best friend. You trust him. Therefore, I trust him."

"Thanks, *Liebchen*. Magdalina recently confided in Frank and me that Gerhard's brother, who recently joined him at the compound, is actually Adolf Hitler from Germany. Mags is the younger sister to Adolf and the older sister to Gerhard. Somehow, Hitler was able to escape Germany and traveled to America. The three of us believe that the Hitler brothers are planning something catastrophic to happen here on American soil."

"Sven, with all the information you've just disclosed my friend, I believe America maybe attacked in the near future," Antonio said with a horrified look on his face.

"This puzzle is strangely beginning to come together somewhat. The warehouse that's located within the compound seemed to have started out very innocent. There were seventy-five of us who were hired to work the assembly lines, producing firearms and ammunition. We were all under the impression that the firearms we were producing was to aid Britain and later for the American military in Europe. However, now that I think about it, strangely all the employees were either German immigrants or of German decent. No goombahs like you, Antonio."

"You mean the Italian perfect race."

"Very funny, between you and Frank, you're surely giving Jimmy Durante and Garry Moore a run for their money. Instead of the *Durante-Moore Show*, we'll call you guys the German-Italian duo. Except, neither one of you can hold a candle to Durante's *schnozzola*."

"Yah, Sven, you should also join the duo. We could become a trio with our two token krauts and a dago."

"Okay, buddy, I think you've had enough bourbon. Let me continue to bring you up to speed. Two years later, noticeable changes began taking place. The compound was built around the warehouse, and an eight-foot wire fence with barbed-wire tops was built surrounding the entire perimeter. Four guard towers were constructed a few days after the fence went up, and uniformed guards and supervisors began popping up all over. We were no longer permitted to speak English, and those who didn't know the German language had to attend mandatory German lessons for two hours daily, seven days a week. Our weekend furloughs to go home were immediately terminated. Overnight, we all became prisoners of the compound.

"Weeks later, a group of German scientists and physicists mysteriously showed up one day and moved in. They took over the left half of the first floor for their science lab, and partitions were suddenly built for privacy. When Gerhard's brother arrived, things got much worse. People with security clearance 2 through 5 all had to wear the gray uniforms and the red armbands with a swastika. However, security clearance 1 workers continued to wear their assigned workmen's uniforms. German Nazi flags with the swastika were suddenly displayed throughout the complex.

"Security got very tight. We all were assigned security-clearance cards. They built a military training facility out back in conjunction with a large barracks building to house the men. Every week, the trucks would drive into the compound with new recruits. The assembly lines started running around the clock, with three shifts of twelve hours per shift, seven days a week. We were pumping out unbelievable amounts of weapons and ammunition, loading them into large crates and then onto the trucks. The trucks were constantly coming and going with these crates packed to the rim. Later, the trucks started coming back with tanks, jeeps, armored cars, and infantry fighting vehicles.

"At that point, it was abundantly clear they were getting ready for an attack. Upon my first attempt to escape, I planned on going straight to the authorities with the intention of trying to warn them. However, I was caught immediately. Fortunately, I was able to weasel my way out of any suspicion. In fact, I ended up moving up another rank, which gave me a little more security clearance to better observe and plan my next strategy. This new security clearance also provided a better opportunity for the actual physical escape."

"Wow, this is much larger than I could ever have imaged. How did the three of you escape?"

"That's actually a cute story," I looked at Antonio and winked.

"I'm all ears, Sven."

"Ironically one evening, I was innocently out back smoking when I witnessed this incredible woman crawling on her hands and knees down a flight of balcony steps. In the two months of Magdalina's incarceration at the compound, she and I became close friends. Within a split second, without giving it any thought, I decided to join her and her friend Frank in their escape and finally implemented what I had been planning since my first botched attempt. That is how the three of us ended up here in the cave. I would assume the cave is probably the safest spot in Somerset County at this point, maybe Philadelphia as well. God forbid, maybe the entire state of Pennsylvania."

"Sven, I have an idea."

"What's that, Antonio?"

"Tomorrow morning, weather permitting, I'll hike down to your father's farm and borrow his telephone. I'm a member of an Italian family consisting of Sicilian muscle based out of Philadelphia. This Sicilian family also has connections with bosses of the Chicago and New York families. With one call, we can potentially have a hundred guys just from the Philadelphia group alone. I'm sure within a couple

LAURA DOTHE HELLWIG

of days, they can be here, all packing Tommy Guns and Molotov cocktails, and catch these Nazi krauts totally by surprise and wipe them off the face of the earth. No offense, guys!"

"None taken, wise guy. So what's your harebrained idea this time, Antonio?"

"My thought is we should first annihilate the Nazis in the compound and free the people. Once the good guys are out, we should then destroy the entire compound. My guys could be in and out before anyone knew what hit them. If we go the route of contacting government authorities, that plan may take too long. By the time they are able to comprehend the knowledge that we've given them, there may not be any more Americans left in the state of Pennsylvania. After all, these Nazi are seeking out, locking up, and deporting people as we speak. Obviously, this is beginning to diminish the Pennsylvanian population. If the authorities can actually comprehend this knowledge, it will probably take them an eternity to act on it. You know these government guys, they're a bunch of donut-eating suits, pushing pencils all day and packing Colt snubnosed revolvers and acting like a bunch of big shots. Once I reach your father's farm, if he's not already aware of the situation, I'll warn him of the dangers lurking in the area, help him get packed, and bring him up here to stay with us."

"I don't know if this is a good idea. Although, I agree my father needs to join us. Frank, can you go with Antonio?"

"Of course, Sven. I've heard many great things about your father. He needs to be safe."

"Thanks, Frank. Antonio, don't forget what our father's pounded into our brains. One of the first rules of survival is the buddy system. Just remember, guys, get down the mountain quickly and as indiscreetly as possible. Be extremely cautious. These idiots are looking for us, and possibly they're in that area. Antonio, you know what the weather is like up here this time of year. Within a blink of an eye, it can change and become treacherous. Take your rifles and plenty of ammo, but remember, don't use the firearms unless it's an emergency. We cannot take the chance that a gunshot will be heard by the enemy.

168

"Antonio, make sure you walk in the direction we used to travel coming up here when we were kids. I'll give you guys three days, one day down and spend the night at my father's. Pack his winter cloths and whatever food and provisions he may have at the farm. The second day, the three of you will return. If you haven't returned by the third day, I'll assume something has gone wrong and I'll come looking for you, walking the illusionary path. Antonio, do you remember our route?"

"Yes, of course, I do."

"Great. Once you start getting close to the bottom, I want you to promise me that you guys will be extremely careful. I cannot stress this more—these guys don't mess around and are extremely dangerous. I'm sure your Italian guys are extremely powerful as well. However, these Nazis aren't human.

"While the two of you are on this mission, I'm going to work on some old-fashioned Indian traps my father taught when I was a teenager. I'll place these traps in the forest one mile around the perimeter of the cave as a precaution, in case the Nazis start to close in. I'll leave the area free of any traps at the arch where the pine tree uprooted fifteen years ago and fell between the two pines. Antonio, do you remember this arch?"

"Sure, it's part of our secret path. I'm not senile yet," I looked at Sven with a snarly look.

"I know, buddy, I don't mean to be such a nudge. I'm just concerned, these traps you won't see, and if you veer off the path and encounter one of them, you're dead. Once the three of you are back here safely, I'll then put a trap under the arch to finish off the entire perimeter. If one of these traps actually catches someone, we should have twenty minutes to prepare to defend our home. Please don't forget—the area will be booby-trapped. Don't veer off the path. Good luck, gentlemen, and Godspeed."

OUR FIRST NEAR-DEATH EXPERIENCE

 Within the two days that Frank and Antonio were absent, Magdalina, Christine, and I were able to finish constructing, digging, and setting the traps around the perimeter of the cave. The bear hide was perfectly cleaned and was now hanging on the rack to extract the moisture. Magdalina and Christine finished the two black bearskin coats from our kill weeks ago and started sewing two pairs of hunting trousers from the deer hides.

Three days have passed rather quickly. Frank and Antonio still weren't back, and I was beginning to become very concerned. The weather overnight changed drastically; it snowed with four feet of accumulation with howling blistery winds. It was late October and we had already experienced our second major snowfall. Alarmingly, I was suddenly haunted with a sense of urgency to go down and look for them.

"Ladies, I'm sorry to leave you. I'm concerned and think it's time to look for Antonio and Frank. I'll be back as soon as possible. Please stay in the cave where it's warm and safe until I get back."

I strapped on the snowshoes, put my hunting knife in my boot, slung one of the shotguns over my shoulder, and buckled a holster with a loaded pistol around my waist. With the arsenal I presently had on my body, I left only one shotgun and one pistol for Magdalina and Christine. I was not feeling warm and fuzzy with the thought of leaving the two girls alone; however, I didn't have a choice.

I had to walk halfway down and assess the situation. After all, if Frank and Antonio managed to get themselves in trouble and were captured, there probably wasn't anything I alone could do to help. I put one of the black bearskin coats on and headed out solo for my long hike down the mountain.

THE 2ND WORLD WAR II

After walking for about an hour, thankfully, I saw Frank and Antonio walking single file, struggling up the mountain, dragging something behind them. As they approached the entrance of the fallen pine tree, I was able to get a better view of what they were dragging. Disturbingly, it was a dead Nazi officer. Fortunately, for us, it had just begun to snow again; however, this time, it was a sleet mixture. This was truly a blessing; once this mess would start to accumulate, our tracks would be covered up and disguised.

"Antonio, are you guys all right?"

"Yah, we got detained somewhat."

"What happened, buddy?"

"Frank and I made great time walking down. However, as we approached the bottom of the mountain, we noticed there was much activity at your father's farm. Frank and I cautiously crept closer to get a better view, lying low in the brush of the woods, and noticed there was an overwhelming amount of Nazi riffraff. Apparently, they have taken over the farm and are using it as a military installation. I'm terribly sorry to say your father was hung from the maple tree alongside the barn. I'm sure he put up quit a fight when those Nazi basterds came to visit. I desperately wanted to cut him down, but it was too dangerous to get any closer.

"Without pause, Frank and I immediately started hiking back up the mountain. We only walked a mile when Frank ditched behind a tree to take a leek, and within those split seconds, I was confronted with this guy. He held a pistol to my head and was saying something in German, gesturing for me to walk down to the farm. As I slowly turned and began to move, Frank came out from behind the trees and strangled this young Nazi with his belt. Frank was smart. If he cut his throat, there would have been a pool of blood in the snow, and with this wet snow presently falling, the blood on the ground would have been diluted, and the stain would have trickled down. It surely would have become very obvious that intruders were in the area. As a result, we could have had the entire Nazi force on our tails in no time and compromise everyone's safety. Frank and I felt the smartest thing was to bring him with us. The plan was to not leave any evidence behind.

Hopefully, this guy is not going to be missed, and if he is, we better be long gone."

"Thank God, you guys are all right. As usual, you did the right thing, Antonio," I said with sadness in my heart and tears in my eyes for my beloved father.

Once the three of us passed through the arch of the fallen pine tree, I finished rigging up my last trap. I tied a nylon line very tautly from an old fishing rod to the fallen pine tree and across to the other tree about six inches from the ground. I then removed the wooden planks that we just walked over to expose a ditch. Frank discarded the planks into the woods, and the three of us replaced them with flimsy tree branches and leaves to disguise the ditch.

"All right, explain this trap you concocted."

"Considering how dense both sides of the forest is for a few miles, with debris, fallen trees, and wild sticker bushes, walking through the arch of the fallen pine tree is, of course, the logical path for someone to take. They'll trip on the ground line and fall into the ditch. This poor slob is immediately stabbed to death with the wooden stacks which are hammered into the ground upright, exposing their sharpened points, resembling arrowheads.

"My god, Sven, I'm glad we're best friends. I wouldn't want to be your enemy."

"Thanks, guys. As a kid, I read too many cowboy and Indian books I think my brain is warped. Although, however warped it maybe, you need to know where the traps are located. I have a total of three ditch traps, the one there and two others at the cave's location. One is at 3:00 o'clock, and the other is at 9:00 o'clock when you're facing the waterfall dead center. The girls and I also have a variety of other traps in between these three. Tomorrow morning, I'll show you both where they're located and explain how they work."

The three of us walked all night single file, taking turns dragging the Nazi body, which fortunately helped to cover up our foot prints. The sense of urgency to get back to the cave suddenly became overwhelming. The snow and sleet were coming down much harder, and we surely didn't want to get stranded out here with this ugly, decaying Nazi.

Once Antonio, Frank, and I arrived at the waterfall, we decided to take the Nazis boots and wool coat before we discard this young man's corpse. We tied a large rock around his torso with the leftover nylon fishing line and threw him into the deep part of the river directly below the waterfall for fish food. Once we had everything cleaned up and all evidence destroyed, we then went back into the cave to warm up and dry off. Thank God, the snow was coming down heavy. The new snowfall would definitely cover up any signs of human footsteps. Once the Gestapo realized one of their own was missing, this could potentially put more fuel on the fire to hunt us down like dogs. Thankfully, we were ready for any intruders. The rifles, shotguns, and pistols were lined up along the wall of the cave, loaded and ready for action.

Within a few days, the snow had accumulated to five feet, and drifted at least eight feet high with blistering winds. Mother Nature had bestowed a blessing upon us. If the Nazis were looking for us, it was virtually improbable for them to get close to our location. As good luck would have it, this bought us sometime. To venture too far into the wilderness with the present conditions as they were, and the chance of more inclement weather unexpectedly popping up at any given time, was suicide. For all intense and purposes, we did an excellent job winterizing the cave. As long as someone continued to feed the fire, the cave stayed nice and toasty. Of course, the challenge had been while we're sleeping. Inevitably, the fire would go out at some point, and we would literally rely on one of us waking up to rebuild it. Notably, that person was normally me.

Amazingly, after all the snow that had fallen last week and the blizzard-like conditions that kick-started an early winter, we woke to an unseasonably warmer picture-perfect day for the month of November. The sun was shining brightly through a clear sky and was beginning to melt the remainder of the snow rather quickly. The five of us decided to take full advantage of this beautiful day. We set up the radio on the tree stump and tuned into the news for the first time in a week. Antonio and Frank were trying their luck at fishing, while Christine and Magdalina took turns washing laundry with my mother's old scrub board in the freezing river. Meanwhile, I was replenishing our water supply by filling jugs of water from the inside of the waterfall and schlepping them into the cave to fill the metal trash can.

With our water can filled for the day, I decided to grab the third fishing rod and help the boys. As I baited my hook with a night crawler, I suddenly stop cold dead when the news program was abruptly interrupted with an emergency report. The five of us quickly stopped what we were doing and ran over to the radio. President Truman was addressing the American people.

> My fellow Americans, yesterday, November 23, 1945, will go down in history with the same magnitude as Pearl Harbor. Nine major military installations on American soil were bombed by the German *Luftwaffe*. This military plan of action was perfectly executed, giving our boys no time to defend their installations. Nine attacks in various states all took place at exactly 0800 sharp. The installation bases that were bombed and destroyed are as follows:
>
> - Naval Station in Norfolk, Virginia;
> - Fort Hood, Texas;
> - Fort Bragg, North Carolina;
> - Fort Campbell, Kentucky;
> - Fort Lewis, Washington;
> - Naval Air Station in Jacksonville, Florida;
> - Air Force Base in McGuire, New Jersey;
> - Dover Air Force Base in Delaware; and the
> - Naval Base in Annapolis, Maryland
>
> This attack was deliberate and very well planned by what seems to be a Nazi organization. This organization is believed to have escaped from Germany before the country's surrender. Loss of American life is astronomical. With so many of our army, air force, navy, and marines currently deployed in Europe and the Pacific, this attack has left us severely crippled. I'm urging all American's to stay at your homes and do not panic. The National Guard has been called to active duty for each

state, along with your local police and fire Departments to ensure the safety of the American people.

Army and Air National Guards, and all reserves are under strict orders to report to the US Capitol Building at once. A strict curfew will go into effect immediately. Please stay tuned for further instructions.

Thank you and God Bless America.

"Wow, this is unbelievable. This attack will surely provoke war on American soil. We need to get as prepared as possible. All the bits and pieces of this crazy puzzle that we've all experienced in different scenarios are now coming together and making sense."

"Sven, you're right. I think it's time I come clean and reveal the knowledge my two brothers have entrusted to me."

"Sure, go ahead, reveal away."

"Adolf was sending money and valuables to Gerhard from Europe well before World War II started. Adolf implemented the well-planned escape of Germany's top scientists, physicists, mathematicians, and SS officers while World War II was actually underway. Later, when it was evident that Germany was losing the war, the same escape plan was used for Adolf and his top-ranking Gestapo officers. It was incredibly hard to believe that my brother could have deported a realistic amount of Nazis to actually pull off a war in United States. However, in our compound alone, as Sven and Frank are well aware, there are probably a thousand American citizens with German heritage forced to undergo strenuous military training and work the assembly lines producing firearms and ammo.

"Realistically, if there are compounds located in other states, doing the same thing, then there's a potential of producing a sizable army. My brothers have been very selective—only young, strong men are forced into training. Obviously, the military training these gentlemen are receiving is for the objective of becoming part of the German Army. Adolf revealed that he has revised his original strategy from what he did in Europe. Instead of sending able-bodied, strong men to deportation or death camps, he wised up and utilized these men for battle. It makes more sense to have them killed fighting on a battlefield than do away with them unproductively in the camps. This still accomplishes the same results and helps to preserve the lives of the Aryan German military. We cannot just sit here and allow this horror to happen. We have to do something and fight back."

"I agree. We need to do something, and pronto!"

"But what, Sven? What can the five of us possibly do to prevent the enviable, especially since we're stuck up here?"

"Once we can get around better, Antonio and I will walk into Meyersdale and place that telephone call to the boss from one of the town merchants. Antonio, I like your idea. I think the three of us should also join the Sicilian muscle to attack and take over the compound and barracks. Depending on how many guys they send us, this is probably very doable. We'll build up our manpower and therefore build up our strength. Once we conquer the compound, we should have all the weapons and ammunition we need. This plan will be an excellent start. As we increase our force, we can start marching into our towns and reclaim them back one at a time. With the bulk of our military presently overseas, it may take a few months to literally get them back on American soil. However, we should get the ball rolling."

Of course, the atmospheric conditions had done a complete about-face, and normal winter weather is once again in full swing. That one beautiful November day was just a teaser. However, no matter how bad the weather might be, the five of us had adopted the routine of sitting by the tree stump to listen to our favorite news program on the radio every Sunday evening at 7:00 p.m. sharp.

Thank you for tuning into our radio program, *You Can't Do Business with Hitler*, with John Flynn and Virginia Moore.

Hours after the attack on our military compounds, President Truman and the US Department of War declared a state of emergency. All military personnel have been ordered to return to the States immediately. Our boys literally have dropped everything and are running home to defend our beloved homeland.

The *USS Enterprise* (CV-6), the Big E, or known also as the Grey Ghost, was the first to sail the North Atlantic Ocean, traveling thirty-three knots and carrying over three hundred men along with the Black Sheep Squadron. Also aboard were five Grumman F6F Hellcats and eleven Corsair "Pirates of the Skies" fighter bomber aircraft. Regrettably, the *USS Enterprise* was torpedoed and sunk by enemy submarines three miles from coastal waters. The *USS Yorktown* (CV-10) was an hour behind the *Enterprise* and was the second carrier to be torpedoed and sunk. She was carrying two hundred and fifty men and eight Northrop P-61 Black Widow Night Bombers, three P-47 Thunder Bolts, and two P-51 Mustangs. At the present we have no word of any survivors.

Two American Douglas O-46 reconnaissance aircraft were seen flying in the vicinity of New York and Washington, DC. Two days later, the same reconnaissance aircraft were spotted flying around Texas and Florida. Thank God, this mission was successful; the two planes were able to return to their carriers unharmed. As information is presented to us, we are dedicated to broadcasting to you.

This is John Flynn and Virginia Moore, signing off. Thank you and God bless America.

With this recent information, even though weather conditions weren't the best, Antonio and I decide to journey back down the mountain. Frank would stay behind with the girls and keep the homefront safe and secure. Antonio and I each put a hunting knife in our boots and a loaded pistol in the waistband of our trousers, strapped on the snowshoes, and bundled up in our black bearskin coats. We placed a decent supply of ammunition in our deerskin knapsacks, and we both slung a loaded rifle over our shoulders.

Thankfully, the sun was shining brightly, which helped warm this bitter cold morning. As Antonio and I began hiking back down the mountain, it didn't take long to realize the snowshoes were helping to make this trip much easier than originally anticipated. Surprisingly, Antonio and I actually made great time, considering the mountain was still covered in a blanket of deep snow. Five hours later, we started to approach Mary's farm. As Antonio and I were crunched down in the brush of the woods, we noticed the property has been seized and turned into a Nazi compound, just as my father's place had been. There was an alarming amount of men and women in gray uniforms with red bands on their left arms walking about. German Nazi flags hung everywhere.

We continued traveling undetected through the dense forest in the direction of Meyersdale. We hope there were no Nazis lingering in town, so we could slide in and assess the area, make our telephone call, and slide out again without being noticed. As we approached town and got a better view, noticeably, there were Nazi German flags hanging everywhere. The town's folk seemed to be going about their business as usual, like nothing was out of sorts. For the life of me, I didn't understand how these people could just walk around, shopping and working like nothing was wrong.

Not to arouse any suspicion, Antonio took off his black bearskin coat and handed it to me. I stayed in the forest at the edge of town as Antonio walked to Craig's Diner to use his telephone. Ten minutes later, Antonio walked out of the diner and back down Main Street and joined me in the forest.

"What wrong, Antonio?"

"This is going to be more difficult than originally anticipated. I was able to get through to the boss, but he informed me that the situation in New York and Chicago is the same as it is here. He advised us to go back to the cave and call him in two months. At the present, the family is struggling with this situation as well. He feels our idea of uniting and taking one town at a time is a good plan. However, the boss is in the process of implementing a nonproliferation treaty with all the other Sicilian coalitions. He needs more time to regroup and get organized. For the first time since our people came to the New World, we are finally going to consolidate with all the different coalitions and work out a plan of action together. Sven, what would you like to see happen here? Not that we have a choice, because what the boss says goes."

"Antonio, whoever the boss is, he seems to be an intelligent man, using good old-fashion common sense. Having the different coalitions unite, in my opinion, is definitely the right way to go. I'm a firm believer that unification brings power in quantities. We'll wait two months, venture back into town, and call him once again. After all, much can happen in two month—this entire ordeal will probably be over. Once our boys are able to penetrate the blockades in the Atlantic Ocean, the United States military will then kick some butt. Meanwhile, I have some money. Let's go into Sam's Market and buy some provisions. The girls will be ecstatic when we show up with potatoes, rice, pasta, and fresh fruits and vegetables. Also, please don't let me forget to buy a wax carton of milk. I don't know how you all feel about just drinking water, vodka, and bourbon every day. I need to have a glass of milk at least with supper a few times."

Antonio waited for me outside Sam's Market, holding my coat this time. Seconds after I entered the store, Craig Miller, an old childhood friend of mine and Antonio, grabbed my arm and inconspicuously walked me quickly to the back storage room.

"Sven, are you nuts? What are you doing here?" I said with such intensity in my voice.

"Nice to see you again, Craig. I'm fine. How about you?"

"The Gestapo has been tearing the town apart, looking high and low for you, another man, and a woman. You can't just traipse in here and buy whatever you want anymore. We have all been furnished weekly ration cards and have to carry mandatory identification papers with us at all times. If you go up to the cashier and try to purchase an item without presenting a ration card, she'll turn you into the authorities. There are Nazi patrols who scout the streets daily.

"I must say, my friend, you're really fortunate that you got this far without getting arrested. You cannot trust anyone, not even your friends. People are rewarded if they rat-fink on someone who speaks negatively about the Nazis or who is suspected of being a rebel. Folks have been turned in and arrested for much less. Rumor is, if you're implicated of something, the Gestapo considers it treason and you're arrested and shipped off to a concentration or death camp. I'm going to take you to my apartment. We can slide out the back from here and slither down the alley to the diner's backdoor. We should then be able to make it upstairs to my apartment without anyone noticing."

"That's fine, Craig, but Antonio is out front waiting for me."

"Holy cow! You two are really gambling with your lives. Stay here out of sight, and wait for me. I'll walk back through the store and buy something, not to arouse any suspicion. Antonio and I will walk down the side of the building to the back alley. We have to hurry and get to my place. A Nazi patrol walked by the front an hour ago and would be coming back through the back alleys very shortly."

"Okay, I'll wait here. You get Antonio."

Craig, Antonio, and I ran down the back alley and up the steps to Craig's apartment without being seen. However, the old lady who lived down the hall in the second apartment must have heard us running up the steps and opened her front door. Craig explained that she had cataracts in both eyes and couldn't see very well, allowing Craig to act as though he was alone.

"Are you all right, Mrs. O'Brien?"

"Yes, I thought I heard a few people running up the steps."

"No, Mrs. O'Brien, that was just me clodhopping up here like an elephant. Go back inside. Everything is all right."

"Will do, dear. Thank you."

"Craig, are you sure she couldn't see us?"

"Honestly, Sven, I don't think so. She has no telephone. For her to rat-fink on us, she'll physically have to leave her apartment, and since she relies on me to help her get around the few times she actually does leave, I think we're safe for now."

"If you say so, my friend."

Mrs. O'Brien went back into her apartment and closed the door. Craig, Antonio, and I quickly crept into his apartment and locked the door behind us. Craig went into the kitchen and graciously brewed some coffee as Antonio and I made ourselves comfortable in the parlor.

"I need to explain what has taken place here while you have been missing in action."

"Do tell, Craig."

"First, I have some bad news, Antonio. Mary was executed, along with four others, by a firing squad. A Nazi patrol drove down Main Street with a loud speaker, announcing that everyone was to meet at my diner. The Nazis literally utilized the brick wall on the right side of building. Mary, Billy, and Zachery, along with Mr. and Mrs. Zielinski, were lined up against the wall and shot. Mary apparently aroused some suspicion and was followed as she left work one evening. They picked her up and Zachery at his garage, as he pumped gas into her car. The entire town had to witness the execution as a scare tactic. If someone tried to help, they're shot in cold blood by armed guards."

"Are you alright buddy?" I looked at Antonio with tears in my eyes, and clearly he's struggling to fight back his tears.

"At any given time, you can walk down Main Street and witness people hanging from ropes. They were implicated by a neighbor or a friend. These people did nothing wrong, maybe just spoke their mind and were overheard. The Gestapo is smart—they scare people into submission. This is how they're able to brainwash and manipulate good God-fearing people. No one knows what crime sweet Mary could have possibly been guilty of to deserve her fate. There have been all sorts of rumors circulating. I personally believe Mary and the others were set up as a patsy.

"Horse farms and private homes located outside of town, southward to the border of Garrett and Allegany counties in Maryland, have been confiscated and are presently used as military compounds and barracks. Dairy and crop farms have been left untouched. However, these farms are visited once a week by Nazi patrols. The owners of these farms are arrested, the older people are executed or put into prison, while the younger men and women are kept on the farms and used as free labor.

"Somerset County is completely German occupied at this point. I don't know what's going on outside of this county. The area is guarded too closely. Presently, we're all prisoners of Somerset. Amazingly, I tried to visit my girlfriend who lives in Bedford County and was refused permission to travel over the county border. I haven't been able to get ahold of her by telephone for weeks, and all personal mail is forbidden. There's actually a guard who sensors our mail in the post office.

"Last week, the Gestapo started coming around to people's homes and are taking possession of their automobiles and trucks. Also any telephone lines coming into our homes and apartments have been disconnected and the actual telephone confiscated. So far, our businesses are able to continue with telephone service. I would assume at this point, the entire state of Pennsylvania is experiencing the same problems."

"Wow, this is incomprehensible. How could the Gestapo accomplish so much in such a short time?"

"I don't know, Sven, but I'm not ready to become a kraut yet. I'll make supper and then we have to get out of here. A Nazi patrol comes door to door sporadically, looking for fugitives. We're safe for now, but I suggest once we eat, the three of us flee as quickly as possible. That's assuming I can accompany the two of you back to the cave?"

"Of course, our cave is your cave."

"Thanks. Living in a cave sounds much sweeter than this town. Furthermore, I like your plan. After we eat, I'll go into the bedroom and pack a duffel bag while you two pack as much food and supplies that I have in my kitchen. On our way out, we can rob the pantry and walk-ins in my diner as well."

"Thanks, Craig. I think Antonio and I can attest to the fact that our diets need to be better balanced."

As Antonio and I proceeded to leave the apartment, out of the corner of my eye, I noticed Craig looking around, scooping the place out, teary eyed. He hesitantly pulled a photograph of his family off the wall and shoved it into his duffle bag. After quietly locking the door, the three of us, with our arms filled with supplies and food, gingerly walked down the staircase and raided the diner's kitchen. Thank God, we managed to escape without arousing any suspicion from Mrs. O'Brien. Craig walked back to the dry-goods storage area and carried out four large boxes to store the food in, allowing us to carry the provisions up the mountain much easier.

Since a Nazi patrol already walked through the alleys thirty minutes ago, we traveled the back alleys as much as we could. For the most part, the light was very limited and we could move about undetected much easier. However, when we encountered a brighter light, Craig shot the light bulb and shattered it with his pellet gun. After fifteen minutes of schlepping the four heavy food boxes down the alley, we reached the edge of town where the forest begins. Thankfully, as the three of us began walking into the forest, I happened to notice two very large tree limbs that had recently fallen. Immediately the light bulb went off in my head.

"Antonio, Craig, wait a second, I have an idea."

"What's your idea this time?"

I immediately pulled out some twine from my pack and my father's old axe and cut the two tree trunks into six 5-foot sections. We took the twine and braided it for extra strength and connected the six logs together, leaving a tail to pull our do-it-yourself sled.

"Oh I get it. Good thinking, Sven."

"Thanks, boys."

We then loaded the four boxes of food and supplies onto the sled and proceeded to pull it up the mountain, making our trip much easier and quicker. After walking a mile into the forest, we were suddenly startled by the sound of human voices that were in the vicinity, prompting the three of us to begin running for dear life. Unfortunately, there was a fresh coating of snow on the ground, which was making our presence quite obvious. As Craig and Antonio continued pulling the sleigh, I ran over to a pine tree and broke off a branch to disguise our tracks. I quickly walked behind, sweeping away any evidence of the sleigh and human footsteps with the tree branch.

"Gee, guys, at this pace, it'll take forever to get to the cave."

"Yah, Sven, just keep on sweeping with that broom. You're doing a fine job, my man."

"Zip it, Antonio. I have no problem switching jobs and making you the girl."

Fortunately, the sound we just heard at the foot of the mountain was slowly dissipating. We quickly continued up the mountain, however, this time, without the stress and urgency the three of us just felt. After four hours of struggling, with Antonio and Craig both pulling the sleigh together, the snow accumulation was becoming unreasonable for passage. Suddenly once again, we were startled by faint sounds echoing through the woods.

"Dear God, we must have been followed. Antonio and Craig, leave the sleigh in this heavy brush and let's head for cover. Worst case, we can retrieve it another day. We're only two miles from the cave. I have numerous traps set exactly one mile from the caves perimeter. We have our rifles and pistols already loaded, and if someone is to encounter one of my traps, Frank will surely hear it."

As we lay low in the brush, freezing our butts off, we noticed a Nazi convoy from a distance tracking us. I can't begin to imagine where they could have come from. It's as though they literally fell from the sky.

"The odds aren't good, guys. There are seven of them and only three of us, and I'm plumb out of ideas. Any suggestions?"

"No, Sven, let's just stay here and sit tight. Maybe they'll go away."

"I hope you're right, Craig."

We continued to lie in the forest brush for hours, watching them. It was hard to tell if they were tracking us or dumb luck fell upon us. Many hours later, Antonio, Craig, and I ended up falling asleep. When we woke the next morning, remarkably there were no visible signs of the Nazi convoy from the night before. The three of us gingerly crept towards the clearing and tried to backtrack to the sleigh's location. Within a split second, we were surrounded by seven Nazis. We were ambushed; these guys were apparently waiting all night for us to resurface.

"Wow, look at this—caught with our hands in the cookie jar. Amazingly, this is one of the oldest tricks in the book, and I totally missed it. Sorry, guys."

"Sven, don't be a fool. There was no way of telling they were still here."

"Yah, but how do we get out of this web?"

"*Halt den Mund und überlassen Sie Ihre Waffen. Legen Sie Ihre Hände auf den Kopf.*"

As instructed Antonio, Craig, and I surrendered our firearms, with the exception of the hunting knives that Antonio and I have hidden in our boots.

"*Folgen Sie uns, wir gehen wieder den Berg hinunter.*"

As we slowly turned to follow the Nazis down the mountain, within a heartbeat, like a gift from God, a buck very innocently ran out of the forest and through the clearing, startling not only the three of us, but the entire Nazi convoy as well. Haphazardly, the Nazis opened fire, missing the deer with bullets flying everywhere. Craig and I dove for cover, while Antonio tackled a Nazi, cutting his throat with his knife.

Frantically, before we had the opportunity to regain our senses, within seconds following the gunfire, we heard rumbling from the top of the mountain. I looked up and saw a powder cloud moving toward us at an alarming amount of speed. Instinctively, I yelled to Antonio and Craig to run horizontally toward the trees and hold up their arms as high as they can in the event they became engulfed in snow.

The Nazi officers spontaneously began running forward down the mountain, as I began to be completely surrounded with the powdery snow from a recent snowfall. I immediately started swimming the backstroke; however, I found myself beginning to panic as the snow began to bury me. I folded my arms across my face to create an air pocket and desperately struggled to move my right arm upright, reaching for the sun.

Minutes later, I felt something grabbing my hand and pulling me to safety. Like an angel sent from heaven, Frank was standing in front of me with a stunned look on his face. After a quick bear hug, we could see Antonio hugging a tree off to the left, slouched over. He was tall and thin and obviously a very fast runner to have made it to the timbers that quickly. Frank and I started frantically searching for Craig. Out of the corner of my eye, I saw a blue ski hat about a yard from the forest. Frank and I sprinted over and began frantically pushing the snow away with our hands. Thank God, that stupid-looking ski hat was still attached to Craig's hand. Frank and I pulled him out of his tomb with such adrenalin force we literally sent him flying through the air. After another big group bear hung, we very cautiously looked around for any Nazi survivors.

For some unforeseen reason, a glistening in the sunlight caught my eye, and I happened to notice what resembled a hand sticking out of the snow a half of mile down the mountain. Impulsively, Frank and I ran down to the object and stood there looking at one another with a blank expression on both our faces.

"Frank, what do you think we should do?"

"Obviously, this is a bad guy. The three of you are accounted for. Leave him. If we save him, we're only going to shot him anyway. Save the bullet. You can't seriously be thinking about saving his sorry *Arsch*."

"I'm sorry, but in good conscience, I have to pull him out. If he's still alive, we can take him prisoner. Maybe we can force some information out of him."

With encouragement not to shoot, Frank immediately aimed his rifle and slid back the bolt to chamber a bullet. As I pulled him out of his snow tomb, we notice this guy was just a kid, who probably just started shaving. I picked up a loaded pistol off the ground and instructed him in German to walk straight ahead. The prisoner and I joined Craig and Antonio, while Frank retrieved a few riffles and revolvers that had not been buried and were glistening in the sunlight. Antonio slowly sat down on a rock, giving the appearance he was about to faint. As he sat down, the right side of his black bearskin coat opened revealing a gunshot wound to his chest.

"Oh my god, Antonio, you're bleeding profusely! Relax, buddy, I'll help you."

I immediately took off my coat and threw it on the ground and tore the sleeve off my flannel shirt to apply pressure to his wound. Craig walked over to the woods to retrieve the sleigh with the food and supplies. Our near-death experience actually worked to our benefit. We accumulated three additional riffles and two revolvers. Unfortunately, however, my father's riffle, which was my favorite, was confiscated and was buried along with those Nazi bastards. Nonetheless, I would stay optimistic and retrieve it among the decayed Nazi bones in the spring after the snow has melted.

"Frank, how did you know we were in trouble?"

"I was down at the river, ice fishing, when I was spooked by the sound of gunfire echoing through the trees. I assumed this gunfire probably had something to do with the two of you. I dropped the rod, picked up my rifle, and ran toward the commotion in the forest. Thank God, I remembered to dismantle your trap. I ran out of the cave's safety perimeter only to see Nazi officers running in one direction, the three of you running in another and that avalanche barreling down the hill."

"Frank, I'm grateful you showed up in the nick of time and saved my sorry *Arsch*."

"Sven, it's my pleasure to have saved your *Arsch* and everything else that's attached."

"You know what, guys, Antonio doesn't look well. We have to get him to the cave and get that bullet out."

Craig struggled with the sleigh, Frank helped Antonio, and I escorted the Nazi kid at gunpoint. Once we reached the clearing in front of the cave, the girls ran out and helped us get Antonio inside, and we gently laid him on the cot. Frank took the rope out of the storage container and proceeded to tie the kid up to the chair. Meanwhile, I grabbed the first aid kit and started rummaging through it, gathering the surgical knife, bandages, and a bottle of peroxide. Craig pulled out a full bottle of whisky from his duffle bag and handed it to me.

Gratefully, Antonio at this point, fell unconscious. Christine placed a bowl of warm water next to the cot and proceeded to clean the wound, exposing the bullet. Thank God, the bullet wasn't deep; it didn't appear as though much damage is done. I held the knife in the fire for a few seconds, wiped the tip off, and poured peroxide over the tip and blade. Instantly, I inserted the sterilized knife into Antonio's wound.

At that very second, he must have started to become coherent. Antonio let out a bloodcurdling scream. Fortunately, however, the bullet dislodged with ease, and I moaned a sigh of relief.

"Sweet dreams, buddy, you deserve it. You survived your first gunshot wound, but wait until you see my surgeon's bill, that will surely kill you."

Christine cleaned and dressed the wound and sat by Antonio's side while he slept. Once the excitement was finished, we turned our attention to our prisoner. Magdalina poured us all a glass of whisky, including the kid.

"*Danke.*"

"*Ihre begruessung.*"

"Wie heisst du?"

"Ich heisse Dieter Mueller."

"Wie alt bist du"

"Nineteen."

"Sprechen Sie Englisch?"

"Yes, but not real well."

This was certainly a feather in the kid's hat. Considering there were only three of us who were fluent in the German language, at least now the entire group could communicate with Dieter.

"First, I will introduce you to everyone. My name is Sven, and these are Christine, Magdalina, Frank, Craig, and the ugly goombah sleeping over there is Antonio. We won't harm you as long as you don't try to escape or act out of stupidity. Trust me, none of us will have a problem slicing your throat from ear to ear, including the girls. I'm proud to say we already have one Nazi at the bottom of the deep hole in the river, feeding our fish. Now to business at hand, what's going on here and why are there Nazis in America?"

"I'm not really sure, and that's the God's honest truth. Two years ago, my father had orders from the *Führer* to report to America, along with other SS Gestapo officers. My father's name is Heinrich Mueller, who used to be the head of the Gestapo in Germany. He is also the Gestapo chief now in America. My mother had just passed away, and my father had insisted I travel with him to America. We shared a small apartment in town, although, he was never home. My father's residence had predominately become the compound. He insisted I learn the English language and try to blend in with the townspeople.

"Everything was going well. I made some friends and just started dating an American girl. Then about a year ago, three SS officers showed up at my apartment and forcibly hauled me into the compound at gunpoint. When my father witnessed me with these guys, he went berserk. He adamantly didn't want his only son involved in any of the nonsense taking place at the compound. He desperately tried to keep me a secret from the Gestapo. That is perhaps the reason he insisted I blend in with the townspeople."

"That makes perfect sense. He thought it was safe here, who could have known," Dieter looked at me and smiled.

"When my mother was alive, she hated the National Socialist Party Regime and, later, the Hitler dictatorship. My father and mother never spoke about politics in our home mainly because their views were so different. In fact, I believe on her deathbed my mother had no idea just how involved my father truly was in this regime. I know my father doesn't approve of the antics taking place in America, but he has to keep his mouth shut and go along with the Gestapo. Believe it or not, there are many of us who feel exactly the same way. Originally I was brought to the compound to undergo military training, with the intent of later moving up the ranks to a top SS officer. When I was ten years old, we were forced to join the *Deutsches Jungvolk* and then at the age of fourteen the Hitler-*Jugend*.

"The Gestapo realized I already had extensive training in Germany, which made me more desirable. The SS officers were also rounding up German-American young men and bringing them in as well for training. These recruits are forced to learn the German language and wear Nazi uniforms. They're brainwashed into becoming traitors of their own country. The Nazis inform them that their parents will be shot on a firing squad if they don't conform. None of us have a choice. Not too long ago, one of the kids from my battalion actually tried to escape, and as punishment, they hung him in front of us. They left his lifeless body hanging from the gallows for two weeks as the black crows and buzzards picked away at his flesh clear down to the bone.

"For the record, I didn't shoot your friend. I wish I could have stopped the guy who did. I don't expect you to believe or trust me. However, I'm on your side and will do whatever I can to help. The *Führer* of Germany murdered and impoverished hundreds of thousands of good people and destroyed the beloved fatherland. Somehow, Hitler was able to escape Europe. He is now starting all over again in this country. However, one terrifying fact this time around, Hitler seems more organized, and the mistakes he made in Germany, which brought a nation buckling to its knees, he's not going to repeat."

WE ARE ALL IN THIS
SINKING SHIP TOGETHER

"So what do you guys think we should do about the kid?"

"Sven, honestly, I think we all feel the same. This is probably your call."

"Gee, thanks Mags. You're all a big help," I said with an inflated ego and a big giant smile on my face.

None of us knew what exactly to make of Dieter. He seemed to be a very nice, intelligent young man. Everything he told us was believable. We had absolutely no reason to mistrust him other than he was wearing a Nazi uniform with the red armband displaying the swastika and was hanging out with the bad guys. In all practicality and fear alike, we just could not convince ourselves to trust him. Unfortunately, for the time being, he'd remain tied up to the chair. However, we all agreed we'd compassionately share our food and water with him daily.

Disturbingly, when Antonio finally woke three days later, after his surgery and the tender, loving care Christine gave him, he was angry with us all. Antonio furiously expressed sheer desire to have Dieter join his Nazi comrade at the bottom of the waterfall. Sadly, who could blame him after what happened to his wife and her family? Although, the same fate was bestowed upon my father, I couldn't blame Dieter.

"Why did you shoot me, and what in the world were you doing here in America dressed like that?"

"I'm sorry, sir, I didn't shoot you or anyone for that fact. My revolver was never loaded."

"Okay, Dieter, then what is your story?"

"There are many of us who were drafted into the Nazi army who adamantly don't agree or support the war effort. We either don't load our revolvers, or if we have to for appearance sake, we load our weapons and mysteriously become a bad aim. I have never in my entire life hurt or shot another human and would love nothing better than to continue going through my life proudly keeping my record intact. I happen to be an excellent marksman with revolvers, shotguns, rifles, bows, and slingshots.

"I grew up in the city of Munich, Germany, and learned to hunt when I was three years old. My father owns a small cabin in the Bavarian Alps, close to Munich. I have hunted bear, deer, lynx, and small game my entire life. On occasion, we would also hunt mouflon, which is a wild sheep as well. Fortunately, that is the extent of my killing experience. I'm not a Nazi. I'm just a boy who was born and raised in Germany during difficult times. If you choose to spare my life, I can be very useful around here. I have the ability to handcraft bows and arrows, along with slingshots to hunt wild game, squirrels, and small rodents. I strongly urge against using any firearms for hunting purposes. This mountain is nothing like the Bayerische Alpen. It's much smaller and has less altitude the sound of gunfire will echo tremendously.

"Despite my father's numerous efforts against my involvement, I was ordered to become part of the Nazi squad in charge of hunting down the three of you. Frank, no offense, but you're not a priority. In fact, we have orders to shoot and kill you on sight."

"Trust me, kid, none taken," we all looked at poor Frank and laughed.

"However, we have strict orders to bring in Sven and Magdalina unharmed for questioning. When Adolf Hitler and his brother, Gerhard, returned from an installation camp in Virginia and were briefed on your escape, they became deranged. For some unknown reason, Magdalina has the largest price on her head. Overnight, security became much tighter. An unrealistic deadline was put into effect for the confidential project the physicists have been working on for the past year. The physicists and scientists have been strictly warned if the deadline is not met, they'll all stand on the firing squad.

"I'm proud to say one of the physicists is a very dear friend of my family. In fact, he's my godfather. My security clearance is higher because my father is Heinrich Mueller, along with the extensive training that I underwent in Germany. This security clearance allows me access into the labs for the purpose of doing odd jobs. I'm known as the token lab rat. I clean the lab every other day and wash the instruments and test tubs daily. I serve coffee and food to the scientist and physicists, since they work around the clock and cannot take the time to go to the mess hall. Gratefully, my father was able to get me this job. His intention now is to keep me safe in the compound. No one has knowledge that Erich Schumann, who is one of Germany's most powerful and influential physicists, is actually a very close friend.

"Mr. Schumann and I secretly meet from time to time in a small storage closet in his lab. Thankfully, he has been keeping me abreast of the current events taking place in the compound. He's convinced, once the project is completed, the Gestapo is going to murder him and his colleagues. At the same time, he has been secretly discussing a plan with my father to smuggle me out of America and into Switzerland, where Erich has a family who fled Germany right before the war broke out.

"The allies have divided the country into four zones. The Soviet Union is occupying the east and will taint the eastern sector with communism and strip whatever industry and worth the land may still have. Thanks to Hitler, we probably now have no chance of American support to rebuild and help feed our people. I fear once President Truman and the United States Congress becomes aware of Hitler's master plan, the fatherland will receive no help or support from any nation."

"What's Hitler's master plan that you're referring too?"

"Sven, I promise you I have no idea. The Hitler brothers' master plan is normal conversation within the compound these days. However, no one seems to know what exactly it means."

"Yah, Dieter, that's really strange. I was there when the compound was first built and never heard anything about a master plan. However, I seem to recall, right before I escaped, hearing some sort of scuttle buff in reference to this master plan. I guess this is something fairly new. So enough about this alleged master plan, how is your father going to get you out of America when we have aircraft carriers being sunk off the coastal line and our boys can't get into the country?"

"My father's evacuation plan out of America is to have me transferred to the compound in Wilmington, North Carolina, and then smuggle me onto the barge that runs from Wilmington to Africa. Africa presently has no Soviet occupation, only some Americans. This route is the longest, with more miles traveled across the North Atlantic Ocean. However, at the present, it's the safest into Europe. Barges have been traveling this route, transporting the Negro people back to Africa for some time now."

"Dieter, it's a shame you left. What a headache that's going to be."

"Yah, you're right, Sven, but there's another reason I had to leave Germany, and it's probably the most important. I was part of a tight-knit group of teenagers called the *Swingjugend*. The National Socialist Party didn't approve of jazz and swing, therefore forbidding any music or dance that wasn't German. We were just kids who loved American jazz and swing. None of us cared a hoot about the politics. We snuck into underground dance halls and clubs just to dance and have fun. We always dressed nicely, but our attire was frowned upon because it was a British style, not the traditional German. We wore our hair longer, and the girls' instead of the traditional German braids, worn their hair down.

"We were viewed by the Nazis as rebellious degenerates against the National Socialist and the Hitler-Jugend. Since all boys from age fourteen to eighteen were forced into this youth group, it was very dangerous for us to be seen and caught at these clubs. The Hitler-Jugend tried to brainwash and scare us into Nazi submission and into their pure hatred for any group of people who weren't Hitler's beloved perfect Aryan race.

"The party opposed our music because they stereotyped jazz with Negro and Jewish musicians, and the swing dance was considered too sexual. Reinhard Heydrich, an associate of my fathers, was in charge of clamping down and therefore exterminating swing and our little organization. Extensive police and Nazi raids of the dance halls and clubs started all over Hamburg and Berlin. Teenage boys and girls were arrested and reprimanded in different ways. Teenagers who were thought to be partisans were hauled off to work or to concentration camps.

"Rumors were circulating that the SS used different tactics of beatings and forced labor to reeducate and deprogram these kids. Horridly, they were sentenced to camps for two to three years. Therefore, many of them ended up dying. Sadly, a very close friend of mine was arrested and thrown into one of the work camps and ended up dying six months later. Fortunately, my girlfriend and I were lucky to escape the raid at the Café Heinze, or I would have been arrested along with him that night. At his funeral, six SS officers showed up and spied on me and my friends. My father knew the SS was watching our house and would ultimately catch up to me sooner or later. His fears of my arrest and the possibility of being thrown into one of those camps were warranted. I had no choice. I was accompanying my father to America come hell or high water."

"Dieter, what are the German physicists and scientists working on? And why is it so time sensitive?"

"Dr. Erich Schumann and Dr. Walter Trinks are working on a nuclear project. There are three main efforts: uranium and heavy-water production, uranium isotope separation, and the Uranmaschine, nuclear reactor. The uranium or plutonium is bombarded by neutrons and split into lighter elements, therefore producing more neutrons and energy. These new neutrons are bombarded with another uranium or plutonium and split and bombard with others, again creating a nuclear chain reaction that creates large amounts of energy. The plutonium isotope and uranium then has to be refined using gas centrifuge. The uranium hexafluoride is spun at an incredibly high speed and is then piped in a cylinder. This is then used as the fissile core of a nuclear weapon.

"These physicists started experimenting with heavy water in Germany years ago and had to put it on hold after the war broke out. After Hitler secretly transported the *Reich* Research Council to America, the production started up again. America obviously beat Germany in the production of nuclear bombs, and with that, we have learned the horrific effects that these bombs caused after Hiroshima and Nagasaki. Erich and his colleagues and I are very concerned how Hitler plans to use these nuclear capabilities.

THE 2ND WORLD WAR II

"So now you have it, my entire life story in a nutshell and everything that I know to date. The way I see it, we're all in this sinking ship together. I can guarantee you I'm not a Nazi. I'm just a young man who was born and raised in Germany, who got into a little trouble and was forced to come to America where it would be safe. I would love nothing better than to help America wipe these Nazi radical, evil bastards off the face of this earth forever. They ruined my country and now they're going to ruin yours as well. Can I please take this redicious uniform off and burn it? I'll sit here in my skivvies if need be."

"Dieter, that won't be necessary. Please let's not give the girls a reason to blush. Let's untie him—he's harmless. You're about my height and build. I have some clothes you can have."

"Thank you, Antonio."

"No problem, but can I ask one question. How do you know so much about nuclear bombs, you're scary?"

"That easy. I'm a science freak. I got straight As in every science and physics class in high school. Plus it didn't hurt having a renowned physicist as a close friend of the family. My entire life, my father was pushing me to follow in Erich's footsteps."

"Well, now that we all know Dieter's entire life story, and I no longer want him feeding our fish, I guess it's my turn to share some information that Craig informed Sven and I of recently. Unfortunately, I have some bad news. My wife, Mary, is dead."

"Nice going, buddy. Did your mother drop you on your head when you were born or something? I'm sorry, ladies, for Antonio's stupidity and bluntness."

"Honest to God, I had no intentions of blurting that out so insensitively. Girls, I apologize. Sven and I had knowledge of this information for a week. Therefore, I've had time to mourn, digest, and come to terms with it."

Christine and Magdalina immediately burst into tears. Antonio went over to Christine and hugged her, while Frank and I went to Magdalina. Thank God, my idiot best friend stopped there and didn't open his big mouth any further. The girls wept for hours. Even Dieter turned away and wiped his eyes several times.

Craig, Dieter, and I made ourselves as comfortable as possible on the floor with the sleeping bags in front of the fire. The girls each had the two larger cots, while Frank and Antonio had the comfort of the two smaller ones. Since we kept accumulating more bodies into our home, the four of us would take turns sleeping on the cave's rock-hard, cold floor.

"Hey, Sven, I have an idea. Tomorrow morning, I'm going to gather a large quantity of leaves and pile them on the floor behind the cots closer to the end of the cave. We can then lay the sleeping bags and blankets on top of the leaves for more warmth and comfort."

"That's a great idea, Antonio. Although the area is large and extends six feet further back, it should still be moderately warm back there. I'm glad to see you using your head for something other than holding up your ears."

At some point, in between the tears, we all ended up falling asleep. Tonight was the first night we trusted Dieter or, more accurately, simply forgot in the midst of all the drama to tie him back up.

Antonio, Dieter, and I were the first of the congregation to rise. We woke up early to a beautiful sunshiny, milder mid-February morning. I decided to walk out to the entrance of the cave to where the meat cooler was stored and assessed our inventory before we all get engrossed in the chores of the day. With taking in one more body, I quickly realized our inventory would need to be built back up. On the other hand, the dry goods that we hauled up the mountain from Craig's apartment and the diner had stocked us up fairly well and should last at least one more month.

"Antonio, you have leaf duty today, and, Dieter, I want you to make two more bows and a decent supply of arrows. Meanwhile, Frank and I will take the two existing bows, the rest of the arrows and head out into the forest to hunt. Craig can take the fishing rods and tackle box down to the river and try his luck at ice fishing since this has been his forte since we were kids. Meanwhile, I'm sure the girls will want to take full advantage of this beautiful day and get laundry caught up."

"You got it, boss."

"Thanks, buddy. I'm looking forward to a little comfort this evening. My back won't survive another eight hours on that rock hard floor. Perhaps when you're finished with the men's sleep area, you can help the others."

"As always, my pleasure, Sven."

"All right, let's not overdue the love here."

"But, Sven, I love you, and I need a kiss."

Antonio playfully plugged toward me with his lips puckered, while Frank simultaneously grabbed my arm, as though Count Dracula's pearly white fangs just appeared. The two of us quickly began walking away from Antonio, towards the forest for our hunt.

"All right, gang, we're going to have a very productive day. Antonio when your finished filling our area with leaves, make sure my sleeping bag is layed out real cozy," Frank and I laughed as we continued to walk away from the Count.

After spending several hours hunting, Frank and I decided to bring back the two deer that we just killed. As we approach the clearing, Craig is fishing in the deep part in front of the waterfall, Dieter has the two bows and a good supply of arrows made, and the girls just finished with the laundry. Antonio on the other hand, is basking in the sunlight on the riverbank watching everyone work.

"Wow, guys, good going. A productive day all around, with time to spare. While we still have daylight, Frank and I are heading out again. Dieter and Antonio can you start to skin the two deer?"

"Sure thing. I'll get on that right away. However, Antonio has other plans."

"Gee, nothing like a little kiss ass?" I looked at Dieter and the two of us cracked up.

"What are you doing, buddy?"

"Christine and I are going for a walk. That is if you still want to go?"

"Yes, of course. It's such a beautiful day, and all I've seen of this mountain is the cave."

"Good point, my dear. I want to show you some extraordinary views that Sven and I came across when we were kids hiking and hunting. This part of the country is so beautiful. The last time I was up here, I was sixteen and Sven was fifteen. I have nothing but very fond memories of this place. Do me a favor—when I die please make sure I'm buried on this mountain. In fact, I'll take you to the exact location."

"Antonio, please don't talk about dying."

"Oh my god, I'm sorry. Once again, let me pull my big foot out of my mouth!"

"Have fun guys, but please be careful. We still don't know if the enemy maybe lerking in the area."

"You got it Sven."

Once again, Frank and I headed back out into the forest to continue our hunt, while everyone else did their own thing. A few hours later, just as Frank and I are running after the doe, I just put an arrow into; we're suddenly startled with the sound of aircraft flying overhead. Minutes later, the faint sounds of gunfire and bombs exploding in the distance makes us stop dead in our tracks, allowing the deer to get away.

"Holy cow Frank, forget the deer, let's get back to the cave," I said in a panic stricken monotone.

As we entered the cave the girls jumped up and ran over to the two of us, with many hugs and kisses. Craig and Antonio both walked over and also hugged us.

"What has happened, does anyone know?"

"Sven, all I know is, Christine and I were sitting up at Casselman Point, when suddenly, our peaceful world was interrupted with the sounds of aircraft approaching in the distance. Without hesitation, we jumped to our feet and ran for the woods. I felt confident that we were out of sight, considering the woods were extremely dense in that location. I found an area where there was a small clearing between the trees, and I was able to identify the planes. There were six P-47 Thunderbolts and four P-51 Mustangs passing over the mountain range. We quickly ran back to the clearing, jumping and screaming and waving to the American pilots. At that point, a sense of pride came over me and shivers went down my spin, with the thought of these Nazi bastards seeing just how powerful the United States Air Force truly is. Once they all passed, Christine and I joyfully ran back down the mountain to the cave."

"Wow, so you really saw these planes that close up? Frank and I were too deep in the forest at the time, we heard them pass overhead, but couldn't see a thing."

"Yah Sven, I felt as though I could touch them. About halfway down is when we heard antiaircraft gunfire and bombs exploding, probably about twenty-five miles northeast."

"We heard that as well, but I couldn't make out exactly where it was coming from. That's the proximity of the Nazi compound," I said with a big smile on my face.

"Anyway, when Christine and I entered the cave Craig, Dieter, and Magdalina were sitting in front of the fire with grins on their faces, happy to see us, but we were all worried about you and Frank."

"Yah, sorry about that guys. Frank and I ventured out a little too far. It took us an hour to get back. Although, don't be mad, we brought back another white-tailed buck and a bobcat, which we left outside laying on the rock ledge behind the waterfall."

"At least with all this excitement, you ran for cover and remembered your cardinal rule—leave behind no evidence of human habitation," Antonio laughed the entire time he blurted out those words.

"Well not quite, there is a doe running around with an arrow in her."

"Good job, my friend."

"Never mind, mister sarcastic. Let's you and I take a little walk outside for a few minutes."

"So, Antonio, what's going on with you and Christine? Where exactly did you take her?" I looked at him with a sly grin on my face.

"Christine and I first hiked the trail through the snow-covered trees to the highest elevation of the mountain. We walked to the location where the huge boulders lay in the clearing of the trees on the summit. I have to tell you, I almost forgot the beauty of that place, we both stood there mesmerized by the picture-perfect view of the snow-covered forest and rolling mountains in the background. Next to her, the scene was spine-tingling."

"Spine–...ting...ling. Antonio, really."

"Yah, buddy, spine-tingling. Anyway, Christine and I then walked three miles to one of my favorite spots, Casselman Point. I lead her to the rocky edge of the mountain which has the best view overlooking the River. Amazingly, there were small ice formations floating down the river resembling tiny ice burgs. It was so peaceful and tranquil there we decided to stay for a while longer. We sat down on the rocks and watched the ice formations floating peacefully down the river while listening to the birds sing. Everything was in perfect harmony. It was inconceivable to comprehend, with all that beauty and peace surrounding us, in actuality, there was nothing but turmoil and conflict outside this tiny area that was ours. Christine and I sat drinking in all that beauty, and for a few precious hours, we forgot about the evil that presently surrounded us.

"Wow, so you're kind of sweet on this girl?"

"Yah, I think that's a safe assumption. What an incredible feeling it was to be that close to her and alone. Strangely, at that point, I found myself slowly wrapping my arm around her and pulled her close to me. I sat gazing into her beautiful brown eyes; it was as though we were the only two people in the world. She was also looking into my eyes, inviting me in, and without a doubt, I didn't need a second invitation. I leaned down, and our lips met. As we sat embraced in a long, passionate kiss, every inch of my body tingled. I hadn't felt this sensation for a while. Next I found myself, very indiscreetly taking the one side of my coat and draped it over my lap to hide what I was really feeling, and you know what I'm talking about. We kissed a few more times and never uttered a sound."

"Good for you, buddy. I'm glad to hear you kept your composure and maintained your status as a gentleman," as the words ran off my lips, I chuckled and slapped Antonio on the back.

"But of course Sven, you know me better than that. Christine then snuggled in between my chest and shoulder and ended up falling asleep, while I was absorbed in the incredible view of a perfect day. However, it didn't take long before my heart and head began painfully struggling with guilt. After all, my wife had only been dead for a few months, and I truly loved her. She was an incredible woman and a good wife; we had two wonderful years of marriage together."

"I know Antonio, it's not fair. But you cannot feel guilty. She's dead and won't be coming back. It sounds like you maybe blessed with a second chance."

"I hope so."

As Antonio and I engaged in an acceptance hug and handshake between best friends, the rest of the gang came out to see what we were up to.

"You know what, this is very interesting. Remember those reconnaissance planes we heard about on the news? I would bet this has something to do with these planes suddenly appearing. This is good. Maybe our boys are finally able to get through the blockades."

"Let's pray, Sven, that that's the case," Magdalina said with joy in her voice and tears in her eyes.

"Alright gang, let's finish up for the day. After we're finished listening to the news this evening, we'll all turn in early and get a good night's sleep. We should get up early tomorrow morning to skin the animals and take care of the meat. If tomorrow's weather ends up like today, I want you guys to help me work on tanning the hides. Craig and Dieter are going to need warm clothing considering we still have a few more brutal winter months ahead.

"Also, Craig, we're completely out of fish. Try your luck again tomorrow with ice fishing in the deep hole where you were today and also the shallower parts of the river. The thought of having fresh fish fillets for supper tomorrow makes my mouth water."

"You got it boss."

It was amazing; we all felt like little kids with ants in our pants with the excitement of today's events. With the awareness of our radio program airing in a couple of hours, we were feeling very impatient for time to pass more quickly. After we finished supper, the seven of us bundled up and walked back outside to the tree stump. We made ourselves as comfortable as possible on the cold ground and placidly waited for our favorite radio program to begin. I poured everyone a glass of whiskey for the anticipated celebration.

Thank you for tuning into our radio program, *You Can't Do Business with Hitler*, with John Flynn and Virginia Moore.

As stated in our last broadcast on February 11, 1946, at 7:00 a.m., several American reconnaissance planes were seen flying over the coastline, taking photographs of the bordering states surrounding the country's perimeter. I'm proud to say this mission was successful, with no loss of life or aircraft. These reconnaissance pilots took many photographs displaying the location of Nazi compounds and installations and recorded their coordinances. At 4:00 p.m. this afternoon, on the day of February 19, US Army Air Force fighter pilots flew over the coastline and dropped Napalm bombs, destroying enemy military installations located in the states of Washington, Montana, Minnesota, Michigan, Pennsylvania, New York, Maine, Virginia, North and South Carolina, Florida, Louisiana, Texas, Arizona, California, and Oregon.

I'm pleased to report this mission was successful. However, one P-47 was shot down in Pennsylvania and one P-15 was shot down in Los Angeles and two in Maine. Once again, American citizens are urged to abide by the curfew restrictions and stay in your homes. As a reminder, all practice air-raid drills and blackouts are no longer taking place since World War II came to an official end in September. However, in the future, if an air siren goes off, you're urged to seek shelter in your cellars or air-raid shelters. City shelters are being constructed in different locations. The US Department of War urges people who live in the suburbs of the cities to build shelters in your backyards. Within the week, American Boeing P-12 biplanes will be flying overhead, dropping instruction leaflets for survival of enemy projectile munitions and artillery assaults.

Please tune in next week to our program, *You Can't Do Business with Hitler*. This is John Flynn and Virginia Moore signing off. Thank you, and God bless America.

"Wow, this is wonderful news. Maybe this nightmare will come to an end. What do you think, Sven?"

"Hopefully you're right, Craig. However, we can't get prematurely optimistic. We still need to stay vigilante and on course."

We woke the next morning to a much colder day with gray clouds hovering, giving the impression it may snow any minute. It was imperative we get the deer and bobcat skins thoroughly cleaned and salt-cured so we can take them back to the cave and hang them from my father's tanning rack to drain all moisture. These hides should be moisture free within ten days. After the skins are moisture free, we'll clean them again for a second time to soften them. The girls can then get started sewing hunting trousers for Craig and Dieter.

Fortunately, with this hunt, we now had enough meat for the seven of us for two weeks. The sun will be setting in an hour, Craig and Antonio started to clean and fillet the three catfish they caught earlier in the river. Catfish was not one of my favorites; however, at this point, it surely beat venison again. We only had enough bear meat for one more supper, and the bobcat was just plain and simply not appealing. Although, Dieter had assured us that if it was prepared properly, it could be very tasty. With that statement, Dieter has now assumed the chef's position of bobcat suppers.

"I think we should take Craig hunting with us sometime this week. Although he's not very talented with rifles and he's terrible with bows, he's an excellent marksman with his pellet gun. I'm thinking maybe we should consider small-game hunting as well."

"Gee, Sven, thanks for the backhanded compliment."

"I'm sorry, you know what I mean," I looked at Craig with a big smile on my face.

"Sven, I almost forgot. I made four slingshots the other day. I was actually thinking the same thing. I figured Antonio, Frank, you, and I could hunt squirrels and any snakes we may be able to find. Even cottontails may be easier with a slingshot. Craig, of course, can use his infamous pellet gun."

"Dieter, I hate to admit to this, but Antonio and I have never hunted with a slingshot. And Frank, of course, has never hunted with anything before our cave days."

"That's all right, guys. There's a first time for everything. I'll be more than happy to show you."

"Yah, but, Dieter, I don't know about this squirrel thing. It sounds as strange as bobcat."

"Sven, I guarantee you'll enjoy squirrel probably much more than bobcat. Believe it or not, squirrel tastes like chicken, and God knows there are enough of them, probably enough to last a lifetime."

"Okay, I believe you, even though I'm feeling a little intimidated with your skills right about now. The three of us will join you in a pretend chicken hunt."

"I don't mean to step on your toes. I'm just thinking a little variety would be a good thing."

"Dieter, lighten up. I'm just yanking your chain."

Although, thinking about how Dieter described the taste of squirrel, I found myself daydreaming about sitting down to a real chicken supper with gravy and mashed potatoes.

What am I nuts? Hmmm... An eight-ounce New York strip medium rare, sautéed mushrooms and onions, baked potato overflowing with sour cream and fresh chives, warm buttermilk biscuits with lots of butter, a case of beer, and a real bed, soft and fluffy with crisp, freshly ironed white sheets and goose down feather pillows. For that fact, while I'm engrossed in this wild daydream, a long, steamy, hot shower and flannel pajamas.

Seconds after I came back to reality, I reminded myself of the gratitude for the food and provisions we presently had and our safe surroundings. Unfortunately, I could imagine there were many people doing much worse than we are at the present time. As I continued to force myself back from that beautiful daydream, suddenly I heard the faint sounds of aircraft approaching from the southwest.

"Quick, guys! Pick everything up off the ground. Grab the fish and meat, and leave the animal hides. Follow me. I know a dense part where we can't be seen."

"Sure, boss, anything you say."

"Antonio, I'm not joking."

Dieter and I stressed to Antonio, Craig, Frank, and the girls the importance of staying cautious. Their first reaction to the sounds of approaching aircraft was to stay in the clearing and jump for joy, show enthusiasm and support to the pilots. I, however, wanted to be more vigilant. After yesterday, with our military blowing up the Nazi compounds, I believe we need to be smart about this.

Thank God, smart we were. As I caught a glimpse of the approaching aircraft through a small clearing among the trees, I noticed a swastika insignia on the sides of the aircraft.

"Sven, I recognize these planes. I remember Erich showing my family the blueprints of a night fighter, also called an all-weather fighter, aircraft in Germany, which was going to be manufactured by Arado Flugzeugwerke when I was a teenager."

"So, what does that mean for us in America?"

"This particular aircraft is an Arado Ar Projekt II, which is a state of the art jet-powered fighter with a cutting-edge design. It was designed with a pressurized two-man cockpit with ejection seats. The design also included wing-mounted jet engines with a retractable landing gear system. The estimated performance speed of this particular aircraft is 466 miles per hour. However, this is very strange. These planes were designed and ready for production in Germany around the time the war took a turn for the worse. In fact, the military factory in Berlin that began to mass produce this aircraft was blown up by the British. This particular model was never completed, which can only mean one thing—German engineers must have also escaped Germany and traveled to America. There has to be a factory some place producing Nazi military aircraft. Sweet Jesus, this cannot be good."

"Dieter, that's a very interesting hypothesis."

"Magdalina, I'm sorry, but I don't believe this is only theory."

"No, actually, Dieter, I agree. I remember witnessing an unbelievable view one evening while I was a prisoner in the compound and was locked in my room. I was looking out the back window from sheer boredom and witnessed three army tanks back off the large delivery trucks. Out of curiosity, I woke up several times in the middle of the night to check on them. They appeared to have sat there all night. However, when I woke the next morning minutes before 0500, I looked out the window once again, but they were gone without a trace. The compound in Somerset is producing a variety of weapons and ammunition that apparently is being shipped all over in those large trucks. Dieter, I think you're right. What are your thoughts, Sven?

You must have seen some peculiar things as well, especially with your security clearance."

"Magdalina, I'm also convinced the Nazis are producing aviation warfare and ground warfare in addition to weapons and ammunition. It makes perfect sense and very clever of the bad guys—produce warfare undercover on American soil, right under the authority's noises."

All night, we took shifts sitting up on guard, waiting for something to happen. Obviously, none of us slept too well. The next morning, we woke to a new coating of snow, very cold with high winds. By midmorning, the winds died down, the sun was shining brightly, and the snowfall had stopped, allowing Craig, Dieter, and I the opportunity to hunt for squirrels. Dieter and I took our bows and slingshots, while Craig utilized his pellet gun. If squirrels indeed tasted like chicken, I was bound and determined to bring back a chicken supper for everyone this evening.

As a result of the recent events, Antonio and Frank stayed behind, guarding the home front. Considering we have no inkling what those jet-powered fighters were up to yesterday, we needed to remain extremely cautious. Craig, Dieter, and I spent the entire afternoon in the forest, freezing our hides off, but the reward was gratifying. We proudly came back to camp with a dozen squirrels. Dieter and I skinned and cleaned our hunt, throwing the bones and debris back into the forest for the smaller mammals to gnaw on. After cleaning the squirrel hides thoroughly, they also made a home on the tanning rack so the girls could show off their creativity in a couple of days.

Surprisingly, Dieter was right—squirrel was very tasty. Magdalina and Christine prepared a wonderful pretend-chicken supper. We were all filled to the gills with a very appetizing meal and were ready to retire early.

The next morning, the weather was the same, allowing the three of us to go back out and hunt the poor squirrels once again. Having predominately lived on bear and venison for months, those poor rodents were a delicacy. After another all-day hunt, we came back with three cottontails and six squirrels. Proudly, we added our new hunt to the meat cooler.

Several uneventful days passed by with no news broadcasted of the Nazi German *Luftwaffe* we saw almost a week ago. It was now Sunday evening, and once again, the seven of us were gathered around the tree stump in front of the waterfall, tuning in to our favorite news program.

> Thank you for tuning into our radio program, *You Can't Do Business with Hitler*, with John Flynn and Virginia Moore.
>
> We have very disturbing news to report this evening. February 26, 1946, enemy aircraft bombed and sank the *USS Randolph* CV-15 and the *USS Ticonderoga* CVS-14. The two aircraft carriers were anchored miles from the coastline, awaiting further orders from the US Department of War. These two carriers were filled with American military tanks and weaponry traveling home from Europe. Hundreds of US Army, Navy, Air Force, and Marine personnel were aboard, waiting for orders of deployment to the coastline. The US Department of War plotted a top-secret plan to send American submarines to the awaiting aircraft carriers and move our military back on land. Fortunately, two American submarines were able to successfully retrieve seventy-five men off each carrier safely, directly before they were spotted by the enemy. Seconds later, Nazi aircraft flew over the coastline, sinking both carriers. Once again, America has experienced a significant amount of fatalities in our coastal waters.
>
> Please tune in next week to our program, *You Can't Do Business with Hitler*. This is John Flynn and Virginia Moore signing off. Thank you and God Bless America.

"My god, this is really serious. We are engaged in the continuation of World War II on American soil."

"Sven, do you really think it's that serious?"

"Yes, I do, Antonio. I know the original plan was to call the boss. However, I'm beginning to question if this is a good idea. I think it's extremely dangerous to consider venturing anywhere near town at this point. Considering the present circumstances, we need to beef up security and become more attentive. I think we should all stay here. The cave maybe the only place in the area that's safe right now. However if you must, I'm going with you."

"Sven, there's no reason for you to put your neck on the line. You have to understand, I have no choice. I have to call the boss as I have been instructed. The only acceptable way out is death."

"But, if it's too dangerous, I'm sure they'd understand."

"Sven, buddy, you don't know how the family works. If you step out of line or do something that allows them to loose trust in you, your fate will be worse with the family than with the Nazis. Weather permitting or not, I will leave first thing tomorrow morning, make the call, and head back immediately. I'll return sometime the following morning. However, if by chance I don't show up the next day, don't come looking for me. I don't want anyone's blood on my conscience."

"Antonio, I'm going with you as well."

"Thanks, Dieter, but I really don't want to bring either one of you into the heart of the lion's den."

"Nonsense, don't be stubborn, Antonio. You of all people know the buddy system. Furthermore, my father and Mr. Schumann were probably in that compound when it was blown up. I love both these men. I believe when my father came to America, he wanted to bear no malice for his sins. I have to go back. They may still be alive and may need my help."

"All right, I give up. Why don't we just bring everyone on this little vacation?" Antonio looked at Dieter and me, with that cocky look of his, while I indiscreetly flipped him the bird.

Christine immediately began to weep and ran out of the cave, with Antonio following directly behind her. As Magdalina gave me those sad puppy dog eyes, I grabbed her hand and the two of us went out as well. Antonio and Christine sat down alongside the river's bed and embraced in another passionate kiss.

As Magdalina and I kept our distance from the two of them, from the corner of my eye I watched to make sure Christine was alright. Antonio seemed to be doing a good job consoling her.

"Sweetheart, I promise I will return to you unharmed."

"You better."

Christine stopped crying and the two of them engaged in another passionate kiss. This was our cue to leave. I took Magdalina's hand once again and led her back into the cave to allow Antonio and Christine some private time.

The next morning, Dieter, Antonio and I inserted hunting knifes in our boots, loaded revolvers in the waistband of our trousers, and slung rifles over our shoulders. Once our arsenal was in place, we immediately put on our black bearskin coats and headed out. The day was blistery cold, with four inches of snow on the ground and a hazy gray sky, and unfortunately, it looked as though it might snow again.

"Guys, listen up. It's really hard to see out here and we're approaching the safety perimeter of my traps. Please stay very conscious and alert. We don't need any of the good guys falling victim to my madness." The three of us laughed and continued to trudge on our way.

This time, the hike down the mountain was burdensome. The snow was heavy, and with each step, we were becoming exhausted. This trip might end up taking us much longer than originally anticipated.

Hours later, as we began to approach the bombed-out compound, the scene was bloodcurdling. There were debris and corpses everywhere. Some of the bodies were literally blown to shreds. Human body parts lay all over. As we walked around looking for any signs of Dieter's father and his friend, we were also looking for the body of Adolf Hitler and his brother. Hopefully, they too were in the compound when it was blown; however, most of the bodies were decimated beyond recognition. As we gingerly walked around back, we notice the large garage off to the left was still intact and the large, long building located three miles at the back of the compound didn't visibly sustain any damage.

"Look at that, guys. I wonder why this place was completely bombed out. However, they left the garage and that building way back there and the smaller one off to the right?"

"Antonio, the building back there was the barracks where a hundred American trainees were housed. The smaller building at the back of the barracks on the right side was where the women workers all stayed. The smaller barracks further down on the left side, which was also destroyed, housed about seventy-five Nazis. Obviously, the

American pilots knew in advance the housing situation back there. My god, I take my hat off to those boys for their acute precision and bombing techniques."

The three of us decided not to take any more chances in the event someone might have survived and might be lurking in the area. We left the war-torn compound and began walking through the forest into town. As we began approaching closer, shockingly, Meyersdale resembled a ghost town. The town wasn't touched by the American bombs; however, there was no activity and no life in sight. Everything was still intact, giving the illusion the townspeople just picked up and walked away. As we strolled around, the town illuminated an eerie atmosphere. Dieter and I stood watch outside, while Antonio apprehensively strolled into the first merchant on Main Street, a men's apparel store. Thankfully, a telephone was sitting on the counter by the dressing room.

After Antonio made his call to the boss, the three of us decided to sneak down the back alley to Sam's Market to see if there was any food left in the store. Surprisingly, the backdoor was unlocked, and we very quietly and cautiously, with pistols drawn, slithered into the store. The store was no different; it was fully stocked like any other business day. We each apprehensively grabbed three large boxes and filled them to the brim with canned items and dry goods. Once again, we cautiously slithered down the back alley, looking as guilty as sin for just breaking one of the commandments—"Thou shall not steal."

As we approached closer to the men's apparel store, noticeably, a man was leaning against the wall, smoking a cigarette. Dieter, Antonio and I immediately dropped the boxes, aimed our rifles, and chambered a bullet.

"Sven, Antonio, stop. This is Dr. Erich Schumann, my father's friend. Erich, how in the world did you survive the attack and what are you doing here in town?"

"Dieter! I thought you were dead. What a sight for sore eyes!"

Dieter and Erich embraced in a manly hug, with tears of joy streaming from their eyes. Dieter politely and proudly introduced us to one of Germany's renowned physicist.

"So, Erich, what happened?"

"Dieter, after the compound was bombed and destroyed, I ventured into town and hid in the upstairs apartment for a week. An hour ago, I saw your friend walk into the store and use the telephone. When he finished his call and left the store, I looked out the back window and was very pleasantly surprised to see a ghost. Dieter, we were all convinced that you had perished with the others in that avalanche. I watched the two of you walk further down the back alley, presumably to pick up supplies, and decided to come out of hiding and wait until you came back this way."

"Erich, where's my father?"

"I'm sorry, son, he died in the blast, as did many others."

"How did you survive?"

"Dumb luck, I would suppose. As you know, we were working around the clock for weeks, and the lack of sleep was beginning to catch up to everyone. We were starting to become careless and were making stupid mistakes. Let's face it—with the nature of our work, we could easily do something wrong and blow up the entire county of Somerset. I decided my colleagues and I would take turns catnapping for a few hours just to rejuvenate. We set up two cots in the corner of the cellar by the steps. At the time of the blast, I was down there sound asleep, along with a friend of mine. Fortunately, that area of the cellar was untouched by the bomb, and thank God, all the ammunition that was previously stored down there was loaded on the trucks and delivered to other locations a few days prior. My friend Klaus and I hid in an area of the cellar among the debris, where we went undetected."

"Undetected? Undetected from whom if everyone died in the blast?"

"I'm getting to that, Dieter. The next day after the bomb was dropped, Hitler, Gerhard, Himmler, and some other bigwigs showed up, assessing the damage. Klaus and I stayed in hiding while they walked about. When it was safe, the two of us moved to another location to see what was going on. I personally witnessed Hitler, Gerhard, and Himmler climb into a Panzerspaehwagen heavy armored car. Klaus Barbie and Adolf Eichmann climbed into the second armored car. Three other high ranking officers, who I didn't

LAURA DOTHE HELLWIG ◀

recognize, got into the third car. There were nine Panzerkampfwagen VI heavy tanks fully loaded and forty Nazi officers with weapons marching into town. Klaus and I followed at a safe distance, walking through the forest out of sight to observe the spectacle. The Gestapo literally paraded down Main Street as Hitler demanded over a loud speaker for everyone to step out into the streets and line up. The people were then escorted at gunpoint to follow the tanks. I have no idea where they took the entire town. Everything here came to abrupt halt.

"Klaus and I later found two young children, crying their eyes out, roaming the streets looking for their parents. We instantly scooped them up and found refuge in this building in the upstairs apartment. Unfortunately, two days later, Klaus died of shrapnel wounds. I carried my colleaque out back and buried him in the tiny yard behind the men's apparel store. To date, the Gestapo has not been back. I cannot imagine they will anytime soon. They left a ghost town behind. With the compound destroyed, there's probably no reason to come back for a while. I've been living here with the children for five days. What happened to you, Dieter?"

"It's kind of a strange story actually. A young Waffen-SS new recruit spotted Craig, who owns the diner down the street, apparently sneaking around with two men whom he hadn't seen in town before. The recruit reported it directly to his superior, and our small regiment was ordered to follow Craig and his two friends up the mountain. The Gestapo hoped these three men would lead us to Magdalina and the two men who escaped the compound. We successfully were able to follow them halfway up the mountain undetected. However, carelessly, this stupid recruit got antsy and became visible and blew our cover. Our regiment immediately captured Craig and his two accomplices. They surrendered their weapons and were taken prisoner.

"Seconds after the capture, a buck came running out of the forest and startled us all. There were bullets flying everywhere, which ended up triggering the avalanche of newly fallen soft snow. Stupid me, I followed the rest of them, trying to out run it, even though I knew better. I was quickly buried. However, I remembered to hold my arms up so someone could see me. Frank and Sven rescued me and took me prisoner. There are seven of us living in a well-camouflaged cave in an obscure area of the mountain. These guys have been living there successfully undetected for seven months. They took me in, first as a prisoner, sheltered and feed me, then later trusted me and adopted me into their world. We all have a unique and trusting relationship. The seven of us work very well together as a team, and we complement one another as a group with our various skills and knowledge."

"Thank God, these guys surely saved a great man."

"Thanks, I cannot begin to tell you how happy I am to see you. Antonio, Sven, I think we should go back to the cave and get the others. If the Gestapo has already been through and they believe that the town is deserted, maybe we should come here and stay, especially since our membership keeps growing. We can literally take over the entire town and have your Italian family join us here for more manpower. At least here we have room for everyone. In all practicality, there's plenty of room for the seven of us in the cave. However, that's probably the limit. We can booby-trap the town's perimeter just as Sven did around the cave. There's also a very prudent fact—Sam's Market has enough food to last us a very long time. We can survive the same way we have been in the mountain with more room, supplies, and comfort. I suggest we leave the cave perfectly intact and booby-trapped, in the event we have to exit quickly and flee into hiding once again."

"Dieter, I think you have a great idea," I looked at Antonio with a sincere expression on my face.

"I agree Sven. The kid's idea is probably the only logical solution right now.

"Yah, nothing can alleviate the fact that the bodies and mouths to feed are multiplying. With Erich and the two children joining us, we would have ten people trying to survive in the cave. Feasibly, it won't accommodate that many people, and we certainly don't have enough supplies. Obviously, we're not going to leave them behind. Furthermore, the Italians will be arriving in Elk Lick in two months, and they'll need a place to stay as well. Once they arrive, we'll have our own battalion right here in town. But right now, we need to leave Erich and the kids and head back while the weather is cooperating.

After we explain the situation to Craig, Frank and the girls, at dawn's early light, the seven of us will traipse back down, and as a group we'll recollect and figure out our next plan of action."

"Erich, is all of this acceptable to you?

"Acceptable, Dieter? You're the answer to my prayers. Godspeed, boys, be very careful, I'll see you in a couple of days."

PAUL TOUVIER: FRENCH NAZI COLLABORATOR

The journey up the mountain was much easier and faster than the trip coming down yesterday. Amazingly, as soon as we were in sight, Christine came running out to greet us, as Frank, Craig and Magdalina began to climb down the rock staircase. Christine must have been sitting by the tree stump for the last couple of hours waiting for us. Like a foolish, lovesick puppy, Antonio dropped his rifle in the snow and ran toward her. In front of us all, they once again embraced and passionately kissed.

"Well, buddy, if the cat wasn't out of the bag before, it is now," I looked at Antonio and gave him one of my famous silly sly grins.

Joyfully, after a warm welcome, we all walked back to the cave for supper. After another scrumptious pretend-chicken supper, we sat around the fire pit, drinking the last of our coffee, discussing the current events. Everyone agreed our home wouldn't feasibly house a total of eleven people comfortably; however, I silently kept my apprehension with living in town in a wideopen, conspicuous area, to myself.

The next morning, we left everything behind, even the meat cooler. The meat was frozen and would stay that way until spring. If everything would work out in town and we decide to stay, we would have to hike backup for the meat sometime in the month of April. The morning turned out to be glorious; the sun was shining brightly, and the snow was melting below our feet with each step we took. Not only had the group made incredible time with the hike down, but spirits were running high with anticipation of new living arrangements and the thought of no longer roughing it in the wilderness.

Thank God, Dieter, Antonio and I remembered the gruesome sight of the compound. As we began to approach the scene from hell, we quickly rerouted the caravan and smartly walked the long way through the dense forest, around the back of the compound. I cannot in good conscience bring the girls pass that grisly sight. We happily continued trudging through the snow past the barracks when a man and an older woman came walking toward us from a large storage shed alongside the barracks. The seven of us simultaneously drew our weapons in perfect continuity.

"Who are you, and what do you want?" I barked out sternly.

"My name is Paul Smith, and this is Miss Helen. The two of us were American prisoners of the compound. I'm a recruit for the army training program, and Miss Helen is one of the assembly-line workers. She is wounded and is presently having much difficulty getting around. It's a miracle she was able to escape serious harm from the destruction of that bomb. After the compound was destroyed, there were a few who got out alive, three of whom were Nazis, who quickly departed in the direction of Meyersdale.

"As you can see, the barracks wasn't affected by the bomb. It is still intact. Thank God, the men and I were in the barracks at the time of the bombing. We were all fortunate to have survived with no casualties. The rest of the men decided to head southwest to the Maryland border, while I agreed to stay behind with Miss Helen. I found her lying among this debris. She apparently was thrown a couple of feet with the impact of the explosion. However, she has some shrapnel wounds that are in need of immediate medical treatment. Miss Helen and I saw the three of you a few days ago, poking around. We were apprehensive. However, we decided if you were to return, we would come out of hiding and confront you. We had to do something. We recently ran out of food, and I had no means of helping her."

"Well, gang, I know we're all thinking the same thing. Let's just vote on it quickly and get on our way."

"Sven, it's the same as Erich and the children."

"Dieter, I know. However, something just doesn't feel right."

"Yah, Sven, probably all those squirrels you ate last night."

"Very funny, buddy. I still don't know who's more the comedian in your duo—you or Frank."

Without giving it much thought, the seven of us agreed that Paul and Miss Helen should join us in our endeavor in town.

"Sven, I have an idea."

"What's that, Craig?"

"Remember the sleigh we built the last time we were here? I think we should build another one to transport Miss Helen. In the condition she's in, she'll never be able to schlepp through the snow, especially with the distance we still have to travel."

"Great idea. Let's get started, guys."

By the time we completed the sleigh and got Miss Helen on it, the weather had drastically changed for the worst. The flurries that started an hour ago had now changed to sleet. Craig, Dieter, and Paul pulled the sleigh with Miss Helen, who was a rather large woman. Without a doubt, the journey into town took unusually longer than normal. We walked into the men's apparel store; Craig, Dieter, Antonio, and the girls went up to the apartment, while Paul and I helped Miss Helen. After assisting her to the sofa, we all settled down on the parlor floor in front of a roaring fire that Erich had blasting all day. It was getting late, and we were fatigued and famished; none of us ate anything all day. The girls immediately went into a very well-stocked kitchen and made some pasta concoction. Erich was smart; he made two trips this morning to Sam's Market with the children, Grace and Tommy, to stock up on food, knowing we would be arriving sometime today.

"Listen up, everyone, we should all get a good night's rest. It's been an incredibly long day. First thing tomorrow, Antonio, Craig, Frank, Dieter, and I will walk down to the drugstore on Main Street. We'll pick up some medical supplies to attend to Miss Helen's shrapnel wounds. Craig and I will deliver the supplies, while Paul and Erich help the girls tend to her. Craig and I will catch up with the three of you and walk back down Main Street, snooping around town to confirm there are no other people lurking, especially Nazis."

We all got up early the next morning. Dieter, Antonio and I put a hunting knife in our boots, a loaded pistol in the waistband of our trousers, and the five of us all hung our rifles over our shoulders and headed out to the drugstore. While walking down Main Street, we passed Sam's Market, which was located in the middle of town.

The drugstore was one of the first merchants, two miles down from Sam's Market. As we began to approach the edge of town, frightfully, we noticed dead bodies lying by the roadside. There were also three people hanging by nooses from the streetlights. Without hesitation, I pulled my hunting knife from my boot and cut them down.

Antonio, Craig, and I proceeded to walk into the drugstore, only to witness the pharmacist, Mr. Thomas slouched over the cash register, shot in the head. I walked through the store aisle by aisle, filling a box with supplies, as Antonio and Craig carried Mr. Thomas outside. Meanwhile, Frank and Dieter were picking up the dead and moving them to the grass next to the store alongside Mr. Thomas. This was the most heinous sight. These people must have tried to fight back and lost their lives in return. I was grateful the girls and the kids didn't come and got a glimpse of this inconceivable aftermath.

We decided to take the money from the register, in case we might need it at a future date. We all agreed to do the same with all the stores and bury it deep in the ground behind the apartment. We certainly didn't want the enemy getting their hands on it. Craig and I delivered the supplies to Paul; Eric and the girls and immediately went back out to help the others dig graves for the dead. On our route back down Main Street, Craig and I stopped at Herman's Hardware Store and picked up some shovels. The perfect spot for a cemetery was directly across the drugstore, where a large lot sat empty due to an old building that was torn down years ago. We carried the bodies across the street and dug their graves. Fortunately, it was not as cold in town as it was up the mountain; the shovels were able to penetrate the soil without too much trouble. Once the bodies of these poor souls were buried and we said an amateur eulogy, it was time to start walking back down Main Street toward the apartment. Along the way, we went through each store one by one, collecting the cash and looking for more dead. We came across a few more and carried them back down the street and buried them as well.

"Dieter, you really had a great idea here. After Craig and I delivered the pharmaceuticals while walking back down Main Street, and after much inner apprehension, I realized this is an ideal location for us all to cohabit. Ideally, with having accessibility to all these different well stocked stores, we no longer have to rough it and live off the land."

First priority was to figure out how to make the area more secure. As Craig and I walked back into the hardware store and returned the shovels, I happened to notice the door to the storage room in the back slightly ajar. Craig and I gingerly walked back to the storage room with a bullet chambered in our rifles and aimed directly at the door. I slowly slithered through the opening with my rifle aimed, only to see an alarming amount of barbed wire rolled up and bound.

When realizing the barbed wire was certainly not a threat, I immediately took the bullet out of the chamber and returned it to my pocket. There were twenty rolls of barbed wire stacked neatly against the wall. I would assume one of the neighboring farms ordered it before all this turmoil went down.

"Craig, this fencing will come in handy. Tomorrow morning, we should move the barbed wire fencing out to the street and begin to construct a security confinement around the entire town."

"Great idea, Sven."

"Obviously, there's not enough to enclose the entire four mile stretch of Main Street. However, after supper, we'll put our heads together and figure something out. At least this is a good start in the right direction. I'm already feeling more comfortable with this move."

The next morning, we all got up at the crack of dawn. Miss Helen stayed with Grace and Tommy, as the nine of us sauntered back to the hardware store. The morning was fairly brisk, but the sun shone brightly, allowing us the opportunity to work the entire day on the fence. Before the sun set for the evening, I looked around at the fruit of our labor and realized that this fencing was a good start to securing the premises. The sturdy barbed wire fence stood five feet tall and was normally used to keep cattle enclosed. It was probably ordered for Mr. Wilson; his farm was the only cattle farm around these parts. Unfortunately, there was only enough fencing to enclose two miles of the town's perimeter.

"Sven, I suggest we go back to the compound. The entire perimeter was enclosed with and eight-foot fence with heavy barbed-wire tops."

"Dieter, great idea. However, first we should go back and bury the dead. Once the compound is cleaned up, we can start digging up the fence and reinstall it to enclose the entire town.

"We also need to take care of the living arrangements. Since Magdalina, Christine, Miss Helen, and the two children occupy the third-floor apartment and the seven of us occupy the second floor, both places are overcrowded. We all want to stay together for security, but we're all sleeping on the floor on top of one another."

The next morning our plans got shuffled around somewhat due to the fact Mother Nature presented herself in full glory once again. The morning started out extremely cold and rainy. We decided not to journey to the compound today; we saved that project for a dryer day. However, I could not help but feel a sense of urgency; at least the cave was completed and the perimeter was secure. I felt confident that we were ready for any intruders. However, now it felt like we were standing here with our pants down around our ankles, in clear view and vulnerable to our enemy.

"Listen up everyone. Since the weather has put a monkey wrench into our day, I suggest Dieter, Antonio, Frank, Paul, and Erich go to compound and bury the bodies. Craig and I will scope out the apartments above the stores for a better living arrangement, and the girls can stay with Miss Helen and the children. This way, we're not wasting any precious time."

As Craig and I ventured down Main Street, we found ourselves in front of Craig's diner. It was an oversized double building, and his apartment was directly above the diner. There was also the second apartment next to his, where Mrs. O'Brien lived. We approached the front door, and Craig nervously pulled out a key from his trouser pocket and unlocked the door.

"Sven, look at this. In the scheme of everything that has happened, the place is exactly the way I left it."

"Yah, at least the Nazis didn't eat here and pollute the place."

I followed Craig up the back staircase and patiently stood in the hallway as he unlocked the door to his apartment. We walked into the parlor, and within seconds, Craig abruptly stopped cold dead in his tracks and ran out to the second apartment. He fumbled for the second key and unlocked the door. As soon as I walked in, I sense the two of us were on the same thought wave. We could knock out the firewall between the two apartments and make it into one extremely large area. Craig's place had two large bedrooms, one water closet, a large parlor, a small dining area, and a kitchen. We could use the diner downstairs. His kitchen could be converted into another bedroom, along with the small dining room. The second apartment had one large bedroom, a kitchen, a parlor, and a water closet. We could convert the kitchen and parlor into two additional bedrooms as well.

So when all was said and done, potentially, the apartment would have seven bedrooms, two water closets, and one parlor with a large brick fireplace. Since the town had recently lost electricity, clearly it was only a matter of time before we would lose natural gas as well. The fireplace was large enough to heat the entire converted apartment. Once we lose the gas for cooking, we'd simply resume the way we cooked in the cave. We could build a large fireplace in the diner downstairs for both heat and cooking and get prepared for the inevitable loss of the natural gas. This was a great idea; this would allow us all to stay together. We could move beds and furniture in from the other apartments on Main Street. This plan allowed us to have some privacy and the convenience and comfort of everyone having their own bed.

The next couple of days, we utilized the bad weather and got started ripping out walls straight away. It took one week for the eight of us, working around the clock, to complete the renovations. The fruit of our labor produced a small bedroom for Miss Helen, the girls share a room, while Grace and Timmy have the smaller room. Dieter and Erich have a room together, Frank and Craig share the fifth bedroom, and Paul was bunked in with Antonio and me in the larger room. Sadly, I could not shake this strange, eerie feeling that would come over me when I was in Paul's presence. We purposely left the seventh bedroom empty, under the pretense of using it for storage.

"Sven, you're not the only one who senses something isn't right with this new guy. I was a prisoner of the army training program as well. I lived in those barracks for nine months. I have to say, I don't remember seeing Paul. Mind you, I could be wrong. There were a hundred of us crammed into those barracks."

"That's interesting you feel this way Frank."

"Why, Dieter, do you?"

"Yes, but for a different reason. I wasn't going to bring it up this soon, but I also have a strange feeling with this guy. I've detected traces of a French accent. If you listen close enough, it almost seems as though he's working very hard to disguise it. I know firsthand how hard it is to erase an accent. Since I have been living in America, precariously, I've tried to eliminate my German accent to blend in as my father requested."

"All right, guys, I'll take the bait. I'm going to play devil's advocate," I said with a worried expression on his face.

"What do you mean, Sven?"

"Although I've had a strange feeling in the pit of stomach with this guy, and it's not the squirrels, there could be a good explanation. Paul could have emigrated from France before the war or escaped after the German occupation of France. Paul may have the same plan as Dieter's father—blend in with the Americans, learn English, and lose the accent. I think we should all keep a very close eye on him."

"Sven, I also agree. However, while we're on the subject of Paul, I also have something I need to tell you."

"What's that, Magdalina?"

"The other day, when you and Craig returned from the drugstore with the medical supplies, Paul was to stay with us. Shortly after you and Craig left, Paul told us there was something else he needed from the drugstore. He meticulously showed us how to clean the wounds and extract metal fragments and assured us he would return directly. Ironically, Paul was gone for most of the day. In fact, he arrived back to the apartment an hour prior to you all coming home for supper. With the help of Mr. Schumann, we took care of Miss Helen."

"Good enough, guys, I'm convinced. I think we should take turns keeping surveillance over him. However, we must be very discreet. I don't want to spook him. Let's see what this guy's all about."

The next morning, we woke to bitterly cold weather; however, the rain finally subsided and the sun began to peek through the heavy clouds. Since the communal apartment was completed, we decided to make a trip to the compound and begin pulling up the fencing. With all the rain we've had in the past week, hopefully the ground was not frozen so our shovels could penetrate easily. The eight of us grabbed shovels from the closet in the diner and draped the riffles over our shoulders. I gave Dieter and the girls each a revolver, while Antonio and I took the two pistols and stuffed them into the waistband of our trousers. We gave Erich the third pistol to stay behind with Miss Helen and the children. Paul was given no weapons, and surprisingly, he didn't say a word. An hour later, we enter the bombed out compound and immediately began fixating on the fence. Our entire group was working well together; we were making incredible progress in a short amount of time. Proudly, we had dug enough fence to complete the perimeter.

"What's wrong with this picture, guys?"

"What do you mean, Sven? We're making incredible progress."

"No, that's not what I mean. The seven of us have been so engrossed with our work. Somehow, Paul has slipped away unnoticed. Dieter, take Antonio and walk back to the barracks. Make sure your guns are loaded and ready if needed."

Thirty minutes later, the three of them rejoined our group. Surprisingly, Paul was looking like a lost puppy, with his tail between his legs, carrying a pair of work boots.

"Sorry, guys, I left my boots in the barracks and thought I should grab them now, so I wouldn't forget later."

"That's all right, Paul. We were just concerned. We have a rule among ourselves. We never travel alone."

"Sure, Sven, I wasn't thinking. I should have told you where I was going."

"No problem. Just remember these are dangerous times we're living in right now, and we all watch each other's backs."

After working the entire day, pulling up fencing, it was now time to enlarge and strengthen the sleigh we made for Miss Helen. I fetched another fallen tree, and Craig, Dieter, and I began to reconstruct Miss Helen's sleigh. Frank, Antonio, and Paul schlepped the sections of fence we just dug up and pilled them next to where we were working.

Once we had the sleigh completed, we placed sections of fence on the new and improved Miss Helen's sleigh. We were all exhausted and frozen to the bone. We decided to hale our load back to town.

As we walked into the diner, we were pleasantly bombarded with a wonderful aroma. The dining area is completely illuminated by candles and oil lamps, giving a heavenly visual effect. Miss Helen and Erich have a hot supper waiting for us. When the girls witnessed Miss Helen walking about, they became ecstatic. Miss Helen was an exceptional cook; she made a wonderful braised beef pot roast with a rich onion-and-red-wine gravy and added a little barley as a thickening agent, mashed potatoes, and carrots.

"Miss Helen, I have to say this is one of the best meals I've ever had."

"Thank you, Sven, but I think you're tired of eating wild game and squirrels."

"Well, that too, but I won't complain if you make this meal again tomorrow."

Thankfully, we were smart enough, when we lost electricity, to unload the freezers and refrigerators at Sam's Market and store the meat and perishables out back in the snow. Presently, there was a good supply of meat, which should last us until midspring. Thank God, there was a large quantity of beef. If I ate another bear, rabbit, deer, or squirrel I swear I'd turn into one.

The following morning, as we work diligently on erecting the fence in town, we were suddenly interrupted with the sounds of aircraft on the horizon. Without hesitation, we all immediately picked up our riffles and scrambled for cover. Dieter and Erich instantly recognized the two planes. They were Messerschmitt Me 210 reconnaissance planes. The pilots circled around two times, and as quickly as they were here, they were gone again.

"Oh my god, this cannot be good. It seems as though these pilots have knowledge of our presence in town. Where did they come from?"

"God only knows, Sven."

"Yah, you're right buddy—God and the Nazis only know."

We immediately ran down Main Street to Craig's apartment. Once inside, we made ourselves comfortable in the parlor, looking at one another horrified.

"What do we do now, Sven? Why were they flying overhead like that?"

"I don't know. All I know is we better pack some warm clothes and as much food that we can fit on the sleigh and get out of here promptly. I suggest we walk back to the compound and hold up in the barracks until we know what's going on. Once we're there, if it doesn't feel right, at sunrise tomorrow, we head up the mountain and deal with the tight accommodations later."

Amazingly, within minutes, we were all packed. We began loading the sleigh with the provisions. The adrenaline must have been running rapidly through all our veins, we made record-breaking time to the compound. As we began to get closer to the barracks, we notice Paul slithering away, like a snake in the grass. Antonio, Frank, and I ran toward him. Paul immediately pulled out a revolver from his coat pocket and stopped us cold dead in our tracks.

At gunpoint, he led us back to the others and confiscated our rifles and pistols. Paul then placed them next to him in a pile on the snow-covered ground. Within a split second, Paul grabbed Magdalina and yanked her closer to him. Relentlessly, we were then ordered to unload the sleigh of the clothing and some of the supplies but keep all the food intact as Paul held the revolver to her head. Once the sleigh was unloaded of the items he didn't want, Magdalina transferred our weapons and ammunition onto the sleigh, as the rest of us stood powerless, taking this all in. Paul then proceeded to walk off with Magdalina and the sleigh. Suddenly and instinctively, Frank hurled himself at Paul, knocking him to the ground. The gun went off, and the five of us pounced on him. I was able to seize his weapon while pulling the hunting knife from my boot and slashed Paul's neck from ear to ear.

Within seconds, we heard heart-wrenching screams from Magdalina echoing throughout the forest. Frank was lying in a pool of blood; she dropped to her knees to cradle him. Frank was dead—the bullet entered his chest in the location of his heart. For seconds, we stood there devastated and paralyzed. Christine and Antonio ran over to Magdalina, pulled her to her feet off the wet snow, and cuddled her. I picked up Frank's lifeless body with tears in my eyes and scurried over to the side of the garage, with Dieter and Craig following closely behind. They helped me carefully place Frank on the cold, snow-covered ground. The three of us ran back to the blood-covered area and frantically started to cover it with a pile of untainted snow. We picked up Paul and threw him into the bombed-out compound and disguised the second bloodstained area.

Very gingerly, Craig, Dieter and I strolled back to the barracks with our riffles aimed at the door. As I very tentatively and slowly opened the barracks' steel enclosure, an overwhelming thick, fowl aroma suffocated the clean, cold, sweet gentle breeze of the day. It was as though this cloud could literally knock us to the ground. As the three of us apprehensively entered through the door with our faces crouched down into our coats, the sight once again was implausible. We suddenly found ourselves surrounded by a scene from an overdramatized horror flick. There were dead decaying bodies lying everywhere, with blood on the ceiling and the walls trickling down to the floor into a deep river of blood. The stench was beyond words.

As we slowly walked around, alarmingly, we noticed these men were literally gunned down and murdered while they slept and didn't have a snowball's chance in hell to defend themselves. Craig and I immediately ran outside into the fresh air and hovered over with extreme embarrassment and preceded to puke our guts up. With all the hunting I had done in my lifetime, killing wild animals and slicing them down the middle, pulling out their gizzards and skinning them, would certainly hold a backseat to decaying murdered human bodies. This cowardly murder scene will play back in my head for the rest of my life.

"Obviously, these men didn't scramble southwest to the Maryland border after the compound was bombed."

"You took the words right out of my mouth, Sven."

"You know, Dieter, in hindsight, how stupid we were to believe everything this stranger told us. There's absolutely no way I will allow the children or the girls to see this horrific sight. These men deserve something better than to be entombed in this building continuing to decay."

"Dieter and I both agree with you, Sven. However, what do you want to do? Should we dig another huge hole to bury them all? There's got to be at least a hundred bodies in here."

"No, Craig, my brain and heart are at war. I don't see any other option. As much as I know, what I'm about to suggest will probably end up coming back and biting me in the butt."

Craig, Dieter, and I ignited the barracks in a flaming blaze that probably could be seen for many miles away.

With all things considered, the urgency to get out of this compound was overwhelming. We had a long journey up the mountain, and the sun would be setting shortly. Antonio and I carefully lifted Frank's body, with tears streaming from our eyes, and removed his beloved black bearskin coat. We laid him attentively back on the ground and covered his face and body with the fur.

As I wiped a tear away, from the corner of my eye, I saw Dieter, Craig, and Erich standing by the garage door, fiddling with the padlock. Dieter stepped back and retrieved the axe that I was using for the sleigh and began to destroy the immense wooden garage doors. Antonio and I quickly walked over and joined them inside the garage.

"Good God in heaven, Sven! Look what we've got here."

"Yah, isn't this interesting?"

Erich informed us that days before the bombs were dropped on the compound, the Nazis were moving crates stored in the cellar to the delivery trucks parked outside the garage. They always kept a good supply of surplus stored in the cellar. Once the three trucks were completely full, they drove away to make their delivery. Erich witnessed the men from the barracks walk over and start loading the excess crates into the garage.

"Sven, I thought it might be intriguing to see if anything was left behind."

"Good going boys. I think we should take a few minutes and rethink this through. Obviously, Paul was working with the enemy. I'm assuming the other day, when he went missing and mysteriously came back with the alleged boots, he contacted the Nazis somehow and gave them our location. That would explain why we saw the two German reconnaissance planes flying over the town earlier. Presumably, he has a radio hidden in the barracks somewhere.

"Gang, the way I see it, we have two choices here—schlepp back up the mountain and cram everyone into the cave, sleeping standing up in rows, or load all this weaponry onto the sleigh and take it back into town. We have time before it gets dark to make a second sleigh. However, we'll have to work all night hauling the loads. Once all the crates are in town, we should than setup the Panzerschreck antitank rocket launchers and bazookas around the perimeter. We need to dig foxholes in front of each of the launchers for easier accessibility and control. This is a gift from God, boys and girls. There are enough weapons here for us to safeguard and defend our town against intruders for a very long time. We have a couple dozen crates of automatic rifles, machine guns, submachine guns, grenade launchers, stick grenade/potato mashers and stick grenades. This is a militant's dream come true."

"Sven, how do you know so much about antitank rocket thing-a-ma-jigs and bazookas?"

"That's easy, Antonio, from the books I read as a child on war and survival. You surely have to remember that."

"Well, that explains it—that's why you're our commandant and token egghead."

"Guys, please don't make fun," I said, while trying to look like a stern and serious commander.

"No, Sven, seriously, you really are our commandant. You must have noticed how we all take direction from you. Frank used to tell us all time how he admired you and was eternally grateful. He adamantly believed if it wasn't for you joining the escape, they would never have been able to successfully pull it off."

"Okay, since obviously I was elected the group's commandant without my knowledge, I think we should take a vote on the next step. My opinion is to proudly defend our home."

With that acknowledged, we unanimously agreed to proudly defend our home even if we have to die doing so. We worked all night transporting the weapons and ammunition. Once the garage was empty, the seven of us stood spellbound while two huge German tanks were staring us in the face. One was a German Panther and the other a Tiger tank that were hidden by at least a hundred wooden crates filled with weapons and ammunition. Erich explained that these German tanks are considered super tanks, more durable than any American or Russian tanks.

"This is going to sound really strange guys. Does anyone know how to drive a tank?"

"Sven, believe it or not, I think I do."

"Magdalina, what are you saying?"

"I worked two years in a military factory, producing munitions, tanks, and armored cars. Of course, I didn't drive them. However, I do understand the fundamentals. We were trained very thoroughly."

"Do you think you can move them out of the garage?"

"Yes, give me a couple of minutes."

"Thank God, I was worried we would have to blow them up. But before we leave, let's all walk over to Frank and say a few words."

We all walked over to where we had buried Frank, everyone of us with tears streaming down our checks.

"Frank, I promise we'll come back my friend and take you home. We'll humbly take you back up the mountain and bury you next to the waterfall, in the area you loved so much. The bear that you so courageously helped me kill, whose hide made the black bearskin coat you so proudly wore, will be buried along with you. Rest in peace, my friend, and go with God. You'll be truly missed."

"That was a nice eulogy, Sven."

"Thanks, guys."

Magdalina immediately broke down in hysterics once again. As an impulsive reaction, I instantly put my arms around her for comfort. Strangely, I was feeling somewhat guilty. I realized early on how Frank felt for her; however, the two of us never spoke of it. Thankfully, Frank was never aware I also had strong feelings for her. It started the minute I met her, when we were both prisoners of the compound and I was assigned to be her supervisor. I would take my feelings for this woman to my grave and let no one know for Magdalina's benefit, even though it had never been obvious to any of us that she might have loved Frank back.

Once Magdalina calmed down with the help of Christine, she jumped into the tank and started fiddling around. It didn't take long before she was able to maneuver the tank out of the garage. She gave me a crash course, and the two of us drove around, practicing maneuvers. When we felt comfortable, Magdalina drove one tank with Christine, Antonio, and Craig, while I drove with Dieter and Erich on the other. Magdalina and I parked the tanks one at each end of town, while the others were setting up the antitank rocket launchers and bazookas around the perimeter. We agreed to wait until sunrise and dig the trenches. Meanwhile, Christine and Magdalina went to bed, while the five of us took two man shifts patrolling the perimeter. Antonio and I volunteered for the first surveillance.

Surprisingly, we made it through an entire night without incident. When the sun began to rise, we immediately went back to work digging the foxholes for the antitank rocket launchers. Once that chore was completed, we continued with the barricade. At the rate we were going, we should have the perimeter secure in a few days and then we can die of exhaustion.

Two days passed by peacefully, and we were beginning to second-guess ourselves. Maybe we jumped the gun and were wrong about Paul. Antonio and I shared our room with him and decided to snoop around somewhat. We lifted the mattress to his bed, and much to our surprise, a manila envelope between the mattress and box spring was suddenly staring us in the face. Inside the envelope were two sets of identification papers. One set read Paul Smith, and the other read Paul Touvier.

"This is very interesting. Who the hell was this man?"

While sharing this information with the others, Erich suddenly developed a frightful pale look on his face and immediately stopped smoking the cigarette that he had just lit. He frantically crushed it out in the ashtray with a trembling hand, totally mutilating the cigarette and reducing it to tiny pieces of raw tobacco.

"Erich, what's wrong?"

"Dieter, you've heard of Paul Touvier, haven't you?"

"No, I don't think so."

"You mean your father never spoke of him?"

"No. Why, who is he?"

"Paul Touvier was a French citizen who became a Nazi collaborator after Germany invaded France. He's a very well-known anti-Semitic French traitor who became Germany's second regional head. Paul worked under Klaus Barbie, head of Gestapo for years. Between Paul and Klaus, they were both dreadfully feared by everyone in Europe. Paul was a ruthless evil man who committed horrific atrocities to mankind. For some reason, Paul Touvier was nicknamed the Hangman of Lyon. When I first saw the vagabond, I thought this guy looked somewhat familiar, but I honesty couldn't put my finger on it. You can rest to be sure—he sold us out and radioed our location to the Nazis. Guaranteed, they'll show up. Klaus Barbie was one of the top-ranking SS officers who were with the Hitler brothers, Himmler, and Eichmann the following day after the bombing. Paul wasn't with that group. I would imagine he was playacting like a Good Samaritan, helping Miss Helen. The Gestapo must have been using him as a spy. I'll bet my last bottom dollar he's the one who shot all those defenseless poor souls in the barracks as they slept."

"Oh my God! Did Paul know who Magdalina is?"

"Antonio, I doubt it. Frank, Christine, you, and I are the only people of this group who know."

"I hope you're right, Sven."

"Unless you told him, Antonio, I know how much you adored him, buddy. None of us trusted Paul from the very beginning. I believe Erich's theory is probably correct. We should count our blessings that the Gestapo hasn't shown up yet. However, one thing is to our advantage; the Nazis don't know Mr. Touvier's dead. I would assume they won't drop areal bombs if they believe he is still with us. Instead they'll attack by ground force.

"Miss Helen, at the first sign of any activity, I want you to take Tommy and Grace downstairs. There's a door in the kitchen by the pantry that leads to the cellar. Magdalina and Christine, I want you both to join Miss Helen and the children."

"Sven, no. I don't mean to be insubordinate. However, I'm more than capable of fighting right alongside the men, if we are to engage in battle. Besides you may need my help with one of the tanks."

"Alright, point well made," I looked at Magdalina with not only admiration but also fear for her safety.

Antonio, Craig, Dieter, and I walked outside and stood in the center of Main Street, pondering Erich's theory about an attack by ground force. It didn't take long to realize that with the layout of this town, in all practicality, the Nazis would surround us.

"Oh my god, I've got an idea."

"What, Sven?"

"One of my favorite books is about an old Cherokee war tactic. The Indians set a very cleaver trap. They allowed the cavalry to surround their village. Once the army was in place, they shot flaming arrows into the sky, which landed on gunpowder that was spread around the perimeter. As a result, the army could not escape outward. The Cherokees then shot a second row of gunpowder also around the perimeter but stringently placed closer to the village. As a result, the army was completely surrounded by fire both front and back and had no way of escaping. Within seconds, the army was engulfed in flames."

"Good lord, Sven, I'm glad you're on our side. This is a prime example of why you have been chosen as our camp commandant."

"Thanks, Dieter. Erich, can you help us with the gunpowder?"

"*Ja*, of course. I've been waiting and praying I could do something useful around here. It's actually a very easy chemical process. I'll get started with this at once. First, I need someone to gather up all the charcoal you can find. The charcoal for the stoves left in some of the apartments will do fine. All I need is potassium nitrate, sulfur powder, and charcoal powder. You guys get the charcoal, and I'll get the rest. I can have this ready in a couple of hours."

"Thank you, Erich. You're worth your weight in gold."

Erich came through and produced the gunpowder as promised. We tested it on a small area, and as predicted, it worked great. Before sunset, we were able to strategically position the gunpowder around the circumference of the town. Erich made enough gunpowder to last us a month. If the Gestapo didn't show up tomorrow, we would simply lay more powder down as needed. Dieter, Antonio, and I made two bows and a dozen arrows for each and placed the bows on a small table we setup in midtown. We also placed on the table, next to the two bows, a container of gasoline, which we siphoned out of an old automobile that was abandoned in the back alley. The girls cut up garments for rags, tied the rags around the arrowheads, and placed them on the table. We were ready for action.

We spent the next morning anxiously waiting in silence. I could feel the Nazis omnipresence in the air. If our flaming-arrow plan didn't work, then Magdalina and I would run for the tanks that were parked at the edges of town. Craig, Antonio, Magdalina, and Erich would assume position in the foxholes and man the antitank rocket launchers and bazookas that they trained on earlier. Dieter and I hovered around the table with the arrows. Christine and Miss Helen were heavily armed in the diner with Grace and Tommy.

We all took turns taking catnaps in the warmth of sun to pass time. I glanced at my watch for the first time today. It was 4:00 p.m., and we only had an hour before sunset. It was not plausible to attack with ground force in the evening. As quickly as my brain assumed we would have to stand guard another night and wait until sunrise to start this process all over, Craig and Dieter spotted three enemy tanks with ground warfare four miles northeast traveling quickly towards us. Dieter and I immediately sprang into action and took our positions alongside the table in the center of town.

"Just remember, Dieter, the timing of this tactic is of upmost importance. We wait until the enemy is at the five-hundred-yard marker."

If Dieter and I could shoot the bows at a perfect forty-five-degree angle, we would hit our target dead-on. As we had done numerous times in our practice runs, and with the ground patrol in position, the first target was hit without fallacy. The new set of arrows were quickly dunked into the gasoline and once again set a flame. Dieter and I, in perfect formation, hit the second target. Our plan worked beautifully. These poor bastards were nothing but sitting ducks. The sounds of human pain and suffering and the smell of burning skin and hair were completely overwhelming to us all.

We waited an hour for the smoke to clear, and as the sun was beginning to set, the awaiting three tanks started barreling toward us. Magdalina and I immediately began to run in opposite directions and jumped into our tanks. Craig, Antonio, Erich, and Dieter jumped back into their foxholes and positioned the launchers. Within twenty minutes of relentless battle, the enemy tanks were disabled. Craig, Antonio, Erich, Dieter, and I ran through our destroyed perimeter barrier toward the tanks, popped their lids, and threw a grenade into each one.

Joyfully, we celebrated our triumph all night long with bottles of vodka and whiskey, which we confiscated from the liquor store next to Craig's Diner. For the first time since this all began, unbelievably, most of us actually slept late. We woke to the inviting aroma of bacon and coffee and ventured downstairs to the diner. Craig and Miss Helen made us a victory breakfast to die for. Once we were finished, the five us picked up our rifles, put our revolvers in the waistband of our trousers, and headed outside to assess the damage.

Thankfully, most of the damage was done to the five-foot barbed wire fencing that we borrowed from the hardware store. The damage done to this fence was no real loss. We would just venture back to the compound and retrieve the eight-foot heavier fence sections and replace them. Eventually, all the five-foot sections would have to be replaced with the better fencing. Once we replace the damaged areas, the entire circumference would be enclosed once again.

As we walked around, noticeably a few stores had structural damage. We decided to enter one store at a time. If the store had heavy damage, we'd transport anything salvageable to another location. We really did luck out; there were only five stores with extensive damage—the drugstore, the bakery, and, on the opposite side of the street, the post office, a ladies' shoes store, and Larry's Printing. We cleaned out the surplus from the drugstore and stored it in the cellar of the diner. Bright and early tomorrow morning, we'd go back to the compound and continue digging up the eight-foot fencing and reconstruct the perimeter barrier.

After relentlessly working all day, we unanimously agreed to stop work and venture back to the diner for an early supper. Once we were finished, we placidly made our way to the parlor and comfortably sat around the fireplace with coffee and a nightcap, tuning in to our Sunday-evening radio program.

Unfortunately, the four-hour, two-man shifts patrolling the area at night still needed to be enforced. Tomorrow morning, we had to get up early and construct a perimeter trap outside the barrier fence. The theory would be the same as it was at the cave. Any intruders would be caught before they get close to our barrier. This trap was practical since there were so few of us for a four-mile span to patrol every evening.

"I don't know about the rest of you, but I'm on pins and needles."

"Sven, loosen up buddy. Your wound as tight as a clock."

"I know, Antonio, but the anticipation of hearing something about our battle in Elk Lick is making me feel like a little kid again waiting for Santa Claus. After all, our conquest with seventy-five Nazi SS soldiers is completely mind-boggling. This should be front-page news."

THE ARYAN MASTER RACE

After waiting for what seemed to be a dog's age, it was finally time for our favorite radio program to begin.

Thank you for tuning into our radio program, *You Can't Do Business with Hitler*, with John Flynn and Virginia Moore.

We have very disturbing news to report this evening, March 27, 1946. The aircraft carrier *USS Essex* CV-9 was bombed and sunk relentlessly by the Nazi *Luftwaffe*. Once again, many American lives were lost. The Essex was anchored in the North Pacific Ocean off the California coastal waters.

The *USS Intrepid* CV-11, also known as the Fighting "I," was also destroyed and sunk in the coastal waters of Massachusetts. The *USS Shangri-La* CV-38 was spotted and destroyed in the Gulf of Mexico, in the coastal waters of Louisiana. The Department of War has made every effort to safely bring these aircraft carriers into different coastal locations, with the expectations of catching the enemy off guard. With the sinking of five US aircraft carriers, it's feared the enemy has a tight guard on the entire United States coastline. As a result, import and export may be impossible. All attempts to bring back American troops have been in vain. The remaining US military army and air force bases have been destroyed as well. Continuous reports had been coming in of German military violence in various areas of America's forty-eight states.

Please organize within your communities and stay vigilant. Once again, American Boeing P-12 biplanes will be dropping instructional leaflets, on war time survival, written by the Department of War. Gen. Douglas MacArthur is urging all abled-bodied American men to step up and join the National Guard. Please report to a staff sergeant of the Guard that has been assigned to your area. You'll need to show proof of citizenship by form of birth certificate and social security. We urge all citizens to tune in each week to our new emergency scheduled times. This program will now air Sunday, Tuesday, and Thursday evenings at 7:00 p.m. sharp. As news becomes available to us, we're dedicated to presenting it to you.

Please tune in Tuesday evening to our radio program, *You Can't Do Business with Hitler.* This is John Flynn and Virginia Moore signing off. Thank you and God Bless America.

"Oh my god, Sven, what do we do now?"

"I don't know, Craig. Maybe you, Antonio, and I should be on the outside and join the Guard. Of course, Dieter and Erich would have to stay here with the girls. They would be lynched by the Americans just for being German. No one will believe they're part of the good guys."

As the group's commandant, this recent news had put my head into a tailspin, giving me feelings of extreme anxiety with the need to fix this.

"Although nothing has been authenticated, America is obviously at war with Germany. What if Japan rejoins forces with Germany in this new quest? Especially considering America dropped two atomic bombs. It would be logical for Japan to seek revenge on America. I find it very peculiar President Truman hasn't declared war. I would assume, with the number of American troops stranded in Europe and with the recent news of more American military bases destroyed, we simply don't have the manpower and equipment needed for retaliation. Seven aircraft carriers sit at the bottom of the Atlantic, Pacific, and the Gulf of Mexico with American military troops and weaponry.

"The United States of America is in serious danger. However, I cannot fathom how Hitler smuggled enough Nazis out of Germany to attack America and how he could win a war with a country this size. There are millions of Americans who are willing and able to defend her against a few smuggled in Nazis and high-ranking Gestapo bastards."

"Sven, logically, that's correct, but trust me, Dieter and I know firsthand how a group of radicals can influence and brainwash everyday, normal, law-abiding citizens."

As we sat in the parlor saddened with this recent news and curious of Erich's statement, once again, I found myself sitting on eggshells with anticipation of Erich's experience and knowledge.

"Erich, would you elaborate on that statement?"

"Sure."

"After the surrender of World War I and the Treaty of Versailles was put into effect, Germany was suffering greatly. Hitler gained notoriety with the National Socialist German Workers' Party, portraying himself as an ordinary, everyday working stiff. In his speeches, he was loud and strong and said the things the German people wanted to hear. He wanted Germany to become a powerful nation, especially after enduring the humiliation of surrender. Those times were eccentric. There were communist, Marxist, and capitalist parties throughout the nation. Germany was in political chaos and the threat of communism was predominate. When the Great Depression hit in Europe, Germany endured extremely hard times. The economy was weak and unemployment was at a staggering high percentage.

"Hitler promised to nullify the Treaty of Versailles, strengthen the economy, and provide jobs. President Paul von Hindenburg, who disliked Adolf Hitler and referred to him as the Austrian corporal, was a senile old man and was persuaded by several influential people to appoint Hitler into power. The German people then voted in his favor, and once von Hindenburg was dead, the Social Democratic Party was abolished and Hitler's dictatorship began. The Nazis spread terror across Europe and inflicted atrocities to mankind. People acted out of fear. German youth were brainwashed, even against their own parents. It didn't take long, with that kind of evil muscle, to destroy a nation of good people.

"The series of progressions Germany experienced is happening in America as well. Good people will do very bad things to survive. It's one thing to die. However, it's entirely different to be tortured or to witness your loved ones murdered or tortured. Sven, a few pockets of militia groups won't make that much of a difference."

"Erich, do you really believe that? If all the American people unite and fight back, we have power in numbers."

"In theory, yes, I agree. However I cannot emphasize this more— if the Hitler brothers seize power, guaranteed a large majority of the American people will reluctantly surrender and end up uniting with the Nazis."

"Erich, that probably makes sense. I believe the American people didn't fully comprehend the politics of World War II. Americans view German people as evil. Germans are hated by many nationalities. German Americans in this country were treated terribly by other Americans. When you hear from someone who witnessed firsthand the actual events that unfolded leading up to the war, it sounds different. I can now understand how the German nation got sucked in and forced to comply. I believe you're right. The same thing the Germans experienced in Europe can realistically happen to the Americans as well.

"We really need to beef up security around here. I suggest tomorrow morning, we begin constructing our perimeter trap. We should dig a narrow six-foot-deep trench one mile from the circumference of the barbed-wire security fence. If someone comes too close, they'll fall in and will have difficulty getting back out. If trucks or tanks get too close, they'll fall partially in. Regardless, this trench should give us plenty of warning.

"Antonio, I suggest while we still have telephone service to call the boss and bring this to his attention. Considering they'll be here in four weeks, I certainly don't want anyone from the Italian family getting caught in our trap. That's not a good first impression."

After a long week of continual digging and many blisters to show for it, the trap was finished and the fence was replaced with eight foot barbed wire sections. The antitank rocket launchers and bazookas remained set up inside the perimeter, with plenty of ammunition for each weapon. Each army tank sat in the vicinity of the entrance and exit of town fully armed and ready to go. Once Antonio's friends arrive, we would have plenty of combined guerrilla muscle and would strategize a new plan.

"People, finish your supper quickly, we need to get upstairs, the president's about to speak".

"All right, Sven, I'll fetch the pot of coffee."

We all grabbed our coffee cups and quickly walked upstairs and got comfortable in front of the blazing fire Dieter just started in the fireplace. Grace and Tommy sat on the floor playing Monopoly, which will keep them occupied for hours. I set up Frank's old radio in the window and pointed the antenna outside for reception.

> Good evening, my fellow Americans. It has been brought to my attention that numerous areas of the country have experienced Nazi military violence. Since it has been proven virtually impossible to bring home our armed forces from Germany, Italy, Japan, China, Africa, and the Pacific, and with our military installations destroyed throughout the country; for all intents and purposes, this has left us somewhat defenseless. While I desperately tried keeping war from tainting American soil, my efforts have been futile.
>
> I have recently learned that nuclear bombs of mass destruction have been strategically placed in the forty-eight states for the sole purpose of coercing an authorized, unconditional surrender of the United States of America to Germany. If this surrender agreement isn't signed within twenty-four hours, the nuclear bombs in each state will be detonated. At 3:00 p.m. this afternoon, April 12, 1946, I learned that the US Capitol building was completely destroyed by enemy forces. This was done as a deliberate warning. After careful consideration, I see no other recourse but to oblige and surrender. Tomorrow morning, at 10:00 a.m., April 13, 1946, I will sign the surrender agreement in the presence of Adolf and Gerhard Hitler in the Oval Office of the White House. Regretfully, I will then step down as your president. The American people will continue to stay in my prayers.
>
> Thank you, and God bless America.

"Oh my god, what the hell are my brothers doing?"

"Your brothers? What do you mean, Magdalina?"

"Adolf Hitler is my older brother, and Gerhard is my younger brother. Gerhard is also Christine's estranged husband. I promise you I had no idea they were planning something of this magnitude. I risked my life to escape, with the intentions of warning the authorities. Unfortunately, once the three of us climbed over the compound fence, we literally had to run and hide for our lives. We're too late to warn anyone. This situation is spinning out of control and is beyond a warning. In hindsight, I surely can see there were warning signs all along. I wish I knew then what I know now. Maybe things would have worked out differently."

"Magdalina, I don't understand why you're torturing yourself? You did nothing wrong."

"Thanks, Erich, I know you're right. However, my heart and head are both very heavy."

"Seriously, if anyone is to feel guilty, it should be me. My colleagues and I produced the nuclear energy for those bombs. In all practicality, how could we have missed the writing on the wall? We could have very easily sabotaged the project, and Hitler wouldn't have the upper hand."

"Yah, great, they would have shot you on the firing squad."

"Sven, I wouldn't care if I died protecting this country. I can assure you my colleagues felt the same."

"None of you can put blame on yourselves. The two men who masterminded this plot, the Nazi antagonists, and the Gestapo are at fault. Once the Italians arrive, we'll all sit down, sort this out, and contemplate a plan. So stop this nonsense right now, all of you. Christine, you didn't tell me you have a husband."

"Antonio, I know, I'm sorry. The entire time as a prisoner in that war relocation camp, I dreamed of the day we would be released. Once we were free, I planned to go back to my apartment in Philadelphia, divorce Gerhard, and use my maiden name, *Luciano*. All I thought of in those four years was starting over with a fresh beginning. I even contemplated returning to New York, where I was born and raised."

"Sweetheart, this is going to be a strange question, but are you related to Salvatore Luciano, better known as Charlie?"

"Yes, Antonio, he's my uncle from Lercara Friddi, Sicily, my father's younger brother. Although, I barely remember him. He was in and out of prison almost the entire time I was growing up. My father didn't approve of his lifestyle and insisted on keeping the family distant from him. I never knew him as *Charlie*. My family always referred to him as Lucky Luciano. Unfortunately, I wouldn't know my uncle if we plowed into each another."

"Wow, what a small world. I have exciting news. You'll all be meeting him shortly, without plowing into him. Mr. Luciano is the boss who will be arriving with his New York associates, along with the family from Chicago with boss Tony Accardo. I propose we forget this guilt-and-blame nonsense and have a peaceful evening listening to the radio."

"Buddy, well said, you took the words right out of my mouth," I looked at my best friend with my famous silly sly grin and slapped him on the back.

"Antonio, I can not tell you how excited I am with the possibility of meeting my uncle. Although, in the same breath, I'm scared to death."

"Please don't worry. I'll bet Mr. Luciano is going to be so happy to see you. Please come over here and sit next to me on the sofa."

"Alright, that would be lovely."

"Sweetheart, when this nightmare is over, I want to go back with you to Philadelphia. Please divorce Gerhard, and if you'll have me, I would be honored to have you as my wife. The two of us can start over together. I love you, Christine, I cannot image living my life without you. Charlie Luciano is your uncle, so I already have my foot in the door. He really likes me and, most importantly, trusts me. I'm sure we'll have his blessing, along with the entire family. I don't have a ring for you, but will you marry me?"

"Oh my god, yes, of course I will. I love you, Antonio."

"Hey, buddy, too bad there's not a jewelry store in town. Christine could be supporting a very affordable rock on her finger, for the amazing price of nothing. Oh well, maybe we should just go to the hardware store and see what we can pick up there."

"Very funny, Sven."

"All kidding aside, congratulations to you both. Any candidates for best man?"

We all stopped what we were doing and ran toward Christine and Antonio and gave them both a huge group hug. What a blessing to finally have something good to celebrate in the wake of all this god-awful turmoil surrounding us. Thank God, my best friend has had the good fortune of a second chance at life. He married well the first time and would be marrying equally well the second time around.

"Let's have a quick toast to honor Christine and Antonio with this vodka before the news program starts."

> Thank you for tuning into our radio program, *You Can't Do Business with Hitler*, with John Flynn and Virginia Moore.
>
> Tonight, we have very sad and disturbing news for the American people. Two days after President Truman signed the surrender agreement with Germany, he was murdered. Adolf Hitler ordered the Gestapo to capture and hang Pres. Harry S. Truman and First Lady Bess until dead. Their bodies hang on display in front of the White House between the center pillars. The people of Washington, DC, are forced to parade down the sidewalks to view this despicable horrific sight. The American flag that so proudly has been displayed for over a hundred years in front of the White House has been replaced with the German Nazi Flag. Nazi banners have been unfurled all over the White House and hang from every streetlight in town.
>
> Groundbreaking news has just come in. On this day, April 21, 1946, at 1:00 p.m., the country of Mexico and the continent of South America were heavily attacked by German *Luftwaffe* flying Arado AR Projekt II jet-powered aircraft loaded with atomic bombs. Apologetically, at the present, we have no word of any survivors.
>
> The Health Department, in conjunction with the War Department, urges all citizens to stay indoors until further notice. Close all windows and doors and tightly seal them. This is a precautionary safeguard against radiation sickness that may travel from Mexico and South America. To date, we don't have complete data of the damage atomic radiation causes and the long-term effects. Radiation sickness caused approximately 15–20 percent of the deaths following the deployment of Little Boy and Fat Man over Hiroshima and Nagasaki, Japan.
>
> Virginia and I humbly apologize this will be our last broadcast. The Gestapo has taken over the studio and has been preparing for our new *Führer*, Adolf Hitler, and *Vorsitzender*,

Gerhard Hitler, to speak to the nation at 11:00 a.m. tomorrow. Using a translator, the *Führer* will enlighten the American people of his future plans and what is expected of every citizen.

Regrettably, this is John Flynn and Virginia Moore signing off for the last time and wishing every American Godspeed.

"Again, like Dieter and I explained, this is the start of how you get an entire nation to buckle to its knees and submit. Sven, I know you're Mr. Fix It and you're used to setting a plan in motion and successfully carrying it through. However, this is much bigger than all of us. I also realize the power of the Italians. Although, gentlemen, I beg to differ. I've seen what the Third *Reich* can do and the immense power they steal. The Italians may not be a match for them. I pray I'm wrong, but I've already lived through this once. You might consider leaving the country."

"Erich, where can we go? Especially with how heavily the coastline is guarded. We're all prisoners in our own country."

"Sven, I wish I had the answers."

"Yah, I'm fresh out of ideas myself."

The next morning, we had another wonderful breakfast that Craig and Miss Helen prepared. The news that was broadcasted last evening, needless to say, was heart-wrenching. Each and every one of us was feeling despondent. I checked Frank's radio twice to make sure we'd get good reception in the diner, while Miss Helen and Magdalina took the children outside to play on the empty lot next to the diner. Even though the public was urged to stay indoors and seal windows, doors, and any cracks, we took a group vote. After confirming our geological location on the map, we all agreed the distance from Somerset County was far enough from Mexico and South America.

"I think our next project will be to build a swing set and a sandbox for these two wonderful children."

"That's a great idea, Sven. There certainly is enough room on the empty lot next to my diner."

"Yah, I know, Craig, and with everything these poor children have been through, losing both their parents, their home, and living with complete strangers, they have never once complained or fussed. Listen up, guys, speaking of Grace and Tommy, I have another idea.

"After we listen to the Adolf Hitler's speech this morning, I'll take Antonio and Dieter with me, and the three of us will canvass a few of our neighboring farms in the area. With any luck, the Gestapo has abandoned this area as well. If this is the case, we'll bring back any cows, horses, chickens, and livestock that may have been left behind. Grace and Tommy should have fresh milk daily, and eggs would be a blessing for us all. The food supply at Sam's Market will start to dwindle very shortly. Once we have the animals in place, and with spring just around the corner, we need to clear the lots where the five merchants were destroyed. We can cultivate the land and plant seeds for the animals and fresh produce."

Thankfully, the morning turned out perfect. The sun was shining brightly and the air had a sweet, warm breeze for a late April morning. We regrouped back into the diner, and Craig started to brew another pot of coffee. The rest of us lounged around, drinking coffee with expectations of Hitler's speech, while the children now played ball in front of the diner where we can watch them.

> *My German fellow countrymen, women, my comrades, this is your new Führer und Reichskanzler*, Adolf Hitler, speaking.
>
> As you are aware, 19 April 1946, the late President Truman resigned from the United States presidency. I have assumed Mr. Truman's presidential position. The United States of America on this day, 22 April 1946, no longer exists. This country is now New Germany. All citizens are required to report to your state's capitol for registration. Since the District of Columbia's capitol was destroyed, those residents are required to report to the White House grounds, where registration will take place.
>
> Upon this registration, you are required to furnish the original copy of your birth certificate, passports, social security cards, and any other documentation for proof of identity and heritage. Once you're processed and upon the completion of registration, you will be given an identity card that you are required by law to carry at all times. Every desirable Aryan adult and child will be granted a German registration card and permanently branded with the swastika on your left forearm.

Newborn babies will be registered in the hospital and will be required by law to report back for the necessary branding at the age of six.

All pure German emigrants and German Americans will be granted Aryan citizenship upon proof of heritage. People born in America with one European ethnic breeding other than German will be granted a level 1 Aryan-German citizenship.

Level 1 citizenship has rules that need to be followed, along with restrictions. Before the level 1 citizenship card and branding are granted, your European heritage has to be approved by Joseph Goebbels, *Reich* minister of propaganda. Level 1 citizens will be awarded new German surnames for the purpose of reproducing. All level 1 citizens are only permitted to propagate with a man or woman of the German-Aryan level. This will ensure through future generations a desired purity of the German pedigree.

Level 2 and 3 undesirables will be taken and detained in concentration camps for holding, which are presently being constructed in all forty-eight states, and later deported.

Level 2 undesirables: Negroes, consisting of any man over the age of sixty and all women and children, will continue to be deported back to Africa.

Level 2 undesirables: Jews, consisting of any man over the age of sixty and all women and children, will be deported to South America.

Level 2 undesirables: Emigrants, consisting of anyone who has more than one European heritage, will be deported back to Europe.

Level 3 undesirables, consisting of homosexuals, handicapped, mentally ill, political prisoners, criminals, and gypsies, will also be taken to the concentration camps for holding and later deported to South America.

Anyone caught forging birth certificates and identity papers will be sent to the death camps, along with any nonconforming individuals. Anyone who doesn't register within the six-month timeframe will be sent to the death camps. All death camps are overseen by Heinrich Himmler, who is dedicated to the purification of the Aryan master race.

Every desirable Aryan and level 1 German citizen will have six months to learn and effectively become fluent in the German language and successfully become a German citizen of the master race. All schools are required, effective immediately, to hold two-hour German lessons daily for all children. Preparatory schools will be set up for all boys and girls from the ages of ten to eighteen. Boys from the age of ten to fourteen are required to join the German Young People group, and teenage boys from the age of fourteen to eighteen are required to join the Hitler Youth. Girls from the age of ten to eighteen are required to join the League of German Girls.

Weekend camps for boys and girls, ages sixteen to twenty, will be set up for the Aryan level only. These camps will serve the purpose of propagation for the offspring of the Aryan master race. Once the babies are born, they will be placed in government group homes and cared for by nursing personnel until the age of ten and then will be transferred to a preparatory school. Anyone wishing to keep their babies may do so once the arrangements have been approved by the *Reich*. All Aryan women over the age of twenty-one, single or married, may volunteer to participate in the propagation program with approval by high-ranking Gestapo leaders.

Lastly, each of the forty-eight states will be renamed with German names and re-territorialize as I see fit. Washington, DC, is now Berlin, and the White House is now my *Führerbunder*. Leaflets will be dropped overhead by Heinkel HD 51 biplanes, reiterating my speech and giving locations for registration for the different states.

Your *Führer und Reichskanzler* of the
German *Reich* and people,
Adolf Hitler

"Holly cow, this guy is certainly deranged. Erich, does he honestly believe he can get away with all this garbage?"

"I believe so. Hitler was able to force the surrender of this great country and lead us into conformity, theoretically, without starting a war and involving any allies that he clearly no longer has. I believe there's a good chance this entire country can successfully become

New Germany and the citizens will become the Aryan *Herrenvolk*, which in English means, the Aryan 'master race.' His plan is excellent. America didn't have any choice but to surrender out of fear of the detonation of nuclear weapons. Regrettably, there's a strong possibility that he can indeed pull this off. I pray that the US Department of War and Generals MacArthur, Bradley, and Eisenhower are planning a top-secret defense—that's if they're all still alive."

THE HITLER BROTHERS' FIVE-YEAR PLAN

 We woke early to another beautiful morning. The birds were singing, and the sun was shining with a delightfully warm spring breeze. After sharing my thoughts, over breakfast, with the group for another new project, Antonio, Dieter, and I decide to leave town by way of the forest to assess the situation at the local farms. The three of us proceeded to get prepared for our journey by each of us placing a hunting knife in our boots and a loaded pistol in the waistband of our trousers and hanging a rifle over our shoulders.

We very gingerly walked past the back of the demolished compound and the burnt-out barracks, staying out of sight through the dense forest. Everything here seemed to be as we left it, with the exception of a small wooden box that was hidden in the bushes behind the barracks. I quickly walked over and picked it up, noticing the inscription on the front was in German. I immediately ran back to where Antonio and Dieter were waiting, placed it carefully on the ground, and cautiously opened the box to reveal a small typewriter housed inside.

"Why would a typewriter be hidden here?"

"Sven, that's no typewriter. It's a German Enigma coding machine used for encryption of secret messages."

"Dieter, are you sure?"

Suddenly it became perfectly clear what that bastard Nazi French traitor was up to. We hid the coding machine in the dense brush of the woods and continued on our way. We'd retrieve it on our way back home; this thing might actually come in handy in the future. After all, the Nazis don't know Paul Touvier was dead, which I believe was to our advantage. I would assume this was why the enemy hadn't come back to this area.

An hour after passing the compound, we approached the Rizzo's farm. Sadly, I noticed Antonio's eyes looking somewhat glassy as we cautiously approached closer with drawn pistols. Using good sense for a change, I decided to keep my big mouth shut and not tease him for having human emotions, as I normally would under different circumstances. After lying in the dead corn field for thirty minutes with no noticeable activity, we decided to walk closer to the house. Antonio informed us that everything seemed to be as it was when he and Christine fled a year ago. The laundry was still hanging on the clothesline as Christine had left it.

We slowly and attentively walked through the house and then the barn. Nothing seemed to be out of place. Unfortunately, the horses were missing, but everything else was intact. We then continued on our way, walking for another hour, and approached the Ackermann's dairy farm. The good Lord must have heard my prayers because out in the meadows, in plain sight, were a dozen cows happily grazing in the sunlight. Very strangely, there were about a hundred cows missing. I could not imagine why the Nazis would have taken a hundred cows and left twelve behind. However, I won't look a gift horse in the mouth.

Again, there seemed to be no activity on this farm, either. With pistols drawn, we discreetly approached the house. As we opened the front door and walked into the parlor, the scene was much different than the Rizzo's. The Ackermann's farmhouse had been transformed into a military compound. There were chairs and desks and empty file cabinets all over the first-floor parlor and dining room, with Nazi flags hanging on the walls. The kitchen was still unblemished; the only thing out of place was a portrait of Adolf Hitler hanging on the wall. The upstairs was the same—empty filing cabinets, desks and chairs throughout, Nazi flags hanging.

After searching the house from top to bottom, we strolled over to the barn. Slowly and squeamishly, we opened the two immense barn doors and walk inside. There was absolutely nothing in here, but a couple of empty stales and bushels of hay. Unfortunately, the horses were missing here as well. As the three of us precariously began to walk out, we were suddenly startled with the sound of rustling hay from one of the stables. The three of us simultaneously chambered a bullet in our rifles and walked back toward the stable. Immediately, we began fishing around in the hay, and lo and behold, a Negro man, woman, and little girl rose from the stable floor with their hands held up high in the air. We immediately approached and frisked the three of them for any weapons.

"Please don't shoot my family. We mean no harm."

"Who are you? Why the hell are you hiding in this barn?"

"My name is Henry Jackson. This is my wife, Geraldine, and our four-year-old daughter, Louise. We escaped from our home in Garrett County, Maryland, three months ago. One evening, while we were all sleeping, the Gestapo showed up in our neighborhood, forcibly barging into people's homes and arresting them while they slept. Fortunately, my aunt called me on the telephone and warned us. The three of us took off on foot in the middle of the night, running toward the mountains. Once we entered the forest, we walked all night and the next two days in the pouring rain and crossed the border to Somerset County, Pennsylvania.

"We stumbled onto this place apparently after the Gestapo suddenly pulled out. My family stayed in the barn, while I snooped around the house. I went through the filing cabinets and saw a thick file containing lists of names of residences in Somerset and neighboring counties. Two days after we arrived here, a Nazi convoy showed up with a large truck and moved out equipment, maps, and emptied the filing cabinets in the house. Thank God, there was nothing in the barn, and the convoy never came back this way. My family and I have been living in this barn for three months.

"You are literally the first non-Nazi human life we've seen the entire time we have been in hiding. Sometimes, horses will stop by and graze for a while. Unfortunately, when I try to get close, they get spooked and run off. I would assume these horses were from some of the neighboring farms in the area."

"Actually, yes they were. Pretty much all these farms had horses at one point. The Nazis probably freed them due to the fact that there's no one to take care of them. We too, would like to catch some of them," Antonio and Dieter both knotted and smiled in agreement.

"My family and I were fortunate—when the Nazis left the farm, they left food in the kitchen and the pantry down in the cellar. However, we've just recently depleted all provisions. I'm a family physician by profession, and I have no weapons for hunting. My wife and daughter are hungry. We are desperate. I was actually considering returning back to our hometown. This is why I've been trying to catch a horse. My wife and daughter cannot possibly make the trip back to Garrett County on foot again.

"I'm grateful we were spared. The Nazis split up Negro families. The women and children are shipped back to Africa, and the men are drafted into the Nazi army. Even though I'm probably the only licensed Negro physician in the state of Maryland, I too would be drafted and, honestly, would make a terrible soldier. I don't have the physical strength or endurance.

"My family and I mean no one any harm. All we're trying to do is survive. Our entire family has lived in America for over two hundred years. We are American citizens. God willing, if you can find it in your hearts to spare us, I promise we'll gladly be on our way and you'll never see us again."

"I apologize if we frightened you. We also mean you no harm. My name is Sven, this is Dieter, and that's Antonio. Trust me, we all have a story as well. As one of our highly respected group members recently stated, 'We are all in this sinking ship together.' I suggest you come back with us and join our little commune. Once we get back to town, Miss Helen and Craig will prepare a meal for the three of you. Presently, our commune consists of seven others, two of whom are children. Grace is six years old, and Tommy is eight. Grace and Tommy are siblings, whose parents were taken away by the Nazis, along with the entire townsfolk. We have reclaimed the town of Meyersdale and have been diligently working to secure it.

"The reason the three of us are having this conversation with you right now is very innocent. We anxiously decided to assess the neighboring farms and bring back any cows or livestock we find. I suggest the three of you accept our invitation and join us. Trust me, if you go back home, you don't know what you would be walking into. I would assume you're going to find a ghost town there as well.

We have plenty of food and water and are more than happy to share whatever we have. Guaranteed, this is a blessing for us all. Having a doctor among us surely will give us peace of mind. We've been very fortunate that no one has gotten sick or critically wounded, with the exception of a little surgery I performed on Antonio, who hasn't settled his bill yet."

"Cute, Sven, check's in the mail."

"Perhaps your wife can help Miss Helen with lessons for the children. They haven't had any schooling for six months. This is something we need to enforce for the children, a more regimented, civilized way of life. We have to get our lives back to some sort of normalcy."

As I glanced at my watch and realized there were three hours left before the sun was going to set, we decide our inspection of the remaining three farms should be postponed for another day. I desperately wanted to get back to Ackermann's dairy farm as quickly as possible, considering none of us were cowboys and knew anything about herding cows. This endeavor might end up taking a considerable amount of time to get these creatures, who weighed at least a thousand pounds each, into town. In addition, we had to take the long route back to pick up the Enigma coding machine. Once we could get the cows into town, Magdalina could show us how to milk them, so Grace, Tommy, and Louise would drink fresh milk tomorrow.

"Dieter, Antonio, first thing in the morning, we'll grab Craig, and the four of us can extend the southwest end of the security perimeter fence. We can put up the remaining five-foot barbed-wire fence to enclose a large area for the cows. With any luck, they'll begin breeding so we can have an abundant supply of beef. This is payday, gentlemen. We've added a doctor and twelve cows to our little commune."

With much effort in the darkness of the night, thankfully, we were able to herd the cows through the security fence and pick up the wood planks, which we used to cross over the trench by the light of a full moon. Henry and Geraldine were exhausted; they took turns carrying their four-year-old daughter for almost the entire trip. Miss

Helen graciously reheated the open-dish chicken potpie she made for supper earlier this evening.

"Miss Helen, once again, kudos for another appetizing meal. How's our squirrel holding up?"

"Oh my goodness, Sven, you know darn right well that was chicken."

"I'm only pulling your leg, dear," I jumped up and threw my arms around her and hugged her tight.

Once supper was through, we decided the Jackson family should spend the night in Antonio's and my room; after all, there were three beds, thanks to Paul, who was rotting away with the other rubbish. Antonio and I would spend the night in the parlor. Tomorrow morning, after we had all eaten a hot breakfast, we would get the Jacksons settled into the two-bedroom apartment next to Craig's Diner, then we would spend the rest of the day securing a home for the cows.

"Antonio, when exactly are your guys coming?"

"I spoke to the Mr. Luciano a couple days ago. They should be here sometime next week."

"I hate to be the bearer of bad news, but we have another priority project, something that we all neglected to think of."

"What's that, Sven?"

"We need to set up a location for your guys to lodge. Since we have no idea how many are coming for this meeting, this potentially presents a challenge. Once the cows are taken care of, we should check the apartments directly across the street, the apartment above the Jackson's place, and the one on the left side of the diner above the liquor store. If a lot of men show up, at least we can keep the group together."

After three long grueling days, the cow project was close to completion. As the rest of the group was diligently finishing up, Craig and I decided to walk across the street and check out the apartments that sit above Carol's Boutique. Craig once again showed off his talents with picking the lock on the front door, allowing us entry into the spacious two-bedroom second-floor apartment.

"Craig, my friend, I just realized you have a God-given talent other than fishing. With your lock-picking skills, you can definitely give up your day job and become a professional burglar."

"Very funny, Sven. What's next, you going to tell me my coffee stinks?"

"If I did that, I'd be shooting myself in the foot my friend."

After walking around the apartment, Craig and I decided that this place was perfect. It was a large two-bedroom with a kitchen, dining room, parlor, and water closet. Since guys wouldn't usually care about privacy or how the place would look like, we would move out the furniture in the parlor and dining room and gut the kitchen, then move in as many beds that would fit comfortably.

"This is great, Craig. If the upstairs apartment is the same as this one, we can probably fit twenty-five guys just in this building alone. Let's go upstairs and check it out. We need to get this project off of our to-do list."

Craig picked the lock once again with ease and opened the door to the rancid smell of death. While gagging, we both pulled our shirts up over our noses and walked around the apartment, scoping the place out. As we squeamishly walked into the master bedroom, a half-decayed elderly man and woman were lying in their bed, both dead from self-inflicted gunshot wounds to the head.

"Oh my god, Sven, that's Mike and Ivy Quinn. They were the sweetest couple alive. When my mother died, Ivy came over every night for two weeks with a care package for supper because she knew I wasn't eating. The two of them would stop by my place a couple times a week, checking up on me. These two were the type to give the shirt off their backs to someone in need. This is horrible."

"This is really sad. I'm sorry for your loss. I assume they felt killing themselves was better than joining the Nazis. Craig, let's wrap what's left of their bodies in the blankets, take them out back, and bury them. We should also take their mattress out back and burn it. There's far too much blood."

"Sure, just give me one minute. I want to open the windows and air the place out."

"Good idea, Craig, I'll help."

The two apartments across the street were completed and set up perfectly within four days. The Italians still hadn't arrived; however, I felt much better knowing that we were prepared for their arrival. It was now the second week of May, and our new priority project was the cleanup and cultivation of the properties where the five buildings once sat. Miss Helen and Geraldine spent every day schooling the three children, while the rest of us, including Dr. Henry, worked painstakingly preparing the five lots for a May 15 planting. With all the new bodies we've accumulated, our food supply was beginning to quickly dwindle.

Tomorrow morning, Dieter, Antonio, Craig, and I were going to venture back up to the cave and retrieve the cooler of meat, which had been frozen for months. Erich, Henry, and the girls would attend to the spring planting. Thankfully, there was a large variety of vegetable seeds at the hardware store. While the four of us were up the mountain, we planned to spend a couple of days small-game hunting and fishing. Unfortunately, bear was still too early.

After three days, we hunted fifteen cottontail rabbits weighing roughly three pounds each with our bows and ten squirrels. Craig also had luck with fishing; he caught five trout. We all agreed to save the rabbit for the first day the Italians arrive. Between Geraldine and Miss Helen, they both had exceptional culinary talents and were quite an asset to our commune. I was sure they would prepare a scrumptious rabbit supper to make a good impression to the Italians.

So far, I hadn't mentioned my concerns to the group about Hitler's last radio broadcast. This conversation would take place when the Italians arrive. I was fearful once the six-month registration deadline for all citizens had come and gone, the Nazis would begin traveling from town to town in search of nonconformists. The Nazis might have abandoned Elk Lick township and the southwest corner of Somerset County; however, they were out there somewhere. I assumed they had moved to the larger towns with a larger population and not as rural as it is here. Chambersburg, Hagerstown, and Harrisburg were the three largest areas northeast in route to the city of Philadelphia. I assumed that entire area was Nazi occupied by now.

The next morning, we woke to thunderstorms with torrential rainfall. After breakfast, we all went back upstairs and lounged around the parlor with our coffee and turned the radio on. Although it was mid-May, Antonio started a small fire in the fireplace to warm the apartment from the dampness of the rain. The only news broadcasted on the radio these days were spoken in German. The public was warned that there were only five months left to register and get branded.

As I watched the children playing peacefully on the floor with Magdalina and Christine, suddenly we were alarmed with the sound of a horn. It almost sounded like a child's bicycle horn. Apprehensively, we jumped up and grabbed the riffles, which were stored seven feet off the ground on top of a large antique chest that sat in Craig's parlor. Christine and Magdalina each had a loaded rifle and a loaded pistol in the holsters buckled around their waist. The girls and children stayed behind, while the rest of us ran down the steps and out the front door in split speed. As we ran down Main Street toward the entrance of town in the direction of the sound, we noticed nine men standing next to three large 1931 Ford Coca Cola delivery trucks. They were holding umbrellas and were dressed in expensive tailored suits. Each truck had a large swastika displayed on the passenger and driver doors and one on the hood. As we stood with our rifles aimed, Antonio immediately ran up further to the gate.

"Hold on, guys, drop your weapons. These guys are the Italians we've been waiting for."

Antonio and I opened the gate and placed the four wooden planks over the trench, allowing the men to cross. Once the men were inside the barbed-wire barricade, the three trucks drove in as well. Antonio and I lifted the wooden planks back up and placed them inside the fence and locked the gate. We quickly walked back into the diner soaked to the bone. Craig started another pot of coffee, while Dieter started our first fire in the newly constructed fireplace in the diner.

"Antonio, are you going to introduce us to your friends?"

"Sure, right away, Mr. Luciano."

"This is Joe Bruno, the boss of the Philadelphia crime syndicate, and Charlie Luciano, the crime boss for New York. The rest of the big muscles are Vito Genovese, Frank Costello, Benjamin Siegel, and Albert Anastasia. As far as these other gentlemen, they'll have to introduce themselves. I apologize I don't know who they are. Some of them are bosses of the other New York families."

"How did you get involved with my uncle?" Christine said lovingly to Antonio, with a gleam in her eyes that could be seen from miles away.

"Five years ago, I was looking for work and moved to New York for a very short time. Mr. Luciano took me under his wing and adopted me into the New York family. A few months later, I met Mary, and we married shortly after. Amazingly, Mary's family was also from Elk Lick. Her father was ill and needed help on the farm. I received permission from Mr. Luciano to move back to Somerset, under the condition that I would help the Philadelphia family when needed and travel back to New York on larger jobs."

"So who do you work for?"

"Christine, technically, my boss is Charlie Luciano. However, the Philadelphia and the five New York families all work well together. This is why I wanted to get all this power together and come up with a plan. Mr. Luciano, not to get off the subject, we have a surprise for you."

"Antonio, please call me Charlie or Lucky. We'll probably be spending a lot of time together, so let's be on a first-name basis. So what's this surprise?"

"I want to introduce you to your niece, Christine Luciano," Antonio said proudly, with a big grin on his face.

"Wow, the last time I saw you, I think you were three years old. You've certainly grown into a beautiful young woman. I'm happy to get acquainted with you. I just wish it was under different circumstances. I heard about your father's death, and I apologize I didn't attend the funeral. Unfortunately, I was incarcerated when he died."

"Mr. Luciano, how in God's name were you able to travel from New York into Elk Lick without being arrested, and where did you get those trucks?"

"Actually, Sven, believe it or not, it was fairly easy. Meyer Lansky has an excellent hand for forgery. We all have fictitious registry papers, birth certificates, work papers, and identity cards. We're all Italian Americans, with only one European heritage and qualify under Hitler's new laws. However, the monkey wrench is once you're registered, they're able to keep tight tabs on your whereabouts and you're required to report to the local courthouse once a month for assessment. Each person is assigned work according to their previous job status. If the authorities feel the work is viable to a better society, then you're permitted to continue working in your field. Although, if they deem the work you performed unworthy of this new society, then you're assigned a new career. I'm sure the Nazis would feel our careers of bootlegging, number racketeering, gambling, and murder undeserving of their precious master plan.

"All the bosses and big muscle have also forfeited from registering, which allows us the power to move about the country easier. The nine of us have work papers stating that we're Coca Cola salesman traveling about the country, visiting food markets and factories with samples of Coke to allegedly entice new business. We stole the trucks in Chicago and had new plates made. Fortunately, at the borders, the Nazi guards favorably passed the trucks through. We all have Hitler's branding on our left forearms, compliments of an Italian artist member of the Chicago family, which we literally have to touch up every two weeks. Once this mess is over, we'll be the only Americans without a swastika tattoo."

"Well, not quite. None of us have that redicious garbage on our arms either."

"Then Sven, that calls for a celebration later."

"That sounds like a good plan of action to me, Mr. Luciano. However, please go on with your story."

"Presently, we have members of the families in Philadelphia, New York City, Chicago, and Atlantic City. These four major families are presently enlisting additional recruits into the various families for more support. I must say, Sven, I'm very impressed with what you all have done in town. This is quite an accomplishment in a short amount of time. Antonio informed me of your recent battle with seventy-five Nazis and three army tanks. I'm very impressed, not only with your combat but survival knowledge as well. It's a shame you weren't born a dago."

"No, I'll let my best friend have the honor of the token dago amongst us."

"It's a good thing Antonio likes you so much, that little comment could get you whacked. However, all kidding aside, you have all been living in seclusion for a year and aren't up to date with the current events. Since most Americans still don't know the German language, it's impossible for Hitler to communicate without a translator. I assume he found it easier to have leaflets printed in English and dropped from biplanes in all the cities and large towns, keeping us abreast of the new Nazi laws and restrictions.

"Small towns, especially in rural areas, farms, and housing developments have been abandoned, and the people have been moved into the cities and larger towns. America is so large that perhaps Hitler is having difficulties controlling the people if they're widely spread out. The county of Somerset and the entire distance from here to Harrisburg are ghost towns. The people were shuffled off to Harrisburg, Chambersburg, and Hagerstown. Then the same thing was done from Harrisburg to Philadelphia. People are literally living in squander in tents that the Nazis supplied. They've all been promised a new home within a year. Row homes are being constructed as we speak in the suburbs of these larger towns. The day of owning a single home, especially a house with any kind of acreage, is obsolete.

"The city of Philadelphia has taken hundreds of dislocated people. Within one year, the Negroes were shipped to Africa while the Jews were shipped to South America. The entire city no longer has any one of the Negro or Jewish population. The younger Negro and Jewish men have all been drafted into the German army and reside at the various military compounds set up throughout the states. With the elimination of the hundreds of Negroes and Jews, this has allowed room for the dislocated Aryans and level 1 Germans.

"Hitler has also enforced a barter system for families and trade for larger companies. Barter and trade vouchers have been printed and have replaced paper money. American paper currency is no longer honored and is being destroyed. All coins are melted down and are being replaced with the Nazi *Reichsmark*. Food ration cards have been issued to families upon registration. Therefore, if you don't register, you're not able to purchase food from any of the markets. Restaurants are set up strictly with the barter method. The Hitler brother's obviously thought their five-year plan thoroughly and very meticulously. It's a good thing I own a restaurant in New York City and Joe owns a deli in Philadelphia, or we all would have starved to death."

"Mr. Luciano, I'm flabbergasted with what the Hitler brothers have achieved in a year."

"Yah, I know, Sven. The American way of life, as we all know it, is a thing of the past. But that's only half of it. All private cars and trucks have all been confiscated. Public transportation and bicycles are the only methods that are permitted for citizens. Company and delivery trucks, ambulances, school and public buses, along with Nazi vehicles, are the only methods of transportation permitted on the highways.

"Adolf Hitler has made it abundantly clear he's not interested in foreign trade. The master plan is that New Germany will be the largest, strongest, and wealthiest independent nation on the earth, with a perfect German-Aryan race and no mongrels. In five years, the American people and our great nation will be completely converted to German, with Adolf Hitler continuing to be the *Führer und Reichskanzler*. The next five years will be devoted to Mexico uniting with New Germany. Gerhard Hitler will become the *SS-obergruppenfüehrer* of Mexico, and Heinrich Himmler will be promoted to *Reichfüehrer-SS* of Mexico.

"Farmers and their families were evacuated from their homes once the crops were harvested. Hitler's plan is to tear down all the private farms in every county and construct new government-owned-and-operated dairy and crop farms, consisting of thousands of acres. Any families who own farms under the new law have donated their land to the government. Work papers have been issued at registration for all farmers to report to the new government-owned farms and work for barter vouchers.

"From what the leaflets have indicated, there's to be one enormous government-owned farm per county and city. The acreage size of these government farms will be determined by the population of each area. We noticed while driving up this way they have leveled out all the smaller townships and counties, which is literally thousands and thousands of miles of potential farmland. They may not venture this far unless they come from the southwest Schwerin, formerly known as Maryland border, and extend Schwerin into Hamburg, formerly Pennsylvania, for the farmland. We should probably take a day and cross over the border and get a better geographical assessment of the area."

"Yes, I agree, Mr. Luciano," I said in a kiss butt sort of way. I think for the time being, I'll keep my wise ass comments to myself. I really don't feel like getting whacked.

"I must say, gentlemen, I'm very concerned with you making your home here in town, considering it's so predominately visible from the air. The Nazis have already been here once for a planned attack on ground—it's only a matter of time before they come back to complete the job. It makes more sense to send aircraft overhead and drop a couple of bombs so the entire town, along with those cows, is annihilated in one quick swoop."

"Mr. Luciano, thank you for bringing us up to speed. Even though we have a radio, which is tuned into the news every day, none of us knew the severity of the events taking place in Pennsylvania, or should I say, Hamburg."

"No problem, Sven. I explained to Antonio last week, once we arrive I would enlighten your group, and then we could put forth full effort into a solution. Unfortunately, this five-year plan isn't only in the state of Hamburg. From what I understand, these events are taking place throughout the entire country."

"Now that we're all together, I also have concerns that I've purposely held off addressing with the others until this meeting."

"What's that, Sven?"

"I also believe the Nazis will come back. So far, we have survived a year, with Magdalina and I both having a very high price on both our heads and with only one fatality. I believe the only reason the Nazis haven't returned to Somerset is because of a man named Paul Touvier. He was a French Nazi traitor and a spy. Foolishly, we accepted him into our group, and two weeks later, I sliced his throat from ear to ear. Which reminds me, Henry, are you and your wife and four-year-old daughter Nazi spies too?"

"Oh my god, Sven, no, of course, not!"

"Henry, lighten up, I'm only kidding. Anyway, I honestly believe the only reason the Nazis haven't conducted an aerial attack is because they believe Paul is still alive. From what Erich has informed us of this guy, he apparently was very valuable to the Gestapo. Days before you gentleman arrived, Dieter, Antonio, and I found this decoding machine hidden behind the Nazi compound barracks. We all witnessed Paul suspiciously hanging out in that area. Obviously, he was communicating with the Nazis through this machine. Dieter and Erich are presently studying it to get a better understanding on how to decode it and send an encryption to the Gestapo. I believe that Paul Touvier is the only reason we haven't been attacked and are still breathing. Obviously, our luck will change at some point. I feel it's in our best interest to send a bogus encryption from Paul Touvier to the Nazis and buy some time."

BACK TO THE BASICS

"I must say, Miss Helen and Geraldine, that was quite an enjoyable rabbit supper the two of you prepared for the Italians' first evening with us. I would think we just made a great first impression. Craig, when this is all over, you know you're going to have to hire our two famous five-star chefs here."

"Oh, Sven, you're such a sweet boy and so full of cow cookies. When it comes to your stomach, I think you'll eat just about anything."

"Gee, thanks, Miss Helen, I love you too. I didn't eat Dieter's bobcat."

"Oh, sweet Jesus, I'm so sorry. I was just kidding."

"Miss Helen, please excuse my best friend's weird sense of humor. I sometimes think he grew up with the apes. He seems to lack human social skills."

"Yah, buddy, at least I don't look like one. Anyway, I suggest we all adjourn upstairs to the parlor and get down to business because Antonio and I could do this all night long."

The bosses followed us upstairs, while the rest of the Italians went back to their apartments to get settled in. Magdalina and Geraldine tucked the three children in for the evening and read them the next chapter in the book, *Black Beauty* by Anne Sewell. Amazingly, after a couple of hours tinkering around, Dieter and Erich had finally understood the basics of the Enigma coding machine and had decrypted the last message. We all agreed, first thing tomorrow, on behalf of Paul Touvier, we'd send a fraudulent, embellished story and keep this sham up for as long as we could get away with it. Once the Nazis figure out Paul was no longer breathing, this would put more fuel to the fire and make the price on our heads much greater.

We had to make sure the entire group had full comprehension of how dangerous it was to continue living in town. Considering we had all put many hours of painstaking labor into securing a safe and comfortable home, it would be extremely difficult to leave these comforts and start living in the cave again. When the Nazis finally get around to gracing us with their presence in Elk Lick for a second time, this entire town would be demolished along with the bombed-out compound and the five farms that spread from the compound to the Schwerin border.

"Can I address the committee?"

"Yes, of course, Sven. What's on your mind?"

"Once we get situated for the third time, we should send another encryption to the Gestapo from Paul, this time stating there was an altercation, prompting him to blow up the diner with grenades, killing us while we slept. Once this encryption goes out, we shall literally blow up Craig's diner with some of the grenades we have in storage. I hate the thought of this. I don't even want to say it, let alone think it, but we have to stage this façade and make it look as authentic as possible. We should dig up eight bodies from the graveyard down the street and scatter them throughout the building. If the Nazis believe we're all dead, then obviously, they won't be in pursuit of us any longer.

"I propose Magdalina, Christine, Miss Helen, Erich, Geraldine, and the children return to the cave. We can take items that'll be needed from town and haul them up the mountain. A single mattress for everyone will fit, especially if we build platforms for the mattresses resembling bunk beds. Blankets, linens, and some of heavy winter clothing that we've accumulated should all be schlepped up as well. We'll pack up all the food, the children's toys, and a good supply of weaponry and ammunition. Our new and improved Miss Helen's sleigh will come in handy for the long haul to the cave. We can pick up some wheels from the hardware store and rig them on to the bottom. This sleigh will help with transporting all this stuff much easier and quicker. Since this is still a democracy among our group, we need to cast a vote."

"Okay, Sven, does this vote include us as well?"

"Yes, of course, Mr. Luciano. We're all in the same boat," and I don't want to get whacked, I said with a little chuckle under my breath.

Thankfully, everyone agreed that this plan was practical. Surprisingly, Henry volunteered to go with the rest of us and join the

Italian Mafia Resistance to help us obliterate the Nazis. We certainly had our work cut out for us, considering Luciano and the other bosses would like to be underway in three weeks. This certainly wasn't the first time we had had an extremely tight deadline, and I was sure it won't be the last, either.

First things first, we rigged the sleigh with wheels and loaded it with crates of ammunition and weapons that we confiscated from the compound a year ago. We made three trips over the next three days to my father's farm. Out back of the house was a very well-camouflaged storm shelter that he and a few friends dug out and built in the early 1920s during the Prohibition years.

My father originally used the cave's location as a distillery. He had a large stile set up nestled in the boulders next to the cave on the other side of the waterfall, camouflaged by the dense forest. He and Antonio's father would bring us up with them when we were young boys from time to time to help them with the moonshine. The four of us literally would live in the cave weeks on end. The hooch shelter was originally designed for the sole purpose of storing large amounts of moonshine to be sold at a later date. This was how my father and Mr. Sabatino made their living during the Depression years. The shelter this time would be utilized for safely storing extra ammunition and weaponry. This would prevent our inventory from being seized by the enemy and would allow anyone of us accessibility when needed.

We left two large crates of assorted guns, grenades, rocket launchers, and two crates of ammunition back in town for the purpose of smuggling these items into Rostock. Some of this armament would be added to the secret storage room inside the wine cellar of Luciano's restaurant. He presently had a large supply of Thompson submachine guns and ammunition stored there. All the Italian families are collecting and stock piling as many guns and ammunition as they can get their hands on and are hiding them in very creative places.

We unloaded the crates of Coca Cola from the three trucks and built a wood plank floor overtop of the existing original truck floor. In between the two floors we laid out as many weapons and ammunition as possible and then sealed the second floor over top. We then loaded the crates of Coca Cola back into the trucks for the facade. Luciano brought two tailored suits, one for Craig and the other for Antonio, who would become Coca Cola salesmen as well. He also brought three Nazi uniforms for Dieter, Frank, and I to wear since we could speak fluent German. Dieter and I were going to pose as Nazis traveling with the Coca Cola salesmen, under the false pretense of observing their operation. We were also given the forged appropriate paperwork to complement our acting roles. With a heavy heart, I placed Frank's uniform between the two floors alongside the weapons.

"Henry, I know you want to join us. However, Luciano didn't know about you. Therefore, you weren't included in this equation. No disrespect, but the color of your skin will make it very difficult to travel with you. Will you please consider staying behind with the others and help Erich see to their safety?"

"Sven, I'm sorry, I don't mean to be insubordinate. This is my home as much as it's yours. My family has lived in America since the 1700s. How long has your family lived in America, twenty years? I have every right to lay my life on the line to defend America as you."

"Oh my god, Henry, of course, you do. I apologize—I meant no harm. I'll personally speak with Luciano and see what we can come up with to change the original plan and safely include you as well."

The only practical plan was to have one of the "Nazis" stay at the back of the truck with Henry, preferably Dieter. On account of Dieter's German accent, if we're stopped and questioned, his speaking role would be greater than the few words I might have to speak. I know the language well; however, I was born in America and never picked up the accent from my parents. The façade was to let Dieter have a pistol drawn on Henry, pretending he captured a Negro runaway and took him prisoner. At the borders, the trucks would be inspected, and if we were randomly stopped on the highway, at least we would have a believable scenario.

Luciano had one other Negro who recently enlisted into the Italian Mafia Resistance in Rostock. This new version of the plan was how we would transport both these men to our battle sites. Temporarily, we had to leave Henry behind in Elk Lick. Once we arrive in Rostock, Meyer Lansky would forge new papers stating

Sammy Davis Jr. and Henry Jackson were prisoners of the Third *Reich*. *Korporal* Frank Hubert was under strict orders to transport these two prisoners to *Generalfeldmarschall* Wilhelm Keitel. Lansky would also have to forge new papers for Dieter changing his name to Frank Hubert. Frank was dead; there was no way of tracing him. This was a very important detail under the circumstances—Dieter's late father, Heinrich Mueller, former head of the Gestapo, was well known and respected within the Nazi regime. We had to change Dieter's name in its entirety to keep a low profile. A low-ranking corporal by the name of Frank Hubert would blend in and not raise any eyebrows.

———

Now that my father's hooch shelter was full of weapons and the trucks were already transformed, we had two weeks to get the rest of the group moved back into the cave and set up. Dieter and I agreed we'd take turns training Craig, Erich, Henry, and Geraldine on marksmanship, both with guns and bows. Magdalina and Christine had already been trained and had proven their abilities to hunt, fish, and defend themselves. This alleviated my conscience and made it easier to leave the rest of the group behind.

Erich had demonstrated real promise, which was impressive, considering he had never been an outdoors type of guy. His entire adult life had been spent in labs, exercising his brain cells, and most of his childhood as well. Antonio, Dieter, and I were beginning to feel much better with our decision to join the Italian Mafia Resistance and try to recapture and restore the United States of America.

"Antonio, I think you and I should walk down to the men's apparel store and retrieve the cash and coins we buried."

"No problem, boss, but what can we possibly do with it?"

"I'm not sure. From everything Luciano has told us, I cannot imagine that American currency still has any value or what purpose it may serve in the world. However, for some strange reason my gut is telling me we should hang on to it and keep it close by."

"Sven, perhaps we should keep the currency for a souvenir. It may actually be worth something greater someday."

"Yah, Antonio, you may have point. We may literally possess the last American currency. Speaking of American currency, I wonder if the Nazis were able to pilfer the US Bullion Depository building in Fort Knox, considering the Fort Knox military compound was bombed and destroyed. Also, if Hitler has knowledge of the Federal Reserve Bank in Manhattan and is aware of the underground vault, this could be devastating to our country's wealth. If these idiots aren't careful, they can bring devastating financial disaster to the entire universe.

"This equation is confusing, considering Hitler has enforced the barter and trade system and has abolished the trade of currency within the country. I would assume the Nazi *Reichsmark* must be on reserve for foreign exchange. This must be part of Hitler's plan of becoming the strongest and wealthiest nation in the world. He is literally hoarding American, German, and several other European nations' gold, precious metals, jewels, and anything of monetary value. I take my hat off to Hitler, his plan was well thought out. It's ingenious how he utilized his brother in America years before he began to execute his plan. He gave Gerhard one of the key roles in this operation. Hitler astonishingly was able to confiscate and remove European wealth a little at a time throughout the years undetected."

"Sven, I think we should leave the American currency with the girls for safekeeping. It may become a souvenir someday, but if America is restored, we'll be one step ahead. We might even be considered entrepreneurs."

"You amaze me, your brain is always in the clouds," I looked Antonio and smiled with approval.

Every day, rain or shine, we loaded the new and improved Miss Helen's sleigh. First trip was for extra weapons and ammunition to be added to our existing inventory stored in the cave, then another two trips with mattresses for everyone. The fourth trip was for clothes, linens and blankets, toys, and all the pharmaceuticals we were able to salvage after the drugstore was destroyed. The last trip was the food and meat we had at the diner and Sam's Market, along with a couple bottles of vodka and whiskey. We left behind enough food for the Italians and for the four of us for the next couple of days before we leave for Rostock. We were not leaving anything behind other than the cows; we decided to allow them the freedom to roam the entire town. There was plenty of grass for the cows to graze and water in the trowel we built. As long as it was safe, the girls plan to travel back down the mountain once a week, check on the cows, and milk them for the children. When their diets would begin begging for beef, this plan would allow the group another option along with their hunt. One cow should last them a couple of months, along with any wild game accumulated.

In our travels, we schlepped up two additional large coolers that we took from the hardware store. This gave the gang three meat coolers, which fitted nicely on the ledge behind the waterfall. I had instructed Magadalina that within two months, the weather would once again start to get cooler. They should then begin hunting and fishing in large quantities to get prepared for the winter, stockpiling meat in all three coolers. Magdalina, Christine, and Erich had been thoroughly trained, with emphasis on black-bear hunting. A black-bear is a very dangerous predator and can stalk and kill a man within minutes. Everyone had been properly trained and had full knowledge of survival techniques to endure another winter in the cave.

"Henry, once we're finished in Rostock, and the new paperwork has been completed along with the changes we made to the original plan, we'll come back with the trucks and pick you up. Magdalina, I'm proudly and humbly handing over my role and title as the group's commandant to you. You have as much knowledge and instinctual survival sense as I do, and I feel it's in the group's best interest to entrust it to you. I don't know what the future has in store for the Italian Mafia Resistance. However, once we're able to secure a better location, you have my word the four of us will be back for every last one of you.

"Dieter, Antonio, Craig, and I have to leave while we still have time to get down the mountain and rejoin the Italians before pitch dark. We're going to take all day tomorrow and clean up the commune, destroy anything we don't want the Nazis to get their hands on, and dismantle and destroy the two army tanks. Before leaving for Rostock the following day, as planned, we'll throw a couple of stick grenades into Craig's building and stage the façade. Wednesday morning before sunrise, we'll leave Rostock, and in eight hours, if everything goes according to plan, we'll be arriving in Elk Lick to pick up Henry. Antonio, hurry up and say your good-byes to Christine. We really have to get going."

"All right, boss, give me ten minutes. Christine, follow me please."

"Antonio, just ten minutes. We have to be on our way," I said sternly to my love sick, best friend, with only sentiment in my heart.

Christine and Antonio quickly walked outside hand and hand to a beautiful sunny, warm early afternoon. Ten minutes later, Dieter, Craig and I said our farewells and began to climb down the rock staircase, for our journey back down the mountain. I immediately walked over to the riverbed, where Christine and Antonio are sitting engaged in a lover's conversation, all googly-eyed.

"Buddy, I'm sorry, we have to go now."

The four of us immediately began to traipse back down the mountain in complete silence.

"Are you all right, my friend?"

"Yah, Sven, this was very difficult this time. Christine was extremely upset. I tried to calm her the best I could, however, that was a very difficult task, considering I'm also terrified of the unknown. There's a small part of me that believes this might be the last time I see her."

"Do not, under any circumstances, say that again. You will, return to her," I said very angrily.

"Alright Sven, point well made. However, I of course, stifled my negative feelings and didn't put my big foot in my mouth this time. Realizing precious time was quickly running out, I pulled the ring from my pocket that Luciano graciously took off his pinky finger, and gave to me for his niece."

"Wow, what a step-up-guy. Luciano may be feeling some sort of immortality at this point as well."

"Yah, probably. Anyway, after asking Christine a second time to marry me, I put the ring on her left finger. After another passionate kiss, once again, I heard myself saying the same words, trying to convince her that I would return and, in the same breath, probably trying to convince myself as well. I have to tell you, this heartfelt moment will stay with me the rest of my life."

"Very good then. I must say Antonio, I take my hat off to Luciano, for his generosity and good sense. Although, it's now time, for business at hand. Guys, let's shake a leg, we're going to run out of daylight soon."

None of us uttered another sound for the rest of the trip. Unfortunately, I could relate to the pain in Antonio's heart. I was deeply in love with Magdalina, and I knew my best friend Antonio had sensed this. It had been an unspoken thing between the two of us. For some strange reason, after Frank's untimely death, I hadn't had the chutzpah to reveal my feelings to her. There was a constant battle playing out in my head. Frank was a very dear friend, and my loyalties to him has been noble; however, he was not coming back, and under these circumstances, I sincerely questioned my sanity. I wonder what the likeliness was of surviving this ordeal. The odds might not be in our favor this time. I believed beyond a shadow of a doubt, it was our patriotic duty to infiltrate in full force every ounce of our being and give up our lives if necessary for the future of America. However, I also thought we were all feeling pretty much the same—these were perilous, unchartered waters we were about to enter into.

Unfortunately, we should have had ended our reunion earlier. We arrived back at the commune late. After a quick bite to eat, the four of us retired for the evening, totally exhausted from the overwhelming amount of miles we have put on our feet in the last few days. Tomorrow morning, we would rise early and work all day to put our plan into effect. In forty-eight hours, come hell or high water, the Italian Mafia Resistance would be trucking out from the place we had called home for the past six months. The thought of the Nazis possibly coming back and demolishing this place was extremely disturbing. I could tell Antonio, Dieter, and Craig were feeling the same sadness as I.

The next morning, we all woke at the crack of dawn and, for the last time, walked through each and every building, collecting anything we might need in the near future. Although, we were so organized and sensible from the very start, this precaution was more or less a neurotic gesture of overkill. As Antonio, Dieter, Craig, and I began to get closer to the northeast entrance of town and approached the graveyard, my insides went numb. This was the part the four of us had been traumatized over ever since I suggested the idea.

There were eight dead corpses that needed to be dug up. With shovels in hand, the four of us stood staring into space, like the bones were going to suddenly jump up and walk down the street to Craig's Diner. The five Italian fellows who escorted us on this endeavor must have read our minds. Thankfully, without hesitation, they grabbed the shovels and started to dig. This was amazing, as the four of us wimps looked on. These guys, without apprehension, dug up the dead and physically picked them up out of their graves with ease and tranquility I had never witnessed before. For such a horrendous job, it didn't seem to faze these guys whatsoever. The Italians gave the four of us the impression of being pros with this type of work. They carried these poor half-decayed souls down the street and laid them alongside the diner, where the children used to play and where the swing set and sandbox never got built. The four of us walked behind with our heads hung low, like puppy dogs that just did something wrong.

"You guys all right?"

"Yah. Are you, Sven?"

"No, I have a fear this grisly site will be etched into my brain forever."

Surprisingly, Vito, one of our fellow Italian Mafia Resistance partisans made a superb supper, which, if I didn't see it with my own eyes, I would have thought Miss Helen and Geraldine were among us. After supper, we all sat around in the parlor of Craig's apartment, drinking heavily, getting silly, and solving the world's problems at least for one evening. Last week, we made it a priority to hold back one case of liquor for our last evening together in the commune.

However, very stupidly, we had now stayed up half the night getting totally shit-faced with the others. The four us decided to use what little sense we still had and called it a night. We were so going to regret this tomorrow morning. We had eight dead decaying bodies that we still had to deal with first thing in the morning. However, maybe a major hangover would be the ticket to this gruesome task that awaited us.

We all woke at different times and very groggily made it downstairs for Craig's morning coffee. Unfortunately, this morning was not a picture-perfect start. It was dingy, with gray clouds overhead, and the smell of rain was predominant. The morning was actually cooler than usual for this time of year. With these unseasonable temperatures for mid-August, my thoughts quickly went to Magdalina and the others up the mountain, where they probably woke to frost. Every last one of us, including the Italians and the bosses, were red eyed and bushy tongued. Craig made the last of the oatmeal for breakfast, which had now left the dry-goods pantry completely empty. We all scarfed it down and drank fresh milk that Craig extracted from the cows earlier and enjoyed several cups of coffee, finishing up the supply.

Now that we were literally two hours behind schedule, we had to get our butts up from the tables, man up, and proceed with the work at hand. The four of us collected our duffels packed with some clothes and our personal effects and headed out the front door. Craig stood in the center of Main Street, calm with no expression on his face, staring at his life's accomplishments about to be obliterated. Loaded with stick grenades, our five Italian grave robbers proceed to toss them into Craig's world. Within seconds, the place was demolished. Once again, the Italians stepped up to the plate. They walked over to the empty lot and picked up the eight human corpses, tear their bones apart, and strategically placed their remains within the ruins. We all jumped into the three Coca Cola trucks and sadly drive out of town.

THE *FÜHRERBUNKER*

Dieter was in the cab of the first truck, and I was in the second, both of us handsomely decked out in our Nazi uniforms, with revolvers holstered around our waists. Craig and Antonio, who were Coca Cola salesmen, were dressed in very attractive tailored suits, sitting in the cab of the third truck alongside Vito, who was driving.

Our first plan was joining together the different families of the Italian Mafia Resistance and meeting in Berlin heavily armed. The plan was to attack the *Führerbunker* perimeter with the rocket launchers and bazookas to gain entry. Once inside, no mercy would be shown and no prisoners would be taken. Our goal was to kill the Hitler brothers, along with Himmler and every Nazi bastard who would show his ugly face.

Once we were done with a thorough walkthrough of the interior of the *Führerbunker*, and all the devil's children were dead, we would reclaim the building and make it a temporary Mafia headquarters. We'd then respectfully cut down the former president and first lady and bury them somewhere on the grounds. All the Nazi banners and flags would be burned, along with any Nazi paraphernalia. The Italian Mafia Resistance would then drive through Berlin in its entirety and reclaim the district. Along the way, we would recruit more partisans for the restoration of the Unites States of America, one state at a time.

Fortunately, our small group made great time driving through Hamburg toward the Rostock border. Once we arrived at the border, we all had to show our identification and work papers. Dieter and I, the two token Nazis, also had to show identification and our military orders to be present with these trucks. A full search was conducted, and the crates of Coca Cola were inspected closely. Thank God, they didn't unload the crates and inspect the truck floor. I was having heart palpitations the entire time the Nazis were in the truck. I had visions of them finding a flaw in the flooring and ripping it up, exposing our smuggled weapons, bottles of alcohol, and a Nazi uniform. If this scenario in my head had actually played out, our group would have been immediately escorted to the nearest firing squad where we all could have been pushing up daisies by now.

After driving on the road for almost eight hours, we finally arrived at Luciano's Restaurant in Rostock City. The three trucks drove alongside the building and into the back alley, where they'll be parked overnight. Vito walked back into the kitchen accompanied by Craig, and the two men began to prepare a pasta supper. Meanwhile, Luciano went upstairs to his private room. Ten minutes later, he walked downstairs with another Italian gentleman and a Negro man, carrying two expensively tailored pinstriped suits. One suit was for Dieter, and the other for me.

Directly before the group was ready for supper, Luciano introduced the two gentlemen who accompanied him downstairs.

"Sven, Dieter, and Craig, this is Meyer Lansky, our token counterfeit specialist of the Italian Mafia Resistance. And this good-looking fellow is Sammy Davis Jr., who is a personal friend. Antonio, I don't believe you ever met Sammy."

"No, I haven't but pleased to meet you."

"Meyer, Sammy, this is Sven, the guy I was telling you about who masterminded the flaming-arrow assault on the Nazis."

"Mr. Luciano, thanks for the recognition. However, I can't take credit for an old Indian war tactic."

Sammy apparently was an entertainer in Luciano's Restaurant before the Nazis. He went into hiding in a cryptic room downstairs in the wine cellar when the Gestapo came through the city interrogating and canvassing people's homes and businesses looking for Negroes and Jews. To date, Sammy hadn't left the restaurant in over a year. Lansky managed the place in Luciano's absence, while Sammy kept the books upstairs in his private room. When we sat down for supper, we would discuss a new plan that would make it possible for Sammy and Henry to come out of hiding.

After the introductions and a brief synopsis of Sammy's post-Nazi life, Craig and Vito placed a large pot of rigatoni with red sauce and fresh parmesan cheese on the counter, accompanied by a large basket of hot buttered garlic bread. Meanwhile, Vito walked down the cellar steps to grab a couple bottles of red wine from the secret room located in the old wine cellar. This sanctuary was built off the right side of the original cellar, disguised behind a mobile wall of solid black walnut wine shelves. In this room, Luciano had a large supply of Tommy Guns and ammunition, along with cases of wine and various bottles of liquor.

Since the Hitler brothers didn't practice and were opposed to drinking, another law went into effect. Bars and restaurants were no longer permitted to serve alcohol. Nazi patrols had gone through every bar and restaurant, seizing alcohol and destroying it. Liquor stores had been closed permanently, and all inventory destroyed. Unfortunately, the country was in Prohibition for the second time in history. The Hitler brothers had succeeded within one year to successfully change a democracy into a totalitarian nation. I now understand why Luciano insisted we clean out the entire surplus from the liquor store and hide what would fit in my father's hooch shelter. The remaining three crates of liquor were hidden outside the cave where Mr. Sabatino and my father's stile was located once during the first Prohibition years.

Shortly after supper and a cup of coffee, the group decided to turn in for the evening. Our plan was to wake before the sun rises and get out on the road for an eight-hour drive back to Elk Lick to pick up Henry, then an additional three-hour drive to Berlin, where we'll meet up with the other Italian families.

"Antonio, don't you find this disturbing? There was no thought put into our sleeping arrangements. Considering we put so much time and effort into making comfortable accommodations for the bosses and some of the Italian muscle men, I have to say I'm a little taken back."

"Sven, don't take it personally. We can surely withstand a hard, cold floor tonight because tomorrow morning, the four of us have a long hot shower reserved. Let's face it—we haven't had that luxury for over a year."

"You're right. I'll keep my simple ass complaining to myself.

The entire group ended up sleeping on the floor and on the booth seat in the restaurant. Luciano, however, retired to a king-size bed in his private room, while Lansky went to his room to spend the entire evening forging papers.

The next morning, like clockwork, we were on the highway as the sun was just beginning to rise. The temperature was already close to eighty degrees. Apparently, Hitler must have been so preoccupied with destroying the world that he never gave any thought to these half-baked Nazi uniforms for the summer months in America. Our group might not have to travel around the country killing Nazis; these uniforms might do the job quite well.

Once in route, we were randomly stopped one time on the highway by a Nazi patrol in Hamburg, an hour away from Somerset County. These guys spent more time frisking the suits and examining the three trucks high and low, inside and out, than the border patrols. Dieter and I each had a loaded German revolver holstered as part of our costume. As usual, the two of us also had our hunting knives in our boots. If we'd run into any problems, it undoubtedly won't be a fair fight. Two pistols and two hunting knives up against a Nazi patrol normally consisting of six men heavily armed, I think the odds would be against us.

As we start to get close to Elk Lick, we decided to drive one truck into town to retrieve Dr. Jackson for security purposes. The two additional Coca Cola trucks drove off the main road and into a patch of forest by the foot of the mountain to await our return. Thus far, it didn't seem as though there had been any Nazi activity in Somerset. As the truck arrived at the trench around the perimeter, the driver honked the horn three times. Magdalina and Christine anxiously unlocked the gate and run toward the truck.

Once Erich and Henry caught up and the four of them approached the trench, Erich and Henry placed the two wooden planks over the hole, allowing Christine to run over the trench into Antonio's arms. Surprisingly, Magdalina followed suit and ran into mine. We very passionately hugged for a few minutes, while my instincts kicked into high gear. With no warning, I found myself leaning down so our lips could meet. Antonio and I wanted nothing better than to tell Luciano and the Italian Mafia Resistance to leave the two of us behind and go save the world without us. However, somehow, in the heat of passion, we both came to our senses and regained equilibrium.

Inevitably, as every good thing must come to an end, and those joyfully minutes flew by, we once again, for a second time, said our good-byes. Magdalina shocked me, first by running up to me and throwing herself into my arms and hugging me so passionately and then so willfully returning a long, sweet kiss. If I'd die this very second, I'd die with a smile on my face from ear to ear. This was the best day of my life. I had a long, hot shower early this morning and a zealous moment with Magdalina. Maybe I had actually died and gone to heaven.

As planned, Dieter, Henry, and Sammy climbed into the back of the first truck. Antonio and I climbed into the cab of the second, while Vito and Craig sat in the cab of the third. Antonio seemed to get great pleasure from teasing me about the highlight of my life. I should have known better and should have switched with Alfonso and traveled with Craig.

"Antonio, I swear if you say one more word, I will open this door and push you out as the truck is barreling down the highway and leave you for the buzzards."

"Sorry, boss, I love picking on a lovesick fool."

"Thanks, buddy, same to you."

At the Schwerin border, formerly Maryland, another inspection was done. This inspection went surprisingly well, with all emphasis placed on Dieter, Henry, and Sammy. Dieter showed the guards the official military orders typed on authentic Nazi letterhead that stated,

17 AUGUST 1946

KORPORAL FRANK HUBERT OF THE *DEUTSCH ARMEE* IS UNDER STRICT ORDERS TO BRING INTO CUSTODY *DOKTOR* HENRY JACKSON *UND HERR* SAMMY DAVIS TO BERLIN FOR QUESTIONING, IN REFERENCE TO ALLEGATIONS OF DESERTION FROM THE *DEUTSCH ARMEE*. *KORPORAL* HUBERT IS TO REPORT DIRECTLY

TO *GENERALFELDMARSCHALL* WILHELM KEITEL AT THE *FÜHRERBUNKER* IN BERLIN.

Once the guards read the signed orders from Wilhelm Keitel, they immediately stopped the inspection of the trucks and apologetically allowed us to resume on our way. This general field marshall must be some Nazi big brass for the guards to get so flustered. This was a great plan, traveling with two Negro men and two armed Nazis. This scheme might prevent any future intense inspections—hats off to Meyer Lansky's counterfeiting abilities. His talents were overwhelmingly tremendous. To the naked eye, there was no difference between the real Wilhelm's signature and Lansky's. This man might be our ticket to surviving within this Nazi regime.

Three hours later, the trucks were again subjected to another border inspection. With Dieter's fabulous acting debut and Lansky's famous Wilhelm signature, once again, the trucks were urged by nervous guards to pass into Berlin. Our truck parked on Pennsylvania Avenue, a mile down the road from the *Führerbunker*. The second truck parked further down a mile from the bombed-out Capitol building. The third truck was parked on Eleventh Street.

The only Nazis we noticed as we passed the *Führerbunker* were the guards on the inside perimeter fence. Craig, posing as a Coca Cola salesman, stopped a pedestrian walking down Eleventh Street, pretending he was lost and in need of directions to underhandedly gain information.

"Sir, I'm not from around here. Could you please tell me when the curfew begins."

"Sure, there's a sundown curfew and a Nazi patrol that walks the streets every evening. For the security of the *Führerbunker*, 1600 Pennsylvania Avenue is heavily patrolled."

After obtaining this information, we decided to move the other two trucks in front of the bombed-out Capitol building. The other families had been instructed to join us with the trucks once the sun had set and the sky had turned pitch black. We would then pull the floorboards up and allow access to the weapons.

Once again, God was looking down on us. This area where we had parked was deserted and dark. The streetlights that ran for three miles on Pennsylvania Avenue were apparently destroyed along with the Capitol building. This atmosphere would allow us the opportunity to get organized without having any witnesses or arousing suspicion.

Luciano posted a goombah three miles northwest down Pennsylvania Avenue and another in the opposite direction as eagle eyes for Nazi patrols. The rest of us unloaded the crates of Coca Cola and hid them in the debris. With crowbars, we yanked up the bogus floorboards and stacked them next to the crates of Coca Cola for safekeeping. Inside the back of the trucks, we assembled the rocket launchers and bazookas and loaded all weapons with ammunition. Everything was set up and ready to attack the *Führerbunker* within seconds of Luciano's command.

At 0300, the three trucks would slowly drive back down Pennsylvania Avenue in the northwest direction, with a group of Italians heavily armed walking alongside the trucks, hidden and out of view of the guards. The trucks would then park on the opposite side of the street in front of the *Führerbunker*. Once Luciano had given the order, the back doors would simultaneously open. We would all jump out with the rocket launchers and bazookas, while the additional Italians would run from the sides of the trucks with Tommy Guns and stick grenades. The plan was to take the Nazi guardsmen by complete surprise. Once the guardsmen were dead, the Italian Mafia Resistance would then infiltrate the *Führerbunker*.

Craig, Dieter, Antonio, and I sat in the dark among the debris of the Capitol building, patiently waiting for 0300 to get started in our quest. The four of us sat together on the Coca Cola crates reminiscing and desperately trying to stay positive. To pass the time, we pleasantly engaged in conversation of our dreams for the future; however, I prayed we hadn't jinxed ourselves by speaking too soon. After all, there might not be a future for us after this morning. It's strange how your mind works when you're questioning your own immortality.

Like clockwork, at 0300 sharp, the caravan began heading down Pennsylvania Avenue toward the *Führerbunker*. It didn't seem as though the Nazis had any idea we were here, setting the stage for an ambush. Within seconds after the trucks were parked and the ignition turned off, Luciano gave the word, and like a well-oiled machine, the back doors opened and we all jumped out with weapons drawn and saddles blazing. The men hidden alongside the trucks joined the rest of us as we all ran across the street to attack the enemy.

Within seconds, the landscape was changed to horizontal lifelessness. We immediately jumped the fence and split into three groups and run up the lawn to the *Führerbunker*. One group ran to the right side of the building around back, while my group infiltrated the front doors, and the third group ran to the left side around back, killing anything on two legs. As planned, we put on our gasmasks and walked around throwing nerve gas into every room of the *Führerbunker*. Once the smoke settled, we split up once again, armed with Tommy Guns, and conducted a thorough check of the entire building. There were dead Nazis all over the interior and exterior of the building. Within two hours, the entire building from head to toe was rechecked and all the dead inside and out were thrown into a pile out back and set ablaze.

"Dieter, help me look for a ladder. You and I need to cut down President Truman and the First Lady."

"Sure, Sven, I thought I saw a storage closet on this floor. I'm sure there's something in there we can use."

"Great. I saw a perfect place out back to bury them."

Dieter and I, very teary eyed and feeling a bit patriotic, cut them down with our hunting knives and carried Mr. & Mrs. Truman to a well-manicured garden. We proudly bury them with respect and admiration that they both deserved.

The sun was beginning to rise, and as instructed Antonio, Vito, and I drove the trucks back to the destroyed Capitol building and began replacing the bogus flooring. All the weapons that we smuggled into Berlin would be temporarily stored in the *Führerbunker*. We would then immediately begin taking sleep shifts, and at 1700, the four of us had orders to meet with Luciano and the other bosses in the Oval Office to discuss our next plan of action.

Our first attack went extremely well, considering it was our first and our enemy outnumbered us considerably. The Italian Mafia

Resistance encountered eight fatalities, and numerous men wounded. Dr. Jackson, with the assistance of Dieter, Craig, and Sammy, along with several other Italians, were attending to everyone's medical needs. Meanwhile, the three of us completed the bogus flooring in all three trucks, drove them back to the White House, and parked them out back. We all grabbed something to eat and slept for a couple of hours, taking turns in our assigned shifts. The Italians from the Atlantic City family presently had the surveillance shift outside on the grounds perimeter.

We all regrouped at 1700 and joined the bosses in the Oval Office. Hanging on the walls were oil paintings of the Hitler brothers and a large Nazi flag behind the former president's desk. After this meeting, the four us were going to take down all this disgusting paraphernalia and burn it. Oddly, we were all experiencing a once-in-a lifetime, memorable moment in the course of history. The twelve bosses, Antonio, Craig, Dieter, and I proudly sit in the president's Oval Office, drinking a victory glass of smuggled whiskey.

"Sven, this will surely be something to tell the kids someday. How many people can actually say they sat in the Oval Office with friends drinking?"

"I must say, you have a point there, my friend. However, you need to marry Christine and get started on that project right away. You're no spring chicken anymore."

After an hour of discussion, the plan Luciano suggested to the bosses was voted favorably. Early tomorrow, the group would get together and work on securing the White House. Once the White House was secured, we would then clean it up from our victory battle both inside and out. As instructed, we would take the jeeps and armored cars and comb the entire District of Columbia one street at a time. We would have leaflets printed, explaining the fall of the *Führerbunker* and Berlin. The leaflets would also explain that the Italian Mafia Resistance had seized Washington, DC, and the White House, therefore restoring the District of Columbia and giving it back to the American people.

We would also encourage all abled-bodied men to join the resistance. Once the group multiplied, the plan was to use the same strategy that we successfully did here and seize Schwerin from the Nazis. Since neither one of the Hitler brothers were in the White House at the time of the attack, we were assuming they fled through the underground escape tunnels built for the presidents.

An ante of a two-million-dollar price tag on both the Hitler brothers' heads immediately went into effect. With the bosses and the various families pulling together and contributing their blood money, the Italian Mafia Resistance was able to raise the two million dollars. This ante should entice the American people to come out of hiding and forget the brainwashing and threats made upon them. The public needed to form a vigilante and hunt these devils down. The Hitler brothers would be the next two corpses hanging between the pillars in front of the White House for every American to walk by and view.

A VISIT WITH FRANK

 Once the White House was cleaned up and secured, and all the Nazi paraphernalia burned and destroyed, we took the next couple of days conducting a hunting expedition for Nazis. The Italian Mafia Resistance split into several groups. Each group had taken sections of the district, literally gunning down these men in the streets, just as they had done to any noncomplying Americans a year ago. One Italian group was capturing and taking Nazis as prisoners back to the White House and escorting them to a torture room. The bosses relentlessly interrogate them for hours for any information on the location of the Hitler brothers. Craig, Dieter, Antonio, and I stayed together and worked as a team. We all agreed to apply two golden rules: (1) no mercy or prisoners, and (2) always enforce the buddy system. None of us had the stomach nor the willingness to participate in human torture and suffering. These Italians might end up a challenge for the Gestapo after all.

Once the leaflets literally came off the printing press with the ink barely dry, we all took stacks and began driving through the streets, throwing them out to the American people.

To my fellow Americans:

The Italian Mafia resistance has successfully attacked and annihilated the Nazis in the White House. In addition, the resistance has gone door to door checking every inch of the Capitol, conducting a thorough and intensive witch hunt for the enemy. The White House and the District of Columbia have been completely redeemed and given back to the American people.

Any abled-bodied men between the age of eighteen and fifty are encouraged to join the resistance, with the intent of refurbishing one state at a time and rescuing the United States of America from German hands. The next state that the Italian

Mafia Resistance will invade is Maryland. Our group has set up temporary headquarters in the White House until such a time the country is sound and a new president has been elected. Anyone interested in joining the resistance, please report to the White House, formerly the *Führerbunker.*

Within hours, hundreds of men were lining up in front of the White House. The people of the district suddenly became very patriotic, and their excitement was overwhelming. What a relief it must be to finally be rid of the Nazi propaganda and brainwashing. People were literally rejoicing in the streets with the news of the triumph over the Germans and the anticipation of becoming an American citizen once again. Festivity was spreading like a wildfire; the people wanted to fight back for the country we all once loved.

When all was said and done, at the end of the day, the Italians successfully recruited a hundred and fifty new men. Many were turned away for various reasons; however, seventy-five of those men were assigned home-front duty. They were in charge of keeping the peace and security of the district until such a time the US Department of War could bring in professional reinforcements, assuming there was still a viable Department of War.

"I don't know how you guys feel, but I'm concerned."

"Why, Sven? We had a victorious first battle."

"Yes, *first*. Luciano's plan worked well. We successfully reclaimed the White House, and the Nazis were terminated in the district. However, with the Hitler brothers and the Gestapo thugs still alive, the next time around will be more difficult. No doubt the Gestapo will be informed of the Italian Mafia Resistance. Theoretically, they won't know what state will be raided next—that is if an American sympathizer doesn't enlighten the enemy with the information from the leaflets. I believe invading Maryland is going to prove more difficult. For Maryland to be as successful as Washington, DC, we have to take the enemy by complete surprise. Surprise is the key ingredient for success—catch them off guard with their pants down. However, the resistance has just informed the public of our next strategy."

Craig, Dieter, Antonio, and I would be joining Luciano and the rest of the bosses for another meeting in the Oval Office at 1700 to discuss our next plan. This would be a perfect time to voice my concerns and see where that would get me, although the bosses seemed to do things their way. I often wondered why Luciano insisted that the four of us attend these meetings.

"Yah, Sven, what would you have done, our commandant and fearless leader?"

"The operation would have to be entirely different. Troops and weapons would be implemented in the north and south, in an undisclosed area in each of the two zones, while the second operation would locate and destroy enemy compounds in both zones. Once this is accomplished and the zones are ready, then we start our battle in both zones and do exactly as we did in the District of Columbia, one state at a time. Let's face it—the Nazis had the entire country set up ahead of time. Of course, their trump card is the threat of nuclear bombs. However, all that threat accomplished was to secure surrender in fear of detonation."

Our entire group was up all night, trying to come up with a better plan; however, as the sun rose the next morning, the plan was still the same with an exception—we were going to split the three trucks up. One truck would enter Maryland straight through Washington, DC, the second from Winchester, Virginia, and the third would drive into Annapolis. All three trucks would not only be loaded with smuggled weapons, but with the additional armed manpower as well. Once a truck arrived at the border, the suits in the cab would present their identification papers, while the others would come out from the back of the truck and ambush the border patrol officers. If the trucks were stopped randomly in the half-hour drive into Maryland, those Nazis would have same fate in store.

Once a truck was in Maryland, the driver would find a suitable location to park, the weapons would be retrieved and dispersed, and the troops would begin walking the streets in the three different locations, exterminating the enemy and any Nazi sympathizers. Once we had freed the State of Maryland, we would recruit more partisans and find more vehicles to transport new recruits. The Italian Mafia

Resistance would then drive back to Washington, DC, get some rest and, in two days, drive back to Elk Lick to retrieve additional weapons from my father's hooch shelter. Once in Pennsylvania, we would do exactly the same as we did in Maryland. Pennsylvania would be seized from the Nazis and would no longer be known as Hamburg. With each state that we would recapture, our weapons would increase, and so would our manpower.

After a couple of hours of sleep, the six of us got ready for our next battle. However somehow we got separated. Originally, it was planned that Dieter and I would travel in two separate trucks due to our German. Craig and Dieter would be in one truck, with Sammy and Henry in the back, and Antonio and I would be in the second. At the last minute, Craig ended up in Vito's truck. This configuration left Dieter alone and went against the promise the six of us made to carry through with the buddy system into battle.

After a long, grueling five weeks, Dieter's battalion and mine were finished, and after talking to Craig on our confiscated *Feldfunksprecher b* German walkie-talkies, our two battalions met up with Craig's at the site where the former Annapolis Naval Academy once sat and helped them finish restoring their area. A week later, the three brigades dispersed to return to the White House. Our battle with the Nazis was a complete success, and the state of Maryland was added to the restoration list.

Vito's truck was the last to arrive at the White House; he pulled around back and parked the truck between the other two. Once Vito got out of the cab, I sensed something was wrong. That eerie feeling in the pit of my stomach came back in full force. Dieter, Antonio, and I quickly ran over to Vito's truck. The three of us stood paralyzed in total skepticism. Vito was actually on the ground, cradling Craig in his arms, sobbing irrepressibly. I helplessly fell to my knees, with tears in my eyes now beginning to run down my cheeks. My first instinct was to man up and stop crying like a little girl; however, it was not working—unfortunately, I had no control on my emotions at this point.

Vito helped me carry Craig into the White House, where we placed his lifeless body on the sofa. Antonio, Dieter, and I helplessly walked back outside to sit in the beautiful fall gardens of the White House in the warmth of the sun. The three of us must have sat there for at least an hour without speaking a word. Surprisingly, Vito came back outside and joined our tearful, melancholic group, and with open arms, we welcomed him into our little clan. I knew how much he cared for my childhood buddy; they had become close friends in a very short time, and for that, I was grateful.

"Vito, what happened to Craig?" I said with much anguish flowing from my heart and soul.

"It's a long story, Sven. Everything started out going according to plan and very smoothly. Once we arrived at the Annapolis border, I stopped for the routine border inspection. Craig and I presented our papers to the guards. As planned, the backdoors of the truck opened and our heavily armed battalion jumped out in full fury and gunned down the enemy. I then drove to an abandoned bombed out bank and parked the truck. As instructed, we assembled the weaponry and proceeded to walk through the streets of Annapolis and kill as much of the enemy as possible.

"It almost seemed as though the enemy were expecting us. My group experienced a much different scenario than how it played out in Washington. Instead of randomly coming across Nazis as we had in the district, this time we encountered a very well-organized battalion, who ambushed us an hour after we arrived. Strangely, this battalion consisted of two German corporals and thirty Negro men all heavily armed. We immediately dove for cover and returned fire. However, this time it was our group that was taken by surprise. We sustained many fatalities."

"That's alarming, getting ambushed that quickly. How in God's name would the enemy know you were arriving at that particular spot, at that particular time? Could this have been a trap?" Vito looked at me with a shocked look on his face.

"I don't know Sven. All I know is the seven of us, managed to get away and took off towards the Chesapeake Bay. It was getting dark, and we ended up staying at an old cabin near the bay. The next morning, we decided to comb the area more cautiously. We stayed away from the roads and advanced through the area more prudently.

In the four weeks we were advancing toward Annapolis, we must have encountered at least six different battalions. These battalions were all the same—one or two Nazis and the rest were Negroes, along with a few white men, whom I assume were Jews. Fortunately, the seven of us were able to exterminate all six of these German battalions. However, the first battalion that killed off most of our men seemed to have magically disappeared. Stupidly, we thought they made their way out of our area and possibly to one of yours. Then five weeks later, you and Dieter radioed me and joined our battalion and helped us finish. Your two trucks headed back to Washington, while the seven of us made our way to our truck.

"However, shockingly, when we arrived at the truck, we were immediately ambushed. The original battalion must have been waiting for us. The seven of us scrambled for cover and returned fire. Craig and I were able to crawl to the back of the truck and unlock the doors. We pulled out one the bazookas, and within a blink of an eye, the entire battalion was extinct. Although, we made a huge error—we should have investigated the area closer. One Nazi survived, and as we started to climb back into the truck, he shot Craig, along with two others. Craig somehow managed to shoot this guy with a few rounds from his pistol, sending him straight to hell. I ran to the passenger side of the truck and helped Craig into the cab. I drove like a maniac, desperately trying to get Craig back to Dr. Jackson at the White House. Regrettably, my efforts were in vain—Craig died on the road. My truck would have arrived an hour earlier, but I had to pull off the side to recollect myself. Twenty-two of us went out, and only four returned."

"Vito, thank you for everything you did to help Craig. Antonio and I are going to miss our childhood friend dearly."

Thankfully, Luciano and the other bosses gave Antonio, Dieter, and me permission to take Craig back to Mount Davis to bury him next to Frank. The bosses were giving us three days, and then they were meeting us at my father's farm in Elk Lick with the entire surplus of weaponry presently stored at the White House. Once all the vehicles and manpower had been transported from the White

House to my father's farm, our third battle would commence in Hamburg to free Pennsylvania.

This particular reunion with our fellow cave people was going to be bittersweet. As much as Antonio and I were anxious to see the girls again, under the circumstances, we were in dismay over this reunion. Everyone loved Craig, and now we would have two resting in peace in our little graveyard next to the waterfall.

Vito and Henry also received permission to join us in our burial ceremony. Minutes before sunrise, the five of us piled into one of Hitler's armored cars out back of the White House and proceeded with the hour drive. Gratefully, we arrived in Elk Lick without incident. Vito parked the armored car in the meadows by the foot of the mountain on my father's farm. We all took turns carefully caring Craig up the mountain. Understandably, it had taken much longer than usual for the four of us to reach the waterfall and the sun is just beginning to set. When we arrived, we encountered Christine and Geraldine playing ball with the children and surprised them with our presence. Geraldine and Louise dropped everything and ran over to Henry with wide open arms, while Christine and Antonio embraced with passion in their hearts. Magdalina and Erich came running out of the cave for the bittersweet reunion. She jumped into my arms, and we entwined in a passionate lip embrace. For a few precious seconds, the world stood still on its axis and life was wonderful. Dieter and Vito stood there, holding Craig, in heartfelt silence.

Within minutes, the rest of the group were feeling the pain as the five of us have for the past twenty four hours. Without a word spoken, the girls immediately walked back into the cave for Craig's black bearskin coat and the shovel. We wrapped Craig in his coat and laid him next to the area of his final resting place. Antonio and I dug his grave and gently placed his cold, lifeless body wrapped in his bearskin in the hole. Mournfully, we all said a few zealous words as we covered him with the earth. This area that we chose for Frank was equally appropriate for Craig. With the entire group teary eyed, we said a prayer and our final farewells.

Strangely, my brain finally caught up to my vision.

"Mags, where's Miss Helen?"

"Sven, I'm sorry to say we have also encountered some difficulties. A couple of days after we got settled in, Miss Helen had a fatal accident. The children were playing *fussball* with Miss Helen and Geraldine, while Christine and I were washing laundry in the river and Erich was fishing. Out of nowhere, a pack of coyotes surprised us with their presence. They were mean and hungry and were licking their chops. When the coyotes showed up, Miss Helen and the children were running for the ball and were close to the perimeter traps. Geraldine started screaming frantically and ran to retrieve the children, while Miss Helen heroically stood with a large stick, trying desperately to fend off the pack. Christine and I immediately dropped what we were doing, picked up our riffles, and ran toward Miss Helen.

"Thankfully, Miss Helen was able to keep the coyotes preoccupied, allowing Geraldine to scoop up the children and run back to the cave. Despite our efforts, tragically, Miss Helen got too close, lost her footing, and fell into the pit. The sharpened stakes pierced through her body mercilessly from front to back. I assumed she died quickly and on impact. I pray she felt no pain—she was a good woman. Erich dug a hole next to the pit, and we safely retrieved her dead body. She is also buried in our little graveyard, alongside Frank and now Craig as well. Reality is now hitting us upside our faces. We're engaged in war, and the probability of this graveyard gaining in size with more casualties of war is tremendous. When all is said and done, none of us may survive this ghastly experience."

"Oh my god, Mags, I wish we could have been here for you. I'm sorry you had to deal with this," I said to this beautiful woman as I too mourn Miss Helen's death.

As suspected, the group willfully accepted Vito as part of our coalition. We all made a solemn pledge—no matter what would happen in the future, we would continue to stick together and protect each other to the best of our ability. If our fate was to fall and perish, so it would be; the same respect would be given. We all would be buried in the little graveyard next to the waterfall.

SCHUMANN AND TRINKS' NAZI A-BOMB

After spending three glorious days with the girls and the joy of having the entire group together, along with Vito, our new addition, it was time to come back to reality. The five of us once again experienced another dreaded teary-eyed farewell as we left our loved ones behind and headed down the mountain to my father's farm. Luciano and the bosses were scheduled to meet with Antonio, Dieter, and I at sunrise tomorrow. By the time we arrived at the farm, the sun had already set. We grabbed a quick bite to eat and decided to turn in early. Heavily armed, we spent the night in the house, taking turns keeping tight surveillance over the farm for any undesirable intruders.

The next morning, when the Italian Mafia Resistance arrived, Luciano and the other eleven bosses requested to meet in the parlor for our private meeting. Henry and Vito quickly joined the others unloading the extra crates of weaponry into the hooch shelter, while the fifteen of us got comfortable with a fire radiating in the fireplace. It was now late September and the cold air was predominant.

Oddly, Luciano began the conversation with current events, not with the group's next plan of action to reclaim Pennsylvania. In the three days we were in isolation, astonishingly, much had actively taken place without our knowledge. Just as Luciano and the bosses had predicted, the White House underwent an aerial bombing last evening. Fortunately for the group, they were well-prepared. There were only a few lingering partisans who were in the immediate area and were sadly killed along with innocent civilians. The three Coca Cola trucks loaded with extra weapons and ammunition, two armored cars, and various work trucks that we confiscated from the district and Maryland had been moved the prior day.

While in Annapolis, we did a thorough search of the naval academy and came across two American patrol boats and a PT boat among the ruins docked in the Severn River perfectly preserved from the enemy attack a year ago. With this knowledge, the bosses sent the remaining Italian Mafia Resistance to Elk Lick one day early to await further orders, while the bosses left the White House and traveled to Annapolis to investigate the three boats. Thank God, we came across these boats, or Luciano and the entire resistance would have been pulverized along with the White House.

"I have to stress how paramount it is going forward. Under no circumstances can the Italian Mafia Resistance whereabouts be known to any outsiders. Not even Americans we think we can trust."

"I agree, Mr. Luciano, that was one of our first mistakes. We shot ourselves in the foot by giving too much information to the public. We also made a serious mistake by trusting the American people. As Erich has stressed, there's always going to be someone who's working with the Gestapo out of fear or bribery. We literally set ourselves up as sitting ducks. Obviously, Hitler didn't care about that particular building. I would assume he's already found a new *Führerbunker*. Since Hitler renamed Washington, DC, as Berlin, I'm inclined to think his new bunker is located somewhere within the capital."

"Yes, I agree Sven. While you boys were taking care of business, the twelve of us had a small meeting and said the same thing. In lieu of everything that has happened in the last twenty-four hours, we're sending a small battalion of men back to Washington, DC, to hunt the Hitler brothers' bunker down and destroy it. Hopefully, this time, the two ring leaders will be at home."

"Mr. Luciano, can my battalion be sent on this mission?"

"No, Sven, we have other plans for your battalion. Henry, Sammy, and Vito are joining the three of you."

"Very good then, what's our next military operation?"

"Unfortunately, with the brothers' newly acquired knowledge, Hitler got his dander up and dropped new leaflets from biplanes to the public yesterday. It's imperative we take the time and rethink our plans through more meticulously because this situation has now become more serious. I want you to read this first. It'll help you understand your next mission. I physically brought one of the leaflets with me for you to read."

My fellow *Deutschen* of the Aryan race:

It has recently come to my attention that there's an insubordinate *Gruppe*, who are known as the Italian Mafia Resistance. This *Gruppe* raided the *Führerbunker* six weeks ago. Fortunately, my *Bruder* and I escaped unharmed, along with my top-ranking Gestapo officers. We're presently conducting business from an undisclosed location. Anyone caught harboring or aiding and abetting this *Gruppe* will face the firing squad, no questions asked. This resistance *Gruppe* has also raided the states of Berlin and Schwerin.

As a result of this turmoil, anyone with Italian ancestry who has registered for *Deutsch* citizenship will be rounded up by the Gestapo, arrested, and taken to concentration camps. I will no longer award Italian Americans the opportunity of becoming part of the *Deutsch*-Aryan race, and the privilege to live in New *Deutschland* will not be permissible.

As a warning to you all, security has heightened. Anyone caught not complying will be shot on sight. If any future problems should arise from this Italian *Gruppe*, the nuclear bombs that have been strategically placed in each of the forty-eight states will be detonated without warning. You can rest to be sure—my *Bruder* and I will not physically be in the country at the time of this detonation. We will, however, return after it's deemed safe and everyone in this country is either dead or infected with radiation poisoning. We'll then resume my five-year plan from scratch, with concentrated efforts on increasing the population. Consider this your first and only warning.

Adolf Hitler, *Führer des Deutschen Reich und Volk*

"Dieter, your friend Erich Schumann, isn't he a German physicist?"

"Yes, Mr. Luciano. Why do you ask?"

"I have an idea that we need to discuss. I want Erich to join your battalion and send your group out hunting down these nuclear bombs and have the man who supplied the juice secretly dismantle them. I assume Erich knows how much nuclear fission he supplied to the Nazis. Therefore, is it realistic he can predict how many weapons were made? And if he can, is it practical to say he can safely dismantle them and release the nuclear energy? Let's face it, gang, once the threat of nuclear bombs are unsanctioned, the enemy will no longer retain the upper hand, making the battlefield more straightforward."

"Mr. Luciano, can I make a suggestion?"

"Sure, Dieter, what's on your mind?"

"This plan is good, and I'm proud to say I am also trained with physics. Between Erich and me, we should be able to dismantle these weapons and release the energy. However, it's impossible for Erich to tell exactly how many weapons were made from the amount of nuclear fission supplied. Schumann and Trinks invented the Nazi A-bomb, which is a more sophisticated miniscule nuclear warhead with a pinch of plasma. This process only uses 150 grams of uranium-233 fissile material, which in actuality is the size of a grape, while the bombs the Americans dropped on Japan used a massive amount of uranium-235-enriched compound.

"The miniature nuclear weapons use uranium-233 coated with Heavy Water. The collision of lithium-6 and deuteride under high pressure causes a beam of issuance of many neutrons. The large fluctuation of neutrons caused by this discharge imitates the effect of a large body of matter through highly confined neutron density. One miniature bomb can wipe out ten city blocks with ease. However, there's no way of telling how many miniature bombs are in each state, and if some are missed, we have no way to know how far the radiation poisoning will travel. I suggest we traipse back up the mountain and bring Erich down and talk with him personally. His equations will be more accurate than mine. This tactic will allow us to proceed with our original strategy."

With that said, Dieter, Antonio, and I were once again looking forward to another reunion with the better half of our group. I was now very concerned. With bringing back Erich, there was no more masculine figure with the girls and the children. I knew in my heart Magdalina and Christine had excellent endurance skills in the wilderness; however, I was scared to death if a Nazi patrol would happen to come across them.

Unfortunately, my concern for the girls' safety was not a priority. Luciano and the other bosses gave us strict orders to bring back Erich only. They had made it abundantly clear to Antonio and me—they could not be concerned about three women and three young children in lieu of everything else. This actually came as quite a shock, considering Christine and Lucky were blood relatives and he genuinely seemed to care about her. However, as Antonio had explained to us several times, you wouldn't want to cross or disobey an order from the bosses and question their final say.

While Antonio, Dieter, and I walked back up the mountain, we were engaged in a very serious discussion for an alternative solution. There was much riding on this. Not only did we promise Henry we would see to Geraldine and Louise's safety, but Antonio and I were in love. The only solution that made sense was to smuggle the six of them out of New Germany. At this point, with everything that was going on in this country, we felt they would all be safer in Europe, especially Magdalina.

The three of us intelligently decide we would have a group discussion in front of a warm fire later and vote on the subject. After all, we were not disobeying Luciano and Siegel's orders; we were just voting on a solution. The girls would take the children and leave on their own accord. Theoretically, none of them were part of this resistance, and technically, there were no direct orders for them to stay in the cave.

By the time the three of us arrived at the cave, it was dark and extremely cold. We warmed ourselves by the blazing fire in the pit, while the girls made something hot to eat. Once we finished our meal, the children were put to bed and the seven of us sat around the warmth of the fire. I pulled the folded leaflet from my inside pocket of my shirt and showed it to the girls. Hitler's sinister message was our tool to begin this difficult powwow. I began the conversation with Luciano, Salvatore, and Siegel's plan for Erich. Agreeably, Erich found the idea to be an excellent plan. The more Dieter and Erich discussed the bosses' plan, no doubt, the excitement in Erich's facial expressions was enough to light up the room. I was sure his ego was considerably bruised with leaving him behind. This task would also give him some peace, hopefully freeing him of any guilt. Already, it's predominately noticeable that Dieter and Erich would be the backbone of this next mission we had been assigned.

After explaining to the girls our fears of leaving them alone, we received mixed reactions. Apprehensively, Magdalina agreed that fleeing the country would be the smartest solution. Geraldine didn't want to leave without her husband, and Christine was dragging her feet as well.

"Ladies, I can guarantee my concerns are warranted due to the rebellious actions of the Italian Mafia Resistance. The Gestapo may have knowledge that we're still alive, which means they'll suspect our involvement with the Italians. If this is the case, the more the resistance infiltrates in this revolution, the greater risk of endangering everyone."

"Sven, as much as I don't want to leave you behind, either, it makes perfect sense for us to flee. Let's face it, ladies, if we're caught, we're all dead. Sven's right, the Nazis are going to realize Paul Touvier is dead at some point and realize we're all still alive. This will give them more reason to hunt us down like dogs. I'm sure every Nazi dreams about getting their hands on me, and, Geraldine, you will be executed along with Louise because you're Negro fugitives. If we can plan a safe way out of this country, I suggest the six of us travel to Leonding, Austria.

"My family home is located in a very rural area outside of town. It's large enough for the six of us to live very comfortably, and it has a large backyard for the children. There's also another option—the Rosenburg farm, which is a thirty-minute walk down the dirt road from my house. Mr. Rosenburg was taken away to a concentration camp and is probably no longer alive. If his daughter, Esther, is still living in this country, his farm is now an abandoned one, which will give us a great opportunity. Esther and I spoke of this dream many times.

"We can live at the Rosenburg farm and utilize it to its full capacity. The fields can be planted with various crops. We can buy animals for meat and eggs and utilize a few cows for fresh milk. I actually have some *Schilling* stored in a secret location, which will give us the opportunity to get set up straightaway. Rosenburg's farm will allow the six of us to be independent and self-sufficient. If Esther returned to Europe, obviously, the farm won't be available to us. However, we can feasibly do the same on a much smaller scale in my backyard. Either way, we'll be safe. The war is over in Europe. Once our men are finished with the war in New Germany, either they join us in Austria or we travel back to America. At least they won't be worrying about us while they're off trying to disable nuclear weapons, kill Nazis, and save the world."

"Mags, please give me the address of your house in Leonding and the Rosenburg farm. When this war is over, Antonio, Henry, and I will come back for you all."

"Sven, please promise me you will."

"Of course, I promise," her sparkling, beautiful blue eyes held me spellbound.

Once Magdalina explained her thoughts with Operation Vamoose in full detail, Geraldine and Christine slowly came around and agreed to leave the country. However, we now had to come up with an arrangement to get all six of them safely out. God forbid, after coming this far, they would be caught fleeing back to war-torn Europe and whatever obstacles await them there.

The sun would rise in two hours, which was our departure time. Erich, Dieter, Antonio, and I had a meeting with the bosses at sunset in my father's parlor. If we were able to leave as planned, we would make it down the mountain with time to spare. This meeting was arranged for the bosses to meet Old Germany's most influential physicist, and in the presence of Erich and Dieter, we would discuss a feasible plan, in full detail, of our next strategy. Magdalina had assured us that between the three of them, they would come up with a plan and successfully execute it.

"Antonio, just throwing it out there, maybe we should indiscreetly talk to the bosses about getting the girls out of the country. I'm sure they could be a huge assistance."

"No, Sven, not a good idea to get them angry. We've already been instructed to leave the women and children behind to fend for themselves, barefoot and pregnant, in the kitchen."

"Antonio, your chauvinistic oxymoron is cute, but I'm serious."

"I know. Luciano promised me once our mission is complete, we can all return to Elk Lick and take care of our business. If the girls cannot come up with a fruitful strategy, they'll simply stay in the cave and wait until we're finished."

"All right, I'll keep my big mouth shut. You obviously know these guys much better than I do."

Once again, as we said our farewells, I put my arms around Magdalina and engaged in a long, succulent kiss. Abruptly, our passionate embrace was interrupted with the reality of our tedious walk to my father's farm. Magdalina tenderly handed me the two addresses in Austria, which she inscribed on the back of the leaflet. For some strange reason at that moment, I genuinely felt a small sense of peace. I knew Magdalina was like me—we were survivalists and did not act in haste. She won't take any unnecessary chances with her life or the others.

Fortunately, we were smart enough to leave the cave early. Erich might be a brilliant, famous German physicist, but he was no outdoorsmen. Surprisingly, he really slowed us down. By the time we got back to my father's farm and warmed up by the fire, we just barely had enough time for a quick supper before our meeting. After the introductions, Erich and Dieter took the next hour explaining to the bosses how these bombs would be dismantled and the energy released. Erich actually made the process sound fairly easy. The hardest part of this plan would be locating the bombs in each state and, of course, not getting blown up.

Now that the resistance had added three armored cars to our collection, our battalion would be using one of the cars and one Coca Cola truck for our newest adventure traveling cross country. The two additional armored cars and the two Coca Cola trucks, along with another work truck we picked up in Maryland, were reserved for the other battalions who would take back Pennsylvania. Dieter and Erich would travel with Sammy and Henry in the armored car, while Vito, Antonio, and I would travel in the Coca Cola truck.

"Mr. Luciano, the orders that Meyer Lansky made up for Dieter and I from General Field Marshal Wilhelm Keitel worked beautifully. We now need to add Erich to these orders."

"Of course, you and Dieter pick out an appropriate name for Erich and ask Meyer to use it."

"Thank you, Lucky."

We left Erich, Vito, and Antonio with the bosses and the entire resistance group in Elk Lick. When we arrived at Luciano's Restaurant, we would also need Lansky to forge a full set of papers for the bosses, Vito and Antonio. Later, he would have to work on new identities for all the Italians in our group, giving everyone a non-Italian name with a new heritage. Dieter drove the armored car, with Sammy and Henry sitting in the backseat handcuffed, as I sat in the front passenger side also in full uniform, with my pistol lying on the dashboard, ready to spring into action. Subsequently, Lansky would have his work cut out for him, forging a full set of papers for fifteen men and official Nazi military orders from Keitel. Since we would already be in New York City and Lansky obviously would need a few days to complete his project, Luciano wanted the four of us to drive to Albany, the capital of New York, and try to locate the bomb. Once Lansky had completed his new assignment, we would then drive to Harrisburg on the way back to Elk Lick. Once in Harrisburg, we would fish around and try to locate the Pennsylvania bomb.

For some strange reason, the bosses believed that Hitler had these bombs located in the capitals of each state. If that is the case, it would make our mission move along much quicker. After all, Hitler had been extremely intelligent for far too long. He had to make a stupid mistake or use poor judgment at some point. It's just the law of averages.

Once we arrived at Luciano's Restaurant, Dieter parked the armored car in the back alley and covered it with an old tarp that Lansky found in the cellar. Lansky closed the restaurant early and made veal parmesan with linguini for supper. While we inhaled our food, I explained the reason we were in need of his services once again.

"Meyer, thank God we came to New York to see you. I can't believe you didn't have knowledge of Hitler's newest leaflet drop."

"Yah, Sven, thanks for coming, this news will surely change the equation here. I'll also have to make a full set of papers for myself with a new name and heritage. Since the restaurant has been registered with the Gestapo as an Italian business, it's time to close up shop and return to Elk Lick with you guys."

"No problem, Meyer, you can sit in the back with Sammy and Henry."

"Thanks."

"You don't need to thank me. I'm glad you're leaving. Unfortunately, before the border crossing, we'll have to put you in the trunk. The border patrol doesn't check anything but our papers when we travel in the armored car."

Sammy escorted the three of us to his private room upstairs so we could turn in early and all get a good night sleep. Tomorrow morning, bright and early, we planned on driving two hours to Albany and stay all day or until we located the bomb. If we found there wasn't a bomb located in the capital, the following day, we would search New York City from top to bottom.

Lansky ended up staying up all night, working on the counterfeit papers. We all felt a sense of urgency to get out of this restaurant before the Gestapo came snooping around, looking for Italians to arrest and cart off to concentration camps. Although, with the sign that Lansky placed in the front window stating that the restaurant was permanently closed, it might buy us some time.

As planned, we woke early the next morning and got started on our road trip. Dieter and I, dressed in our Nazi uniforms, and started the charade once again. With Sammy and Henry in the backseat, we proceed with our two-hour drive to Albany. Incredibly, we passed a few Nazis traveling in jeeps on the highway, but no one stopped us for a random check. I assumed we weren't stopped considering we're traveling in an armored car, which gave the appearance that we're big shots.

Amazingly, an hour after we arrived in Albany, we were able to locate the bomb. Sitting in plain sight for everyone to view, the bomb was housed on the grounds of the New York State Capitol building on State Street. It literally sat there like some historic monument, with no visible Nazis guarding it.

"I have got to tell you, gang, once again I tip my hat to Hitler. With this bomb sitting here in plain view, the people are reminded daily to conform."

"You're right Sven, theoretically, these bombs don't need surveillance. Only a highly trained scientist or a physicist can sensibly and safely deactivate the nuclear energy. That is, of course, if they understand the entire process. And I say *entire* process because if you leave out one element, *bang!*"

"Yah, Dieter, if I understand Erich correctly, the outer casing of the bomb is very durable. This thing can probably sit here as a monument for an indefinite amount of time. With any luck, the other forty-seven bombs are located in their capitals as well."

Thankfully, we had a very productive day. We weren't stopped by any Nazi patrols; we breezed on through to Albany and then back to New York City. Dieter drove the car around back, and we replaced the tarp. As the four of us approached the backdoor of the restaurant, we noticed the door was slightly ajar. Dieter and I pulled out our pistols from their holsters and chambered a round and armed Henry and Sammy with the extra revolver we each carried in our boots.

Very cautiously, the four of us entered the restaurant and saw a wounded Nazi lying at the top of the wine cellar steps. Dieter immediately pulled out his hunting knife from his other boot and sliced the Nazi's neck wide open. Dieter and Sammy then proceeded to walk down the steps to the wine cellar, while Henry and I searched the restaurant and kitchen. After conducting a thorough search, Henry and I walked upstairs to the two private rooms, which were totally ransacked. Still with our weapons drawn we made our way down the steps to the cellar. There was blood everywhere—on the walls, the floor, and a trail leading up the steps. We gingerly walked into the cellar to see Dieter and Sammy looking over the bodies of three dead Nazis.

Off to the right where the secret room was located, Lansky's dead body lay on the cold cellar floor in a pool of blood with his shotgun lying beside him. The solid black walnut wine rack was slightly open, exposing the door behind it. Sammy walked over and opened the wine rack further; he took out a set of keys from his trouser pocket and unlocked the door. Papers lay scattered about on the stone floor. The Tommy Guns, ammunition, and alcohol were still perfectly intact. We picked up the forged papers, which Lansky apparently threw into the room, and somehow he was able to lock the door while shooting the four intruders. I would assume the guy upstairs, whose head was hanging by a few threads, with blood gushing out like a waterfall, was the Nazi who was capable of taking down our friend after Lansky shot the four of them and killed his three buddies.

We decided to leave immediately. This patrol was only four men, but my fear was when these guys were missed, the Gestapo would show up in full magnitude. Sammy carried Lansky's dead body out back to bury him. Dieter, Henry, and I carried a couple crates of weapons and ammunition out back to the armored car and began unloading the contents into the trunk. Sammy locked the door and closed the black walnut wine rack. The remaining weapons should be safe, even if the Gestapo came to the restaurant and ransacked the entire place. The only thing down here were empty wine racks, a significant amount of blood, and three dead bad guys.

We all stood over Lansky's grave while Sammy said a few heartfelt words to a man who was very special to him and who had a small place in all our hearts as well. Although Meyer Lansky was a powerful part of the crime syndicate and had no qualms about it, had done some really bad things throughout the years, he was also a very likeable man and one hell of a counterfeiter. Luciano and Siegel were going to take his death very hard. These three men had been very close and had been working together since they were young boys.

Dieter and I decided to let Sammy explain to Luciano the tragedy that took place in his restaurant. All our concentrated efforts now needed to go toward locating the next bomb hopefully housed in Harrisburg. At least we had some good news to report to the bosses. One bomb had already been located, and hopefully, the second one would stand out and bite us in the butts as well.

A YELLOW BELLY

It was late October, and we already had an accumulation of four feet of snow in the mountains with blistery cold winds. I wrapped the wool blanket around me as I climbed out of bed and throw two more logs onto the fire in the pit. Unfortunately, the children were still sleeping. I almost wanted to wake them; I couldn't wait to see the expression on their faces when they see how much snow had accumulated last evening. Geraldine and Christine started preparing breakfast, while I continued sewing the black bearskin coat for Geraldine.

Gratefully, last week after an all-day fishing extravaganza, we witnessed another bear strolling happy go lucky into our camp. Somehow, he was able to bypass Sven's security traps and came to pay us a visit. I had to say I was rather proud of myself; I dropped him cold dead with two shots. However, when Geraldine saw the huge bear waltzing into our area, she picked up the children and ran screaming into the cave. As much as Christine and I had loathed it, we had to seriously reprimand her. The way she reacted had put us all in serious danger. Black-bears hadn't gone into hibernation yet. The chance of another one strolling into camp, looking for food, was great. Once again, Christine and I lectured Geraldine and the children on how to avoid a bear attack and survive on this mountain.

After enjoying a hot breakfast, we all bundled up and walked outside for some recreational time with Tommy, Grace, and Louise. We spent a glorious hour building a five-foot snowman. We all started to get frozen to the bone and quickly scampered back to the toasty warmth of the cave. I threw a few additional logs onto the fire as the six of us gathered around the flames, taking in its warmth and watching the beauty of the dancing blaze.

"Christine and Geraldine, thanks for suggesting we go outside and play. What a wonderful hour—we just had the pleasure of spending time together, doing nothing of monetary value. For the first time in over a year, the children actually experienced the innocence of childhood and the simple pleasures of a fresh snowfall."

However, once we were all dry and warm again, the fun and games were over, and it was time to get back to reality. Christine and Geraldine spent the rest of the afternoon schooling the children, saving the last two hours for me. I now instructed a daily two-hour German class for the five of them. No matter what the case might be, if we stay here or travel back to Austria, the five of them needed to be fluent in the German language. Unfortunately, the English language might end up becoming obsolete.

"Listen up, ladies, an idea occurred to me while we were playing with the children. We need to seriously discuss a plan to flee the country."

"Sure, what's your idea?"

"This morning was a wake-up call. Winter has arrived. Christine and I know all too well Mother Nature will soon present herself in full furry. While we can still travel down the mountain, I suggest we walk to Sven's farm and ask the Italians if we can borrow a vehicle. If three women and three young children take them by complete surprise, and we're literally standing there looking pathetic and helpless, they may lend us a helping hand. Especially Mr. Luciano, considering Christine is a blood relative."

"Yah, but, Mags, we really don't know one another."

"Yes, but isn't it worth a try? All we're asking is to borrow a confiscated vehicle. Once we have transportation, we should travel back to Gerhard's apartment building and talk to Richard and get some advice. He has always given me the impression that he's very resourceful and has some shady connections."

"You're right about Richard. I don't know about shady connections. However, he is very resourceful."

"Yah, Christine, and what's good about this plan is we're already in Pennsylvania. Obviously, we won't encounter any border stops traveling to the city. However, we do need to be prepared. If we're stopped on the highway for a routine inspection, we'll have to engage in bloodshed to get out of the situation. After all, none of us have identification papers—the three of us are fugitives.

"Geraldine, Tommy, Grace, and Louise should lie on the backseat of the vehicle and out of view of any passing vehicles on the highway. We don't want to arouse any suspicion, and we can't be seen with a Negro woman and child. In fact, Christine and I should dress as men. Two women in a car will also arouse suspicion. We'll sit up front armed with loaded rifles and take a few stick grenades. If we're stopped, I'll simply unscrew the base cap of the stick grenade, pull the cord and throw the grenade out window. In one quick second, the bad guys will be blown to smithereens, and we won't have to worry about wasting bullets."

"Mags, I think your idea is good. You're beginning to scare me— you sound more and more like Sven every day."

"Thanks, I'll take that as a compliment," I looked at Christine and gave her a wink.

"Please do. I agree Richard is definitely shrewd. If anyone can get three women and three children safely out of the country, it would be him. But may I ask one question? Who's going to drive? I don't know how."

"Oh my God, I don't, either."

"Ladies, relax. I can drive. However, you want me lying in the backseat with the children because of the color of my skin."

"Geraldine, yes, this is a serious situation we have here. Do you remember the three of you fleeing your home in the middle of the night in the pouring rain not too long ago? And the three months you were hiding in that barn with not enough to eat? If the guys hadn't come by on their expedition that day, you all would have been dead by now. Geraldine, you don't understand the power of these Nazis and how relentless they are. Sven and I know all too well. We witnessed firsthand and watched them execute and torture people for no reason."

"Magdalina, I apologize. I seriously didn't mean anything disrespectful with my big mouth. I do realize how serious our situation is. I also realize I'm not gifted like you and Christine, natural survivalists with incredible instincts and endurance in the wilderness. My family will never be able to thank you all enough. You saved our lives and welcomed us with open arms into your commune. The entire group has shown us hospitality and generosity beyond words. Please let me do something to help our cause. I can drive. I've been driving since I was ten years old and could reach the pedals. In fact, I grew up on a small farm right outside of Elk Lick in Meyersdale. I know this area real well. I suggest we travel through as many of the fields and back dirt roads leading to Philadelphia as possible. Once we get close to the city, we should abandon the car and travel at night on foot."

"You're a lifesaver. Maybe someday you can teach me how to drive?"

"That's a deal, Mags."

"I'm so excited. I've always wanted to drive but was always too chicken to try."

After supper, the three of us sat in front of the fire, discussing different alternatives to an escape, while the children finished their homework. However, with each alternative we came up with, we always go back to our original plan. Tomorrow morning, if the weather allowed us passage down the mountain, we would leave for Sven's farm at daybreak. This next journey the six of us were about to venture into was going to be tough, especially for the children.

The next morning, we woke to a beautiful sunny, cold day. We all got something to eat and bundled up for our long trip. We wrapped the children in wool blankets over their deerskin coats for extra warmth. Christine and I placed a loaded pistol in the waistband of our trousers, slugged a loaded rifle over our shoulders, and put plenty of ammunition and three stick grenades in each squirrel-skin knapsack. On our way out of the cave's entrance, I opened the meat cooler and grabbed some frozen fish, bear meat, and venison and placed them in both knapsacks as well. When the children weren't looking, I smashed the tall snowman to the ground and covered up any signs of human inhabitance at the waterfall, and very encouragingly, we set out on our journey.

Remarkably, we made incredible time. Tommy, Grace, and Louise never complained, nor did they stop for a break that I didn't initiate. As we approached the foot of the mountain outside of Sven's farm, Geraldine and the children quietly lay low in the brush. Christine and I made our way closer to the farmhouse prudently, looking for the enemy.

There actually seemed to be no activity on the grounds or in the house and barn. As we advanced closer with our pistols drawn, Christine and I proceeded to walk very gingerly into the kitchen and into an ambush. Lucky Luciano, Bugsy Siegel, and Joseph Bonanno were standing in front of us, while four men advanced around to the back of the house and stood at the kitchen door, all aiming a weapon at the two of us. In a huge sigh of relief from both parties, we all disengaged our weapons and put them away.

"Christine, what the hell are you doing here? I thought I told you to stay in the mountains where it's safe."

"I know, Uncle, but after speaking with Antonio and the boys, we discussed the possibility of traveling back to Austria. Magdalina has connections to a farm where we can live in peace and work the land. This endeavor won't only be for survival but for a business as well. We plan to sell our crops, eggs, and meat to a local market in town. I have a German friend in Philadelphia who may be able to help us safely escape. Magdalina and I are hoping we can borrow the armored car behind the barn so we can drive to the city. Once we're in a safe, secluded area, we'll abandon the car for you to retrieve at your convenience."

"Christine, where's Geraldine and the children?"

"They're at the foot of the mountain, hiding in the brush."

"Bugsy, take a couple of guys and bring Geraldine and the kids back to the house."

"Listen up, girls, I'm not feeling real warm and fuzzy about your idea. If a Nazi patrol passes you on the highway, guaranteed, you'll be stopped and arrested. I realize it can't be easy living in a cave in the wilderness, especially with no men and three young children. However your plan may end up backfiring. I will, however, lend you the armored car. I want you both to know if there was more we could do to help, we sincerely would have given it. Presently, the Nazis are searching and arresting anyone of Italian heritage and sending us to concentration or death camps. Therefore, we're as sought out as you are, making it extremely dangerous for anyone to be in our presence.

"Christine, please accept this money to help with your journey. From what I understand, even though American currency is no longer accepted in this country, other countries aren't aware yet of the full magnitude of what's happening and are still honoring it. We have heard through the grapevine that there are underground ratlines for Americans to escape as long as you have money to pay. We have also been informed that some of the barges which are allegedly deporting Hitler's undesirables aren't necessarily following the full plan. Apparently, there are some corrupt captains who literally stop at midpoint from New Germany to Europe and discard their cargo in the middle of the North Atlantic Ocean to feed the sharks."

"Oh my god, Uncle, that's horrible!"

"Yes, but I also have some good news. Antonio's battalion has successfully disarmed the bomb in New York and the bomb in Pennsylvania, with kudos going to Erich and Dieter. My boys are now in Maryland locating and disarming that bomb, and then they will travel the Southern states one at a time. The bombs are disarmed, the energy released, and the casings replaced to give the appearance that they're intact and haven't been tampered with. Christine, I look forward to the day this is over and the two of us can get to know one another. You have my blessing, and as the Germans say, '*Auf Wiedersehen.*'"

After a late supper with Mr. Luciano, Christine, Geraldine, and I got prepared for our five-hour trip to the city by way of moonlight. As we said our good-byes I slipped Mr. Luciano the addresses in Leonding, Austria. Surprisingly, he seemed very humble and gracious to receive it. Mr. Luciano and Mr. Siegel carried the children from the parlor to the car and laid the three of them on the backseat of the spacious armored car as they slept. Geraldine jumped behind the wheel as Christine and I got into the passenger side. All three of us were dressed as men, thanks to the bosses. We thanked them for their hospitality and, of course, their helping hand and spun off in the cold night air. God was once again on our side. The brightness of the moon and the stars fully illuminating the sky would make our travels easier without the usage of the car lights.

We arrived at the outskirts of the city four hours before the sun rose. Geraldine parked the car in a small area of the woods next to an old half-demolished factory building. Tommy, Grace, and Louise were still asleep, and the three of us decided to get out of the car to stretch our legs. We stood in the freezing darkness of the early morning air, with a flashlight and a map of the city that Mr. Costello had given us.

While Christine, Geraldine, and I were diligently studying the map and planning our route to the apartment building on foot, we were suddenly interrupted with what resembled headlights approaching very quickly. My heart fell down to my feet in sheer panic. The three of us ran around to the backside of the car, opened the door, and dragged the children out. Geraldine took the three children and dashed further into the woods, while Christine and I immediately jumped back into the car. We took our pistols from the waistband of our trousers, chambered a bullet, and laid them on the seat underneath our thighs. Both rifles, also with a bullet chambered, lay on the floor by our feet. I immediately reached into the squirrel-skin knapsack and pulled out two stick grenades.

Within seconds, the moon illuminated enough light to see that the jeep quickly approaching has a swastika on the hood and four men dressed in Nazi uniforms. With trembling hands and a nauseous feeling in my stomach, without hesitation, I unscrewed the base cap, pulled the cord and tossed a grenade at the oncoming jeep. Within a blink of an eye, there was a loud explosion and the jeep flew in the air in fragments, while the four men were tossed in different directions with severely mutilated bodies.

Yards away, we could hear the faint cries of one of those mutilated bodies. Christine and I jumped out of the armored car and ran up to a young man moaning with excruciating pain, lying in a pool of blood. One leg was completely blown off and his other leg had nothing left but exposed muscle and thigh bone. Without a second thought, I aimed my rifle and shot this poor soul in the head and put him out of his misery. Christine and I ran back to the car and took cover, with our rifles pointing at the jeep's debris. My body was trembling as tears flowed down my checks and a nauseous feeling overpowered every inch of me. The horror my brain had witnessed literally dropped me to my knees while I vomited out my supper. Christine and I stood there for what seemed to be an eternity, paralyzed to move.

It wasn't until Geraldine and the children came out of woods and joined us in our zombie state that we snapped out of it and regained our senses. Remarkably, our plan worked very well. I was not sure when the Nazis spotted us; however, they surely received a fate they weren't expecting.

"How could this be? Geraldine, Christine, did either one of you see that coming? I realize we're all extremely fatigued, but how could the three of us not notice a jeep?"

"Yah, it's as though they literally dropped from the sky. Thank God, we brought the grenades."

"Ladies, we really need to get out of here, pronto. There's no way of telling how far the sound of the explosion may have traveled. I used only one grenade, so now we're down to five. These five grenades have got to last us until we get to Gerhard's apartment building."

With only walking a short time, the three of us felt as though we're ready to collapse, however we have to push on while it's still dark. Fortunately, we didn't encounter anymore confrontation and were able to stay on track with the timing of our arrival. The sun was just beginning to rise as we entered the apartment building through the backdoor. Christine and I ran down the hall to Richard and Jutta's apartment with overwhelming excitement. With adrenaline pouring through my body and lack of sleep hindering my good judgment, I pounded fiercely on his door. Minutes later, Richard greeted us in his bathrobe, obviously woken out of a sound sleep. Christine and I lunged at him with big bear hugs and tears streaming down our eyes. Richard immediately grabbed us and hurled us into his apartment and rather abruptly closed the door.

"Oh my god, look at you two. What a sight for my weary eyes. I thought you both were dead. What are you doing here? Don't you realize how extremely dangerous it is for you to be here, especially you, Magdalina? For the past year, this building has been under high-security surveillance. The Hitler brothers have surprised us with a personal visit several times throughout the year looking for you. The only information I had was that you were both arrested and taken to a war relocation camp five years ago. Please have a seat. You both look exhausted. I'll wake Jutta to start a pot of coffee and make some breakfast."

"Richard, thanks. However, there is a woman with three young children out back hiding. Can I please bring them in to join us as well?"

"Yes, of course. You get them while I wake my wife. Christine, please make yourself at home."

I ran back down the hallway and out the backdoor to retrieve Geraldine and the children. Like a bat out of hell, the five of us quickly made our way to Richard's apartment. I closed door and locked it behind us. At this point, Jutta was up, also in her bathrobe, making a pot of coffee. I ran into the kitchen and gave her a kiss on the cheek and hugged her tightly. What a wonderful reunion this had turned out to be. After we all enjoyed Jutta's delicious breakfast, the children curled up on the floor in front of the fire with pillows and fell back asleep. The five of us sat in Richard's spacious parlor, mesmerized by the warmth of a crackling fire, drinking a second cup of hot percolated coffee. Christine, Geraldine, and I feel asleep before we were able to finish our coffee. Jutta and Richard kindly kept the children occupied and allowed us the time to sleep.

We pleasantly woke to the apartment engulfed in a phenomenal aroma of beef braising all day. Needless to say, I was famished after smelling this wonderful, distinctive smell as I slept and devoured Jutta's supper within seconds. Once we finished supper, we all adjourned back into the parlor for coffee and a piece of plum cake that Jutta had also prepared for our welcoming. As we settled in and got comfortable, we realized it was time to seriously discuss business at hand.

"Magdalina and Christine, I have to warn you the Gestapo continues to conduct random inspections of the complex looking for you both. These surprise inspections aren't as predominate as they had been in the past. However, it's still very dangerous for you to be here. Geraldine and Louise are also in serious danger. They're probably the last two Negroes in Philadelphia."

"Yes, Richard, we know. That's why we're here. I'm hoping you can help us all flee the country."

After sharing the past five years with Richard and Jutta and bringing them up to date, beginning with Ingrid's betrayal and ending with our journey back to Philadelphia, several hours already passed.

"Magdalina, I agree with Sven. Under the circumstances, the only sensible option is to get the six of you out of the country. I wish Jutta and I could flee with you. However, I have an important obligation. I've become a key figure of an organization known as the American Underground Ratline. We assist people wanting to flee the country to the American-occupied zones in Old Germany. Once an individual is in the American sector of Frankfurt, we then have a group of American military men who are stranded assisting individuals with our ratline at the other end. Safe passage is assured to American citizens to Czechoslovakia, Austria, Hungry, Belgium, Luxembourg, Netherlands, Denmark, and Sweden. An individual also has the choice of staying in any of the American sectors in Old Germany. However, these areas are war-torn and poverty stricken. The French and British zones and, of course, the Soviet and Polish-occupied zones are not an option. We also have a ratline from Africa to Munich for any American Negroes who were deported and didn't want to live in Africa.

"Within the past year, the Hitler brothers have allowed three barges to sail from Boston, Hannover—or as we know it, Massachusetts—exporting agricultural goods and grains to help the starving German citizens in Old Germany. These barges usually leave port from Old Germany once every four months. The captain of one barge was a personal friend of my late brother, Hans. Carl and Hans had a small involvement in an unsuccessful assentation attempt on Hitler's life during World War II in Old Germany on July 20, 1944. According to Carl, about two hundred people, both military and civilians, were arrested and executed within that year. Most had no involvement whatsoever. Somehow by the grace of God, Carl escaped persecution. However, sadly, my brother was shot in a firing squad, along with other no-name participants in the courtyard at the Bendlerblock."

"Richard, I'm so sorry for your loss. Oh my god, that's horrible."

"Thank you, Magdalina. Anyway, Carl wrote me of my brother's untimely demise in October 1944. After that first letter, we managed to stay in touch through the mail for the next two years until Hitler enforced his No Written Correspondence Law in New Germany. All mail within the country is subject to censorship, while mail delivery overseas has been totally abolished. Once the American Underground Ratline was established, I decided to travel to Hannover and personally met Carl and recruit him. His barge has been a perfect alibi to smuggle Americans out of the country. His barge sails out of the Boston Harbor across the North Atlantic Ocean and into the port of Antwerp, Belgium, which is a port at the heart of Europe. The ratline begins in Antwerp, Belgium, which is a neutral nation. The refugees are then transported by trucks from Belgium through the tip of the French sector in Old Germany and then into an American-occupied sector, with the end of the ratline in Frankfurt. I'm proud to say we have successfully smuggled out hundreds of American Jews, Negroes, and, recently, quite a few people of Italian heritage.

"Rumors have been circulating for the past year. Some of the ships that Hitler has set up for deportation never make their destiny. Apparently, there are a few corrupt captains who literally sail to a halfway point in the middle of the Atlantic Ocean. The crew then forces the refugees overboard, and they're left to drown. This is one of the reasons we're so passionate about our ratline. I can go to my Maker knowing we've saved thousands of lives."

"I cannot tell you how proud I am, of this work you're doing," I looked at Richard and gave him a huge kiss on the cheek."

"Thank you Magdalina."

"First thing tomorrow, I'll walk down to the print shop I once owned and have Wolfgang forge paperwork for the six of you. As luck would have it, Carl's barge is due into the Boston Harbor next Monday, and we have a significant amount to accomplish in less than a week. However, first things first, we need to get the six of you out of here and to a safe location. There's an abandoned building around the corner that was once a bank. A year ago, the Nazis cleaned out all banks in the city and threw grenades into the buildings, destroying them. You should be safe there. Once a building is destroyed, the

Nazis seem to have no more interest in them. We'll set you up in the cellar so that you can have a small fire burning in the dark of the night. No one is out past curfew. Therefore, you can safely stay warm. However, please don't burn during the day and keep a low profile. Normally, no one is around that area during the day. Nevertheless, I don't want to take any chances. I'm not worried about Nazi patrols in that immediate area. I'm more worried about Nazi sympathizers who may suspect your presence in the building."

"Richard, whatever happened to Ingrid?"

"Mags, the next day after you were arrested, Ingrid packed her belongings and moved into her fiancé's house somewhere in the suburbs. We said our good-byes, and I honestly never expected to see her again. From what I understand, she married Hermann Goering, a leading member of the Nazi party and has made quite a name for herself within the Nazi regime. I don't know how a person can do a total flip-flop overnight, but she sure as hell did. The Ingrid we all knew was a sweet and kind, beautiful young woman from Austria. Somehow, hooking up with Goering turned her into a monster overnight. She's in charge of a small propaganda outfit. She heads a group that travels around the city coercing people to rat out their family, friends and neighbors. From what I've heard, with every so-called nonconforming person she arrests, somehow she's personally involved with their execution. And with every arrest and execution, she is rewarded.

"What's even more disturbing, I've also heard that Ingrid mimics an evil Nazi from Old Germany during World War II, Ilse Koch, better known as the Bitch of Buchenwald. Apparently, Ilse was known to parade around naked with a whip in front of male prisoners. If a man glanced at her, he was immediately beaten or executed. We also heard she would have anyone who had an interesting tattoo killed and use their skin for a lampshade in her home, just as the real Ilse had allegedly done in Old Germany. Ingrid Goering has become a feared name in the average household. She has shown up here several times, interrogating me for any information I would have on you and Christine, which makes me believe she may actually be working for Gerhard."

"Well, isn't that a hoot? My so-called Jewish best friend is nothing but a backstabbing, hypocritical traitor and a lying sack of cow minure. I wonder how her precious, high-ranking Nazi husband would feel if he knew her real name is Esther Ingrid Rosenburg. My god, what would her poor father think of how she has tarnished his good name? Mr. Rosenburg was such a good man. If that concentration camp didn't kill him, this news of his only child would. When we get to Austria, if Mr. Rosenburg is still alive, none of us will ever speak of Esther in his presence."

Early the next morning, before sunrise, we enjoyed a hot breakfast that Jutta prepared for our send-off. Geraldine helped Jutta wash and dry the dishes, while Christine and I gathered our belongings, along with the extra blankets and pillows from our apartments. We woke the children, helped them get dressed, and bundled them up for the start of a chilly late October morning. Geraldine and the children kissed and hugged Jutta and thanked her for her generous hospitality. Christine and I waited until after the gang was finished. We both threw our arms around her in a tight squeeze and genuinely cried, knowing we'd never see her again.

Richard quickly led us out the backdoor of the complex, and very indiscreetly, we hustled for a mile around the corner to the abandoned bank. We carefully made our way down to the cellar of the destroyed building to set up camp. Thank God, we only had four days before we would leave for Boston. This was going to be very difficult with three young children. Jutta gave the children a deck of cards, pads of blank paper, pencils, and a full set of colored pencils to help keep them occupied. She also gave us three romance novels from her personal collection to keep the three of us occupied. In the four days we would be stranded in this half-blown-up building, I wanted to put all concentrated efforts into our German lessons. This would serve as a constructive way to pass the time and get prepared for our future. Richard helped us get set up and quickly left the building moments before sunrise. He didn't want to take any chances of being seen coming or going from this location.

Thankfully, the children immediately fell back to sleep, while Christine, Geraldine, and I sat in the dark, dingy, and moldy smelling half-demolished cellar we were now calling home for the next four days. We had to put full effort into making the best out of this horrible situation we were presently in. The end result would surely make all this worthwhile. Strangely and very disturbingly, a flash from the past haunted me. I remember saying those exact words to Ingrid way back when.

After four very long, uneventful, problematic days finally passed with much anticipation, Richard was due sometime early this morning. He would be bringing our new identification papers and a woman's very fair liquid foundation and baby powder for Geraldine's and Louise's facial and neck skin. We had to pass them off as white Aryan Germans since we all had to take public transportation to Boston. Wolfgang would be accompanying Richard so he could temporarily tattoo our left forearms with the swastika as well. It was imperative all the details were taken care of for this charade.

The six of us sat patiently waiting for an hour. The sun was rising, and Richard was late. With every last bone in my body, I sensed something's wrong. However, we were paralyzed—we were depending on Richard and his partner, Wolfgang, to get us out of here. As more time passed, Christine, Geraldine, and I began to panic. We were literally up against the clock. We had to catch the 11:00 a.m. bus to Boston. If we missed this bus, we would have to live in this purgatory for another four months to wait for the next barge to sail into the Boston Harbor.

Thirty minutes later, Richard and Wolfgang came strolling into the cellar, accompanied by a small parade of Nazis following them at gunpoint. My stomach turned into a tight knot, and my hands began to shake. My brain was in slow motion. I could not for the life of me figure out how to get out of this one. Foolishly, earlier this morning, the three of us hid our rifles in the corner of the cellar under heavy cement debris. The five stick grenades were in the two squirrel-skin knapsacks next to us on the floor, which we couldn't get too. Christine and I were armed as usual; however, there were six Nazi men and only two of us. Then out of the clear blue, you could have knocked me over with a feather—in slithers, like a snake in the grass, was our infamous Jewish Nazi queen bee.

Esther turned as pale as a ghost and did a double take when she saw Christine and me standing there with our hands up in the air. Within a blink of an eye, we could hear Geraldine walking back down to the cellar, with Tommy, Grace, and Louise following behind her. Five minutes earlier, she had taken the children to the water closet, which was still in working condition on the first floor. Instinctively, I screamed for her to run for cover, while at the same time, Esther hit me upside my face with the handle of her gun and knocked me off my feet. She then grabbed two of her escorts and proceeded to run up to the first floor after Geraldine.

While the four Nazis guarding us seemed to be preoccupied with the commotion on the first floor, Christine and I looked at one another with the same thought and discreetly pull our pistols from the waistband of our trousers and simultaneously shot three of them dead. That quickly, I heard another gunshot and immediately felt a painful, burning sensation on my right side directly under my ribs. Within seconds, I fell to the floor in excruciating pain and immediately lost consciousness.

Minutes later, I woke to see Richard slumped over me, holding a torn piece of his shirt applying pressure to my bleeding wound. Sadly, Wolfgang lay dead next to the Nazi that he barehandedly strangled after he had been shot as well.

"Magdalina, I'm taking your pistol and a stick grenade. Stay put, and apply pressure to the wound."

Richard immediately ran upstairs to the first floor along with Christine, in pursuit of Esther and the other two Nazis. They should not get away, or we would have an entire battalion on our tails within the next hour. At that point, I must have blacked out once again.

Abruptly, I woke to the sounds of gunfire in the distance. I was suddenly consumed with an uncanny feeling of immortality. I had visions of everyone dead, including the children, and I was left here literally bleeding to death in slow motion. My brain was telling my body to stand up and get the hell out of here; however, I didn't have the strength to move a muscle. I guessed there would be no fairytale happy ending here today.

Once again, I blacked out. Very strangely, however, as though I was conscious and coherent, somehow I could feel my body slowly floating in peace and tranquility in a forward motion to a warm and desirable place. Subconsciously, I found myself desperately wanting to continue. Then suddenly, within seconds of that unexplainable spiritual experience, I regained consciousness and saw Richard picking me up in his arms. I wanted to say something but didn't have the strength to utter a sound. My body felt as though I weighed nothing and I was nothing but a rag doll. Once again, everything went black.

An hour later, I woke to the warmth of a crackling fire and the tender, loving care of Jutta in her parlor. Apparently, while I was unconscious, Richard carried me back to his apartment and was able to dislodge the bullet and finally removed it. Christine and Jutta thoroughly cleaned and dressed my wound as well as any doctor could have. A sense of gratitude came over me, along with shock that I had somehow cheated death. Be that as it may, I felt agonizing pain penetrating from my chest especially as I take a breath of air.

"Magdalina, you're out of danger, but you're going to be in a lot of pain. The bullet entered below your ribs and ricocheted off the bone, cracking three ribs. I tightly wrapped some heavy gauze around your torso. This should alleviate some of the pain."

"Thank you, Richard."

As I looked around the room, I noticed Grace, Louise, and Tommy sitting on the floor by the fire in a very mournful mood. I slowly tried to rise; however, with the pain and weakness and the confused daze I was in, it was impossible. Realizing what I was trying to do, Christine and Jutta helped me sit upright on the sofa.

"There's something I need to tell you."

"What is it, Christine?"

"Sadly, Geraldine was shot and killed by Esther moments after she was pursued. Unfortunately, the three children witnessed her fall to the ground and die immediately. Directly after Geraldine was shot, Richard grabbed Esther and tackled her to the ground, confiscating her weapon in the process. Per Richard's request, with a gun to Esther's head, the other two Nazis dropped their weapons and immediately raised their hands in the air. I retrieved their weapons, and we escorted the three of them behind the demolished bank where Richard ordered them to sit on the ground.

"Subsequently, we didn't know what to do. However, we were smart enough to realize we couldn't let them go. Richard aimed the gun and killed one of the men, while the second tried desperately to flee the scene. Richard ran after him, eventually putting a bullet through his brains, while I guarded Esther at gunpoint. Strangely, for the few seconds Esther and I were standing there face to face, I felt an uncanny urge to ask her why. While I was so absorbed with that thought tantalizing my brain, she slowly pulled out a cyanide capsule from her sleeve, swallowed it, and immediately died like a yellow belly. I would assume she got her just due and was on her way for a long visit with the devil."

THE AMERIKANER
UNDERGROUND RATLINE

For the children's sake, I desperately struggle to keep myself from crying or showing any negative emotions; however, at times, I was unsuccessful. With Geraldine's ill-timed death, somber feelings for Frank, Craig, and Miss Helen overwhelmed me with grief. When I absolutely couldn't control my emotions any longer, I cried into a pillow to muffle the sound of agonizing pain with every tear. I was sure Louise didn't understand her mother's passing and that she would never return. Once we get to Europe and were settled in our new home, I would sit down with Louise and help her understand and cope with her loss. I also wanted Louise to understand that I would take full responsibility for her well-being until her father returns from war. That's the least I could do for Geraldine. Although we hadn't known the Jacksons that long, Geraldine would be sadly missed.

My thoughts of Geraldine were suddenly interrupted by the sound of Richard's voice reminding us that it was now 10:00 a.m. We had exactly one hour to pull it together and walk down to the bus stop. With the amount of pain and weakness I was experiencing, I felt like a slow-moving tortoise and thought I would surely be a great hindrance. Graciously, Jutta helped me off the sofa and into the water closet so I could clean up. My trousers were torn, and I was covered with blood and dirt from head to toe. Jutta kindly handed me one of her dresses and a new pair of nylons and tenderly lent a helping hand, cleaning me up and getting me dressed.

Meanwhile, Christine took Louise into the kitchen where the light was bright and applied the foundation and baby powder to her face and neck. It was very cold outside. Thankfully, her entire body would be bundled, including her hands with a pair of gloves Jutta gave her. Regrettably, with Wolfgang's death, none of us had the opportunity to be temporarily branded. Even though Richard and Jutta were both branded and legally registered, Richard assured us that in all the times he traveled in the winter months, the guard just checked each passenger's identification papers. If a guard suspected something was wrong with the paperwork, the next step was taking off the layers of clothing to check the left forearm for the branding.

"Girls, due to our recent set of circumstances, Jutta and I have decided to join you on the bus to Boston. Once the bus arrives at the Boston depot, we'll continue on until it arrives at Portland, Maine. My friend Wolfgang owned a small cabin nestled in the woods right off the water. Obviously, it will not take long before Esther and her Nazi thugs are missed. When the Gestapo comes looking for her, thankfully we'll all be long gone. Once we're there, if a reason warrants fleeing the country, this is an ideal place to do so. There's a small motorboat that Wolfgang had moored directly in front of his cabin. All Jutta and I will need to do is to sail directly across to the province of Nova Scotia and later into Canada. The Nazis have left Canada and her provinces untouched. Hitler wants to form an ally with Canada, just as America once had."

"That's great. I'm happy you're leaving. Why not come with us? There's plenty of room at the Rosenburg farm."

"No, Magdalina, I can't. I'm dedicated to the underground ratline. I'll run the ratline from Portland, instead of Philadelphia."

"I understand. However, I'll give you both addresses. You and Jutta are always welcome."

Quite surprisingly, we were ready to go with time to spare. Jutta handed me aspirin, some extra heavy gauze, peroxide, and badges for my ribs and gunshot wound. I stuffed it all into the squirrel-skin knapsack, along with my pistol and the rest of the ammunition and the five grenades. Richard locked the apartment, and we made it down the street to the bus stop minutes before it arrived. Richard graciously handed Christine and I each barter-trade voucher slips for the children and the two of us. We got on the bus and paid for our fare. I sat with Louise, while Christine sat with Tommy and Grace. If the guard gave me any trouble about my new Negro daughter, he would certainly be in for quite a surprise. I was in no mood for anymore of this nonsense. My pistol had been loaded with a full clip, and I had quick accessibility to retrieve it.

Christine and I purposely kept the children awake last night, so they should be fatigued and sleep the entire trip. We also packed their pillows and blankets; this would help keep Louise well hidden and won't look out of place. Once the children got comfortable in their seats, they immediately knotted off. The Nazi guard came back to where we were seated and visually examined us all and checked our identity papers as the children slept. I must say Christine did a wonderful job with Louise. If I didn't know better, I would have believed she was a perfect Aryan German girl. I prayed we would be able to pull this façade off without anyone else getting hurt.

After a long six-hour bus trip, the bandage on my wound was full of blood and had to be cleaned and the dressing changed. The bus stopped at the Boston bus depot and allowed everyone a five-minute break. We woke the children and quickly departed. Christine and I hugged Richard and Jutta with much sadness.

"Listen up, girls, before we depart, I have to explain the rest of the Esther saga. After I carried Magdalina back to my apartment and dislodged the bullet, I went out back and buried Geraldine in the corner of the tiny yard where the perennials come up every spring. I then quickly walked over to the building where Esther had taken her life, picked up her lifeless body, and walked back to the alley at the back of the apartment complex. I threw a rope over a limb on the maple tree and hung her dead body with a sign tied around her neck."

My true identity is Esther Ingrid Rosenburg, and my husband is Hermann Goering.

I immediately broke down in tears. Unfortunately, I was experiencing some very nostalgic feelings. I had known Esther my entire life; she was my best friend and was always a good person. It was almost as though the Nazis gave her a drug and possessed her body and soul. With all the turmoil I was feeling deep inside, I allowed myself guilt free to mourn the Esther I once knew and loved.

I was also very sad we broke our promise and failed to bury Geraldine at the waterfall in our little graveyard. However, under the circumstances, it would be inconsequential to go back to the cave for another burial. Someday, when this war would be over and New Germany would be America once again, Christine and I would travel back and dig a grave for her black bearskin coat.

The five of us sadly watched Richard and Jutta climb back on the bus. Christine and I knew in our hearts that this would be our final good-bye and we would never see them again. Christine, Tommy, Grace, Louise, and I stood on the sidewalk, waving as the bus pulled away. Once the bus was out of sight, we quickly ran into the water closet at the bus depot. Christine helped me clean and change the dressing on my wound and rewrapped the gauze around my ribs tightly.

The clock was ticking; we now had only two hours to walk to the Boston Harbor. We had to hustle and get there on time. Captain Carl had no idea that two women and three young children were about to be stowaways in his barge.

Thank God, we planned this entire trip out to the last detail. By keeping the children awake all night, they slept the entire six-hour trip from Philadelphia to Boston. The children were bright eyed and bushy tailed and rejuvenated for our two-hour journey. Although I had also slept the entire bus trip, I felt as though I was literally a ball and chain wrapped around Christine and the children. My injuries had reduced me to nothing but an inconvenience. However, Christine had been a saint as usual; she was an incredible crutch and was helping me every inch of the way.

Fortunately, we made it to the harbor in enough time to introduce ourselves to Captain Carl. After explaining our situation, I handed him Richard's handwritten letter, asking for asylum. Once the Captain read Richard's letter, he graciously escorted us to the stern, port side of his barge. There was a large very inconspicuous area snuggled among the crates of fertilizer, vegetable seeds, wheat, corn, and rice which has already been loaded onto the barge. In this corner lay a thick bed of hay, some wool blankets and pillows, a large folded-up canvas tarp and two large barrels of fresh drinking water. There was also a large metal barrel placed at the center of the hay, with stacks of firewood along the perimeter. At the bow of the barge were many wooden crates filled to the brim with coal to power the steam tug.

Captain Carl graciously welcomed us to our new home for the next five to six weeks. I immediately handed him the one hundred dollars Mr. Luciano gave Christine for our trip and made ourselves comfortable lying in the hay. Captain Carl didn't want to take a chance of being seen by any Nazi patrols in the harbor or by any German sympathizers.

An hour later, Captain Carl's small crew was finished loading the additional crates onboard, and we slowly sailed out of the Boston Harbor. Christine and I sat in the hay balling our eyes out.

"Christine, I cannot begin to explain how very betrayed I feel. I traveled such a long distance under horrific conditions to get here, worked extremely hard to learn the language, and here we are, going right back to where I started from. My head and heart are in a tug of war, with negative thoughts of Esther and me making a huge mistake leaving Austria twelve years ago."

"Mags, you listen to me. None of this is your fault. If the two of you didn't leave, Esther also would have been carted off to a concentration camp. Coming to America in actuality saved her life."

"You're right, I know you are. I'll come to terms, with all of this, I promise."

Once we sailed out of the harbor, Captain Carl allowed us to freely walk about. He very kindly handed the children two fishing rods that he stored onboard the steam tug and showed them how to cast a line.

It was now imperative that we forget the *Englisch* language *und* speak only *Deutsch*. Captain Carl *und* his crew of four were all from Old *Deutschland und* didn't speak *Englisch*, leaving me the only one of our *Gruppe* able to communicate with them. Between our *Deutsch* lessons, the pads of paper, colored pencils *und* the fishing rods, the *Kinder* were happy *und* content.

Once we got further out to sea, the air became much colder *und* the winds began to gust, with tiny snowflakes flying about. The crew immediately started a fire in the metal barrel, and we all happily congregated around the fires warmth. Later that evening, the five of us comfortably fell asleep with smiles on our faces, under a clear sky, allowing the stars to brighten up the darkness, nestled within a *Bett* of clean *Heu*.

This trip was unbelievably pleasant *und* extremely organized. If it rained, the crew would assemble the large tarp resembling a tent. Captain Carl made sure each day we all had enough to eat *und* generously shared his personal container of *Milch* with the *Kinder*. This entire experience had by far exceeded all my expectations. The first trip Esther *und* I made on the steamship *Rotterdam* was a nightmare as far as comfort *und* accommodations, *und* of course, there was never enough to eat. I tip my hat to Richard *und* Captain Carl for a very well-planned, organized, *und* humane ratline.

Captain Carl stressed that on this particular trip, he wanted to arrive into the Belgium Port in a record-breaking four weeks, instead of the normal six weeks. He was concerned the Nazis might retaliate with Esther's death *und* end up searching for us not only by land but by sea as well. From time to time on these trips, he had witnessed *Deutsch* naval vessels in these waters. However, for some strange reason, he had never been stopped for a random inspection.

"Captain Carl, I'm sure the reason you haven't been stopped is per the request of Adolf Hitler. The three barges that have been set up to make this journey are probably off limits to the small newly formed *Deutsch* Navy."

"Yes, Magdalina, you're probably right. However, I'm still anxious with this trip. If by fluke the navy has a patrol already out in the *Ozean*, we could be in some hot water. We need to quickly get as far out as possible."

"Captain, you have nothing to worry about. I still have five stick grenades in my knapsack for safekeeping, *und* I sure as *Hölle* know how to use them. I feel sorry for the poor *Schwein* who would have the unfortunate luck of coming after us at this point. We have survived many dangerous situations, and I'm like a tiger mother these days."

After five weeks, still in record-breaking time, we sailed into the port at Antwerp, Belgium. I woke the *Kinder, und* we scurried to collect our belongings. I was ecstatic to no longer needing my sea legs and no longer bearing negative feelings over leaving New *Deutschland*. Christine *und* I were actually feeling excited with our new adventure.

"Ladies, since we arrived in port one week early, the other end of the Ratline isn't expecting us *und* is therefore not prepared for our arrival. The trip from Belgium to Leonding, Austria, is ten hours. I suggest we all pile into my truck *und* spend the night at my *Haus* in Frankford, which is only three hours from here. Tomorrow morning, I'll personally drive you to your location."

Once again this perfect gentleman, who was a kind *und* generous soul *und* our knight in shining armor, came to our rescue. We all piled into his truck *und* proceeded on our way. As we drove through the streets of Belgium, I was alarmed at the countryside. We noticed some areas that were bombed *und* the evidence of war left behind, while other areas seemed as though war never took place.

"Captain Carl, I'm confused. It doesn't look as though the war was that bad. With everything we heard in America, I imagined Europe to be in ruins."

"Magdalina, you haven't seen anything yet. Belgium maintained a neutral stand. However, it was still invaded by the *Deutsch* on 10 May 1940. King Leopold III surrendered eighteen days after the initial attack, realizing that to continue fighting would be hopeless, *und* he desperately didn't want any more bloodshed. However, during the time Belgium was Nazi occupied, two resistance groups, the White Brigade *und* the Fifty-Ninth Brigade of Geheim Leger, continued to courageously fight as an *underground* force *und* are favorably known as aiding *und* assisting the allies. Compared to *Deutschland*, this is a cakewalk."

"Captain Carl, I apologize. Once again, I put my foot in my big mouth."

Three hours later, when we arrived at the Belgium-*Deutsch* border, we showed our fraudulent identity papers *und* crossed over into a bloodcurdling sight, something from the depths of *Hölle*. The closer we were getting to Frankford, the harder it was for any of us to take in this dreadful sight without feeling a sense of despair *und* hysteria. Old *Deutschland* was nothing but dust *und* dirt, bombed-out shells of buildings, bricks, cement, *und* war debris lying everywhere in the streets. There were *Deutsch* citizens *und* orphaned *Kinder* who were displaced, living in the streets among the filth, literally starving to death. Because there was such a shortage of men, *Deutsch* women, known as the *Trümmerfrauen* (rubble women), were desperately cleaning up the streets with whatever they could find, most of them engaged in this strenuous physical manual labor with only their bare hands. This sight was heart wrenching. The countryside, which was once so incredibly beautiful, was now in total chaos *und* ruin. I could not believe my *Bruder* was responsible for all this pain *und* suffering *und* loss of life.

"Unfortunately, ladies, this horrendous sight is a common scenery throughout the entire country. The other two captains *und* their crew of the emergency-relief barges are all very dedicated *und* passionate with their work as I am *und* my crew. Everything has been destroyed, *und* there's no fuel or natural resources. Fortunately, the two farm trucks that we're using for the ratline *und* the distribution of food have been converted to wood gasifiers *und* are powered by syngas fuel. We drive around the countryside distributing crates of corn, wheat, rice *und* flour *und* the agricultural crates are filled with fertilizer *und* vegetable seeds to help the *Vaterland* feed its people. Unfortunately the *Gruppe* isn't able to distribute in the Soviet occupied Sectors in the east. Tragically, there are thousands of *Deutsch* people stuck in these Sectors who are suffering greatly. These people in the east *und* the Polish occupied Zones are starving; *und* there's nothing that can be done to help them.

"To add more salt on the wound, horses that were used for the *Deutsch* cavalry *und* any farm horses, thoroughbreds, *und* mules within the country were confiscated, used, *und* abused *und* left for dead. With an alarming shortage of *Deutsch* horses *und* mules, this has also hindered travel *und* tilling farm fields for crops. What little Hitler is allowing to be imported into Old *Deutschland* is just a Band-Aid. I fear the Hitler *Brüder* will get bored *und* tire of their small charitable contributions to Old *Deutschland und* abandon the idea at some point."

"Captain Carl, they can't. These poor people need help."

"Magdalina, my organization will continue to do everything in our power, trust me."

"*Danke*, Captain. Christine *und* I also want to help," I said to him very sincerely.

After drinking in this inhumane, grisly sight, *und* Esther's death opening a door, I was very enthusiastic with the five of us taking over the Rosenburg farm. We would till *und* cultivate the land *und* plant our crops this coming spring. My compassionate feelings convinced me that Christine *und* I would do whatever we could to help with this cause. We would only sell for profit what we had to in order to keep the farm producing. The rest of the food would be donated to the people of Old *Deutschland*.

For some strange reason, Canada very generously had been shipping food to hundreds of millions of people who were facing starvation due to the war. When World War II ended in Europe, they fed Italy, Japan, *und* the Soviet Union; however, charitable aid was banned to *Deutschland*.

Three hours later, we pulled up to the ruins of Captain Carl's apartment building *und* gingerly walked up one flight of stairs to his second floor apartment. The building was destroyed but not demolished by an *Amerikaner* aerial attack two weeks prior to the surrender. Fortunately, the apartments were still salvageable. Through the past year, the captain was able to fix his place up so it was habitable, along with three other neighbors. Slowly, they were working to restore the rest of the building back to the way it was before the war. Incredibly, this seemed to be the only building still standing on his block.

Since Captain Carl confessed that he was a lousy cook, Christine *und* I went through his *Küche und* concocted a bratwurst stew with peas *und* potatoes. This was pretty much all the food he had, *und* the peas were from his garden, wrapped in an old newspaper in the icebox freezer. He apologetically explained that everyone who lived in this building all share what little food, tools, *und* supplies they had for survival. They all shared a vegetable garden in a large patch of cultivated soil out back this past summer, which had helped them get through some tough times. The two trips he made from New

Deutschland, he brought home each time a crate of food to share with his neighbors.

"Christine *und* Magdalina, I want you to understand something. The one hundred dollars you gave me for your trip will be donated to the *Amerikaner* Underground Ratline. This money helps many innocent *Amerikaner* citizens escape New *Deutschland*. This organization accepts donations from those who are able to give. However, for the many people who don't have the means, they're never turned away. There has been entirely too much inhumane behavior in Old *Deutschland*, Russia, Poland, *und* New *Deutschland*. It's now time to set things right *und* coexist as *Gott* intended."

"I agree, Captain Carl. Christine *und* I are grateful to her Uncle for giving us that money. We're proud to have had the privilege to contribute to the cause."

"*Danke, Mädchen, und* if you please, stop calling me Captain Carl. Using my title is appropriate while I'm at sea. However, on land, it's just plain Carl. Since both your men are in New *Deutschland*, fighting with the resistance, you have my word when I'm not at sea, I'll be stopping by at least once a week to make sure you're all doing well. I'll also make myself available for the spring planting *und* fall harvest. You're going to need as much help as possible. I can assure you this work is relentless *und* backbreaking. If the two of you are willing to sacrifice *und* work that hard, I want to do all I can to help you. Besides, any friend of Richard is a friend of mine for life."

"*Danke*, Carl. Christine *und* I are forever in your debt."

We all woke early *und* piled back into Carl's truck. After a seven-hour drive, Carl stopped in front of my *Eltern Haus* in Leonding. I gratefully handed him both addresses. Christine *und* I both promised Carl that by the end of this coming summer, we would be in full swing to help the starvation cause in Old *Deutschland*.

We said our temporary good-byes *und dankte* him for all his generosity *und* assured him that he's always welcome in our *Zuhause*. The five of us stood by the front door of my *Haus*, waving *Auf Wiedersehen* to a new member of our little world.

PART 3

SETTING IT RIGHT ON MY DEATH BED

THE BOMBSHELL

"So you see, *Fräulein* Neumann, there really wasn't anything different I personally could have done to change the way history was meant to unfold."

"Magdalina, of course not, none of this was your fault. This is one of the reasons I believe this book has to be written. The world deserves to know the truth, and I have every intention of writing the actual events."

"*Fräulein* Neumann, *danke.*"

"May I ask one question before we continue?"

"Sure anything."

"What's up with your *Schlafzimmer* and all this artillery?"

"What artillery? You mean the hunting knife in my boot on the floor next to my *Bett* or the loaded pistol under my mattress, or maybe you're referring to the five stick grenades in my squirrel-skin knapsack under the *Bett*? Then there's always the rifle slung over the *Bett* post. Could this possibly be the artillery you're referring to? You know the saying. You can't teach an old dog new tricks."

"Very funny, *mein Liebe*. Magdalina please continue."

Christine *und* I immediately took over the Rosenburg farm; in fact, we moved into the *Haus* the next day after we arrived in Leonding. We followed through with all the plans we made while we were in transit with the Underground Ratline. That first spring of 1948, we plowed *und* cultivated the land *und* planted our crops until our fingers bleed. There was enough *Schilling und Reichsmark*, or better known these days as *Deutsche Marke*, in Esther's *und* my treasure boxes to purchase some chickens for their eggs.

Unfortunately, that summer, eight months after the five of us arrived in Europe *und* our farm was just barely producing, my *Brüder* recanted *und* terminated the export of goods to Old *Deutschland*. Needless to say, that action brought more stress *und* anxiety to generate enough food to help the cause. After all, that first season, we all were rookies *und* were learning with our new career as farmers. However, with Carl suddenly having more free time on his hands, he moved into my *Eltern Haus* to be closer to the farm, which he also slaved over daily.

Our first season as farmers, we were able to produce enough to scrape by *und* ended up making a very small profit to further production for the following season. *Gott sei Dank*, as planned, there was a small amount of produce that Carl *und* three of his guys distributed to the most impoverished areas in Old *Deutschland*. After two years, our chickens bred considerably, giving us enough to slaughter for meat while keeping the rest for breeding *und* producing eggs. During that second year, we also saved enough *Schilling* to purchase a few pigs *und* cows.

I could not begin to explain how hard those first two years were, especially for two single women raising three *Kinder* on our own *und* farming the land. Tommy, Grace, *und* Louise were such a blessing from the first time they came into our lives. My beloved *Kinder* had always been such a huge help on this farm. They woke at the crake of dawn every *Morgen*, did their chores, *und* went to *Schule* all day, only to come home to more chores.

"My three *Kinder* are as perfect as perfect can be."

"That's so sweet, Magdalina. You're actually bringing tears to my eyes."

"Hogwash, let's go on and finish this before I die," I chuckled in silence.

Another reason we succeeded, Christine always had a good head for business. She developed a congenial business relationship with the market in town *und* sold our crops, eggs, *und* chicken. Years later, we were also able to slaughter some of our pigs *und* cows to sell that meat to the market as well. Again, as promised to Carl that first day in 1948, we only sold enough to keep our business going; the rest were donated, which we faithfully continued to do for another ten years.

"Magdalina, I humbly have to admit that's what prompted me to write this book. I was four years old when my *Vater* died in the war, leaving my *Mutter und* me as one of those impoverished families. Your generosity literally saved our lives. I would have starved to death if it wasn't for your organization. By the way, whatever happened to the rest of your *Gruppe*?"

"*Fräulein* Neumann, I cannot begin to tell you what it means to actually look someone in the eye that we were able to help. *Danke* for sharing that with me."

Four years after Christine, Tommy, Grace, Louise, *und* I arrived at the Rosenburg farm, we had an unexpected visit. An old, beat-up rust bucket of a truck that was also converted to a wood gasifier pulled into our driveway one hot *und* rainy September afternoon. There were no words to describe the feeling that came over me when I saw Sven, Dieter, *und* Dr. Jackson strolling to the back of the *Haus*.

"This is amazing. I can clearly see it as though it was yesterday. In fact, I have butterflies in my stomach right now just thinking about that glorious day."

"Please go on."

Carl, Christine, *und* I were in the fields along with the *Kinder*, picking corn, when we heard Sven's voice yell for us. We immediately stopped what we were doing *und* ran towards the *Haus*. My husband was standing there with a big stupid, silly grin on his face looking ridiculous as I enthusiastically gave him a huge black-bear hug that wouldn't end. Pleasantly, the *Kinder* remembered the three of them *und* followed suit. However, it took Louise a few minutes before it registered that her *Vater* was humbly standing there in tears. Christine, on the other hand, stood in front of us pale *und* unresponsive. I think she knew before any words were spoken.

We all quit work early that day *und* went into the *Haus* to hear their story. My husband's best friend, Antonio, was killed, along with Erich *und* Vito, on their mission dismantling a nuclear Nazi A-bomb. Sadly, there were only three more states that still had viable bombs. Earlier in the day, the *Gruppe* located the Wyoming bomb in an old cornfield next to an elementary *Schule*. The *Schule* sat too close to the road, so the safest area to park the Coca Cola truck *und* the armored auto was four miles past the *Schule*. They parked the vehicles in a field among the dead cornstalks in one of the government-owned farming locations.

In the pitch darkness of the night, Erich, Antonio, *und* Vito took a flashlight along with the toolbox *und* walked ahead to the bomb's location. Their plan was to leave Henry, Sammy, *und* my husband standing guard with the vehicles. Fifteen minutes later, Dieter finished what he was doing *und* grabbed his rifle and the second flashlight *und* proceeded to catch up with Erich *und* his entourage. As Dieter began to get closer, he saw eight Nazis passed out in the playground of the elementary *Schule*. Dieter frantically ran back to the truck to retrieve the stick grenades that he carelessly left behind.

Apparently, that small Nazi *Gruppe* had something grand to celebrate. The bomb that Erich had just begun working on was yards away from where these guys were sleeping. Unfortunately, they woke before Dieter was able to retrieve the grenades, giving the Nazis the advantage of catching Erich, Antonio, *und* Vito off guard.

"The way my husband described it, there was suddenly an incredible force of energy literally lifting the four of them off their feet."

When Dieter, Sammy, Henry, *und* Sven woke, they landed a mile further down the road. By the grace of *Gott*, somehow the four of them managed to cheat death that cold, dark evening. They immediately ran back to the truck *und* the armored auto *und* quickly drove to the bomb's location. Regrettably, once the dust settled somewhat, there was no trace of human life. The Nazis were saved one *Hölle* of a hangover, but sadly, we lost three more members of our family. When the guys looked around, everything for miles was leveled. Sven described an eerie thick cloud hovering overhead, which scared the daylights out of them. All they could think about was Japan *und* what little was known of radiation sickness. Dieter drove the Coca Cola truck, while my husband drove the armored auto *und* frantically as though the vehicles had wings they accelerated out of there like a bat out of *Hölle*.

The vehicles seemed to have a direction of their own; the gang found themselves heading back to Elk Lick. With the recent shock of just losing three more friends, none of them were in the right mind-set, especially my husband with Antonio's death. The guys walked back up the mountain *und* buried Antonio's *und* Erich's black bearskin coats. The three of them retrieved six river rocks *und* took the next two weeks chiseling Frank, Craig, Miss Helen, Antonio, Erich *und* Vito's initials in the rocks. They then placed each rock upside down *und* marked everyone's grave. Sadly, our little graveyard next to that beautiful waterfall had slowly begun growing in size. At that time, they had no idea that Geraldine also perished. Unfortunately, we were never able to go back *und* bury her bearskin coat *und* mark her grave.

Two weeks later, the four of them ventured back down the mountain to Sven's farm, looking for the Italians. It was clear the resistance hadn't been there for some time *und* a battle had taken place on the premises. My husband went back to the hooch shelter *und* grabbed two cases of stick grenades *und* more ammunition. Dieter, Henry, Sammy, *und* Sven decided to finish the job. Dieter felt very confident, after helping Erich *und* studying his technique, that the three of them could successfully dismantle the last three bombs.

So off they went; Dieter *und* my husband dressed in their Nazi uniforms, while Henry *und* Sammy sat in the back of the armored auto. They all agreed they were through with pussyfooting around *und* walking on eggshells. At the border crossings or if the auto was randomly stopped, they simply would catch the Nazis by surprise, toss a grenade, *und* be done with it. They drove days across country to the *Amerikaner* names of Oregon, Washington, *und* Montana, successfully dismantling *und* releasing the energy of the last three bombs. Once this task was completed, the guys decided to travel back to Luciano's Restaurant for further instructions, hoping that the Italian Mafia Resistance relocated there.

Once they arrived at the Restaurant, Frank Costello, Benjamin Siegel, *und* Albert Anastasia were the only three bosses still alive out of the original twelve of them. Sadly, *Herr* Luciano *und Herr* Salvatore were the first two bosses to get picked off. Almost all the Italians *und* their recruits who were sent out in different squadrons to take back Philadelphia were bushwhacked or randomly caught *und* executed. The Italian Mafia Resistance suffered great loss in the two years that Sven's battalion was off dismantling the miniature nuclear Nazi A-bombs.

After learning of the Italian's great loss in the number of recruits *und* Luciano's fate, Sven, Dieter, Sammy, *und* Henry were completely discouraged *und* broken. Sammy decided to stay behind at Luciano's Restaurant with Siegel, Costello, *und* Anastasia, while Dieter, Henry, *und* Sven agreed to temporally leave the country. Not only were they tormented with *Herr* Luciano's death, but Sammy's as well, which they heard through the grapevine. As it turned out, shortly after they left New York City, they learned of Sammy's fate. Weeks after Sammy was dropped off at the restaurant, he was captured and hung on the gallows, along with many other good Negro men who were considered deserters of the *Deutsch Armee*.

Although the guys never spoke of it through the years, I believe the three of them had overwhelming feelings of dishonor *und* guilt over the fact our resistance *Gruppe* was killing fellow *Amerikaner*. In the battles the Italian Mafia Resistance were engaged in, they were predominately killing brainwashed *Amerikaner* Negroes *und* Jewish men *und* very few Nazis.

Again, my *Bruder* was very smart this time around; he trained *und* utilized his undesirables for the frontline *und* only used a few low-ranking Nazi officers to guide these brigades. He inevitably made false promises to the Negro men. If they were loyal *und* fought for New *Deutschland*, once the resistance was annihilated, the Negroes would be granted special retribution *und* would be permitted to live among the *Deutsch*-Aryan race. These men were promised they all would be treated as equals, as opposed to the prejudice hatred *Amerikaner* people inflicted on the Negroes, treating them like second-class citizens.

With Luciano dead, the guys agreed to tackle the situation slightly different. They decided to travel to Europe *und* recruit any castaways who were exiled from *Amerika* and were interested in becoming a partisan of Italian Mafia Resistance. Once they had a sizable *Armee*, the new resistance would travel back to New *Deutschland* to continue with the reservation battle. However, once the three of them traveled from Africa to Austria *und* witnessed firsthand the devastation in Europe *und* the starving, impoverished people, they sadly realized it was probably a lost cause.

The despairing fact was, if the *Amerikaner* people had united *und* fought back, eventually, we could have saved *Amerika*. The pockets of recruits who joined the Italian Mafia Resistance and laid their lives on the line *und* proudly died for Lady Liberty, unfortunately, weren't enough. There's power in numbers. It was a shame the *Amerikaner* people allowed this to happen.

"Magdalina, so what happened then? Since the nuclear bombs were no longer a threat, did Dieter, Dr. Jackson, *und* Sven go back?"

"Regrettably, no. Shortly after the guys fled, my *Brüder* lost interest in deporting undesirables out of New *Deutschland*. Anyone left in the holding camps at that point were simply executed. However, from what I understand, there were many groups of Jewish and Negro people who were able to escape the camps and fled the country through the underground ratline."

Adolf enforced another new law, making it impossible for anyone to travel to or from New *Deutschland*; importing *und* exporting stopped as well. Antisubmarine nets were placed in the coastal waters as well as minefields *und* torpedo nets to enforce this new law. Of course, all exporting of relief food *und* supplies had stopped three years prior to the guys escape. No vessels were permitted within twenty kilometers of the coastline. If a foreign vessel got too close *und* somehow maneuvered through the minefields, the *Deutsch* Navy would sink the vessel by either *unterseeboot* or the two *Amerikaner* PT *Boote* from Annapolis that Luciano never had the opportunity to confiscate *und* unfortunately ended up in enemy hands.

"Wait a minute, Magdalina, you never told me how Sven, Dieter, *und* Dr. Jackson escaped."

"I'm sorry, your right."

Sven, Dieter, *und* Henry were very fortunate that New *Deutschland* was still deporting Negro women, elders, *und* Kinder at the time of their escape. In the dead of night, they snuck onto a barge permitted to sail from New *Deutschland* to Africa. With the help of the prisoners, the three of them stayed hidden from the captain *und* his crew. We found out later, they literally escaped on the last barge; nothing was coming in or out of the country—she was locked up tight as a drum.

Adolf finally had his new *und* improved, humungous *Deutschland* for his perfect Aryan race. From what I've heard, everything he set out to do in the Hitler *Brüder* five-year plan, he remarkably accomplished. Adolf *und* Gerhard were untouchable.

However, Mexico was never joined with New *Deutschland* as originally planned. Adolf used the Native *Amerikaner* Indians as laborers for the first year *und* later had them secretly deported to Mexico to a nuclear-destroyed, bombed-out country. Because of the 1851 Indian Appropriations Act, later known as the Indian Reorganization Act, Native *Amerikaner* Indians were an easy target for the Nazis. The Indians were already rounded up *und* forced to live on reservations by the *Amerikaner* federal government; this, of course, allowed the Nazis to waltz in *und* take control. These poor people were used and abused, then were literally thrown into a strange nation that was tainted with radiation poisoning. Most of the country's natural resources *und* plant life were destroyed, along with a majority of the wild game.

"Sadly little has been spoken about the Native *Amerikaner* Indians. *Fräulein* Neumann, you may want to check into this someday."

"*Ja*, of course, now that I'm aware of more displaced *Amerikaner*. Let's pray these people survived."

"*Danke, Fräulein*."

However, with all the prudence *und* success that Adolf *und* Gerhard accomplished, stories were circulating throughout Europe of my *Brüder* paranoia, which caused them to begin making stupid mistakes. Probably one of the most potentially severe mistakes was the Negro *und* Jewish men who became traitors of *Amerika und* were loyal to Adolf *und* New *Deutschland*. Sadly, anyone who survived was taken to the death camps.

"Magdalina, when did you *und* Sven get married *und* what happened to everyone else?"

Sven *und* I married six months after the boys joined us in Austria. We lovingly raised Tommy, Grace, *und* Louise as our own *Kinder*. Shortly after we were married, my husband became the mayor of Leonding *und* passionately practiced peace *und* respect for all mankind. His principle until the day he died at the age of seventy-two was, "Treat others as you want to be treated."

Christine continued to live on the farm with us. Two years later she *und* Carl married. Once they were married we kept enough profit to have a small *Haus* built outback for them. Christine *und* Carl devotedly worked the farm every day for the rest of their lives. Sadly, on Christine's deathbed, she confided that although she loved her late husband Carl in her own way, Antonio was always her true love. He held a special place in her heart for the rest of her life. Her heart ached in silence. I buried Christine with the ring that *Herr* Luciano gave to Antonio for Christine's engagement.

"Now, do you want to hear the bombshell," I looked at *Fräulein* Neumann as she squirmed in her seat.

"*Ja*, of course, I'm on pins *und* needles."

"Okay, hold on to your pantyhose because this is beyond imagination."

Throughout the three years we were living in survival mode, *und* all the endurance, twists, *und* turns of actually surviving The 2nd World War II *und* successfully escaping New *Deutschland*, nothing on this God's green earth could have prepared any of us for the phenomenon of the century.

One year after Christine *und* Carl were married, the same old, beat-up rust bucket of a truck drove down the dirt road *und* parked out front of the *Haus*. Sven, Christine, Carl, Dieter, *und* I just sat down to supper after a long day in the fields when surprisingly, there was a thump on the front door. When I opened the door I saw a strange but familiar face of a disfigured man, glaring at me with tears in his eyes. Every ounce of my being went numb, *und* the blood literally drained from my head—then my world went black. When I finally woke, Antonio Sabatino was sitting on the sofa in front of a roaring fire, engaged in conversation with my husband *und* the others. By the grace of God, Antonio barely survived the nuclear bomb explosion that mutilated Erich, Vito, *und* the drunken Nazis.

"*Oh mein Gott*, Magdalina, I don't think *bombshell* is a strong-enough word."

"That's why I wanted to prepare you. To this day, I find it hard to believe that this truly happened. Sometimes, I think it's just a wild dream."

Apparently when Antonio, Erich, *und* Vito arrived at the bomb site, they realized the hacksaw was missing from the toolbox. Since Antonio was the tallest, leanest, *und* could run like a roadrunner, he started sprinting back to the Coca Cola truck to retrieve it. Minutes later, the celebrating Nazis regained consciousness from their drunken stupor *und* confronted Erich *und* Vito at gunpoint. Erich had the bomb's shell completely removed *und* began dismantling it when he must have panicked *und* mistakenly triggered it off, pulverizing everything within ten kilometers. As Antonio was running toward the truck, all he remembered was an incredibly loud sound, the earth shaking under his feet like an earthquake, *und* a tremendous force literally hurling him through the air like a piece of paper in a seventy-five-mile-an-hour windstorm.

Antonio woke two months later in the loving care of a group of Lakota Indians, who somehow managed to escape their reservation after their home was invaded by the Nazis. There were twenty-nine adults and ten children who took refuge in the Rocky Mountains. Six months later, two other tribes, the Crow *und* Shoshone, consisting of fifteen adults and six children, also took refuge in the mountains with the Lakota. The three tribes successfully put aside their differences and pulled together to coexist.

Antonio suffered numerous broken bones *und* radiation burns over 80 percent of his body. During the two years Antonio was recovering *und* living with the Indians, he befriended a young man who was part of the Lakota tribe. He was named Tatanka, but George was his *Amerikaner* name. George was actually affiliated with Richard *und* successfully smuggled out many Indians who were prisoners in the Hitler *Brüder* work camps the year before they were deported to Mexico. Unfortunately, George was never able to get his family out, *und* as a result, they were deported to a slow death sentence. However, the Indians George was able to get out of the Nazi camps were taken to his secret location in the Rocky Mountains and later to British Columbia.

When Antonio was well enough to travel a great distance, George personally escorted him from Wyoming to Montana, where a man who was involved with Richard's old ratline then took Antonio straight threw into British Columbia. Antonio was then successfully smuggled onto a vessel waiting in the Gulf of Alaska in the Pacific *Ozean* through his new ratline that Richard created in Canada. The trip was much longer *und* unrelenting, from Canada to Norway *und* from Norway to Europe, than the more direct ratline we had originally taken.

"Wow, that's quite a story. What ever happened to George?"

"I'm sorry, I really don't know. We've never heard anything more about George or the Native *Amerikaner* Indians."

None of us ever spoke of it, but in my heart, I still believe the only reason Antonio survived *und* went through all his pain *und* suffering, along with the torment to travel to Austria, was for the love he had for Christine. The next morning after Antonio arrived, Dieter drove him to Munich to his *Väter* cabin located in the Bavarian Alps. Sadly, Antonio only lived for another two years. The kid Antonio literally wanted to dump into the deep part of the Casselman River while wearing cement shoes, to join his fellow Nazi for fish food, devotedly lived with him the entire time *und* took excellent care of a slowly dying man. We buried Antonio in a remote area in the Alps that resembled Casselman Point in New *Deutschland*, overlooking the tops of the trees and autumn leaves.

After Antonio's death, Dieter became a farmer once again *und* lived with us from the start of our spring planting until after the autumn harvest. During the winter months, he continued to travel back to Munich *und* lives in his cabin. Dieter also became an active advocate for feeding the starving *Deutsch* people *und* spent fifteen years passionately *und* zealously supporting the cause.

"Magdalina, whatever happened to Dieter. Is he still alive?"

"*Ja*, actually he still maintains the same routine. Dieter has a share in the business, just as Christine, Carl, Sven, *und* I had. The only difference now is everyone's dead, *und* I've been sick for three years, so I've stepped back. Now the farm belongs to Dieter, Tom, *und* Grace, who have proudly kept this old place as viable as ever. Strangely, after all these years, I actually got shivers down my spine. It's sad *Herr* Rosenburg wasn't here to see the good his farm has done for so many people *und* the amount of lives that were saved."

"I believe he's looking down from heaven *und* is very proud of what you all accomplished here."

"*Danke*, that's a very sweet thought," I turned away so *Fräulein* Neumann couldn't see my tears.

"Don't you think it's time we stop the formalities *und* you address me by my first name?"

"I'm sorry, what is your name, dear?"

"Please call me Ella. Oh my goodness, while I'm thinking of it, before we quit for the day, I still need to know about Dr. Jackson *und* Louise. Whatever became of them?"

Since Carl moved out of my *Väter Haus und* lived with Christine, Henry moved in the next day after arriving in Austria. He immediately set up a medical practice in the parlor *und* later had a clinic built in town. Henry was the only family practitioner in Austria *und Deutschland* for many years. People traveled for miles to see him. He treated everyone who was in need of medical care, whether or not they had the means to pay.

"He proudly never turned anyone away. Trust me, I have a chicken coup to prove it."

Louise continued to live with us *und* shared a *Schlafzimmer* with Grace. Henry played an active role in her life. However, my husband *und* I primarily raised her as our own. After my *Kinder* graduated high *Schule*, Tommy *und* Grace took over the farm, while Louise continued on *und* graduated medical *Schule*, following in her *Väter* footsteps.

"She is presently a partner with Henry, who is semiretired from the Jackson Clinic located in Linz. I'm proud to say, Ella, those of us who survived the ordeal all walked away with a life-altering experience. We all gained more empathy *und* compassion for our fellow humans who were in need due to circumstances beyond their control. I believe we made a small difference.

"Once I'm dead, my *Kinder* know to plant me in between my beloved husband *und* my *Eltern* in front of the large fir tree in the graveyard across from my *Eltern Haus*. However, someday, if it's possible to safely return to New *Deutschland*, Tom, Grace, *und* Louise are well aware of my final wishes. They're to hike up the mountain to the waterfall *und* bury Geraldine's, Christine's, Antonio's, their *Väter*, *und* my black bearskin coats, which we left in the cave, in our little graveyard in Mount Davis of Elk Lick, Pennsylvania."

"Magdalina, if your *Kinder* ever have the opportunity to travel back to New *Deutschland*, I would love to accompany them. Out of respect, nothing would bring me greater pleasure than to participate in this endeavor."

"Ella, *danke*, I'm honored. Is this all right with the three of you?"

"Of course, *Mutti*. Maybe while we're all there, Ella can take photographs of the cave *und* waterfall. Photographs would probably help people have a better understanding of how you all lived *und* survived."

"Gracie, that's a wonderful idea, especially since the cave is so unique. Ella, there's one more thing I'd like to share, some information I acquired a year ago. But I have no idea what relevance it may have in the future. This has nothing to do with the history book, Tom, Grace, *und* Louise are already aware *und* are trying to get to the bottom of it."

"Alright, please continue."

Years ago, I befriended an *Amerikaner* woman of Polish heritage with some Italian in her blood as well. Sara was an *Amerikaner* citizen from Oregon, who was exiled from New *Deutschland* when my *Brüder* were still transporting level 3 undesirables back to Europe. After church on 5 May 1945, Sara joined the pastor *und* his pregnant wife, who was her best friend at the time, along with five Sunday school students for a picnic at Gearhart Mountain. Sara *und* Pastor Mitchell began to unload the auto when the two of them witnessed Elsie Mitchell *und* the five *Kinder* come across a deflated hot air balloon in the field. The six of them were instantly blown up *und* killed.

When the authorities researched the incident, they secretly confided that Japan launched approximately nine thousand fire balloons, or better know these days as hydrogen balloons, carrying bombs aimed for *Amerika*. The launch was successful due to strong currents of winter air flowing at a high altitude *und* speed. This balloon project took place between November 1944 *und* April 1945 *und* was considered the fourth attack Japan made on *Amerika*. In that year, approximately three hundred balloons bearing bombs successfully landed in various states in *Amerika* and some in Canada. The attack was classified; the US Department of War kept this news unpublicized *und* a secret from the public for the purpose of fooling Japan into believing the project was unsuccessful *und* Japan's military would lose interest *und* void any future attempts.

"Now here's the kicker," once again I see Ella squirm in her seat.

Very innocently, last spring, I was out back reading when I happened to glance up at the sky *und* noticed three hydrogen balloons floating by. Moments after witnessing this, I instantly remembered the story Sara told me about the Japanese hydrogen balloons. A shiver went down my spine as I found myself questioning if the balloons could be carrying bombs *und* for what reason.

Although it's been thirty years, a sudden fear came over me for two reasons. Japan was experimenting with biological weapons in the 1940s, *und* a threat of bio warfare would be devastating. Also, the Soviet Union could be a threat, considering Stalin didn't want any involvement in World War II. In fact, a treaty, the Nazi-Soviet Non-Aggression Pact of Friendship, was signed on 23 August 1939, between the *Deutsch* Foreign Minister Ribbentrop *und* the Soviet Foreign Minister Molotov. This treaty stated that both countries would not attack each other, *und* it was valid for ten years. However, my *Bruder* broke the treaty in less than two years *und* invaded the Soviet Union on 22 June 1941. Not only for the natural resources, but Eastern Europe would be a great place to expand his empire where more Germans could settle.

"Gee, your fears may be warranted. After all, there could be some animosity built up."

"Exactly, Ella."

With the atrocities, the inhumane treatment *und* suffering of both military *und* civilians, that were inflicted on the Soviet Union *und* *Deutschland* by each other during World War II, it was questionable. This could also be coming from Japan, who might be holding a grudge due to the devastation the atomic bombs caused on two of their major cities

I pray there would be no more retaliation or rivalry between any nations in Europe *und* New *Deutschland*. Perhaps someday after my *Brüder* are dead, New *Deutschland* would acquire a democratic government with a good *Präsident* who would serve the people. In light of all our knowledge *und* technology these days, I don't believe the world can survive another world war.

This novel is the first in a three part series:

Book one: The 2nd World War II
Book two: The 2nd World War II, Civil War
Book three: The 2nd World War II, The New World